I'm Tracy Beaker. This is a book all about me. It's the most incredible heart-rending story.
Honest. And I bet some great movie magnate spots it and turns it into a film and I'll get to be the star. (Just like my mum.) I suppose I'd better let Peter have a small part in my film. But not Louise or Justine. *No way!* Cam can write the script if she likes. Cam is . . . But if you want to know who she is you'd better turn over the page and begin reading. There's some funny bits and some rude bits and some sad bits and I think it's the best book ever. But then I would do, seeing as I helped write it.

Tracy is ten years old. She lives in a Children's Home but would like a *real* home one day. Meet Tracy, follow her story, and share her hopes for the future in this beautifully observed, touching and often very funny tale.

www.kidsatrandomhouse.co.uk/jacquelinewilson

Also available by Jacqueline Wilson:

Available from Corgi Pups, for younger readers:

THE DINOSAUR'S PACKED LUNCH
THE MONSTER STORY-TELLER

Available from Young Corgi Books:

LIZZIE ZIPMOUTH

Available from Doubleday/Corgi Yearling Books:

BAD GIRLS
THE BED AND BREAKFAST STAR
BURIED ALIVE!
THE CAT MUMMY
CLIFFHANGER
THE DARE GAME
DOUBLE ACT
GLUBBSLYME
THE ILLUSTRATED MUM
THE LOTTIE PROJECT
THE MUM-MINDER
SECRETS
SLEEPOVERS
THE STORY OF TRACY BEAKER
THE SUITCASE KID
VICKY ANGEL
THE WORRY WEBSITE

Collections:

THE JACQUELINE WILSON COLLECTION
(includes *The Story of Tracy Beaker* and
The Bed and Breakfast Star)
JACQUELINE WILSON'S DOUBLE-DECKER
(includes *Bad Girls* and *Double Act*)
JACQUELINE WILSON'S SUPERSTARS
(includes *The Suitcase Kid* and *The Lottie Project*)

THE JACQUELINE WILSON DIARY

Available from Doubleday/Corgi Books, for older readers:

DUSTBIN BABY
GIRLS IN LOVE
GIRLS UNDER PRESSURE
GIRLS OUT LATE
GIRLS IN TEARS
LOLA ROSE

CORGI YEARLING BOOKS

THE STORY OF TRACY BEAKER
A CORGI YEARLING BOOK : 0 440 86624 3

First published in Great Britain by Doubleday

PRINTING HISTORY
Doubleday edition published 1991
Corgi Yearling edition published 1992

Set in 12/14pt Century Schoolbook by
Falcon Graphic Art Ltd, Wallington, Surrey.

Corgi Yearling Books are published by Random House Children's Books,
61–63 Uxbridge Road, Ealing, London W5 5SA,
a division of The Random House Group Ltd,
in Australia by Random House Australia (Pty) Ltd,
20 Alfred Street, Milsons Point, Sydney, NSW 2061, Australia,
in New Zealand by Random House New Zealand Ltd,
18 Poland Road, Glenfield, Auckland 10, New Zealand
and in South Africa by Random House (Pty) Ltd,
Endulini, 5a Jubilee Road, Parktown 2193, South Africa.

Printed and bound in Great Britain by
Cox & Wyman Ltd, Reading, Berkshire.

To Bryony, David, Miranda,
Jason and Ryan

My Book About Me

ABOUT ME

My name is Tracy Beaker

I am 10 **years** 2 **months old.**

My birthday is on 8 May. It's not fair, because that dopey Peter Ingham has his birthday then too, so we just got the one cake between us. And we had to hold the knife to cut the cake together. Which meant we only had half a wish each. Wishing is for babies anyway. They don't come true.

I was born at some hospital somewhere. I looked cute when I was a little baby but I bet I yelled a lot.

I am cms tall. I don't know. I've tried measuring with a ruler but it keeps wobbling about and I can't reach properly. I don't want to get any of the other children to help me. This is my private book.

I weigh kgs. I don't know that either. Jenny has got scales in her bathroom but they're stones and pounds. I don't weigh many of them. I'm a little titch.

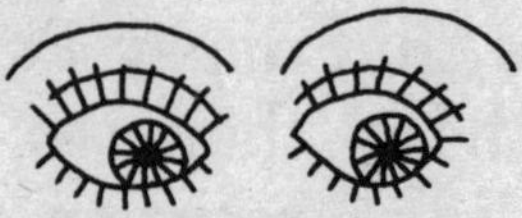

My eyes are black and I can make them go all wicked and witchy. I quite fancy being a witch. I'd make up all these incredibly evil spells and wave my wand and ZAP Louise's golden curls would all fall out and ZAP Peter Ingham's silly squeaky voice would get sillier and squeakier and he'd grow whiskers and a long tail and ZAP . . . there's not room on this bit of the page, but I've still got all sorts of ZAPs inside my head.

My hair is fair and very long and curly. I am telling fibs. It's dark and difficult and it sticks up in all the wrong places.

My skin is spotty when I eat a lot of sweets.

Stick a photo of yourself here

I'm not really cross-eyed. I was just pulling a silly face.

I started this book on I don't know. Who cares what the date is? You always have to put the date at school. I got fed up with this and put 2091 in my Day Book and wrote about all these rockets and space ships and monsters legging it down from Mars to eat us all up, as if we'd all whizzed one hundred years into the future. Miss Brown didn't half get narked.

MORE THINGS ABOUT ME

Things I like

My lucky number is 7. So why didn't I get fostered by some fantastic rich family when I was seven then?

My favourite colour is blood red, so watch out, ha-ha.

My best friend is Well, I've had heaps and heaps, but Louise has gone off with Justine and now I haven't got anyone just at the moment.

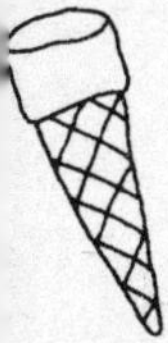

I like eating everything. I like birthday cake best. And any other kind of cake. And Smarties and Mars Bars and big buckets of popcorn and jelly spiders and Cornettos and Big Macs with french fries and strawberry milk shakes.

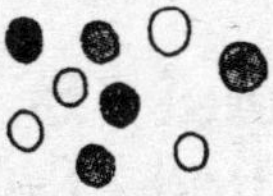

My favourite name is Camilla. There was a lovely little baby at this other home and that was her name. She was a really sweet kid with fantastic hair that I used to try to get into loads of little plaits and it must have hurt her sometimes but she never cried. She really liked me, little Camilla. She got fostered quick as a wink. I begged her foster mum and dad to bring her back to see me but they never did.

I like drinking pints of bitter. That's a joke. I *have* had a sip of lager once but I didn't like it.

My favourite game is playing with make-up. Louise and I once borrowed some from Adele who's got heaps. Louise was a bit boring and just tried to make herself look beautiful. I turned myself into an incredible vampire with evil shadowy eyes and blood dribbling down my chin. I didn't half scare the little ones.

My favourite animal is Well, there's a rabbit called Lettuce at this home but it's a bit limp, like its name. It doesn't sit up and give you a friendly lick like a dog. I think I'd like a Rottweiler – and then all my enemies had better WATCH OUT.

My favourite TV programme is horror films.

Best of all I like being with my mum.

Things I don't like

the name Justine. Louise. Peter. Oh there's heaps and heaps of names I can't stand.

eating stew. Especially when it's got great fatty lumps in it. I used to have this horrid foster mother called Aunty Peggy and she was an awful cook. She used to make this slimy stew like molten sick and we were supposed to eat it all up, every single bit. Yuck.

Most of all I hate Justine. That Monster Gorilla. And not seeing my mum.

MY OWN FAMILY

Stick a photo of you and your family here

This was when I was a baby. See, I was sweet then. And this is my mum. She's ever so pretty. I wish I looked more like her.

The people in my own family are My mum. I don't have a dad. I lived with my mum when I was little and we got on great but then she got this Monster Gorilla Boyfriend and I hated him and he hated me back and beat me up and so I had to be taken into care. No wonder my mum sent him packing.

My own family live at I'm not sure exactly where my mum lives now because she has to keep moving about because she gets fed up living in one place for long.

The phone number is Well, I don't know, do I? Funny though, I always used to bag this toy telephone in the playhouse at school and pretend I was phoning my mum. I used to have these long long conversations with her. They were just pretend of course, but I was only about five then and sometimes it got to be quite real.

Things about my family that I like I like my mum because she's pretty and good fun and she brings me lovely presents.

MY FOSTER FAMILY

There's no point filling this bit in. I haven't got a foster family at the moment.

I've had two. There was Aunty Peggy and Uncle Sid first of all. I didn't like them much and I didn't get on with the other kids so I didn't care when they got rid of me. I was in a children's home for a while and then I had this other couple. Julie and Ted. They were young and friendly and they bought me a bike and I thought it was all going to be great and I went to live with them and I was ever so good and did everything they said and I thought I'd be staying with them until my mum came to get me for good but then . . . I don't want to write about it. It ended up with me getting turfed out THROUGH NO FAULT OF MY OWN. I was so mad I smashed up the bike so I don't even have that any more. And now I'm in a new children's home and they've advertised me in the papers but there weren't many takers and now I think they're getting a bit desperate. I don't care though. I expect my mum will come soon anyway.

MY SCHOOL

My school is called It's Kinglea Junior School. I've been to three other schools already. This one's OK I suppose.

My teacher is called
Miss Brown.
She gets cross
if we just call
her Miss.

Subjects I do Story-writing. Arithmetic. Games. Art. All sorts of things. And we do Projects only I never have the right stuff at the Home so I can't do it properly and get a star.

I like Story-writing best. I've written heaps of stories, and I do pictures for them too. I make some of them into books. I made Camilla a special baby book with big printed words and pictures of all the things she liked best, things like TEDDY and ICE-CREAM and YOUR SPECIAL FRIEND TRACY.

I also like Art. We use poster paints. We've got them at the Home too but they get all gungy and mucked up and the brushes are useless. They've got good ones at school. This is a painting I did yesterday. If I was a teacher I'd give it a gold star. *Two* gold stars.

My class is 3a.

People in my class I can't list all their names, I'd be here all night. I don't know some of them yet. There's not much point making friends because I expect I'll be moving on soon.

Other teachers Oh, they're all boring. Who wants to write about them?

I get to school by going in the Minibus. That's how all the kids in the home get to school. I'd sooner go in a proper car or walk it by myself but you're not allowed.

It takes **hours** **mins** It varies. Sometimes it takes ages because the little kids can't find their pencil cases and the big ones try to bunk off and we just have to hang about waiting.

Things I don't like about school
They all wear grey things, that's the uniform, and I've only got navy things from my last school. The teachers know why and I don't get into trouble but the other kids stare.

BEING IN CARE

My social worker is called Elaine and sometimes she's a right pain, ha-ha.

We talk about all sorts of boring things.

But I don't like talking about my mum. Not to Elaine. What I think about my mum is private.

IF I WAS . . .

older, I would live in this really great modern house all on my own, and I'd have my own huge bedroom with all my own things, special bunk beds just for me so that I'd always get the top one and a Mickey Mouse alarm clock like Justine's and my own giant set of poster paints and I'd have some felt tips as well and no-one would ever get to borrow them and mess them up and I'd have my own television and choose exactly what programmes I want, and I'd stay up till gone twelve every night and I'd eat at McDonald's every single day and I'd have a big fast car so I could whizz off and visit my mum whenever I wanted.

a policeman, I would arrest the Monster Gorilla and I'd lock him up in prison for ever.

a kitten, I would grow very long claws and sharp teeth and scratch and bite everyone so they'd get really scared of me and do everything I say.

yelled at, I would yell back.

invisible, I would spy on people.

very tall, I would stamp on people with my great big feet.

very rich, I would buy my own house and then . . . I've done all that bit. I'm getting fed up writing all this. What's on the next page?

MY OWN STORY

Use this space to write your story

THE STORY OF TRACY BEAKER

Once upon a time there was a little girl called Tracy Beaker. That sounds a bit stupid, like the start of a soppy fairy story. I can't stand fairy stories. They're all the same. If you're very good and very beautiful with long golden curls then, after sweeping up a few cinders or having a long kip in a cobwebby palace, this prince comes along and you live happily ever after. Which is fine if you happen to be a goodie-goodie and look gorgeous. But if you're bad and ugly then you've got no chance whatsoever. You get given a silly name like *Rumpelstiltskin* and nobody invites you to their party and no-one's ever grateful even when you do them a whopping great favour. So of course you get a bit cheesed off with this sort of treatment. You stamp your feet in a rage and fall right through the floorboards or you scream yourself into a frenzy and you get locked up in a tower and they throw away the key.

I've done a bit of stamping and screaming in my time.

And I've been locked up heaps of times. Once they locked me up all day long. And all night. That was at the first Home, when I wouldn't settle because I wanted my mum so much. I was just little then but they still locked me up. I'm not fibbing. Although I do have a tendency to tell a few fibs now and again. It's funny, Aunty Peggy used to call it Telling Fairy Stories.

I'd say something like — 'Guess what, Aunty Peggy, I just met my mum in the back garden and she gave me a ride in her flash new sports car and we went down the shopping arcade and she bought me my very own huge bottle of scent, that posh *Poison* one, just like the bottle Uncle Sid gave you for your birthday, and I was messing about with it, playing Murderers, and the bottle sort of tipped and it's gone all over me as I expect you've noticed, but it's my scent not yours. I don't know what's happened to yours. I think one of the other kids took it.'

You know the sort of thing. I'd make it dead convincing but Aunty Peggy wouldn't even listen properly. She'd just shake her head at me and get all cross and red and say, 'Oh Tracy, you naughty girl, you're Telling Fairy Stories again.' Then she'd give me a smack.

Foster mothers aren't supposed to smack you at all. I told Elaine that Aunty Peggy used to smack me and Elaine sighed and said, 'Well sometimes, Tracy, you really do ask for it.' Which is a lie in itself. I have never in my life said 'Aunty Peggy, please will you give me a great big smack.' And her smacks really hurt too, right on the back of your leg where it stings most. I didn't like that Aunty Peggy at all. If I was in a real fairy story I'd put a curse on her. A huge wart right on the end of her nose? Frogs and toads coming wriggling out of her mouth every time she tries to speak? No, I can make up better than that. She can have permanent huge great bogeys hanging out of her nose that won't go away no matter how many times she blows it, and whenever she tries to speak she'll make this terribly loud Rude Noise. Great!

Oh dear. You can't win. Elaine, my stupid old social worker, was sitting beside me when I started writing THE STORY OF TRACY BEAKER and I got the giggles making up my brilliant curses for Aunty Peggy and Elaine looked surprised and said, 'What are you laughing at, Tracy?'

I said, 'Mind your own business' and she said, 'Now Tracy' and then she looked at what I'd written which is a bit of a cheek seeing as it's supposed to be very private. She sighed when she got to the Aunty Peggy part and said, 'Really Tracy!' and I said, 'Yes, really, Elaine.' And she sighed again and her lips moved for a moment or two. That's her taking a deep breath and counting up to ten. Social workers are supposed to do that when a child is being difficult. Elaine ends up doing an awful lot of counting when she's with me.

When she got to ten she gave me this big false smile. Like this.

'Now look, Tracy,' said Elaine. 'This is your own special book about you, something that you're going to keep for ever. You don't want to spoil it by writing all sorts of silly cheeky rude things in it, do you?'

I said, 'It's my life and it hasn't been very special so far, has it, so why shouldn't I write any old rubbish?'

Then she sighed again, but sympathetically this time, and she put her arm round me and said, 'Hey, I know you've had a hard time, but *you're* very special. You know that, don't you?'

I shook my head and tried to wriggle away.

'Yes, you are, Tracy. Very very special,' Elaine said, hanging on to me.

'Then if I'm so very very special how come no-one wants me?' I said.

'Oh dear, I know it must have been very disappointing for you when your second placement went wrong, love, but you mustn't let it depress you too much. Sooner or later you'll find the perfect placement.'

'A fantastic rich family?'

'Maybe a family. Or maybe a single person, if someone really suitable came along.'

I gave her this long look. 'You're single, Elaine. And I bet you're suitable. So why don't you foster me, eh?'

It was her turn to wriggle then.

'Well, Tracy. You know how it is. I mean, I've got my job. I have to deal with lots of children.'

'But if you fostered me you could stop bothering with all the others and just look after me. They give you money if you foster. I bet they'd give you lots extra because I'm difficult, and I've got behaviour problems and all that. How about it, Elaine? It would be fun, honest it would.'

'I'm sure it would be lots of fun, Tracy, but I'm sorry, it's just not on,' Elaine said.

She tried to give me a big hug but I pushed her hard.

'I was only joking,' I said. 'Yuck. I couldn't stand the thought of living with you. You're stupid and boring and you're all fat and wobbly, I'd absolutely hate the idea of you being my foster mum.'

'I can understand why you're angry with me, Tracy,' said Elaine, trying to look cool and calm, but sucking in her stomach all the same.

I told her I wasn't a bit angry, though I shouted as I said it. I told her I didn't care a bit, though I had these silly watery eyes. I didn't cry though. I don't *ever* cry. Sometimes people think I do, but it's my hay fever.

'I expect you're going to think up all sorts of revolting curses for me now,' said Elaine.

'I'm doing it right this minute,' I told her.

'OK,' she said.

'You always say OK,' I told her. 'You know: OK, that's fine with me, if that's what you want I'm not going to make a fuss; OK Tracy, yes I know you've got this socking great axe in your hand and you're about to chop off my head because you're feeling angry with me, but OK, if that's the way you feel, I'm not going to get worried about it because I'm this super-cool social worker.'

She burst out laughing then.

'No-one can stay super-cool when you're around, Tracy,' she said. 'Look kiddo, you write whatever you want in your life story. It's your own book, after all.'

So that's that. This is my own book and I can write whatever I want. Only I'm not quite sure what I do want, actually. Maybe Elaine *could* help after all. She's over the other side of the sitting-room, helping that wet Peter with his book. He hasn't got a clue. He's filling it all in *so* slowly and *so* seriously, not writing it but printing it with that silly blotchy biro of his, trying to do it ever so carefully but failing miserably, and now he's smudged some of it so it looks a mess anyway.

I've just called Elaine but she says she's got to help Peter for a bit. The poor little petal is getting all worried in case he puts the wrong answers, as if it's some dopey intelligence test. I've done heaps of them, intelligence tests. They're all ever so easy-peasy. I can do them quick as a wink. They always expect kids in care to be as thick as bricks, but I get a hundred out of a hundred nearly every time. Well, they don't tell you the answers, but I bet I do.

TRACY BEAKER IS A STUPID SHOW-OFF AND THIS IS THE SILLIEST LOAD OF RUBBISH I'VE EVER READ AND IF SHE'S SO SUPER-INTELLIGENT HOW COME SHE WETS HER BED LIKE A BABY ?

Ignore the stupid scribble up above. It's all lies anyway. It's typical. You can't leave anything for two minutes in this rotten place without one of the other kids spoiling it. But I never thought anyone would stoop so low as to write in my own private life story. And I know who did it too. I know, Justine Littlewood, and you just wait. I'm going to get you.

I went over to rescue Elaine from that boring wimpy little Peter and I had a little peer into his book and I nearly fell over, because you'll never guess who he's put as his best friend. Me. *Me!*

'Is this some sort of joke?' I demanded. He went all red and mumbly and tried to hide what he'd put, but I'd already seen it. *My best friend is Tracy Beaker*. It was down there on the page in black and white. Well, not your actual black and white, more your smudgy blue biro, but you know what I mean.

'Go away and stop pestering poor Peter,' Elaine said to me.

'Yes, but he's putting absolute rubbish in his book, Elaine, and it's stupid. I'm not Peter Ingham's best friend!'

'Well, I think it's very nice that Peter wants you to be his friend,' said Elaine. She pulled a funny face. 'There's no accounting for taste.'

'Oh, ha-ha. Why did you put that, Peter?'

Peter did a little squeak about sharing birthdays and so that made us friends.

'It does *not* make us friends, dumbo,' I declared.

Elaine started getting on at me then, saying I was being nasty to poor little Peetie-Weetie and if I couldn't be friendly why didn't I just push off and get on with my own life story? Well, when people tell me to push off I generally try to stick to them like glue, just to be annoying, so that's what I did.

And then Jenny called me into the kitchen because she made out she wanted a hand getting the lunch ready, but that was just a *ploy*. Jenny doesn't smack. She doesn't even often tell you off. She just uses ploys and tries to distract you. It sometimes works with the thicker kids but it usually has no effect whatsoever on me. However, I quite like helping in the kitchen because you can generally nick a spoonful of jam or a handful of raisins when Jenny's back is turned. So I went along to the kitchen and helped her put an entire shoal of fish fingers under the double grill while she got the chip pan bubbling. Fish fingers don't taste so great when they're raw. I tried nibbling just to see. I don't know why they're called fish *fingers*. They don't have fingers, do they? They ought to be fish *fins*. That Aunty

Peggy used to make this awful milk pudding called tapioca which had these little slimy bubbly bits and I told the other kids that they were fish eyes. And I told the really little ones that marmalade is made out of goldfish and they believed that too.

When Jenny started serving out the fish fingers and chips, I went back into the sitting-room to tell everyone that lunch was ready. And I remember seeing Louise and Justine hunched up in a corner, giggling over something they'd got hidden. I don't know. I *am* highly intelligent, I truly wasn't making that up, and yet it was a bit thick of me not to twig what they were up to. Which was reading my own life story and then scribbling all over it.

A little twit like Peter Ingham would tell, but I'm no tell-tale tit. I shall simply get my own back. I shall think long and carefully for a suitable horrible revenge. I don't half hate that Justine. Before she came Louise and I were best friends and we did everything together and, even though I was still dumped in a rotten children's home, it really wasn't so bad. Louise and I made out we were sisters and we had all these secrets and—

One of these secrets was about a certain small problem that I have. A night-time problem. I've got my own room and so it was always a private problem that only Jenny and I knew about. Only to show Louise we were the bestest friends ever I told her about it. I knew it wasn't a sensible move right from the start because she giggled, and she used to tease me about it a bit even when we were still friends. And then she went off with Justine and I'd sometimes worry that she might tell on me, but I always convinced myself she'd never ever stoop that low. Not Louise.

But she has told.

She's told Justine, my worst enemy. So what am I going to do to her? Any ideas ticking away inside my head?

Well, I could beat her up.

Tick, tick, tick.
I could deliver a karate chop death blow.

Tick, tick, tick.

I could get my mum to come in her car and run her over, squashing her hedgehog-flat.

Tick, tick, tick. Hey! Tick tock. Tick tock. *I* know. And I also know I'm not leaving this book hanging about. From now on I shall carry it on my person. So, ha-ha, sucks boo to you, Justine Littlewood. Oh you're going to get it. Yes you are, yes you are, tee-hee.

I'm writing this at midnight. I can't put the light on because Jenny might still be prowling about and I don't want *another* ding-dong with her, thanks very much. I'm making do with a torch, only the battery's going, so there's just this dim little glow and I can hardly see what I'm doing. I wish I had something to eat. In all those Enid Blyton school stories they always have midnight feasts. The food sounds a bit weird, sardines and condensed milk, but I could murder a Mars Bar right this minute. Imagine a Mars Bar as big as this bed. Imagine licking it, gnawing away at a corner, scooping out the soft part with both fists. Imagine the wonderful chocolatey smell. I'm slavering at the thought. Yes, that's what those little marks are on the page. Slavers. I don't cry. I don't *ever* cry.

I acted as if I didn't care less when Jenny had a real go at me. And I don't.

'I think you really do care, Tracy,' she said, in that silly sorrowful voice. 'Deep down I think you're really very sorry.'

'That's just where you're wrong,' I insisted.

'Come off it now. You must know how you'd feel if your mother had bought you a special present and one of the other kids spoilt it.'

As she said that I couldn't help remembering being in the first Home, long before the dreaded Aunty Peggy or that mean hateful unfair Julie and Ted. My mum came to see me and she'd brought this doll, a doll almost as big as me, with long golden curls and a bright blue lacy dress to match her big blue eyes. I'd never liked dolls all that much but I thought this one was wonderful. I called her Bluebell and I undressed her right down to her frilly white knickers and dressed her up again and brushed her blonde curls and made her blink her big blue eyes, and at night she'd lie in my bed and we'd have these cosy little chats and she'd tell me that Mum was coming back really soon, probably tomorrow, and—

OK, that sort of thing makes me want to puke now but I was only little then and I didn't know any better. The housemother let me cart Bluebell all over the place but she tried to make me give the other kids a go at playing with her. Well, I wasn't going to let that lot maul her about, so of course I didn't let them hold her. But I came unstuck when I started school. You weren't allowed to take toys to school, only on Friday afternoons. I cried and fought but they wouldn't let me. So I had to start leaving Bluebell at home. I'd tuck her up in my bed with her eyes closed, pretending she was asleep, and then when I got home from school I'd charge upstairs into our crummy little dormitory and wake her up with a big hug. Only one day I woke her up and I got the shock of my life. Her eyelids snapped open but her blue eyes had vanished inside her head. Some rotten lousy pig had given them a good poke. I couldn't stand it, seeing those creepy empty sockets. She stopped being my friend. She just scared me.

The housemother took Bluebell off to this dolls' hospital and they gave her some new eyes. They were blue too, but not the same bright blue, and they didn't blink properly either. They either got stuck altogether or they flashed up and down all the time, making her look silly and fluttery. But I didn't really care then. She was spoilt. She wasn't the same Bluebell. She didn't talk to me any more.

I never found out which kid had done it. The housemother said it was A Mystery. Just One Of Those Things.

Jenny didn't call it a mystery when Justine went sobbing to her because her silly old Mickey Mouse alarm clock had got broken.

Clocks break all the time. It's not as if it's a really flash expensive clock. If I'd been Jenny I'd have told Justine to stop making such a silly fuss. I'd have stopped up my ears when that sneaky little twerp started going on about me. 'I bet I know who did it too, Jenny. *That Tracy Beaker.*'

Yes, she sneaked on me. And Jenny listened, because she came looking for me. She had to look quite a long time. I kind of suspected what was coming, so I cleared off. I didn't try to hide in the house or the garden like one of the little kids. I'm not that dumb. They can flush you out in five minutes no matter where you are. No, I skipped it out the back door and down the road and went for a wander round the town.

It was great. Yes, I had the most amazing time. First I went to McDonald's and had a Big Mac and french fries with a strawberry milk shake and then I went to the pictures

and saw this really funny film and I laughed so much I fell out of my seat and then I went off with this whole crowd of friends to an amusement arcade and I kept winning the jackpot on the fruit machines and then we all went off to this party and I drank a whole bottle of wine and it was great, it just tasted like lemonade, and this girl there, we made friends and she asked me if I'd like to stay the night, sharing her twin beds in this fantastic pink and white room, in fact she said I could stay there permanently if I really wanted and so I said . . .

I said: 'No thanks, I'd sooner go back to my crummy children's home.' ?

Of course I didn't say that. Well, she didn't say it either. I sort of made her up. And her party. I didn't go down the amusement arcade. Or to the pictures. Or McDonald's. I *would* have done, but I couldn't, on account of the fact I ran off with no cash whatsoever.

I said I tell fibs sometimes. It makes things more interesting. I mean, what's the point of writing what I really did? Which was loaf about the town feeling more and more fed up. The only thing I could think of to do was sit in the bus shelter. It got a bit boring. I pretended I was waiting for a bus and I tried to think of all the places I'd like to go to. But that began to depress me because I started thinking about Watford, where my mum said she lived. And last year I got all the right money together (which created a few problems afterwards as I sort of borrowed it without asking) and sussed out the journey and got all these trains and buses and all the rest of it, so that I could pay my mum a visit and give her a lovely surprise. Only it was me that got the surprise because she wasn't there, and the people who lived in that house said she'd moved on about six months ago and they didn't have a clue where she'd gone now.

So it's going to take a bit of organized searching to find her again. I could catch a different bus every day for the rest of my life and maybe not find her. It's hard when you haven't got a clue where to look.

I was still scrunched up in the bus shelter when a familiar white Minivan hoved into view. It was Mike, come looking for me. Mike looks after us with Jenny. He isn't half a bore. He doesn't often get cross but he whinges on about Rules and Responsibility and a whole lot of other rubbish.

So by the time I'd got back to the Home I was sick to death of the subject, but then Jenny came into my bedroom and *she* started. And she assumed it was me that broke Justine's clock though she had no proof whatsoever. I told her so, and said she just

liked picking on me, and it wasn't fair. She said I'd feel better if I owned up to breaking Justine's clock and then went to say sorry to her. I said she had to be joking. I wasn't the slightest bit sorry and anyway I didn't didn't *didn't* break Justine's rotten clock.

That isn't necessarily a fib. I don't absolutely one hundred percent *know* that I broke it. All right, I did go into her bedroom when she was in the bathroom, and I did pick up the clock to look at it. Well, she's always going on about it because she's got this boring thing about her dad. She makes out he's so flipping special when he hardly ever comes to see her. The only thing he's ever given her is that stupid tinny old alarm clock. I wanted to look at it to see if it was really so special. Well, it wasn't. I bet he just got it from Woolworth's. And it certainly wasn't made very carefully because when I twiddled the knobs to make the little Mickey on the end of the hands go whizzing round and round he couldn't keep it up for very long. There was this sudden whir and clunk and then the hand fell off altogether and Mickey fell too, with his little paws in the air, dead.

But he might have been about to take his last gasp anyway. That hand might well have fallen off the next time Justine touched the stupid clock to wind it up.

I'm not going to say sorry no matter what.
I wish I could get to sleep.
I'll try counting sheep . . .

I *still* can't get to sleep and it's the middle of the night now and it's rotten and I keep thinking about my mum. I wish she'd come and get me. I wish anyone would come and get me. Why can't I ever get a good foster family? That Aunty Peggy and Uncle Sid were lousy. But then I could suss them out and tell they were lousy right from the start. Anyone who smacks hard and serves up frogspawn for your pudding is certainly not an ideal aunty. But last time, when I got fostered by Julie and Ted, I really thought it was all going to work out happily ever after, and that it was my turn to be the golden princess instead of a *Rumpelstiltskin*.

They were great at first, Julie and Ted. That's what I called them right from the start. They didn't want to be a prissy aunty and uncle. And Julie said she didn't want me to call her Mum because I already had a mum. I thought such a lot of Julie when she said that. She wasn't exactly my idea of a glamorous foster mum – she had this long wispy brown hair and she wore sludge-coloured smocky things and sandals – and Ted looked a bit of a wimp too with his glasses and his beard and weirdo comfy walking shoes, not so much

Hush Puppy as Shut-your-face Hound-Dog – but I thought they were the sort of couple you could really trust. Ha!

Because I went to live with them and I thought we were getting on really great, though they were a bit boringly strict about stuff like sweets and bedtimes and horror videos, but then Julie started to wear bigger smocks than ever and lolled about on the sofa and Ted got all misty-eyed behind his glasses and I started to realize that something was up. And so I asked them what it was and they hedged and pulled faces at each other and then they looked shifty and told me that everything was fine and I knew they were lying. Things weren't fine at all.

They didn't even have the guts to tell me themselves. They left it to Elaine. She'd only just started to be my social worker then (I've had heaps because they kept moving around and leaving me behind and I got passed on like a parcel). I wasn't that keen on Elaine in those days. In fact I was really narked with her, because I'd had this man social worker Terry before her and he used to call me Smartie and he used to give me the odd tube of Smarties too, and I felt Elaine was a very poor substitute.

I wish I hadn't thought of those Smarties. I wish I had some now, I'm simply starving.

I'm sure Elaine marked me down as Sulky and Non-co-operative in her little notebook. The day she told me the Julie and Ted Bombshell I'm sure she scribbled TRACY TOTALLY GOB-SMACKED. Because Julie was having her own baby, after years of thinking she couldn't have any kids.

I didn't get it at first.

'So what's the problem, Elaine?' I said. 'We'll be a proper family then, four of us instead of three.'

Elaine was having difficulties finding the right words. She kept opening her mouth and closing it again, not saying a sausage.

'You look just like a fish when you do that, did you know?' I said cheekily, because my heart was starting to hammer hard against my chest and I knew that when Elaine eventually got the words out I wouldn't like the sound of them.

'The thing is, Tracy . . . Well, Julie and Ted have loved fostering you, and they've got very fond of you, but . . . you see, now they're having their own baby they feel that they're not really going to be able to cope.'

'Oh, I get it,' I said, in this jokey silly voice. 'So they're going to give the boring old baby away because they can't cope with it. And keep me. Because they had me first, didn't they?'

'Tracy— '

'They're not really going to dump me, are they?'

'They still very much want to keep in touch with you and— '

'So why can't I go on living with them? Look, I'll help all I can. Julie doesn't need to worry. I'll be just like a second mum to this baby. I know all what to do. I can give it its bottle and change its soggy old nappy and thump it on its back to bring up its wind. I'm dead experienced where babies are concerned.'

'Yes, I know, Tracy. But that's the trouble. You see, when Julie and Ted first fostered you, we did tell them a bit about your background, and the trouble you had in your first foster home. You know, when you shut the baby up in the cupboard— '

'That was Steve. And he wasn't a baby. He was a foul little toddler, and he kept mucking up our bedroom so I tidied him up into the cupboard just for a bit so I could get everything straightened out.'

'And there was the ghost game that got totally out of hand— '

'Oh that! All those little kids *loved* that game. I was ever so good at finding the right hiding places and then I'd start an eerie sort of moan and then I'd jump out at them, wearing this old white sheet.'

'And everyone got scared silly.'

'No they didn't. They just squealed because they were excited. *I* was the one who should have been scared, because they were all the ghost-busters you see, and I was the poor little ghost and— '

'OK, OK, but the point is, Tracy, it makes it plain in your records that you don't always get on well with little children.'

'That's a whopping great lie! What about Camilla? I looked after her at that children's home and she loved me, she really did.'

'Yes, I'm sure that's true, Tracy, but— Well, the thing is, Julie and Ted still feel they don't want to take any chances. They're worried you might feel a bit uncomfortable with a baby in the house.'

'So they're pushing me out?'

'But like I said, they still want to keep in touch with you and maybe take you out for tea sometimes.'

'No way,' I said. 'I don't want to see them ever again.'

'Oh Tracy, that's silly. That's just cutting off your own nose to spite your face,' said Elaine.

That's such a daft expression. How on earth would you go about it?

It wouldn't half hurt.

It hurt a lot leaving Julie and Ted's.

They wanted me to stay for a few months but I couldn't clear out of there quick enough. So here I am in this dump. They've tried to see me twice but I wasn't having any of it. I don't want any visitors, thanks very much. Apart from my mum.

I wonder where she is. And why didn't she leave a forwarding address at that last place? And how will she ever get to find me here? Yeah, that's the problem. I bet she's been trying and trying to get hold of me, but she doesn't know where to look. Last time I saw her I was at Aunty Peggy's. I bet Mum's been round to Aunty Peggy's and I bet that silly old smacking-machine wouldn't tell her where I'd gone. So I bet my mum got really mad with her. And if she found out just how many times that Aunty Peggy smacked me then wow, ker-pow, splat, bang, I bet my mum would really let her have it.

I don't half want my mum.

I know why I can't sleep. It's because I'm so starving hungry, that's why. Crying always makes me hungry. Not that I've been crying now. I don't *ever* cry.

I think maybe I'll try slipping down to the kitchen. Jenny's bound to be fast asleep by now. Yeah, that's what I'll do.

I'm back. I've had my very own midnight feast. And it was absolutely delicious too. Well, it wasn't bad. I couldn't find any chocolate, of course, and that was what I really fancied. But I found an opened packet of cornflakes and got stuck into them, and then I tried raiding the fridge. There weren't too many goodies. I didn't go a bundle on tomorrow's uncooked mince or yesterday's cold custard, but I poked my finger in the butter and then dabbled it in the sugar bowl and that tasted fine. I did quite a lot of poking and dabbling actually. I know Jenny might notice so I got my little finger nail and drew these weeny lines like teethmarks and then did some paw prints all over the butter, so she'd think it was a mouse. Mice do eat butter, don't they? They like cheese, which is the same sort of thing. Of course this is going to have to be a mountaineering mouse, armed with ice-pick and climbing boots, able to trek

up the grim north face of the Frigidaire. And then it's got to develop Mighty Mouse muscles to prise open the door of the fridge to get at the feast inside.

Maybe Jenny will still be a teensy bit suspicious. But I can't help that. At least she didn't catch me while I was noshing away at my midnight feast.

Someone else did though. Not in the kitchen. Afterwards, when I was sneaking up the stairs again. They're very dark, these stairs, and they take a bit of careful negotiating. One of the little kids is quite likely to leave a teddy or a rattle or a building brick halfway up and you can come an awful cropper and wake the entire household. So I was feeling my way very very cautiously when I heard this weird little moaning sound coming from up on the landing. So I looked up, sharpish, and I could just make out this pale little figure, all white and trailing, and it was so exactly like a ghost that I opened my mouth to scream.

But Tracy Beaker has a lot of bottle. I'm not scared of anybody. Not even ghosts. So I clapped my hand over my mouth to stop the scream and pattered right on up the stairs to confront this puny little piece of ectoplasm. Only it wasn't a ghost after all. It was just snivelling drivelling Peter Ingham, clutching some sheets.

'Whatever are you up to, creep?' I whispered.

'Nothing,' Peter whispered back.

'Oh sure. You just thought you'd take your sheets for a walk in the middle of the night,' I said.

Peter flinched away from me.

'You've wet them, haven't you?' I said.

'No,' Peter mumbled. He's a useless liar.

'Of course you've wet them. And you've been trying to wash them out in the bathroom, I know. So that people won't guess.'

'Oh don't tell, Tracy, please,' Peter begged.

'What do you take me for? I'm no tell-tale,' I said. 'And look, you don't have to fuss. Just get Jenny on her own in the morning and whisper to her. She'll sort it all out for you. She doesn't get cross.'

'Really?'

'Truly. And what you do now, you get yourself some dry sheets from the airing cupboard, right? And some pyjamas. Goodness, you don't know anything, do you? How long have you been in care?'

'Three months, one week, two days,' said Peter.

'Is that all? I've been in and out of care nearly all my life,' I said, getting the sheets for him. 'So why are you here now then? Your mum and dad get fed up with you? Can't say as I blame them.'

'They died when I was little. So I lived with my nan. But then she got old and then– then she died too,' Peter mumbled. 'And I didn't have anyone else so I had to come here. And I don't like it.'

'Well, of course you don't like it. But this is a lot better than most children's homes. You ought to have tried some of the places I've been in. They lock you up and they beat you and they practically starve you to death and then when they do give you meals it's absolutely disgusting, they pretend it's meat but it's really chopped up worms and dried dog's muck and— '

'Shut up, Tracy,' Peter said, holding his stomach.

'Who are you telling to shut up?' I said, but not really fiercely. 'Go on, you'd better shove off back to your room. And put your dry pyjamas on. You're shivering.'

'OK, Tracy. Thanks.' He paused, fidgeting and fumbling with his sheets. 'I wish you would be my friend, Tracy.'

'I don't really bother making friends,' I said. 'There's not much point, because my mum's probably coming to get me soon and then I'll be living with her so I won't need any friends here.'

'Oh,' said Peter, and he sounded really disappointed.

'Still. I suppose you can be my friend just for now,' I said.

I don't know why I said it. Who wants to be lumbered with a silly little creep like that? I'm too kind-hearted, that's my trouble.

There wasn't much point in getting to sleep, because when I did eventually nod off I just had these stupid nightmares. It's as if there's a video inside my head and it switches itself on the minute my eyes close and I keep hoping it's going to be showing this great comedy that'll have me in stitches but then the creepy music starts and I know I'm in for it. Last night was the Great Horror Movie of all time. I was stuck in the dark somewhere and there was something really scary coming up quick behind me so I had to run like mad. Then I got to this big round pool and there were these stepping stones with people perching on them and I jumped on to the first one and there was no room at all because that fat Aunty Peggy was spread all over it. I tried to cling to her but she gave me a big smack and sent me flying. So then I jumped on to the next stepping stone and Julie and Ted were there and I tried to grab hold of them but they just turned their backs on me and didn't even try to catch me when I fell and so I had to try to reach the next stepping stone but I was in the water doing my doggy-paddle

and it was getting harder and harder, and every time I swam to a stepping stone all these people prodded at me with sticks and pushed me away and I kept going under the water and . . .

. . . and then I woke up and I know that whenever I dream about water it spells Trouble with a capital T. I had to make my own dash to the airing cupboard and the laundry basket. I was unfortunate enough to bump into Justine too. She didn't look as if she'd slept much either. Her eyes seemed a bit on the red side. I couldn't help feeling a bit mean then, in spite of everything. So I gave her this big smile and I said, 'I'm sorry about what happened to your alarm clock, Justine.'

I didn't exactly tell her that *I* did it. Because I still don't know that it really was me. And anyway, I'd be a fool to admit it, wouldn't I? But I told her that I was still sorry, just like Jenny had suggested.

Only there's no point trying to be nice to pigs like Justine Littlewood. She didn't smile back and graciously accept my apologies.

'You'll be even sorrier when I've finished with you, Tracy Beaker,' she hissed. 'And what have you been doing, eh? Wet the bed again? Baby!' She hissed a lot more too. Stupid insulting things. I'm not going to waste my time writing them all down. Words can't hurt me anyway. Only I can't help being just a bit worried about that threat. What's she going to do to get her own back for the clock? If only we had poxy locks on our bedroom doors. Still, at least we've got separate bedrooms in this Home, even though they're weeny like cupboards.

It's new policy. Children in care need their own space. And I want to stay in my own space, doing all this writing, but Jenny has just put her head round my door and told me to buzz out into the garden with the others. And I said No Fear. Being in a Home is lousy at the best of times, but I just can't stick it in the school holidays when you're all cooped up together and the big ones bully you and the little ones pester you and the ones your own age gang up on you and have secrets together and call you names.

'How's about trying to make it up with Justine?' Jenny suggested, coming to sit on my bed.

So I snorted and told her she was wasting her time, and more to the point, she was wasting *my* time, because I wanted to get on with my writing.

'You've done ever such a lot, Tracy,' said Jenny, looking at all these pages. 'We'll be running out of paper soon.'

'Then I'll use the backs of birthday cards. Or bog roll. Anything. I'm inspired, see. I can't stop.'

'Yes, you've really taken to this writing. Going to be a writer when you grow up, eh?'

'Maybe.' I hadn't thought about it before. I was always sure I was going to be on telly with my own chat show. THE TRACY BEAKER EXPERIENCE and I'd walk out on to this stage in a sparkly dress and all the studio audience would clap and cheer and all these really famous celebrities would fight tooth and nail to get on my show to speak to me. But I reckon I could write books too.

'Tell you what, Tracy. We've got a real writer coming round some time this afternoon. You could ask her for a few tips.'

'What's she coming for?'

'Oh, she's doing this article for a magazine about children in care.'

'Oh that boring old stuff,' I said, pretending to yawn but inside I start fizzing away.

I wouldn't mind my story being written up in some magazine. A book would be better of course, but maybe that could come later. I'd have to be careful what she said about me though. Elaine the Pain made a right mess of my newspaper advert. I was Child of the Week in the local paper. If she'd only let me write it I'd have been bowled over by people rushing to adopt dear little Tracy Beaker. I know just how to present myself in the right sort of way.

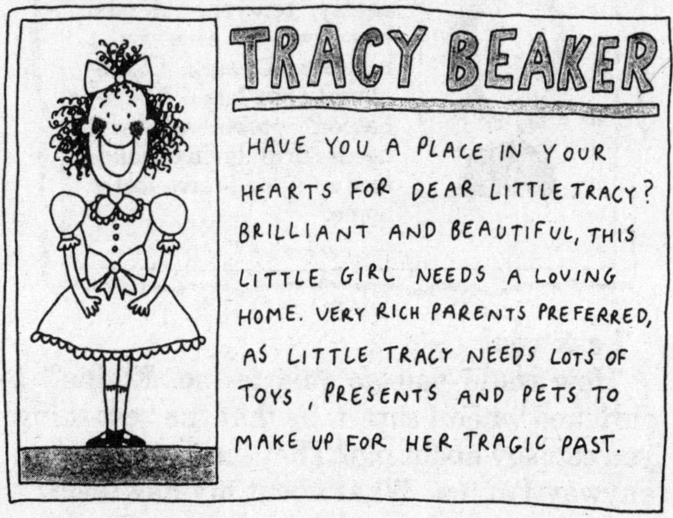

Elaine is useless. Doesn't have a clue. She didn't even let me get specially kitted out for the photograph.

'We want you looking natural, Tracy,' she said.

Well I turned out looking too flipping natural. Hair all over the place and a scowl on my face because that stupid photographer kept treating me like a baby, telling me to Watch the Birdie. And the things Elaine wrote about me!

TRACY

Tracy is a lively, healthy, chatty, ten-year-old who has been in care for a number of years. Consequently she has a few behaviour problems and needs firm loving handling in a long-term foster home.

I ask you!

'How could you *do* this to me, Elaine?' I shrieked when I saw it. 'Is that the best thing you can say about me? That I'm *healthy*? And anyway I'm not. What about my hay fever?'

'I also say you're lively. And chatty.'

'Yeah. Well, we all know what that means. Cheeky. Difficult. Bossy.'

'You said it, Tracy,' Elaine murmured.

'And all this guff about behaviour problems! What do I do, eh? I don't go round beating people up? Well, not many. And I don't smash the furniture. Hardly ever.'

'Tracy, it's very understandable that you have a few problems— '

'I *don't*! And then how could you ask for someone to handle me *firmly*?'

'And lovingly,' said Elaine. 'I put loving too.'

'Oh yes, they'll tell me how much they love me as they lay into me with a cane. Honestly, Elaine, you're round the twist. You're just going to attract a bunch of creepy child-beaters with this crummy advert.'

But it didn't even attract them. No-one replied at all.

Elaine kept telling me not to worry, as if it was somehow my fault. I know if she'd only get her act together and do a really flash advert there'd be heaps of offers. I bet.

But maybe I'm wasting my time nagging Elaine. This woman who's coming this afternoon might be just the chance I've been waiting for. If she's a real writer then she'll know how to jazz it all up so that I sound really fantastic. Only I've got to present myself to her in a special way so that she'll pick me out from all the others and just do a feature on me. So what am I going to do, eh?

Aha!

Not aha. More like boo-hoo. Only I don't ever cry, of course.

I don't want to write down what happened. I don't think I want to be a writer any more.

I tried, I really did. I went flying up to my bedroom straight after lunch and I did my best to make myself look pretty. I know my hair is untidy so I tried scragging it back into these little sticky-out plaits. Camilla had little plaits and everyone cooed over them and said how cute she looked. I thought my face looked a bit bare when I'd done the plaits so I wetted some of the side bits with spit and tried to make them go into curls.

I still looked a bit boring so I decided to liven my face up a bit. So I sneaked round to Adele's room. She's sixteen and she's got a Saturday job in BHS and she's got a drawer absolutely chock-a-block with make-up. I borrowed a bit of blusher to give myself some colour in my cheeks. And then I thought I'd try out a pink glossy lipstick too. And mascara to make my eyelashes look long. I tried a bit on my eyebrows too, to make them stand out. And I put a lot of powder on to be

like the icing on a cake. I thought I looked OK when I'd finished. Well, at least I looked different.

I changed my clothes too. I didn't want this writer to see me in a scrubby old T-shirt and skirt. No way. It had to be posh frock time. Only I don't really have a posh frock of my own. I did try on a few of Adele's things but somehow they didn't really suit me.

So then I started thinking about all the other girls. Louise had this really fantastic frock that she got a couple of years ago from some auntie. A real posh party frock with smocking and a flouncy skirt and its own sewn-in frilly white petticoat. It was a bit small for her now, of course, but she could just about squeeze into it for special days. And Louise and I are about the same size.

I knew Louise would go spare if she saw me parading around in her best party frock but I decided it might be worth it if I made a great impression on the writer woman first. So I beetled along the corridor towards her room, but I didn't have any luck. Louise was in her room. With Justine. I heard their voices.

They were discussing me, actually. And nappies. They were snorting with laughter and normally I'd have marched right in and punched their silly smirky faces but I knew if I got into a fight Jenny would send me to my room and make me stay there and I'd miss out on meeting the woman writer.

So with *extreme* self-control I walked away, still musing on what I was going to wear. I know it's summer, but I'd started to feel a bit shaky and shivery so I put on this mohair sweater that Julie knitted me for Christmas. When Julie and Ted dumped me I vowed not to have anything to do with them and I even thought about cutting up the mohair sweater into little woolly hankies but I couldn't quite do it. It's a pretty fantastic sweater actually, with the name Tracy in bright blue letters. That way it's obvious it's mine, specially made for me. Of course it's a bit tickly and prickly, but my mum once said you have to suffer if you want to look beautiful.

She's always looked beautiful. I don't half wish I took after her. I wasn't too bad as a baby. I was still quite cute as a toddler. But then I went off in a big way.

Still, I was trying my hardest to look OK. I only had my old skirt to wear with my mohair sweater, and there were dark blue stains all down one side where a biro exploded in my pocket, but I couldn't help that. The woman writer might just think it was a tie-and-dye effect. And at least the blue matched the lettering on my jumper.

I kept on prinking and preening in my room. I heard all the other kids go clattering downstairs. I heard Louise and Justine go giggle-snigger-titter along the corridor. My face started burning so that I didn't need my blusher. Then I heard Adele rampaging around because some rotten so-and-so had been in her room and rifled through all her make-up and mucked it all up. I decided to hang about in my room a bit longer.

I heard the front door bell. I heard Jenny talking to someone down in the hall. I heard them go into the sitting-room. I knew it was time to make my Entrance.

So I went running down the stairs and barging into the sitting-room with this great big smile on my face. It's no use looking sad or sulky if you want people to like you. Mum always tells me to give her a big smile. Even when she's saying goodbye to me. You can't look gloomy or it just upsets people and they don't want any more to do with you.

You've got to have this great big s-s-s-m-m-m-i-i-i-l-l-l-e-e-e.

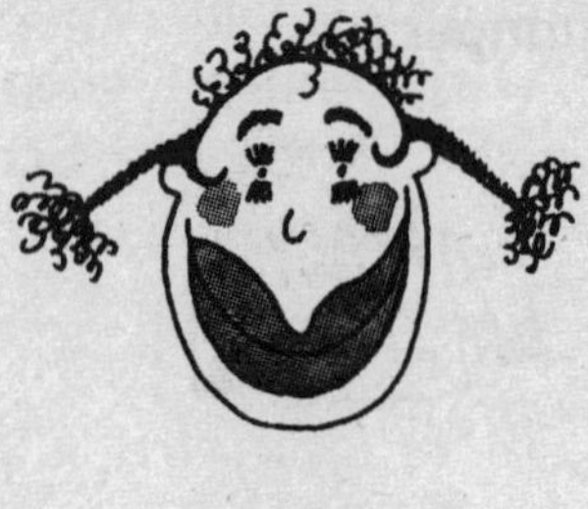

Everyone looked up at me when I went into the sitting-room. And they all smiled too. Just for a moment I was daft enough to think they were all smiling back at me. But then I saw they were the wrong sort of smiles. They were smirks. And Justine and Louise nudged each other and giggled and spluttered and whooped. And Adele glared at me. Peter Ingham was the only one with a proper smile. He came over to me. He was blinking a bit rapidly.

'You look . . . nice, Tracy,' he said.

But I knew he was lying. It was no use kidding myself. It was obvious I looked a right prat. Jenny's pretty laid back about appearances but even she looked shocked at the sight of me. And it looked like all that effort was for nothing, because she didn't seem to have the woman writer person with her after all.

I've seen women writers on chat shows on the telly. They're quite glamorous, like film stars, with glittery frocks and high heels and lots of jewellery. They look a bit like my mum, only nowhere near as pretty of course.

The woman with Jenny looked like some boring social worker or teacher. Scruffy brown hair. No make-up. Scrubby T-shirt and rumpled jeans. A bit like me on an off-day, grown up.

I decided to slope off back to my bedroom. It seemed sensible to steer clear of Adele anyway. But Jenny caught hold of me by the back of my jumper.

'Hang about, Tracy. I thought you wanted to meet Cam Lawson.'

'Who?' I said.

'You know. The writer. I told you,' Jenny hissed. Then she lowered her voice even more. 'Why are you wearing your winter jumper when it's boiling hot today? And what on earth have you done to your face?'

'She thinks she looks pretty,' said Justine, and she clutched Louise and they both shrieked.

'Pipe down, you two,' said Jenny. 'Tracy. Tracy!' She hung on to me firmly, stopping me barging over to that stupid pair of titterers so as I could bang their heads together. 'Leave them, Tracy. Come and meet Cam.'

I wanted to meet this Cam (what sort of a silly name is that?) even though she didn't look a bit like a *proper* writer, but I sort of hung back. I'm usually the last person to feel shy, but somehow I suddenly didn't know what to say or what to do. So I growled something at Jenny and twisted away from her and stood in a corner by myself, just watching.

Peter came trotting after me. Justine and Louise were still having hysterics at my appearance. You could tell they'd actually got over the giggles by this time, but Justine kept going into further false whoops and Louise was almost as bad.

'Don't take any notice of them,' Peter whispered.

'I don't,' I said crossly.

'I like your jumper,' said Peter. 'And your make-up. And the new hairstyle.'

'Then you're mad. It looks a mess. I look a mess. I look a mess *on purpose*,' I said fiercely. 'So you needn't feel sorry for me, Peter Ingham. You just clear off and leave me alone, right?'

Peter fidgeted from one foot to the other, looking worried.

'Clear off, you stupid little creep,' I said.

So of course he did clear off then. I wondered why I'd said it. OK, he *is* a creep, but he's not really that bad. I'd said he could be my friend. And it was a lot better when he was with me than standing all by myself, watching everyone over the other side of the room clustered round this Cam person calling herself a writer.

She's a weird sort of woman if you ask me. She was chatting away and yet you could tell she was really nervous inside. She

kept fidgeting with her pen and notebook and I was amazed to see she bites her nails! She's a great big grown-up woman and yet she does a dopey kid's thing like that. Well, she's not great big, she's little and skinny, but even so!

My mum has the most beautiful finger-nails, very long and pointy and polished. She varnishes them every day. I just love that smell of nail varnish, that sharp peardrop niff that makes your nostrils twitch. Jenny caught me happily sniffing nail varnish one day, and do you know what she thought? Only that I was inhaling it, like glue sniffing. Did you ever? I let her think it too. *I* wasn't going to tell her I just liked the smell because it reminds me of Mum.

I'll tell you another weird thing about Cam Whatsit. She sat on one of our rickety old chairs, her legs all draped round the rungs, and she talked *to* the children. Most adults that come here talk *at* children.

They tell you what to do.

They go on and on about themselves.

They talk about you.

They ask endless stupid questions.

They make personal comments.

Even the social workers are at it. Or they strike this special nothing-you-can-say-would-shock-me-sweetie pose and they make stupid statements.

'I guess you're feeling really angry and upset today, Tracy,' they twitter, when I've wrecked my bedroom or got into a fight or shouted and sworn at someone, so that it's *obvious* I'm angry and upset.

They do this to show me that they understand. Only they don't understand peanuts. *They're* not the ones in care. I am.

I thought Cam Thing would ask questions and take down case histories in her notebook, all brisk and organized. But from what I could make out over in the corner she had a very different way of doing things.

She smiled a bit and fidgeted a lot and sort of weighed everybody up, and they all had a good stare at her. Two of the little kids tried to climb up on to her lap because they do that to anyone who sits down. It's not because they *like* the person, it's just they like being cuddled. They'd cry to have a cuddle with a cross-eyed gorilla, I'm telling you.

Most strangers to children's homes get all flattered and make a great fuss of the littlies and come on like Mary Poppins. This Cam seemed a bit surprised, even a bit put out. I don't blame her. Little Wayne in particular has got the runniest nose of all time and he likes to bury his head affectionately into your chest, wiping it all down your front.

Cam held him at arm's length, and when he tried his burrowing trick she distracted him by giving him her pen. He liked flicking the catch up and down.

She let little Becky have a ride on her foot at the same time, so she didn't feel left out and bawl. Becky kept trying to climb up her leg, pulling her jeans up. Some of Cam's leg got exposed. It was a pretty ropey sort of leg if you ask me. A bit hairy for a start. My mum always shaves her legs, and she wears sheer see-through tights to show them off. This Cam had socks like a schoolgirl. Only they were quite funny brightly patterned socks. I thought the red and yellow bits were just squares at first, but then I got a bit closer and saw they were books. I wouldn't mind having

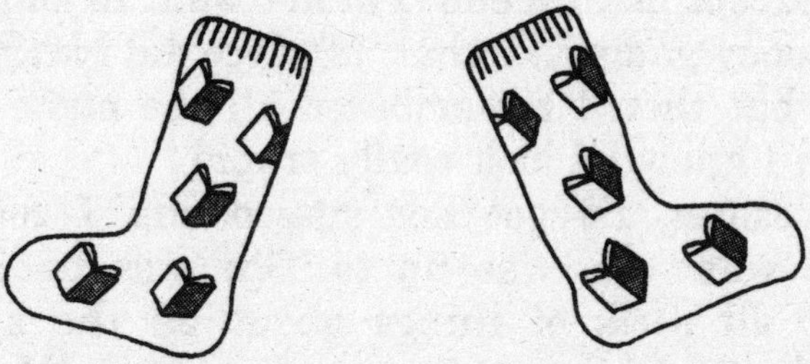

a pair of socks like that myself, if I'm going to write all these books.

She's written books. Old Cammy. Cammyknicker, ha-ha. The other kids asked her and she told them. She said she wrote some stories but they didn't sell much so she also wrote some romantic stuff. She doesn't look the romantic type to me.

Adele got interested then because she loves all those soppy love books and Cam told her some titles and the boys all tittered and went yuck yuck and Jenny got a bit narked but Cam said she didn't mind, they were mostly yuck but she couldn't help it if that's what people liked to read.

Then they all started talking about reading. Maxy said he liked this book *Where the Wild Things Are* because the boy in that is called Max, and Cam said she knew that book and she made a Wild Thing face and then everyone else did too.

Except me. I mean, I didn't want to join in a dopey game like that. My face did twitch a bit but then I remembered all the make-up and I knew I'd look really stupid.

Besides, I'd got her sussed out. I could see what she was up to. She was finding out all sorts of things about all the kids without asking any nosy questions. Maxy went on about his dad being a Wild Thing. Adele went on about love, only of course real life wasn't like that, and love didn't ever last and people split up and sometimes didn't even go on loving their children.

Even little creepy Peter piped up about these Catherine Cookson books that his nan used to like, and he told Cam how he used to read them to her because her eyes had gone all blurry. And then *his* eyes went a bit blurry too, remembering his nan, and Cam's hand reached out sort of awkwardly. She didn't quite manage to hold his hand, she just sort of tapped his bony wrist sympathetically.

'My nan's dead too. And my mum. They're both together in heaven now. Angels, like,' said Louise, lisping a bit.

She always does that. Puts on this sweet little baby act when there are grown-ups about. Like she was a little angel herself. Ha. Our little Louise can be even worse than me when she wants. She's had three foster placements, no, was it four? Anyway, none of them worked out. But Louise always swore she didn't care. We used to have this pact that we'd do our best not to get fostered at all and we'd stay together at the Home till we got to be eighteen and then we'd get them to house us together. In our own modern flat. We'd got it all planned out. Louise even started thinking about our furniture, the ornaments, the posters on the walls.

And then Justine came and everything was spoilt. Oh how I hate that Justine Littlewood. I'm glad I broke her silly Mickey Mouse alarm clock. I'd like to break her into little bits and all.

Anyway, Louise lisped on about angels and I'll give that Cam her due, she didn't go all simpering and sentimental and pat Louise on her curly head and talk about the little darling. She stayed calm and matter-of-fact, and started talking about angels and wondering what they would look like.

'That's simple, Miss. They've got these big wings and long white nighties and those gold plate things stuck on the back of their heads,' said Justine.

'Draw one for me,' said Cam, offering her pen and notebook.

'OK,' said Justine, though she can't draw for toffee. Then she had a close look at the

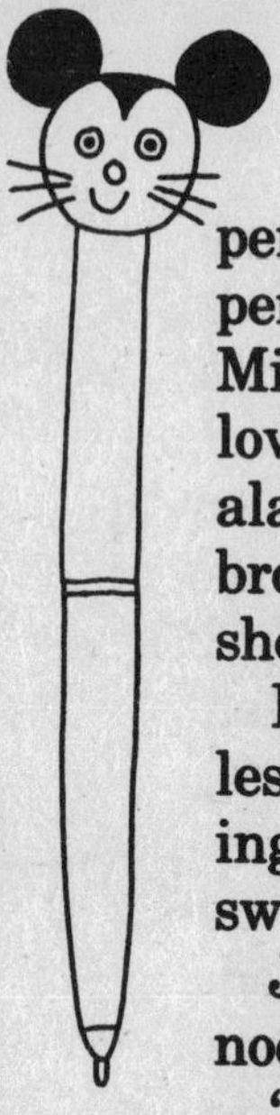

pen in her hand. 'Here, it's a Mickey Mouse pen. Look, Louise, see the little Mickey. Oh Miss, where did you get this pen? It's great! I love Mickey, I do. I've got this Mickey Mouse alarm clock, my dad gave it me, only some *pig* broke it deliberately.' Justine looked over her shoulder and glared at me.

I glared back, making out I couldn't care less. And I *couldn't*. My face started burning, but that was just because of my mohair sweater.

Justine drew her stupid angel and Cam nodded at it.

'Yes, that's the way people usually draw angels.' She looked at Louise. 'So is this the way you imagine your mum and your nan?'

'Well. Sort of,' said Louise.

'Is that the sort of nightie that your nan would wear? And what about the halo, the gold plate bit. Would that fit neatly on top of her hairstyle?'

Louise giggled uncertainly, not sure what she was getting at.

'You draw me what you think your mum and nan look like as angels,' said Cam.

Louise started, but she can't draw much either, and she kept scribbling over what she'd done.

'This is silly,' she said, giving up.

I knew what Cam was on about. I'd have

done a really great drawing of Louise's mum and nan in natty angel outfits. Like this.

'I'll draw you an angel, Miss,' said Maxy, grabbing at the pen. 'I'll draw me as an angel and I'll have big wings so I can fly like an aeroplane, y-e-e-e-o-o-o-w, y-e-e-e-o-o-o-w.' He went on making his dopey aeroplane noises all the time he was drawing.

Then the others had a go, even the big ones. I got a bit nearer and craned my neck to see what they'd all drawn. I didn't think any of them very inspired.

I knew exactly what I'd draw if she asked me. It wouldn't be a silly old angel.

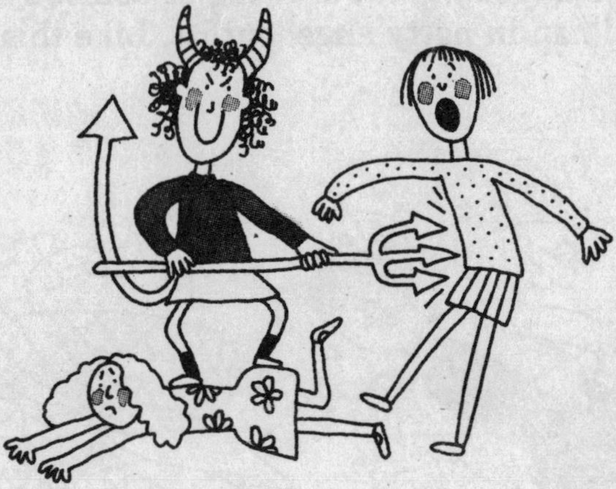

Then Cam looked up. She caught my eye. She did ask me.

'Have a go?' she said, dead casual.

I gave this little shrug as if I couldn't care less. Then I sauntered forward, very slowly. I held out my hand for the pen.

'This is Tracy,' said Jenny, poking her big nose in. 'She's the one who wants to be a writer.'

I felt my face start burning again.

'What, her?' said Justine. 'You've got to be joking.'

'Now Justine,' said Jenny. 'Tracy's written heaps and heaps in her Life Book.'

'Yeah, but it's all rubbish,' said Justine, and her hand shot out and she made a grab underneath my jumper, where I was keeping this book for safety. I bashed out at her but I wasn't quick enough. She snatched the book from me before I could stop her.

'Give that here!' I shrieked.

'It's rubbish, I tell you, listen,' said Justine, and she opened my book and started reading in a silly high-pitched baby voice "Once upon a time there was a little girl called Tracy Beaker and that sounds stupid and no wonder because I *am* stupid and I wet the bed and—Oooowwww!" '

Things got a bit hazy after that. But I got my book back. And Justine's nose became a wonderful scarlet fountain. I was glad glad glad. I wanted her whole body to spout blood but Jenny had hold of me by this time and she was shouting for Mike and I got hauled off to the Quiet Room. Only I wasn't quiet in there. I yelled my head off. I went on yelling when Jenny came to try and calm me down. And then Jenny went away and someone else came into the room. I wasn't sure who it was at first because when I yell my eyes screw up and I can't see properly. Then I made out the jeans and the T-shirt and the shock of hair and I knew it was Cam Whosit and that made me burn all over until I felt like a junior Joan of Arc.

There was me, throwing a hairy fit, and there was her standing there watching me. I don't care about people like Jenny or Elaine seeing me. They're used to it. Nearly all children in care have a roaring session once in a while. I have them more than once, actually. And I usually just let rip, but now I felt like a right raving loony in front of her.

But I didn't stop yelling all the same. There was no point. She'd already seen me at it. And heard me too. She didn't try to stop me. She wasn't saying a word. She was standing there. And she had this awful expression on her face. I couldn't stand it. She looked sorry for me.

I wasn't having that. So I told her to go away. That's putting it politely. I yelled some very rude words at her. And she just sort of shrugged and nodded and went off.

I was left screaming and swearing away, all by myself.

But I'm OK now. I'm not in the Quiet Room any more. I stayed in there ever such a long time and I even had my tea in there on a tray but now I'm in my bedroom and I've been writing and writing and writing away and it looks like I can't *help* being a writer. I've written so much I've got a big lump on the longest finger of my right hand. You look.

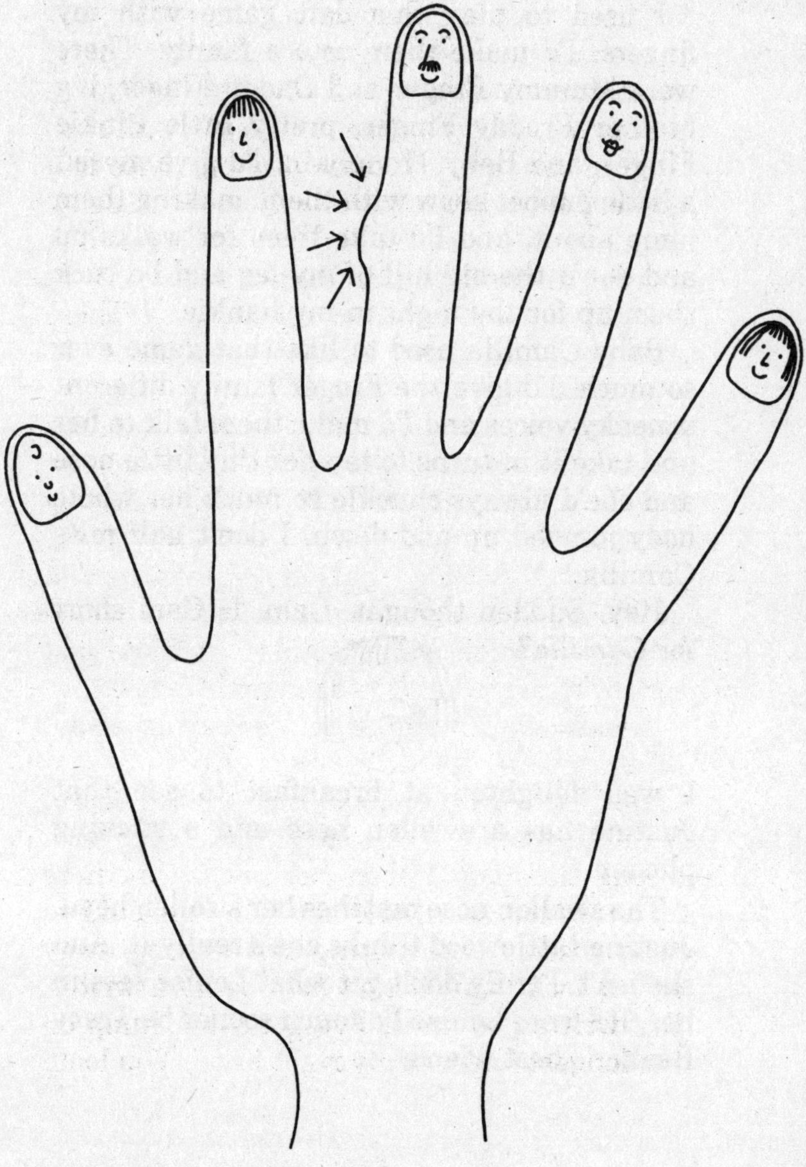

I used to play this daft game with my fingers. I'd make them into a family. There were Mummy Finger and Daddy Finger, big brother Freddy Finger, pretty little Pinkie Finger, and Baby Thumbkin. I'd give myself a little puppet show with them, making them jump about, and I'd take them for walks up and down the big hill of my leg and I'd tuck them up for the night in my hankie.

Baby Camilla used to like that game ever so much. I'd give the Finger family different squeaky voices and I'd make them talk to her and take it in turns to tap her tiny little nose and she'd always chuckle so much her whole body jumped up and down. I don't half miss Camilla.

Hey. Sudden thought. Cam. Is Cam short for *Camilla*?

I was delighted at breakfast to see that Justine has a swollen nose and a sticking plaster.

The swollen nose matches her swollen head. Justine Littlewood thinks she's really it. And she isn't. I truly don't get what Louise sees in her. If *I* were Louise I'd much sooner be Tracy Beaker's best friend.

What really gets me is that I was the one who palled up with Justine first. She turned up at the Home one evening, all down and droopy because her mum had cleared off with some bloke and left Justine and her two little brothers and her dad to get on with it. Only her dad couldn't get on with it, and the kids got taken into care. The brothers got into a short-term foster home because they were still nearly at the baby stage and not too much bother. But Justine didn't get taken on too, because they thought she'd be difficult.

I generally like kids who are difficult. And I thought I liked the look of Justine. And the sound of her. Because after the first droopy evening she suddenly found her tongue and she started sounding off at everyone, getting really stroppy and swearing. She knew even more swear words than I do.

She was like that all week but she shut up on Sunday. Her dad was supposed to see her on Sunday. She was sitting waiting for him right after breakfast, though he wasn't supposed to be coming till eleven o'clock. Eleven came and went. And twelve. And then it was dinnertime and Justine wouldn't eat her chicken. She sat at the window all afternoon, not budging.

My tummy went tight whenever I looked at her. I knew what it was like. I used to sit like that. Not just here. I used to wait at both my crummy foster homes. And the children's homes in between. Waiting for my mum to come.

But now I've got myself sorted out. No more dumb sitting about for me. Because my mum's probably too far away to come on a quick visit. Yeah, that's it, she's probably abroad somewhere, she's always fancied travelling.

She's maybe in France.

Or Spain, she likes sunshine.

What am I thinking of? She'll have gone to the States. Maybe Hollywood. My mum looks so great she'd easily get into the movies.

You can't hop on a bus and visit your daughter when you're hundreds and thousands of miles away in Hollywood, now can you?

All the same, even though I don't sit waiting, I always go a bit tingly when there's a knock at the door. I hold my breath, waiting to see who it is, just in case . . .

So I could understand what old Justine was going through. I didn't try to talk to her because I knew she'd snap my head off, but I sort of sidled up to her and dropped a lollipop on her lap and backed away. It wasn't exactly my lollipop. I'd snaffled several from little Wayne. His dopey mum is younger than Adele and she hasn't got a clue about babies. Whenever she comes she brings Wayne lollipops. Well, they've got sticks, haven't they? We don't want little Wayne giving himself a poke in the eye. And he's normally so drooly that if you add a lot of lolly-lick as well he gets stickier than Superglue. So it's really a kindness to nick his lollies when he's not looking.

'But why did you want to give one to that Justine?' Louise asked. 'She's horrible, Tracy. She barged right into me on the stairs yesterday and she didn't even say sorry, she just called me a very rude word indeed.' Louise whispered it primly.

'Um. Did she really say that?' I said, giggling. 'Oh she's not so bad really. And anyway, I didn't give her the *red* lollipop. I saved that for you.'

'Thanks, Trace,' said Louise, and she beamed at me.

Oh we were like *that* in those days.

I kept an eye on Justine. She didn't budge for a good half hour, letting the lollipop lie in her lap. And then I saw her hand creep out. She unwrapped it and gave it one small suspicious lick, as if I'd poisoned it. But it must have tasted OK because she took another lick, and then another, and then she settled down for a good long suck. Lollipops can be very soothing to the stomach.

She didn't say thank you or anything. And when she eventually had to give up waiting and go to bed she stalked off by herself. But the next day at breakfast she gave me this little nod. So I nodded back and flicked a cornflake in her direction and she flicked one back, and we ended up having this good game of tiddlyflakes and after that we were friends. Not best friends. Louise was my best friend. Ha.

She moaned at first.

'Why do we have to have that Justine hanging round us all the time?' she complained. 'I don't like her, Trace. She's dead tough.'

'Well, I want to be tough too. You've got to be tough. What do you mean, *I'm* tougher than Justine,' I said, sticking my chin out.

'Nutter,' said Louise.

It started to get to me though. I started swearing worse than Justine and Jenny got really mad at me because Maxy started copying me and even little Wayne would come out with a right mouthful when he felt like it.

So then I started the Dare Game. I've always won any dare. Until Justine came along.

I dared her to say the rudest word she could think of when the vicar came on a visit. And she did.

She dared me to go out in the garden stark naked. And I did.

I dared her to eat a worm. And she did.

She dared *me* to eat a worm.

I said that wasn't fair. She couldn't copy my dare. Louise opened her big mouth and said that I hated worms. 'Then I dare her to eat *two* worms,' said Justine. So I did.

I *did*. Sort of. It wasn't my fault they made me sick. I did swallow them first. Justine said I just spat them out straight away but I *didn't*.

I thought hard. I happen to be a crack hand at skateboarding. Justine's not much good at getting her balance and her steering's rotten. So I fixed up this skateboard assault course round the garden, with sloping benches and all sorts. And I dared Justine to have a go. So she did.

She fell over a lot. But she kept getting up and carrying on. So I said she was disqualified. But Louise said Justine should still win the bet if she completed the course. And she did.

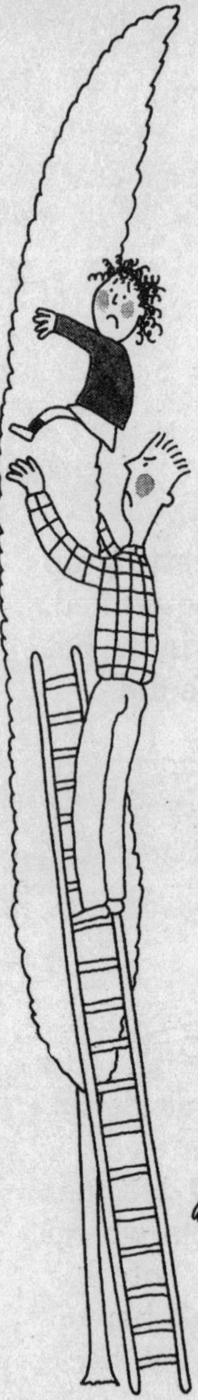

Then Justine dared me
to climb the tree
at the end of the garden.
So I did.
It wasn't *my* fault
I didn't get right to
the top. I didn't ask
that stupid Mike to
interfere. But Justine said
I'd lost that dare,
and Louise backed her up.
I couldn't believe my ears.
Louise was *my* friend.

We couldn't do any more dares because Jenny PUT HER FOOT DOWN. You don't argue when she does that.

The next day Justine's famous dad put in an appearance at long last. Justine had gone on and on about how good-looking he was, just like a pop star, and he actually had an evening job singing in pubs, which was why he couldn't be at home to look after her and her brothers. Well, you should have seen him. Starting to go bald. Pot belly. Medallion. He wasn't *quite* wearing a frilly shirt and flares, but almost.

You wouldn't catch me wanting a dad like that. But Justine gave a weird little whoop when she saw him and jumped up into his arms like a great big baby. He took her on some dumb outing and when she got back she was all bubbly and bouncy and showing off this . . . this present he'd bought her.

I don't know why, but I felt really narked at Justine. It was all right when she didn't get a visit, like us lot. But now I kept picking on her and saying silly sniggery things about her dad. And then she burst into tears.

I was a bit shocked. I didn't say anything *that* bad. And I never thought a really tough girl like Justine would ever cry. *I* don't ever cry, no matter what. I mean, my mum hasn't managed to come and visit me for donkey's years and I don't even *have* a dad, but catch me crying.

And then I got another shock. Because Louise turned on me.

'You are horrid, Tracy,' she said. And then she put her arms right round Justine and gave her a big hug. 'Don't take any notice of her. She's just jealous.'

Me, jealous? Of Justine? Of Justine's dopey dumb dad? She had to be joking.

But it didn't look like she was joking. She and Justine went off together, their arms round each other.

I told myself I didn't care. Although I did care a little bit then. And I did wonder if I'd gone over the top with my remarks. I can have a very cutting tongue.

I thought I'd smooth things over at breakfast. Maybe even tell Justine I hadn't really meant any of it. Not actually apologize, of course, but show her that I was sorry. But it was too late. I was left on my own at breakfast. Louise didn't sit next to me in her usual seat. She went and sat at the table by the window – with Justine.

'Hey, Louise,' I called. And then I called again, louder. 'Have you gone deaf or something?' I yelled.

But she could hear me all right. She just wasn't talking to me. She wasn't my best friend any more. She was Justine's.

All I've got is silly squitty twitty Peter Ingham. Oh, maybe he's not so bad. I was writing all this down when there was this tiny tapping at my door. As if some timid little insect was scrabbling away out there. I told this beetle to buzz off because I was busy, but it went on scribble-scrabbling. So eventually I heaved myself off my bed and went to see what it wanted.

'Do you want to play, Tracy?' he said.

'Play?' I said witheringly. 'What do you think I am, Peter Ingham? Some kind of infant? I'm busy writing.' But I'd been writing so much my whole arm ached and my writing lump was all red and throbbing. Oh, how we writers suffer for our art! It's chronic, it really is.

So I did just wonder if it was time for a little diversion.

'What sort of games do *you* play then, little Peetle-Beetle?'

He blinked a bit and shuffled backwards as if I was about to squash him, but he managed to squeak out something about paper games.

'Paper games?' I said. 'Oh, I see. Do we make a football out of paper and then give it a kick so that it blows away? What fun. Or do we make a dear little teddy out of paper and give it a big hug and squash it flat? Even better.'

Peter giggled nervously. 'No, Tracy, pen and paper games. I always used to play noughts and crosses with my nan.'

'Oh gosh, how incredibly thrilling,' I said.

Beetles don't understand sarcasm.

'Good, *I* like noughts and crosses too,' he said, producing a pencil out of his pocket.

There was no deterring him. So we played paper games after that.

I suppose it passed the time a bit. And now I've just spotted something. Right at the bottom of the page, in teeny tiny beetle writing, there's a little message.

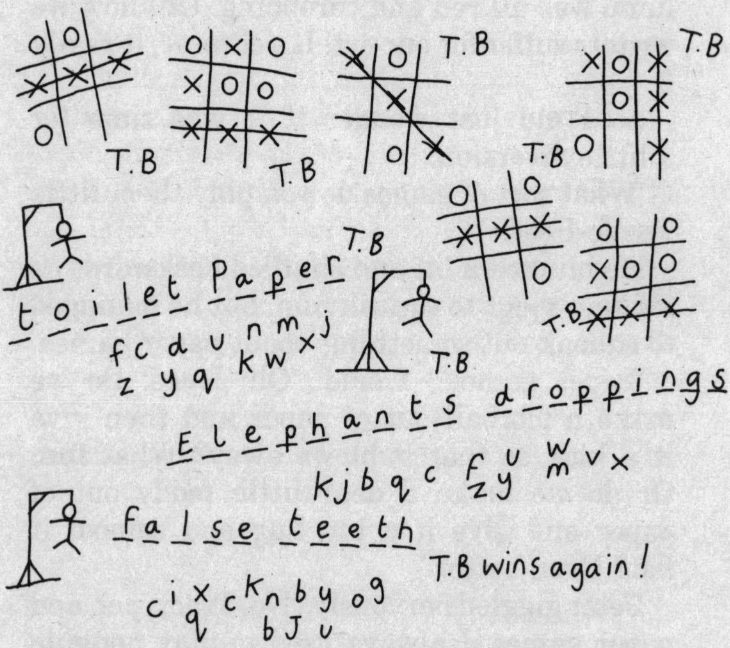

Justine Littlewood's Father
met my nan
At the sewage works
he said to her [redacted]

Censored!

I don't half like
you, Tracy.
signed Peter Ingham.

Guess what! I've got a letter!

Not another soppy little message from Peter. A real private letter that came in the post, addressed to Ms Tracy Beaker.

I haven't had many letters just recently. Oh, there have been plenty of letters *about* me. Elaine's got a whole library of files on me. I've had a secret rifle through them and you should just see some of the mean horrid things they say about me. I had a good mind to sue them for libel. Yeah, that would be great. And I'd get awarded all these damages, hundreds of thousands of pounds, and I'd be able to thumb my nose at Justine and Jenny and Elaine and all the others. I'd just clutch my lovely lolly in my hot little hand and go off and . . .

Well, I'd have my own house, right? And I'd employ someone to foster me. But because I'd be paying them, *they'd* have to do everything *I* said. I'd order them to make me a whole birthday cake to myself every single day of the week and they'd just have to jump to it and do so.

I wouldn't let anybody else in to share it with me.

Not even Peter. I had to share my *real* birthday cake with him. And he gave me a nudge and said 'What's the matter, Tracy? Don't you feel well?' just when I'd closed my

eyes tight and was in the middle of making my birthday wish. So it got all muddled and I lost my thread and now if my mum doesn't come for me it's all that Peter Ingham's fault.

Well, maybe it is.

But I'd still let him come round to my house sometimes and we could play paper games. They're quite good fun really, because I always win.

Who else could I have in my house? I could try and get Camilla. I'd look after her. I could get a special playpen and lots of toys. I've always liked the look of all that baby junk. I don't suppose I had much of that sort of thing when I was a baby. Yeah, I could have a proper nursery in my house and when Camilla wasn't using it I could muck about in there, just for a laugh.

I wonder if Camilla remembers me now? That's the trouble with babies.

I wonder if Cam *is* short for Camilla? That's who my letter was from.

I was a bit disappointed at first. I thought it was from my mum. I know she's never written to me before but still, when Jenny handed it to me at breakfast I just clutched at the envelope and held it tight and shut my eyes quick because they got suddenly hot and prickly and if I was a snivelly sort of person I might well have cried.

'What's up with Tracy?' the other kids mumbled.

I gave a great swallow and sniff and opened my eyes and said, 'Nothing's up! Look, I've got a letter! A letter from— '

'I think it's maybe from Cam Lawson,' Jenny said, very quickly indeed.

I caught my breath. 'Yeah. Cam Lawson. See that? She's written me my own personal letter. And she's not written to any of you lot. See! She's written to *me*.'

'So what does she say then?'

'Never you mind. It's *private*.'

I went off to read it all by myself. I didn't get around to it for a bit. I was thinking all these dopey things about my mum. And I had a bad attack of hay fever. And I didn't really want to read what Cam Lawson had to say anyway. She saw me having my hairy fit. I was scared she'd think me some sort of loony.

Only the letter was OK.

10 Beech Road
Kingtown

Dear Tracy

We didn't really get together properly when I came on my visit. It was a pity because Jenny told me a bit about you and I liked the sound of you. She said you're very naughty and you like writing.

I'm exactly the opposite. I've always been very very good. Especially when I was at school. You wouldn't half have teased me.

I'm not quite so good now, thank goodness.

And I hate writing. Because it's what I do for a living and every day I get up from my cornflakes and go and sit at my typewriter and my hands clench into fists and I go cross-eyed staring at the blank paper - and I think - what a stupid way to earn a living. Why don't I do something else? Only I'm useless at everything else so I just have to carry on with my writing.

Are you carrying on with your writing? You're telling your own story? An actual autobiography? Most girls your age wouldn't have much to write about, but you're lucky in that respect because so many different things have happened to you.

Good luck with it.

Yours,

Cam

Lee Road Dumping
Ground for Difficult Kids

Dear Ms Lawson,

Jenny says that's what I should call you, Ms Lawson, although you wrote Cam at the bottom of your letter. What sort of name is Cam? If you're called Camilla then I think that's a lovely name and don't see why you want to muck it up. I had a friend in this other home called Camilla and she liked her name. I had a special way of saying it, Ca-miiii-lla, and she'd always giggle. She was only a baby but very bright.

Why don't you mind me being naughty? Actually, its not always my fault that I get into trouble. People just pick on me. Lots of people, but I won't name names because I don't tell tales, not like <u>some</u> people.

Do you like my drawing? I liked yours, I thought they were funny. What do you mean, you hate writing?

I think that's weird when it's what you do. I like writing. I think it's ever so easy. I just start and it goes on and on. The only trouble is that it hurts your hand and you get a big lump on your finger. And ink all over your hand and clothes and paper if some clueless toddler has been chewing on your felt tip.

Are you having trouble writing your article about us? I could help you if you liked. I can tell you anything you need to know about me. And the others. How about it?

Yes I am still writing my autobiography. I like that word. I asked Jenny and she said it's a story about yourself, and that's right, that's exactly what I'm writing. I'd let you have a look at it but it's strictly personal. Don't take any notice of what that moron Justine read out. There are some really good bits, honest.

Yours

From your fellow writer

Tracy Beaker

R.S.V.P

That means you've got to reply.

10 Beech Road.

Dear Tracy,

Thanks for your lovely letter. It made me laugh. Do you know what? I think you're a born writer.

I could do with some help on my feature. Are you around next Saturday morning? Hope to see you then.

Cam.

I *hate* Camilla. I used to get teased rotten at school for having such a soppy name.

The dumping Ground.

Dear Camilla,

It's not a soppy name. You've got to be proud of it. You want to try having a name like Tracy Beaker. Excuse this crummy writing paper. Jenny lent me the first lot but she says I'm costing her a small fortune in paper and can't I give it a rest. So I borrowed this from one of the little ones. Isn't it yucky? I know.

This is Goblinda the Goblin and she's going to gob all over these daft fairies.

Yes, I'll help you out on
Saturday. If I'm there, of course.
My Mum often comes to take me out.
Although she may be abroad just now. I think
she's going to take me on a trip abroad too. But it
mightn't be for a while, so I'll see you on Saturday
morning probably. About what time? We have
breakfast at 8.30 on Saturdays and I always
eat quickly so about 8.35?

Yours, from your fellow - hang on, I'm
not a fellow
Yours, from another lady writer,

Tracy

R.S.V.P
So as I know what time to start waiting.

10 Beech Road

Dear Sister Writer,

See you Saturday morning. 8·35 impossible.

I look like this at 8·35.

How about 10·35?

Cam. Sorry. Camilla. Ugh!

P.S. I love Goblinda. Put her in a story.

Imagine staying in your bed half the morning. She is lazy. And she was late even then. It was 10.41 before she turned up. I'd practically given her up. She's supposed to be a professional writer and yet she can't even keep an appointment on time.

She's pretty hopeless if you ask me. She didn't half muck up this morning. I'd got it all worked out. I was ready to fill her in on all the facts. Mostly about me, of course. But I thought maybe she might fancy interviewing Peter too, to balance things up. A girl's point of view, and a boy's. No need to bother with any of the others.

Cam's got this dinky little tape recorder and after just one minute of instruction I mastered all the mechanism and had great fun fast-forwarding and rewinding and playing back. I had a little go first, trying out all my different accents, doing my Australian G'day routine and my American gangster and my special Donald Duck, but then I decided we'd better get down to business and as I'm not the sort of girl to hog the limelight I said Peter could go first.

He backed away from the tape recorder as if it was a loaded gun.

'Don't be so silly, Peter. Just act normal and speak into it.'

'What shall I say?' Peter squeaked.

I sighed impatiently. 'Just tell Cam your life story.'

'But I haven't got a story. I couldn't think of anything to put when Elaine gave me that book,' said Peter. 'I lived with my nan. And she died. So I came here. That's all there is.'

'That's OK, Peter. Don't let Tracy bully you into it. You don't have to say anything,' said Cam.

'What a cheek! I'm not a bully. Huh, *I* was the kid who always *got* bullied. This other Home I was in, there was this huge great teenage bloke, and he was a really tough skinhead and he had these bovver boots and I filled them up with custard for a joke and he didn't see the funny side of it

and yet he didn't half look hilarious, all this frothy yellow liquid squishing up his trouser legs – so anyway, from then on my name was mud, and he really had it in for me. The things he used to do!'

I was about to launch into a long account but typical typical that Justine Littlewood came barging over.

'It's not fair, Miss. You're letting that stupid Tracy show off like mad, and you're not giving any of us a go.'

'You shut your face, blabbermouth,' I said. 'She's not come to see you lot. She's come to see *me*. A strictly private appointment. So clear off. Isn't that right, Cam?'

'Well. Yes, I've come to talk to you, Tracy. But we could all have a go on the tape recorder for a bit,' she said.

What a gutless creep she is. She was there just to see *me*. We had a proper business appointment. All she had to do was tell Justine and the others to buzz off. It wouldn't have mattered if Peter stayed, because he's not really any bother. But the others! It was useless. Practically the whole morning was wasted. She let them all muck around on the tape recorder and then some of the littlies wanted another go drawing with her Mickey Mouse pen, and then Jenny came in with coffee for Cam and coke for us and it was like some big party. Only I didn't feel like the birthday girl. I felt squeezed out to the edge again.

After a bit I stomped off. I kept looking back over my shoulder and I thought she didn't even notice. But then she sidled up. She still had baby Becky on one hip and little Wayne clinging to her leg like a limpet. She gave me a dig in the back with her Mickey Mouse pen.

'Hey,' she said softly. 'Shall we get started on your interview now, Tracy?'

'Well, you've got all these other kids. Why waste your time with me?' I said acidly. 'I mean, I'm only the one you were *supposed* to see.'

'Tell you what. Let's go up to your room. Just you and me. How about it?'

'OK,' I said, yawning and shrugging. 'If you really want. I've gone off the idea now. But if you insist. Just for a minute or two.'

It took her a while to dump the baby and prise Wayne away, and then all the others kept clustering around, saying it wasn't fair. So do you know what she did? She said they could do interviews on her tape recorder. And she put *Justine* in charge of it.

'You aren't half making a mistake there, Cam. You're crazy. They'll wreck it in two minutes,' I said.

'No they won't. Justine will work it. And everyone take a two-minute turn. Introduce yourselves first, and then say whatever you want. But don't worry, Peter, you don't have to.'

'You are stark staring mad,' I said. 'Look, if anyone's in charge of that tape recorder it's got to be me. I'm the only one who knows how to work it properly.'

'Well, show Justine,' said Cam. 'Then she'll be able to work it too.'

'I'm not showing *her*,' I said. But in the end I did. And of course Justine was clueless and didn't catch on and I kept sighing and groaning and she got narked and gave me a push and I clenched my fist ready to give her a thump but Cam got in between us and said, 'Look, I'll run through it. Here's the record button, Justine, right?' and *eventually* Justine got the hang of it. I don't know why she's called Littlewood. Little*brain* would be far more appropriate.

Then Cam and I went up to my room and left them to it.

'You thought you'd found a way of getting Justine and me to make friends,' I said. 'But, ha-ha, it didn't work, did it? Because we're always going to be deadly enemies.'

Cam laughed at me. She laughed at the notice taped on my bedroom door too.

'It's OK. You can come in. You're my guest,' I said, opening the door for her.

My room looked a bit of a tip actually. I hadn't got round to making the bed and the floor was littered with socks and pyjama tops and bits of biscuit and pencil sharpenings, so she had to pick her way through. She didn't make a big thing of it though. She looked at all the stuff I've got pinned to my noticeboard, and she nodded a bit and smiled.

'Is that your mum?' Cam asked.

'Isn't she lovely? You'd really think she was a film star, wouldn't you? I think she maybe *is* a film star now. In Hollywood. And she'll be jetting over to see me soon. Maybe she'll take me back with her, and I'll get to be a film star too. A child star. The marvellous movie moppet, Tracy Beaker. Yeah. That would be great, eh?'

I spun around with a great grin, doing a cutsie-pie curtsey – and Cam caught on straight away and started clapping and acting like an adoring fan.

'I hope you're still going to be a writer too,' she said. 'Have you done any more about Goblinda?'

'Give us a chance. I've been too busy doing my autobiography,' I said.

'I suppose this autobiography of yours is strictly private?' Cam asked, sounding a bit wistful.

'Of course it is,' I said. But then I hesitated. Elaine the Pain has seen bits of it. And Louise and Littlebrain. And I did show a bit to Peter actually, just to show him how much I'd done. So why shouldn't I show a bit to Cam too? As she's a sort of friend.

So I let her have a few peeps. I had to be a bit careful, because some of the stuff I've written about her isn't exactly flattering. She came across a description of her by accident, but she didn't take offence. She roared with laughter.

'You really should be the one writing this article about children in care, Tracy, not me. I think you'd make a far better job of it.'

'Yes, have you made a start on this article yet?'

She fidgeted a bit. 'Not really. It's difficult. You see, this magazine editor wants a very touching sentimental story about all these sad sweet vulnerable little children that will make her readers reach for a wad of Kleenex.'

'Yeah, that's the right approach.'

'Oh come off it, Tracy. None of you lot are at all *sweet*. You're all gutsy and stroppy and spirited. I want to write what you're really like but it won't be the sort of thing the editor wants.'

'And it won't be the sort of thing *I* want either. You've got to make me sound sweet, Cam! No-one will want me otherwise. I've gone past my sell-by date already. It gets hopeless when you get older than five or six. You've stopped being a cute little toddler and started to be difficult. And I'm not pretty either so people won't take one look at my photo and start cooing. And then it's not like I'm up for adoption so people can't ever make me their little girl, not properly.'

'You're not up for adoption because you've still got your mum?'

'Exactly. And like I said, she'll be coming for me soon, but meanwhile I'd like to live in a proper homey home instead of this old dump. Otherwise I'll get institutionalized.'

Cam's eyebrows go up.

'I know what it means and all. I've heard Elaine and some of the other social workers going on about it. It's when you get so used to living in an institution like this that you never learn how to live in a proper home. And when you get to eighteen you can't cope and you don't know how to do your own shopping or cooking or anything. Although I can't see me ever having that problem. I bet I could cope right this minute living on my own. They'd just have to bung me the lolly and I'd whizz off down the shops and have a whale of a time.'

'I bet you would,' said Cam.

Then Maxy started scratching at my door

and whining and complaining. I told him to push off, because Cam and I were In Conference, but he didn't take any notice.

'Miss, Miss, it's not fair, them big girls won't let me have a go on the tape, I want a go, Miss, you tell them to let me have a go, they're playing they're pop stars, Miss, and *I* want a go.'

Cam smiled and sighed, looking at her watch.

'I'd better go back downstairs. I've got to be going in a minute anyway.'

'Oh that's not fair! Aren't you staying? You can have lunch with us lot, Jenny won't mind, and it's hamburgers on Saturday.'

'No, I'm meeting someone for lunch in the town.'

'Oh. Where are you going then?'

'Well, we'll probably have a drink and then we'll have a salad or something. My friend fusses about her figure.'

'Who wants boring old salad? If I was having lunch out I'd go to McDonald's. I'd have a Big Mac and french fries and a strawberry milkshake. See, I'm not the slightest bit institutionalized, am I?'

'You've been to McDonald's then?'

'Oh, heaps of times,' I said. And then I paused. 'Well, not actually *inside*. I was fostered with this boring family, Julie and Ted, and I kept on at them to take me, but they said it was junk food. And I said all their boring brown beans and soggy veggy stews were the *real* junk because they looked like someone had already eaten them and sicked them up and – well, anyway, they never took me.'

'No wonder,' said Cam, grinning.

'I am allowed to go out to lunch from here, you know.'

'Are you?'

'Yes. Any day. And tell you what, I really will work on that article for you. I could work on it this week and show you what I've done. And we could discuss it. Over lunch. At McDonald's. Hint, hint, hint.'

Cam smacked the side of her head as if a great thought has just occurred to her.

'Hey, Tracy! Would you like to come out with me to McDonald's next week?'

'Yes please!' I pause. 'Really? You're not kidding?'

'Really. Next Saturday. I'll come and pick you up about twelve, OK?'

'I'll be waiting.'

And so I shall. I'd better send her a letter too, just in case she forgets.

The dumping ground.

Dear Camilla,

I'm working hard on the article. I'll show you on Saturday. Remember we have a lunch-date. At 12. To go to McDonald's.

From your co-writer Tracy Beaker.

P.S Goblinda says if you took her to McDonald's she'd be ever so good and wouldn't gob once.

I know she said twelve o'clock. And she's not exactly the most punctual of people. She mightn't get here till ten past. Even twenty or half past. So why am I sitting here staring out of the window when we've only just had breakfast?

I hate waiting. It really gets on my nerves. I can't concentrate on anything. Not even my writing. And I haven't done any writing in this book all week because I've been so busy with my article for Cam. I've got it all finished now and even though I say it myself I've done a really great job. She can just bung it at her editor and no-one will be any the wiser. I should really get the whole fee for it myself. But I'm very generous. I'll share fifty fifty with Cam, because she's my friend.

Old Pete's my friend too. We've been bumping into each other in the middle of the night this week, on a sheet sortie. Mostly we just had a little whisper but last night I found him all huddled up and soggy because he'd had a nightmare about his nan. Strangely enough, I'd had a nightmare about my mum and it had brought on a bad attack of my hay fever. Normally I like to keep to myself at such moments as some stupid ignorant twits think my red eyes and runny nose are because I've been crying. And I never *ever* cry, no matter what.

But I knew Peter wouldn't tease me so I huddled down beside him for a bit and when I felt him shivering I put my arm round him and told him he was quite possibly my best friend ever.

He's just come up to me now and asked if I want to play paper games. Yeah, it might pass the time.

Oh charming! Peter and I had just got started and I was about to win the first game when Elaine the Pain comes buzzing in. She's here dumping off some boring new kid and now she wants to have a little chat with Peter.

'Well, tough, Elaine, because *I'm* having a little chat with Peter right now,' I said.

'Now now Tracy,' said Elaine.

'Yes, *now*,' I said.

Elaine bared her teeth at me. That smile means she'd really like to give me a clip around the ear but she's going to make allowances for me.

'I expect you're feeling a bit het up this morning, Tracy, because of this writer coming to take you out. Jenny's told me all about it. It'll be a lovely treat for you.'

'You bet. And it'll be a lovely treat for her too because I've written this article for her.'

'Well, I might have a little treat up my sleeve for Peter here,' Elaine said, and she shuffled him off into a corner and started talking to him earnestly.

She's still talking to him. She's keeping her voice down. But I can have very large waggly ears when I want. Elaine's going on about these people she knows. An older couple whose children have all grown up. And now they're a bit lonely. They'd like to look after someone. A little boy. Maybe a little boy just like Peter.

So that's it. Little Peetie-Weetie is obviously going to get fostered and live Happily Ever After.

Well, that's good, isn't it? Because he's my best friend.

No, it's bad, because he won't be able to be my best friend any more if he goes off and gets himself fostered.

And it's not fair. He's hardly been here any time. I've been here ages and ages and no-one ever wants to foster me now.

Still, who wants to be fostered by some boring older couple anyway? Older might mean really ancient. And crabby. And strict. They'd never wear jeans or write funny letters or take Peter to McDonald's.

I wish Cam would hurry up and come for me. Although it's nowhere near time. It's daft me sitting here by the window like this. Waiting.

Justine is hovering behind me. I think she's waiting for her dad. I hope she won't tell him about the little accident to her Mickey Mouse clock. He might come and beat me up. Even though the clock's all mended now. Jenny took it in to this shop and they sorted it. I was glad to see old Mickey tick-tocking round and round again. Justine caught me looking and she gave me this great fierce push that nearly knocked me over and told me that if I so much as touched her clock again she'd duff me up good and proper. Honestly! My fists clenched and I was all set to have a real go at her because no-one talks to Tracy Beaker like that, but then I remembered my lunch date. Jenny isn't best pleased with me at the moment. If I got into a punch-up with Justine then she mightn't let me go out with Cam.

So I Kept Calm. I smiled at Justine in a superior sort of way.

'Really Justine, do you always have to resort to violence?' I said.

My superior willpower was wasted on Justine. She just thought I was chicken.

'Cowardy cowardy custard,' she's mumbling under her breath now. 'Tracy Beaker's got no bottle.'

I shan't take any notice of her. I shall just sit here writing. And waiting. It's not *that* long now. Only it seems like for ever.

I used to sit like this. When I waited for my mum. I wonder when she will come. I had that awful dream about her. I was out having lunch with Cam in McDonald's and it was really great and we were having a smashing time together when I looked up at the clock and saw it had gone one o'clock, and

it suddenly rang a terrible bell in my head, and I remembered that my mum was coming to take me to lunch at one o'clock, and I just went panic panic panic.

I charged off to try to get back to the Home in time and I got a bus but they chucked me off because I didn't have enough money and then I ran into Aunty Peggy and she chased after me to give me a good smacking and Julie and Ted tripped me up and Justine caught me and threw me in a river and I couldn't swim and I was drowning . . . and then I woke up. Wet.

So OK, I know it was only a dopey old nightmare. But what if it was some kind of *premonition*??? What if my mum really comes for me today and I miss her because I'm having lunch with Cam?

I'll have to talk to Elaine.

Well, I've talked. Sort of.

'Can I have a little chat, Elaine?' I said.

'Tracy. I'm still having a little chat with Peter.'

'You've *had* a little chat with Peter. Correction. You've had an extremely long and boring endless conversation with him. And you're my social worker just as much as his. So could you *please* come and have a little chat with me. It's sort of urgent.'

Elaine sighed. She ruffled Peter's hair and gave him a little chuck under the chin. Then she came over to me at long last.

'What is it then, Tracy?'

I swallowed, not sure how to put it.

'Tracy, are you just winding me up?' said Elaine.

'No! It's just ... Look, about my mum. She doesn't know I'm here, does she?'

'Well. No, I don't think so.'

'But if she wanted to find me she could, couldn't she?'

I said it in a whisper but Justine heard.

'Who'd ever want to come looking for you, Tracy Beaker?' she said.

'You shut your mouth!'

Justine pulled a hideous face and Louise giggled. Then she tugged at Justine's sleeve.

'Come on. Let's see what that new girl's doing. She's got two whole suitcases with her, so she must have heaps of clothes.'

But Justine wanted to stay at the window so Louise wandered off by herself. I knew Justine was still listening for all she was worth (honestly, some people have no decency whatsoever) but I had to keep on asking Elaine.

'If my mum wanted she could go round to that old children's home. And they could tell her where I am now, couldn't they?'

'Yes, of course they would,' said Elaine. 'Don't worry, Tracy. Each time you get moved on somewhere else, there's a special record kept. So if your mum wants to see you then it's easy. They look up your name and file number and find your present address.'

'Good,' I said.

'What's up, Tracy? You still look a bit worried.'

'I'm OK.'

Only I don't feel OK. What if my mum does come today? And I'm out having lunch with someone else? Will she wait for me? Or will she get fidgety and fed up and zoom off again? And I'll get back here and Jenny will say, 'Oh, by the way, Tracy, your mum called when you were out, but she couldn't wait for you. She was all set to take you back to Hollywood with her but she had this plane to catch so she couldn't hang about.'

What am I going to do?

Maybe she won't come today. She hasn't ever come before. And yet, what if she did? I *wish* I hadn't had that dream. Dreams *can* come true.

I feel sick. Maybe I don't really want to go to McDonald's after all.

See that? It's real blood.

I'm not going to get to go to McDonald's now, whether I want to or not. I've had a fight. I'm in the Quiet Room.

This is how it happened. I went over to Peter. I whispered in his ear.

'Would you like to go to McDonald's with Cam?'

Peter scrunched up his neck because my whispers can be a bit tickly.

'You mean, go with you?'

'No. Go instead of me. I've kind of gone off the idea. It's OK, I'll tell Cam when she comes. She quite likes you, so she won't mind taking you instead.'

Peter looked worried.

'I can't, Tracy. I'm going out too. With these people.'

'What, with this boring older couple?' I said.

Elaine raised her eyebrows at me but I took no notice.

'I bet they won't take you to McDonald's,' I said.

'Why don't *you* want to go, Tracy?' Elaine asked. 'I thought you were so looking forward to it.'

'Yes, but . . . I want to stay here. Just in case.'

Elaine is a pain but she's also quite quick at putting two and two together.

'Tracy, I don't think your mum will be coming today,' she said quietly.

'Oh. I know that. Only I had this dream. She did in the dream.'

'Yes, I'm sure she did. And I expect it was a lovely dream but— '

'No, it was a perfectly foul dream because I wasn't here to see her and— '

'And you woke up blubbing with a soaking wet bed, *baby*,' Justine muttered.

'I told you to shut *up*,' I said, getting really riled.

'I'd go out with your writer friend, Tracy,' said Elaine.

'Mm. Well. I'm not sure I really want to now, anyway.' I glare at Peter. 'Why do you have to be seeing this boring old couple today, eh? You could see them any old time. You go and have a Big Mac with Cam.'

Peter wriggled. Elaine put her hand on his shoulder. He looked up at her and then at me.

'Sorry, Tracy. I want to meet them. Aunty Vi and Uncle Stanley.'

'Of course you want to meet them, Peter. And Tracy is going to meet her writer,' said Elaine.

'No, I'm not.'

'*I'd* go,' said Justine. 'Only I can't, because of my dad. I'm going out to lunch with him.'

'You were supposed to be going out with him last Saturday. Only he never turned up,' I said.

'OK, but he does come *sometimes*. Not like your famous mum. She's never ever ever come for you,' said Justine.

'Oh yes she has!' I yelled. 'She's come for me lots of times. She's going to come and take me away for good, we're going to Hollywood together and – will you stop *laughing* at me, you great big pig.'

'You're so stupid,' Justine gasped. 'Your mum's not a film star. Louise told me about your mum. She's nothing. And she's never coming for you. She hasn't been near you since you were little. I bet she's forgotten all about you. Or she's had heaps of other kids and doesn't want to think about that boring ugly Tracy ever again.'

So I hit her. And I kept on hitting her. And I don't care. I've made her nose bleed again. She's hurt me a bit too, but I don't care. And now I'm stuck in the Quiet Room and it's gone twelve and one of the other kids will get to go out to lunch with Cam instead of me and I don't care. At least it won't be Justine.

Maybe my mum *will* come.

There's someone outside the door. It's opening. *Is it Mum???*

No. It wasn't Mum. It never is. It was Cam, of course.

I took one look at Cam and burst into tears. Well, I would have done, if I was a crying sort of person.

'Oh dear,' said Cam. 'I don't seem to have a very good effect on you, Tracy.'

She sat right down on the floor beside me, waiting for me to quieten down a bit. Then she dug in the pocket of her jeans and found a crumpled tissue. She passed it to me and I mopped up my hay fever.

'Now,' said Cam. 'What do you want to do?'

'I haven't got any choice, have I? I'm stuck here.'

'No you're not. You can still come out to lunch with me. I've asked Jenny. Elaine explained why you got upset.'

'She doesn't know! I hate the idea of you lot all blabbing away about me,' I said fiercely.

'Yes, it must get a bit annoying,' said Cam. 'Still, at least it means you're the centre of everyone's attention. Here, you've still got a runny nose. Good job you weren't wearing your make-up this time.'

'Are you laughing at me?'

'Just a little tease. Coming?'

'You bet.'

Only I *still* felt bothered about my mum, even though I knew it was silly. I knew she almost definitely wouldn't be coming. I knew deep deep down that Justine was maybe right about her. But I still worried.

'My mum,' I mumbled.

'You're scared she'll come and you won't be here?' said Cam. 'OK. Tell you what we'll do. You can phone home when we're out. To check she's not arrived. And if she *has* I'll whisk you straight back. How about that?'

'That sounds great,' I said.

So Cam and I went off together for our lunch appointment after all. She's got this ancient grass-green Citroën which made a bit of a change from the Minivan.

'My mum wouldn't be seen dead in this sort of naff car,' I said. 'She drives a Cadillac you know.'

'Mm,' said Cam.

I squinted at her. 'You're just nodding to be nice to me, aren't you?' I said. 'You don't really believe my mum's got her own Cadillac.'

Cam looked at me. 'Do you believe it, Tracy?'

I thought for a bit. 'Sometimes.'

Cam nodded again.

'And sometimes I know I'm sort of making it up,' I mumbled. 'Do you mind that? Me telling lies?'

'I make things up all the time when I write stories. I don't mind a bit,' said Cam.

'I've got that article with me. I've written it all. You won't have to bother with a thing. Shall I read a bit to you? You'll be really impressed, I bet you will. I think I've done a dead professional job.'

So I started reading it to her.

'You can see the signs of suffering on little Tracy Beaker's elfin face. This very very intelligent and extremely pretty little girl has been grievously treated when in so-called Care. Her lovely talented young mother had to put her in a home through no fault of her own, and in fact she might soon be coming for her lovely little daughter, but until then dear little Tracy Beaker needs a foster family. She is deprived and abused in the dump of a children's home— Why are you laughing, Cam?'

'Abused?' Cam spluttered.

'Look at my hand. My knuckles. That's blood, you know.'

'Yes, and you got it bouncing your fist up and down on poor Justine's nose,' said Cam. 'You're the one who deprives and abuses all the others in your Home.'

'Yes, but if I put that no-one will want me, will they?'

'I don't know,' said Cam. 'If I were choosing, I'd maybe go for a really naughty girl. It might be fun.'

I looked at her. And went on looking at her. And my brain started going tick tick tick.

I was mildly distracted when we got to McDonald's. I ate a Big Mac and a large portion of french fries, and washed it down with a strawberry milkshake. So did Cam. Then she had a coffee and I had another milkshake. And then we sat back, stuffed. We both had to undo our belts a bit.

I got out my article again and showed her some more, but she got the giggles all over again.

'I'll give myself hiccups,' she said weakly. 'It's no use, Tracy. I think it's great, but they'll never print it. You can't say those sort of things.'

'What, that Tracy Beaker is brilliant and the best child ever? It's true!'

'Maybe! But you can't say all the other things, about Justine and Louise and the rest.'

'But they're true too.'

'No, they're not true at all. I've met them. I like them. And you certainly can't say those things about Jenny and Mike and your social worker and all the others. You'd get sued for libel.'

'Well, you do better then,' I said huffily. 'What would you put?'

'I don't know. Maybe I don't want to do the article now anyway. I think I'd sooner stick to my stories, and blow the money.'

'That's not a very professional approach,' I said sternly. 'Maybe you ought to give up writing. Maybe you ought to do some job that gives you a whacking great allowance. Looking after someone. You get an allowance for that.'

Cam raised her eyebrows.

'I can barely look after myself,' she said.

'Well then. You need someone to look after you for a bit,' I said. 'Someone like me.'

'Tracy.' Cam looked me straight in the eye. 'No. Sorry. *I* can't foster you.'

'Yes, you can.'

'Stop it. We can't start this. I'm not in any position to foster you.'

'Yes you are. You don't need to be married, you know. Single women can foster kids easy-peasy.'

'I'm single and I want to stay single. No husband. And *no kids.*'

'Good. I hate other kids. Especially boring little babies. You won't ever get broody, will you, Cam?'

'No fear. Holding that little Wayne was enough to douse any maternal urges for ever,' said Cam.

'So it could be just you and me.'

'No!'

'Think about it.'

Cam laughed. 'You aren't half persistent, girl! OK, OK, I'll think about it. That's all. Right?'

'Right,' I say, and I tap her hand triumphantly. 'Can I phone home now? I sound like E.T., don't I? We've got through two videos of that already. So, can T.B. phone home? Only she doesn't have any change.'

Cam gave me ten pence and I went to the phone by the Ladies and gave Jenny a buzz. My heart did thump a bit when I was waiting for her to answer. I felt a little bit sad when she told me that Mum hadn't come. Even though that was the answer I was really expecting.

But I had other things to fuss about now. I whizzed back to Cam.

'Well? Have you had your think? Is it

OK? Will you take me on?' I asked eagerly.

'Hey, hey! I've got to think about this for ages and ages. And then I'm almost certain it's still going to be no.'

'*Almost* certain. But not absolutely one hundred percent.'

'Mm. What about you? Are you absolutely one hundred percent sure you'd like me to foster you?'

'Well. I'd sooner you were rich. And posh and that, so that I could get on in the world.'

'I think you'll get on in the world without my help, Tracy.'

'No, I need you, Cam.'

I looked straight at her. And she looked straight at me.

'We still hardly know each other,' she said.

'Well, if we lived together we would get to know each other, wouldn't we, Cam? Camilla. That sounds classier. I want my foster mum to sound dead classy.'

'Oh Tracy, give it a rest. Me, classy? And I told you, I can't stick Camilla. I used to get teased. And that's what my mum always called me.' She pulled a face.

I was shocked by her tone and her expression.

'Don't you . . . don't you *like* your mum?' I said.

'Not much.'

'Why? Did she beat you up or something?'

'No! No, she just bossed me about. And my father too. They tried to make me just like them and when I wanted to be different they couldn't accept it.'

'So don't you see them any more?'

'Not really. Just at Christmas.'

'Good, so they'll give me Christmas presents, won't they, if I'm their foster grandchild?'

'Tracy! Look, it really wouldn't work. It wouldn't work for heaps of practical reasons, let alone anything else. I haven't got room for you. I live in this tiny flat.'

'I'm quite small. I don't take up much space.'

'But my flat's really minute, you should see it.'

'Oh great! Can we go there now?'

'I didn't mean— ' Cam began – but she laughed again. 'OK, we'll go round to my flat. Only I told Jenny I'd take you back to the Home after lunch.'

'T.B. can phone home again, can't she?'

'I suppose so. Tell Jenny I'll get you back by teatime.'

'Can't I come to tea with you too? Please?'

'Tell you what. We could pretend to be posh ladies just to please you and have afternoon tea. About four. Although I don't know how either of us could possibly eat another thing.

And then I'll take you back to the Home by five. Right?'

'What about supper? And look, I could stay the night, we're allowed to do that, and I don't need pyjamas, I could sleep in my underwear, and I needn't bother about washing things, I often don't wash back at the Home— '

'Great! Well, if you ever lived with me – and I said *if*, Tracy – then you'd wash all right. Now don't carry on. Five. Back at the Home. That'll be quite enough for today.'

I decided to give in. I sometimes sense I can only push so far.

I phoned, and Cam spoke to Jenny for a bit too.

'T.B.'s phoned home twice now. Like E.T. Do you know what E.T. got?' I said hopefully. 'Smarties.'

'You'll be in the Sunday papers tomorrow, Tracy. THE GIRL WHOSE STOMACH EXPLODED,' said Cam.

But she bought me Smarties all the same. Not a little tube, a great big packet.

'Wow! Thanks,' I said, tucking in.

'They're not just for you. Take them back and share them with all the others.'

'Oh! I don't want to waste them.'

'You're to share them, greedyguts.'

'I don't mind sharing them with Peter. Or Maxy. Or the babies.'

'Share them with everybody. Including Justine.'

'Hmm!'

She stopped off at another shop too. A baker's. She made me wait outside. She came out carrying a cardboard box.

'Is that cakes for our tea?'

'Maybe.'

'Yum yum. I'm going to like living with you, Cam.'

'Stop it now. Look Tracy, I seem to have got a bit carried away. I like seeing you and I hope we can go out some other Saturdays— '

'Great! To McDonald's? Is that a promise?'

'That really is a promise. But about fostering . . . I'd hate you to build your hopes up, Tracy. Let's drop the subject now and just be friends, OK?'

'You could be my friend *and* my foster mum.'

'You're like a little dog with a bone. You just won't let go, will you?'

'Woof woof!'

I'm getting good at making her laugh. I like her. Quite a lot. Not as much as my mum, of course. But she'll do, until my mum comes to get me.

Her flat came as a bit of a shock, mind you. It really is weeny. And ever so shabby. It's in far worse nick than the Home. And you should see her bedroom. She leaves her pyjamas on the floor too!

Still, once I get to live there I'll get her sorted out. Help her make a few improvements.

'Show me your books then,' I said, going over to the shelves. 'Did you write all this lot?'

'No, no! Just the ones on the bottom shelf. I don't think you'll find them very exciting, Tracy.'

She was dead right there. I flicked through one, but I couldn't find any pictures, or any funny bits, or even any rude bits. I'll have to get her to write some better books or she'll never make enough money to keep me in the style to which I want to become accustomed.

Maybe I'll have to hurry up and get my own writing published. I got Cam to give me a good long go on her typewriter.

It took me a while to get the hang of it. But eventually I managed to tap out a proper letter. I left it tucked away on Cam's desk for her to find later.

DEAR CAM, I WILL BE THE BESTEST FOSTER CHILD EVER. YOU'LL SEE. WITH LOVE FROM TRACY BEAKER, THE GIRL WHOSE STOMACH DIDN'T EXPLODE.

It did nearly though. Guess what she bought for tea! A birthday cake, quite a big one, with jam and cream inside. The top

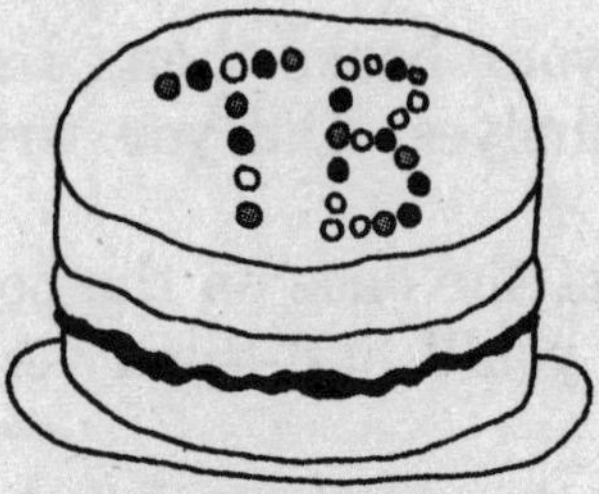

was just plain white, but she took some of my Smarties and spelt out T.B. on the top.

'So that it's all my cake,' I said happily.

'Aren't I going to get a slice?' asked Cam.

'Oh yes. Of course. But I don't have to share it with anyone else. I had to share my proper birthday cake with Peter, wasn't that *mean*!'

'I thought Peter's your friend.'

'Well. He is. But still. You don't want to share your birthday cake even with your bestest friend ever,' I said.

Only I started thinking about it all the time I was chomping my way through my first great big slice. And my second slice with extra jam and cream. And my third weeny slice. And my nibbles at a bit of icing.

'This is much better than that birthday cake at the Home, you know,' I said.

'Good.'

'Peter's gone out with this dumb sounding old auntie and uncle today,' I said.

'Has he?'

'But I bet they won't take him to McDonald's. Or buy him his own special cake.'

'Maybe not.'

'Well, seeing as we are friends, Peter and me, and we share a birthday, and we shared that other birthday cake – maybe we *ought* to share this one too,' I said. 'Shall I take a slice back for my friend Peter?'

'I think that would be a good idea,' said Cam. 'I'll wrap up a slice for Peter. And another slice for you. Just so long as you promise me you won't throw up all night.'

'Of course I won't. Here, can I do the cutting this time? Because if this is like a birthday cake I get a wish, don't I?'

So Cam gave me the knife and I closed my eyes and wished really really hard.

'I bet you can't guess what I wished,' I said to Cam.

'I bet I can,' said Cam.

'I'll tell you if you like.'

'Oh no. You're supposed to keep birthday cake wishes secret,' said Cam.

I pulled a little face at her. Then I thought.

'Here, if this is a sort of birthday, then it's a pity there aren't any presents too.' I paused. 'Hint hint hint.'

'Do you know what you are, Tracy Beaker? Absolutely shameless.'

But it worked!

Cam looked all round her room and stared for a while at her bookshelves. I thought I was going to end up with a boring old book. But it was much much better. She went to her desk and picked up her Mickey Mouse pen.

'Here we are, Tracy. Happy Unbirthday,' she said, and she pressed the pen into my hand.

Just for a moment I was lost for words. And that doesn't happen very often to me. I was scared I might even get another attack of my hay fever. But I managed to grin and give her the thumbs up sign and show her that I was ever so pleased.

We got back to the Home at five. On the dot. Trust her to be punctual at the wrong time. I made a bit of a fuss on the doorstep. I sort of clung a bit. It was just that I was enjoying myself so much that I wanted to go *on* enjoying myself. That's not being difficult, is it?

But it's still OK. She's coming next Saturday. She's promised. Twelve o'clock. We have a date, me and my future foster mum. I'm going to make that wish come true.

It took me a bit of time to calm down after we'd said goodbye. I missed out on tea, but it didn't really matter, seeing as I'd had more than half my cake and the McDonald's lunch and the Smarties. There were still quite a few Smarties left. Just no red ones. Or pink or mauve or blue. They're my favourite colours. But there were plenty of the boring ones to share with the others.

When I came out of the Quiet Room I collected my Smarties and the two slices of cake. They'd got a bit squashed as I was saying goodbye to Cam, but Jenny helped me spruce them up a bit and put them on a plate.

I went to find Peter. He was up in his room, sitting on his bed, looking a bit quiet.

'Oh oh,' I said. 'This older couple. They didn't turn up?'

'Oh yes. They did,' said Peter.

'But they were pretty awful, yes? Never you mind, Pete, see what I've got for us? Look, really yummy cake.'

'Thank you, Tracy,' said Peter, and he took his slice absent-mindedly. 'No, they aren't awful, Auntie Vi and Uncle Stanley. They're nice, actually.'

'I bet they didn't take you to McDonald's.'

'No, we went and had fish and chips. My nan and I always used to go and have fish and chips. With bread and butter and a cup of tea.'

'Boring! I had a Big Mac and french fries and a strawberry milkshake, two actually, and then Cam bought me these Smarties and then she bought me this really incredible cake and even put my name on the top. It was my extra special cake and I could have eaten it all up myself but I asked her to save a big slice for you. So I did. And you haven't even started on it yet. Don't you like it? It was meant to be your big treat.'

'Oh, it's lovely, Tracy,' said Peter, munching politely. 'It's ever so good of you. I told Auntie Vi and Uncle Stanley all about you and said that you were my best friend. They want to meet you very much.'

'Well, it's no use them getting interested in me. I'm going to be fostered by Cam, you wait and see.'

'Really? That's wonderful. You see, I think Auntie Vi and Uncle Stanley want to foster me, Tracy. That's what they said. They want to take me almost straight away.'

'So you're zooming off and leaving me in this dump, are you?' I said. 'Terrific!'

'Well. I don't *want* to leave you, Tracy. I told them that. But if you're going to be fostered too . . .'

'Yeah, yeah, well Cam's desperate to have me, but you shouldn't always rush into these things you know, Peter. You should think it over carefully.'

'I know. That's what I've been trying to do,' said Peter. 'Tracy. No matter who fosters me, who fosters you, we can still stay best friends, can't we? And visit each other lots? And write letters?'

'I'll write you letters with my very own

special Mickey Mouse pen. Want to see it?'

'Oh Tracy, you didn't nick it from Cam, did you?'

'Cheek! What do you take me for? She gave it to me, dumbo. I told you she's dotty about me. OK, we'll make a pact. We'll stay best friends no matter what. Here, you're leaving all the icing. Don't you like it?'

'Well, I was saving the best bit till last. But you have it, Tracy. I want you to have it, really.'

It's quite good, sharing a cake with your best friend.

Then I went round the whole Home with the packet of Smarties. I gave one each to everyone. I even gave one to Louise and the new girl. They were upstairs together, trying on the new girl's clothes.

Justine was downstairs. At the window. Her dad hadn't turned up. She had a new sticking plaster on her face. She was sniffling.

I looked at her. My heart started going thump thump thump. I went up to her. She turned round, looking all hopeful. She thought I was Louise. But it looks like Louise might have a new best friend now. Louise is like that.

Justine jumped a bit when she saw it was me.

'What do you want, Tracy Beaker?' she mumbled, wiping her eyes.

'I've got something for you, Justine,' I said.

I thought I was going to give her a Smartie. But you'll never guess what I did. I gave her my Mickey Mouse pen.

I must be stark staring bonkers. I hope Cam can get me another one. Next Saturday. When I see her. When she tells me that she's thought it all over and she wants to be my foster mum.

This started like a fairy story. And it's going to finish like one too. Happily Ever After.

ABOUT THE AUTHOR

JACQUELINE WILSON was born in Bath in 1945, but has spent most of her life in Kingston-on-Thames, Surrey. She always wanted to be a writer and wrote her first 'novel' when she was nine, filling countless Woolworths' exercise books as she gew up. She started work at a publishing company and then went on to work as a journalist on *Jackie* magazine (which was named after her) before turning to writing fiction full-time.

Since 1990 Jacqueline has written prolifically for children and has won many of the UK's top awards for children's books, including the Smarties Prize in 2000 and the Guardian Children's Fiction Award and the Children's Book of the Year in 1999. Jacqueline was awarded an OBE in the Queen's Birthday Honours list, in Golden Jubilee Year, 2002.

Over 10 million copies of Jacqueline's books have now been sold in the UK and approximately 50,000 copies of her books are sold each month. An avid reader herself, Jacqueline has a personal collection of more than 15,000 books.

She has one grown-up daughter.

'A brilliant young writer of wit and subtlety whose stories are never patronising and are often complex and many-layered'
THE TIMES

'Jacqueline Wilson has a rare gift for writing lightly and amusingly about emotional issues'
BOOKSELLER

'Wilson writes like a child, and children instantly recognize themselves in her characters. The tone of voice is faultless, her stories are about the problems many children face, and her plots work with classic simplicity . . . a subtle art is concealed by alertness, and some might call that genius'
DAILY TELEGRAPH

DOUBLE ACT
Jacqueline Wilson

No-one can ever be like a mother to us. NO-ONE. NO-ONE AT ALL. ESPECIALLY NOT STUPID FRIZZY DIZZY ROSE.

Ruby and Garnet are ten-year-old twins. Identical. They do *everything* together especially since their mother died three years earlier. But can being a double act work for ever? When so much around them is changing . . .

'Wonderfully perceptive'
BOOKS FOR CHILDREN

'Hilarious' THE TIMES

WINNER OF THE 1995 CHILDREN'S BOOK AWARD

WINNER OF THE SMARTIES PRIZE

0 440 863341

'Our whole lives have been shaken up.

Dad really has bought a bookshop! He didn't even take us with him to check it out first. He went away for the weekend with Rose, and when he came back he said, "Guess what! I've bought a shop."

We just stared at him stunned. He's been acting so crazy. Not like a dad at all. Especially not our dad . . .'

Ruby and Garnet are ten-year-old twins who do *everything* together. But can being a double act work for ever? Especially when everything around them is changing – beginning with Dad and his new friend, Rose . . .

Double Act is Jacqueline Wilson's seventh title to be published by Corgi Yearling Books. Other titles include *The Suitcase Kid*, which won the 1993 Children's Book Award, and *The Illustrated Mum*, which won the Guardian Children's Fiction Award.

Also available by Jacqueline Wilson.

Available from Corgi Pups, for younger readers:

THE DINOSAUR'S PACKED-LUNCH
THE MONSTER STORY-TELLER

Available from Young Corgi Books:

LIZZIE ZIPMOUTH

Available from Doubleday/Corgi Yearling Books:

BAD GIRLS
THE BED AND BREAKFAST STAR
BURIED ALIVE!
THE CAT MUMMY
CLIFFHANGER
THE DARE GAME
DOUBLE ACT
GLUBBSLYME
THE ILLUSTRATED MUM
THE LOTTIE PROJECT
THE MUM-MINDER
SECRETS
SLEEPOVERS
THE STORY OF TRACY BEAKER
THE SUITCASE KID
VICKY ANGEL
THE WORRY WEBSITE

Collections:

THE JACQUELINE WILSON COLLECTION
(includes The Story of Tracy Beaker and
The Bed and Breakfast Star)
JACQUELINE WILSON'S DOUBLE-DECKER
(includes Bad Girls and Double Act)
JACQUELINE WILSON'S SUPERSTARS
(includes The Lottie Project and The Suitcase Kid)

THE JACQUELINE WILSON DIARY

Available from Doubleday/Corgi children's books for older readers:

GIRLS IN LOVE
GIRLS UNDER PRESSURE
GIRLS OUT LATE
GIRLS IN TEARS

Double Act

Jacqueline Wilson

Ruby illustrated by
Nick Sharratt

Garnet illustrated by
Sue Heap

CORGI YEARLING BOOKS

For Anne, Derek, Thorne and Franca Dorothy

DOUBLE ACT
A CORGI YEARLING BOOK : 0 440 86623 5

First published in Great Britain by Doubleday,
a division of Random House Children's Books

PRINTING HISTORY
Doubleday edition published 1995
Corgi Yearling edition published 1996

Corgi Yearling Books are published by Random House Children's Books,
61–63 Uxbridge Road, London W5 5SA,
a division of The Random House Group Ltd,
in Australia by Random House Australia (Pty) Ltd,
20 Alfred Street, Milsons Point, Sydney, NSW 2061, Australia,
in New Zealand by Random House New Zealand Ltd,
18 Poland Road, Glenfield, Auckland 10, New Zealand
and in South Africa by Random House (Pty) Ltd,
Endulini, 5a Jubilee Road, Parktown 2193, South Africa.

Printed and bound in Great Britain by
Cox & Wyman Ltd, Reading, Berkshire

ONE

We're twins. I'm Ruby. She's Garnet.

We're identical. There's very few people who can tell us apart. Well, until we start talking. I tend to go on and on. Garnet is much quieter.

That's because I can't get a word in edgeways.

We are exactly the same height and weight. I eat a bit more than Garnet. I love sweets, and I like salty things too. I once ate thirteen packets of crisps in one day. All salt-and-vinegar flavour. I love lots of salt and vinegar on chips too. Chips are my special weakness. I go munch munch munch gulp and they're gone. So then I have to snaffle some of Garnet's. She doesn't mind.

Yes I do.

I don't get fatter because I charge around more. I hate sitting still. Garnet will hunch up over a book for hours, but I get the fidgets. We're both quite good at running, Garnet and me. At our last sports day at school we beat everyone, even the boys. We came first. Well, I did, actually. Garnet came second. But that's not surprising, seeing as I'm the eldest. We're both ten. But I'm twenty minutes older. I was the bossy baby who pushed out first. Garnet came second.

We live with our dad and our gran.

Dad often can't tell us apart in the morning at breakfast, but then his eyes aren't always

open properly. He just swallows black coffee as he shoves on his clothes and then dashes off for his train. Dad works in an office in London and he hates it. He's always tired out when he gets home. But he can tell us apart by then. It's easier in the evening. My plaits are generally coming undone and my T-shirt's probably stained. Garnet stays as neat as a new pin.

That's what our gran says. Gran always used to have pins stuck all down the front of her cardi. We had to be very careful when we hugged her. Sometimes she even had pins sticking out of her mouth. That was when she did her dressmaking. She used to work in this posh Fashion House, pinning and tucking and sewing all day long. Then, after . . .

Well, Gran had to look after us, you see, so she did dressmaking at home. For private customers. Mostly very large ladies who wanted posh frocks. Garnet and I always got the giggles when we peeped at them in their underwear.

Gran made all our clothes too. That was *awful*. It was bad enough Gran being old-fashioned and making us have our hair in plaits. But our clothes made us a laughing stock at school, though some of the mums said we looked a picture.

We had frilly frocks in summer and dinky pleated skirts in winter, and Gran knitted too – angora boleros that made us itch, and matching jumpers and cardis for the cold. Twinsets. And a right silly set of twins we looked too.

But then Gran's arthritis got worse. She'd always had funny fingers and a bad hip and a naughty knee. But soon she got so she'd screw up her face when she got up or sat down, and her fingers swelled sideways and she couldn't make them work.

She can't do her dressmaking now. It's a shame, because she did like doing it so much. But there's one Amazing Advantage. We get to wear shop clothes now. And because Gran can't really make it on the bus into town, we get to *choose.*

Well. Ruby gets to choose.

I choose for both of us. T-shirts. Leggings. Jeans. Matching ones, of course. We still want to look alike. We just want to look normal.

Only I suppose we're not really like the normal sort of family you read about in books. We read a lot of books. Dad is the worst. He keeps on and on buying them — not just new ones, but heaps of old dusty tomes from book fairs and auctions and Oxfam shops. We've run out of shelves. We've even run out of floor. We've got piles and piles of books in every room and you have to zig-zag around them carefully or you cause a bookquake. If you have ever been attacked by fifty or a hundred very hard hardbacks then you'll know this is to be avoided at all costs. There are big boxes

of books upstairs too that Dad hasn't even properly sorted. Sometimes you have to climb right over them to get somewhere vital like the toilet.

Gran keeps moaning that the floorboards won't stand up to all that weight. They do tend to creak a bit. Dad gets fussed then and agrees it's ridiculous and sometimes when we're a bit strapped for cash he loads a few boxes into our old car and takes them to a second-hand bookshop to sell. He does sell them too – but he nearly always comes back with another lot of bargains, books he couldn't possibly resist.

Then Gran has another fierce nag and Dad goes all shifty, but when he brings her a big carrier of blockbuster romances from a boot fair she softens up considerably. Gran likes to sit in her special chair with lots of plumped-up cushions at her back, her little legs propped up on her pouffe, a box of Cadbury's Milk Tray wedged in beside her, and a juicy love story in her lap. They're sometimes very *rude*, and when Garnet and I read over her shoulder she swats us away, saying we'll find out something we shouldn't. Ho ho. We found it all out *ages* ago.

Dad reads great fat books too, but they're not modern, they're all classics – Charles Dickens and Thomas Hardy. If we have a look at Dad's book we wonder what the Dickens they're on about and they seem *very* Hardy, but Dad likes them. He also likes boys' adventure books – really old ones where the boys wear knickerbockers and talk like twits: 'I say, old bean', and 'Truly spiffing', and 'Tophole'.

Garnet likes old books too – stuff like *Little Women* and *What Katy Did* and all those E. Nesbit books. And she reads twin books too. Books like *The Twins at St Clare's*. And all the *Sweet Valley Twins*. I read them too, because you can read them nice and quickly. But the books *I* like best are true stories about flashy famous people. Actors and actresses. I skip everything boring and just read the best bits when they're on telly and making movies and all over the front of the newspapers, very flashy and very famous.

We're going to be famous too someday, you bet. So I've started writing our life-story already. It's funny, Garnet is usually the one who writes stuff. Her writing's neater than mine. So often I get her to do my schoolwork. She doesn't mind.

Yes I do.

I was rifling through one of the boxes of books upstairs and right at the bottom there was this lovely fat red book. Ruby red, with a leather spine and one word picked out in gold lettering: ACCOUNTS.

I thought it was the title but when I opened it up there were just all these blank pages.

I asked Dad what had happened to the story and he said it wasn't a proper book at all. Accounts are sums. You add up everything you've bought. That's keeping accounts.

'Only I don't like keeping accounts. I just feel guilty seeing how much I've spent,' said Dad. 'You can have it to scribble in, twins.'

So I'm scribbling away.

I'm not.

Yes you are. I keep letting you have a turn. And I'm not just writing about me, I'm writing about us. Giving an account of ourselves. Hey, Garnet, find a dictionary and look up the word 'account'.

Account: 1. A verbal or written report, description, or narration of some occurrence, event, etcetera.

Yeah! That's exactly what I'm doing. Writing an account of our lives.

Everything's a bit boring right this minute but maybe soon we'll somehow get our big chance and we'll achieve our lifetime's ambition and be actresses.

I don't want to be an actress.

Of course we want to be actresses. Honestly, Garnet, give over jogging me. (She can be a bit stupid and shy at times. She doesn't think we'll ever make it as flashy film stars, but I keep telling her all we need is CONFIDENCE. She keeps going on at me now, saying she doesn't want to be a star. Well, that's mad. She can't mean it. Who on earth wouldn't want to show off all day in front of the camera and go to posh parties every night with all the other stars?)

We'll live in our own flash flat with masses

of flowers in every room and huge boxes of chocs to dip into whenever we fancy, and we'll wear ruby-red sequin frocks and ruby jewellery to match – OK OK, Garnet, you can have garnets, only they're not as precious and valuable and sparkly, *are* they?

That's not what you wanted to say? Well, what *do* you want to say then? All right. You write your bit now. Go on. Here you are. Get cracking. You write about you.

I don't know what to put.

I'm not used to writing about me. It's always us. I do like writing though. I was a bit annoyed when Ruby bagged this beautiful red book and started scribbling all that stuff. I thought we could maybe use it to write down our plays. We've always played these pretend games together right from when we were little. We pretend to be other people and make things up. It used to seem so real that it would get muddled into our ordinary life. It can still seem real for me, but Ruby often mucks about and won't play properly. She doesn't like going over and over a play, she just wants me to keep making up new ones for us. She doesn't seem to realize it's hard work. And if we keep starting on new plays then some of the best old plays get forgotten. I want to write them down properly to keep them safe.

I like making up plays and I don't mind acting them out when it's just Ruby and me and we're totally private and imagining it so it could almost be actually happening, but I can't bear proper *acting.*

Ruby and I were twin sheep in the nativity play when we were still in the Infants and it was one of the most truly awful experiences of my life.

Not the most awful, of course.

That was when

Look, you're not writing any of that sad stuff, I won't let you. This is me again. Ruby. Garnet's just gone off, all humpy because I happened to scratch her a tiny little bit when I snatched the pen. I asked her nicely first. And it's my turn now. You have to be able to take turns fairly when you're twins.

That stuff she wrote is daft anyway. What's the point of writing plays down in books? You should *play* plays. And she's got to be an actress because that's what we've always wanted to be, and while we're still trying to get famous we can do adverts and game shows on the telly. Identical twins are a Mega-Novelty.

Garnet can't reject Fame just because of

that one unfortunate experience being a sheep when we were little.

She got so worked up and nervous when we had to perform that she wet herself. On stage. In front of everyone. But it didn't really *matter*. I don't know why she still gets all hot and bothered if I happen to bring it up. It was dead appropriate, actually, because that's what real sheep do all the time. They don't hang around the stable with their back legs crossed, holding it in. They go all over the place. Which is what Garnet did. And everyone thought it was ever so funny. Except Garnet.

Got to go now. I can smell Sunday dinner. Yorkshire pud, yummy yummy yummy in my tummy.

Ruby! You mean pig. You've put about me being the sheep!

Look, *you* were the one who mentioned it first. You went on and on about it.

Yes, but I didn't say what happened. It was my most painful and humiliating secret. And now you've told, Ruby.

I haven't *told*. I've written. And this accounts book is secret. Just for us. We can write everything down in it. All our secrets.

Yes, but you haven't written down your *secrets. You've written down mine.*

Oh, quit fussing. Let's go and eat. I'm starving.

Gran's a bit cross because Dad's ever so late back from his car-boot sale and she's had the dinner turned down low for the last half-hour and her Yorkshire is going all sad and soggy.

Like some silly twin. Come on, Gran's calling.

Dad should have been back ages ago. He is

all right, isn't he?

Of course he is. You are an old worryguts, Garnet. He'll have just bought up an entire bookstall, that's all, and he'll be having trouble stuffing them all into the car. You know what he's like.

Yes, but he's not usually as late as this. And he likes Gran's Sunday dinners as much as we do. What if he's had an accident?

Oh, Garnet, shut up. Coming, Gran.

TWO

We haven't been able to write a proper account because tons and tons of stuff has been happening. And now I suppose I should write it all out and yet I don't know where to start. You have a go, Garnet. Go on.

I don't want to go on. I want to stop. No. I want to go backwards. Back past the day Dad was late back from the boot fair. Back past the ordinary us twins and Dad and Granny day after day part. Back through the awful bit when Mum died and

STOP IT STOP IT STOP IT

No, Ruby. We can't stop now. We've got to remember. And don't you see? We've got to make Dad remember. And then he'll stop seeing Rose.

Ah. All right. But tell it quickly. The bit about Mum. Tell it as if it was a story and not real so that it won't hurt so much.

Once upon a time a man called Richard fell in love with a girl called Opal. Opals are beautiful stones that shine all different colours. But some say opals are unlucky. This girl Opal was beautiful and she shone and Richard knew he was lucky lucky lucky to have met her.

Richard loved Opal. He sometimes mucked about and called her Oh Pal. Because he said she was his pal. And he gave her an opal ring.

Where's that ring? Remember how we used to be allowed to try it on? But I haven't seen it for ages. Oh no. Oh Garnet, you don't suppose Dad will give it to *Rose*?

No! Of course not. Gran's got it safe in her jewel box and she says we'll get it when we're grown up.

Which one of us? It ought really to be me, seeing as I'm the eldest. But I'll let you borrow it sometimes. If you're careful.

I'm *the careful one. Look, you've interrupted my story now.*

Go on then. You got to the ring bit. Dad gave Mum the ring.

Richard gave Opal a beautiful opal ring, milky-white but with all different pinks and blues and greens and purples, sparkling like magic whenever it caught the light.

They got their own flat.

They got married.

They had twin daughters.

Which is which? I'm that one, the baby with Mum.

No, that's me. You're the baby with Dad. I drew it so I should know.

Well, I can't help that. The baby with Mum is the biggest baby, you just look and see. And *I* was the biggest, we both know that. That's baby Ruby. I'll show you.

It doesn't matter anyway. OK, you're the baby with Mum.

Right. Well. Mum held you too, of course. She held me and then she held you and Dad held me and then

And then we grew up a bit and we could toddle around and we didn't need to be held. Though we still had cuddles with Mum. We sat on her lap. Both of us together. I can remember.

You're just remembering that photograph. Hey, let's stick it in the accounts book.

It's not just the photo. I can remember. She felt so soft and yet her arms could hold you so

tight you felt safe. And there was her flowery smell, and her curly hair tickled. She tickled us too, remember? Round and round the garden and then she'd tickle us under our arms and we'd go all squirmy. Remember that, Ruby?

(She's gone all quiet. She can't stand remembering because it makes her so sad and she can't ever stand being unhappy. She won't ever cry. That's one of the few ways people tell

us apart. If one of us has gone all red and watery-eyed then it's me.

I think I might cry a bit when I write this next part. I'll go back to doing it like a story. And I'll scribble it down ever so quickly.)

The twins started school, and Opal and Richard went to work and at the weekend they did fun things like going swimming and shopping and they had days at the seaside. All the normal nice family things. But then everything stopped being normal and nice. Opal got a bit sick. Then she had to go into hospital. She was all right for a bit after that. But then she got sick again. She couldn't work any more. She lay on the sofa at home. Gran had to meet the twins from school. Richard stopped working and looked after Opal. But she couldn't get better. She died. So they stopped being a family.

There. I've written it. Do you want to read what I put, Ruby? No, she doesn't. It was three years ago. When we were seven. But we're ten now and it's all right again. We can't ever be our old family but we're a new family now. Gran lives with us and she's not like a mother, but then no-one can ever be like a mother to us. NO-ONE. NO-ONE AT ALL. ESPECIALLY NOT STUPID FRIZZY DIZZY ROSE.

This is Rose.

No, THIS is Rose.

Yes, that's Rose. Only she's even worse than that. What does Dad see *in her? He's the only one that likes her. Gran doesn't like her one little bit.*

Gran's face when Dad turned up with Rose that Sunday! We all just stared at her. And Dad came out with all this guff about how she'd helped him when his bag of books broke, and then surprise surprise her car wouldn't start so he'd given her a lift and they'd popped into a pub for a quick drink on the way home and she was all set to have a sandwich for her lunch and Dad said he'd got a proper roast-beef-and-Yorkshire job cooking for him at home and she went Oooh it's ages since I had a proper Sunday dinner like that so guess what, folks. He brought her back. To share our Sunday lunch.

'There's no problem, is there, Gran?' Dad said.

'No, of course not. Do come and sit down at the table, Rose. There's plenty of food. I'm afraid the beef will be a bit overdone and I can't take pride in my Yorkshire today. It *was* lovely and light and fluffy, but . . .'

'But I waylaid your son-in-law and kept him down the pub and mucked up your meal,' said Rose, and she actually laughed. 'Sorry about that,' she said, though she didn't look the *slightest* bit sorry.

Gran had to smile back at her through gritted teeth like it was funny.

We didn't smile though, did we, Garnet?

She couldn't take the hint though. She chatted away to us, nattering on about telly programmes and pop records and stuff, as if she'd known us years and years. And she kept trying to remember which of us was which.

'Now, you're Garnet, right?' she said to me. 'And you're Ruby,' she said to Garnet.

'Yes,' we said. 'Right.'

'Wrong,' said Dad, laughing uneasily. 'That's Ruby. And that's Garnet. They're a pair of jokers. Even Gran and I get confused at times.'

'Speak for yourself,' Gran said huffily. 'I'm sorry the beef was so dry. Though it would have been just cooked through a treat an hour or so ago. Anyway. Apple pie and cream? Help me clear the plates, girls.'

We helped her clear and when we came

back with the pudding plates I sat in Garnet's chair and she sat in mine. Rose was none the wiser. She nattered away to me, calling me Garnet, and she jabbered stuff to Garnet, calling her Ruby.

'Yes, I'm beginning to be able to tell you apart,' she said. 'You're Ruby. And you're Garnet. Yes. Right.'

'Well. Not *quite* right,' said Dad. He came out with this false ho-ho-ho as if it was a great joke. 'Stop teasing poor Rose, twins. I'm afraid they've swopped seats. They're always doing it. I'd just call each girl "Twin"and be done with it, Rose.'

'Oh, I think that's awful,' said Rose. 'I couldn't stand that if I were a twin.'

Well, certainly twin Roses would be AWFUL.

'You're two separate people who just happen to be sisters, aren't you, Garnet and Ruby. Or Ruby and Garnet. Whichever. I've got muddled.'

'We like being called Twin,' I told her.

'That's what they call us at school,' said Garnet.

'We *are* twins . . .' I said.

'So we like . . .' said Garnet.

'Being called . . .' I said.

'Twins,' we said simultaneously.

Rose raised one eyebrow and gave a little nod.

'OK OK,' she said. 'Got it.'

She stopped trying to be so matey with us then. She tried complimenting Gran on her apple pie but Gran stayed as dried up as the dinner and barely said a word. So Dad did all the talking, on and on, saying all this silly stuff and pulling faces and telling stupid stories.

He didn't sound like Dad at all.

It was as if *he'd* swopped with a new twin dad.

He didn't go back to being our dad even when we'd got rid of Rose at last.

'Well, what did you think of her?' he asked eagerly.

I looked at Garnet. She looked at me. I raised one eyebrow. She raised one too. Then we both turned sideways and pretended to be sick.

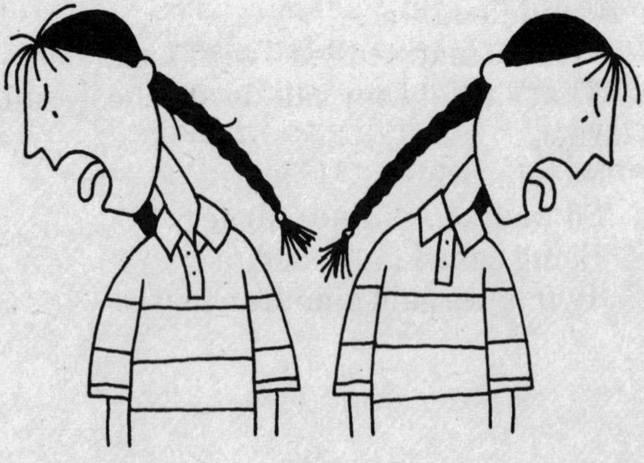

'All right, all right. You've done enough clowning around for one day,' Dad said crossly.

'Yes, don't be so rude, Ruby and Garnet,' said Gran – but she didn't sound a bit cross.

'Did you like Rose, Gran?' Dad asked.

'Well. She seems nice enough. I suppose. A bit . . . pushy, inviting herself to lunch like that.'

'No, I invited her,' said Dad. 'I didn't think you'd make such a big deal about it, actually. You've always said you wished I'd socialize a bit more, bring a few friends home, not stay so wrapped up in the past.'

'Yes, dear. And I mean that. I'm only too pleased that you want to bring people back. Though if you could have just phoned to give me a bit of warning . . . And you do want to go a bit carefully with that type of woman.'

'What do you mean, *type*?' said Dad, really angry now.

'Now, Richard, don't get in such a silly state,' said Gran, as if he was our age. 'It's just that she seems a bit eager. She's never set eyes on you before today and yet she's all over you, even trying to act like one of the family.'

'I've known Rose for months, if you must know,' said Dad. 'She's got her own bric-a-brac stall in the arcade – we're forever bumping into each other at boot fairs. I've always wanted to get to know her better, she's so bubbly and warm and friendly. I don't know how you can talk about her like that – she's a lovely girl.'

'Girl!' said Gran. 'She'll never see thirty again.'

'Well, neither will I,' Dad shouted. 'And it's about time I started making the most of my life, OK?'

He stormed off out of the house, slamming the door. There was a horrible silence after he'd left. Garnet got hold of my hand and squeezed it tight. She looked like she was going to cry. *Gran* looked like she was going to cry too.

We were all shocked by the row. We don't ever have rows in our family.

It's all that Rose's fault.

Yes, it's all Rose's fault. She started all the changes. She comes every Sunday now. And in the week sometimes. And Dad goes out with her in the evenings and when they come back in the car, they KISS.

THREE

I hate changes. I want every day to be the same. I've always been like it, even before Mum died.

I couldn't stand our first day at school.

Everybody stared at us because we were different. And the whole day *was different. We couldn't play our own games and talk in our*

own private language. It felt like we couldn't even be twins, because the teacher sat me on one side of the classroom and Ruby on the other. She said it was so she could tell us apart.

I felt as if she'd somehow torn us apart. I didn't feel a whole person at all. I felt like a half, as if an arm and a leg and most of my head were the other side of the room stuck to Ruby. I didn't know how to think without her.

Well, naturally. I'm the oldest. I'm the DOMINANT twin. That's what they call the one that's born first. That's me. I'm the Big Cheese. You're just the Little Crumb.

You didn't like us being separated either, Ruby. You didn't cry

You did.

but you were ever so naughty and so we got sent to the headteacher and she said, 'Why are you so unhappy, Garnet? Why are you so naughty, Ruby?' and we said, 'We want to sit together.' And she said, 'Is that all? Simple!'

And it was simple. We sat together. I didn't cry any more. And Ruby wasn't naughty. Well, she was, *but not so much.*

But it still took me ages and ages to get used to school. But now it's OK. Everyone's so used to us they don't stare. We're just The Twins. That's the way we want it. We sit together in every lesson. We're always partners. We sit next to each other at lunch. We even go to the loo together.

We're good at lessons. We sometimes come top, especially when we have to write stories or do a project.

But we like Drama best. We're absolutely fabulous at Drama. Well. *I* am. Garnet goes all red and gets her words mixed up.

Don't start, Ruby.

Well, you do. Only you wouldn't if you'd stop being so shy. I don't know why you're so shy. *I* never feel shy.

Look, I just want to write about

You've been writing for ages and ages and you keep waffling on about us back in the Infants and who's bothered about baby stuff like that? Write about what's happening now. All the horrible bit.

Well, give me the pen.

Say please then. Hey! Get off!

'Are you two girls having a fight?'

That's Gran. She's seen us snatching the pen from each other.

'You can share nicely if you try. Now you're going to have to remember all I've taught you when you go. *She's* not the type to bother with good manners.'

'Oh,Gran. I don't want to go!' I said, and I

flung myself on to her lap.

'Watch my hip! And my knee! Ruby, you great lump, get off of me,' said Gran – but she cuddled me close all the same.

'Can I come and join in the cuddle too?' I asked.

I sat on the arm of the chair so I didn't hurt Gran's other hip and knee, but she reached out and pulled me properly on to her lap.

We clung tight. I started crying.

'Stop it, Garnet,' said Ruby, and she pinched me hard. Her face was all screwed up. She was scared I'd make her start crying, even though she never cries. Gran's eyes were all watery too.

'Dear oh dear,' she said, sniffling. She patted us with her poor hands, the fingers all slipping sideways with arthritis. She fumbled up the sleeve of her cardi for her hankie and mopped my face and hers, and then pretended to blow Ruby's nose.

'We'd better turn off the waterworks. I don't want a puddle in my chair,' said Gran.

'Oh Gran, please please please come with us,' Ruby begged.

'Now don't you start, young Ruby. You know it's all settled and decided.'

'But we'll miss you so, Gran!' I said, nuzzling into her warm woollen chest.

'And I'll miss both of you, my girls. But you can come and stay with me on visits – you can sleep either end of the sofa and bring your sleeping bags – and I'll maybe come to this new place for Christmas.'

'Not maybe. You've GOT to come.'

'We'll see. Of course, there's probably no point. She doesn't have a clue about cooking. She probably won't even bother to have a proper turkey.'

'So why can't we all come to you for Christmas, Gran, and then we can have Christmas dinner the way you do it, with cranberry sauce and little chipolatas and chestnut stuffing, yummy yummy,' said Ruby.

'That oven in my new flat is so small it would be hard put to cook a chicken in it,' said Gran. 'Sorry, pet. No more Christmas dinners.'

'No more roast potatoes with special crispy bits and Christmas pud with little silver charms and traffic-light jelly, red and yellow and green,' Ruby wailed.

'I think you're going to miss my cooking more than you'll miss me,' said Gran, shaking her head. 'Come on now, you're both squashing me something chronic. You'd better get back to your writing. Is it something for school?'

There's no point doing anything for school. Because we won't be going there much longer. We've got to go to a new school. In a new place. In a new life. And we're going to hate it.

It's all her fault. We hate her. WE HATE HER.

Yes. We hate her. It all started when Dad met Rose. She kept coming round upsetting us. Barging in. Changing things.

She changed Dad. It isn't just the way he acts, all loopy and lovey-dovey, yuck yuck yuck. She's changed his clothes. He always used to wear just ordinary Dad clothes. Jumpers. Trousers. Suits and white shirts on weekdays, with stripy ties. She started with the ties. She bought him this bright red flowery number.

Then it was Marilyn Monroe. And Mickey Mouse. Dad looked a bit of a cartoon himself in all these daft ties. She didn't stop there. Oh no.

Would you believe, Donald Duck underpants!

At least they were hidden under his trousers. She started on his shirts next. Green stripes. Red check. Blue polka dot.

She said they brightened up his dull old suit.

She was worse with his weekend clothes. She made him give his tracksuit and his comfy old cords to Oxfam. She said they were old man's clothes. She's turned Dad into a new man. A new stupid trendy twit of a dad

in black jeans and
denim jackets and
lumberjack shirts.

She even calls him a new name. Rick. It's Rick this, Rick that. Sometimes it's even Ricky. It doesn't half make you feel Sicky.

Gran can't bear it either.

'His name's *Richard*,' she hissed one day. 'We've always called him Richard. No-one ever calls him Ricky or Rick.'

She said it in the sort of voice that makes Garnet squirm. But Rose isn't the squirmy sort. She just smiled.

'*I* call him Rick,' she said.

Gran scowled and sucked her teeth.

'Oh dear,' said Rose sympathetically. 'Is the pain really bad today?'

Rose is the Pain.

But Gran is in pain too. Her arthritis has got horrid. Sometimes she can't even get out of bed and Ruby and I have to help her. And it takes her ages and ages to get down the stairs with her hip. And up the stairs to the loo. And when she's in her chair she gets stuck and we have to heave, Ruby one side, me the other.

How is she going to manage without us helping her?

She's moving to sheltered housing. We thought that meant she was being housed in a bus shelter.

It's not as bad as that. It's a little flat on the ground floor and she's going to have a Home Help and an Alarm Button.

I feel as if I have an Alarm Button inside me and it's going off all the time.

We're moving too. Garnet and me. And Dad. And *Her*. Dad lost his job. It's called Being Made Redundant. Dad said he didn't care. He'd always hated that boring old office. But he looked a bit shocked all the same.

'So how are you going to manage without your boring old salary?' said Gran, sniffing. 'Oh, Richard, you're such a fool. How could you spoil all your chances like this? And you've got the twins to think of, too.'

'It wasn't my fault,' he said.

'You've never shown the right attitude. And since you've taken up with that Rose, you've turned into . . . into a *hippy*.'

'Oh, for goodness sake—'

'Those silly ties and shirts were the last straw. Of course they got rid of you. So what are you going to do now? Have you looked at the Jobs Vacant in the papers?'

'I don't want that sort of job any more,' said Dad. 'I've been thinking. They're giving me quite a bit of cash as my redundancy pay. It's my chance for a whole new start. We could sell up here, get a little shop in the country somewhere. A bookshop. You've always been on and on at me to sell some of my books!'

'You're talking nonsense,' said Gran. 'Well, count me out.'

Count us out too, Dad! Garnet and me. We

don't want to be part of any of this.

We don't want to move to a silly old shop in the country! We don't want to leave Gran. We don't want to leave all our friends. We don't want to leave our school. We don't want to leave our old lives. We don't want to live with you. Not if it means we've got to live with *her*. Because she's coming too. Rose.

We wish she'd get greenfly and mildew and wilt.

FOUR

If our writing's a bit shaky, it's because we're doing this account in the van.

We feel shaky. Our whole lives have been shaken up.

Dad really has bought a bookshop! He didn't even take us with him to check it out first. He went away for the weekend with Rose, and when he came back he said, 'Guess what! I've bought a shop.'

We just stared at him, stunned. He's been acting so crazy. Not like a dad at all. Especially not our dad.

We're used to him saying, 'Guess what! I've bought another box of books.'

But you don't buy a book*shop* just like that. You're meant to hang around for months, getting it surveyed and seeing solicitors.

'It's all simple,' said Dad. 'This sweet old couple are retiring and are happy to move out straightaway. If I can't sell our own house, I'll let it out to students for a bit. Your gran's got her sheltered flat all worked out. Rose only rents her room, and she can shut up her stall in the arcade any time, so she hasn't got any problems either.'

We're the ones with the problems. Garnet and me.

We don't even get considered.

'Why didn't you take us with you to see if *we* like it?' I said.

'You'll love it,' said Dad. 'The village is right out in the country, beside a river, with hills all around. It's a real story-book place. There's a pond with puddleducks straight out of Beatrix Potter. There's just this one street of shops. Ours is in the middle. We'll fit it out with shelves and Rose can have the window for her bric-a-brac. She's got all sorts of ideas for getting it done up. And there's plenty of room upstairs. You two can have the attic for your bedroom – you'll like that.'

Sarah Crewe gets stuck in an attic in A Little Princess *and she has to act like a servant to all the girls in her school. Though at least she got to* stay *in her school.*

We've had to leave our school.
It was awful saying goodbye.

But it was much worse saying goodbye to

Ruby doesn't want to write it. She always leaves the worst bit to me. I don't want to write it either.

Oh, Gran. We do miss you. We miss you ever so ever so much. You used to get cross and you were strict and sometimes you even smacked, but you didn't hurt because of your poor hands and you couldn't help being strict because you're old and you were only cross when we were naughty.

But we do so wish you were with us now. You could be cross and strict and smack all the time and we wouldn't mind a bit.

You didn't get cross and strict and smack when we took you to your new flat. But you weren't all happy and smiley. You looked so small and scrunched up and sad and it was so awful.

We helped you put your chair and your china cabinet and all the rest of your stuff in your new room, but they didn't look right. They didn't look yours. It didn't look like a home.

This funny old man next door came round to say hello and he gave you a bunch of flowers he'd grown in his garden. Dad teased you and said you'd got yourself a boyfriend already, but you wouldn't smile. And when Dad said he hoped you'd be really happy in your new flat and he was sure it was all for the best, you just sniffed. You didn't say anything, but you looked at Dad and it was as if you were shrieking: Who are you kidding?

You didn't even kiss Dad properly goodbye, just gave him your cheek. And we don't blame you either, Gran.

You kissed us. And we kissed you. Lots and lots.

We didn't talk to Dad either. We're still not speaking to him properly. Or Rose. We don't need to. We can just speak to each other. In Twinspeak, so they can't understand.

Garnet and I have this special language. We've got heaps of made-up words for things. Sometimes we don't use words at all, we use signs. Little tiny things like widening our eyes or putting our heads slightly to one side. We signal to each other and then both start up a pretend coughing fit or sneeze simultaneously or shriek with manic laughter.

Rose isn't used to this. It doesn't half make her jump.

'Pack it in,' says Dad.

I glance at Garnet.

'Pack it in what, Dad?' we say simultaneously.

'Less of the cheek,' says Dad, taking one hand off the steering wheel and swatting at us.

'How do they *do* that?' Rose asks.

'How do we do what?' we say.

'Stop it! You're giving me the creeps. Can you really read each other's thoughts?' she says, shivering.

'Of course they can't,' says Dad.

'Then how can they say the same thing at the same time in that weird way?' Rose says, peering at us.

'I don't know,' says Dad, shrugging.

'*We* know,' we say, and we raise our eyebrows and make our eyes glitter in a mysterious and mystic manner.

We wait until Rose turns round again and starts fiddling with the old van radio, trying to tune it to a station. I point to it and nudge Garnet. We both start singing loudly, our timing spot on.

Rose gasps.

'Cut it out, twins,' says Dad sharply.

I turn my fingers into pretend scissors and

make lots of cutting movements. Garnet does the same.

'Oh, very funny,' says Dad, not at all amused.

When he's concentrating on the road, I change the scissors to a dagger and mime a sudden bloody attack on Rose. Garnet does likewise, only she's not quite quick enough. Dad sees, so Garnet shakes her arm quickly, making out she's got cramp.

'What are you playing at, you two?' says Dad.

We blink at him and shrug.

Dad sighs with exasperation, and then takes one hand off the steering wheel and puts his arm round Rose.

I nudge Garnet and we both make a very rude noise.

Dad's hand tightens on Rose's shoulder, but he doesn't say anything. She doesn't say anything either. Neither do we. The radio keeps buzzing and fading and going funny.

I feel a bit like that too. Maybe I'm starting to feel car-sick. Well, van-sick. Ooh good, if I'm going to throw up then I shall aim at Rose.

Ruby was sick. She managed to hit Rose. And me.

Only little splashes on you.

You're not supposed to be writing, in case you get sick again.

I did great, didn't I?

Yes, but I'd sooner you didn't do it again. Rose got through a whole box of tissues, mopping away. Dad had to stop at the next service station and we had to go to the Ladies. I washed and Ruby washed. Rose positively scrubbed and changed her sweater and jeans, scrunching the stained smelly stuff into a plastic bag.

'I think you two belong in the bag too,' she said, sighing. 'Look, I *don't care if you act like idiots, but it isn't half upsetting your dad.'*

We didn't say anything. But Ruby smiled, even though she was still sick and shivery.

'Don't you want your dad to be happy?' said Rose, looking at Ruby and then at me.

Not with you!

'He's had a really tough time the last few years. You two were only tiny so you probably didn't realize, but he nearly went to pieces after your mum died.'

We stared at her silently, hating her. How dare she! We felt like we were in little pieces too.

'It was really tough for him, but he kept on going for your sake. He did his best to get on with your gran, even though she can be so difficult at times.'

How does she have the nerve *to criticize our gran!*

'He didn't have any fun, he never went out anywhere, he was so lonely,' she said.

How could he possibly have been lonely? He had us!

'He kept slaving away at that boring old job in the city, even though it nearly drove him crazy. He was like this old old man even though he's barely thirty.'

She's mad. He's our dad. He is *old.*

'But now he's got this big chance. A whole new life. Something that he's always wanted.

And he's been like a little kid – so excited. But you two are spoiling it all. Can't you see that?'

Yes, we can see it. That's what we want. It's not us that's spoiling anything. She's got it all wrong. It's her. It's her it's her it's her.

FIVE

We're here. And we hate it.

Yes. We hate it.

It's the worst place in the whole world, and we're stuck here with the worst people. Stuck stuck stuck.

Well, the place itself *isn't that bad.*

Yes it is!

No, wait, Ruby. I don't mean the shop. Or the village. But the countryside itself is OK, isn't it? Especially the hills. I hated going for a walk with Rose and Dad, but when we were up in the hills and we saw all the sheep and the wild ponies and we got right to the top and we were almost up in the sky and we could see for miles and it felt like we could just step off the edge and fly—

Will you put a sock in it, Miss Arty-Farty Show-Off. All this sky-and-fly stuff! You sound like you're writing a poem for school. 'My-day-in-the-country'. Boring! And the country's boring too. Grey hills and grey fields and grey trees and grey rain.

Rose doesn't think much of it either. She's still all smarmy with Dad, but we're wearing her down – and this certainly isn't her dream place to live. She got seriously fed up when I accidentally on purpose waved that branch near the washing line and snagged all her stupid tights and the village shop only sells

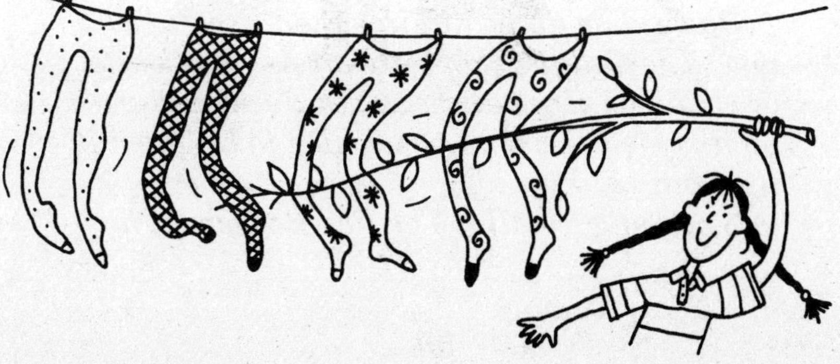

pale beige old-lady tights. Old Rose could have sold her soul for a Sock Shop then.

She hates the Superstore too. Because it doesn't have any decent fruit or veg and the bread's sliced up in bags.

Yes, but Dad says he'll grow raspberries and tomatoes and runner beans in the back garden and he's going to have a go at making our own bread.

Do me a favour, Garnet! Dad can't even make *toast*. Gran was always going on about how hopeless he was.

Dad says that was because she never let him try his hand at anything. She always said, 'Come on now, out from under my feet, stop cluttering up my kitchen.' Oh dear. We do miss Gran so. We wish she was here.

No, we wish *we* were *there*. Instead of here in this hateful dump. We don't fit in.

Dad's shop doesn't fit in either. Especially now. The antique shops are all painted white or cream or very pale beige. Dad's shop started off dirty white too, so he decided to brighten it up a bit.

'I'm going to call it The Red Bookshop,' he

said. 'Because of my three girls. Rubies are red, Garnets are red, and Roses are red. So let's go the whole hog and paint it red too.'

He motored miles and miles to the nearest Do-it-Yourself Store in Hineford and came back with pots of stinging scarlet paint. We were supposed to help Rose wash the front of the shop and rub the peeling paint, but after about ten minutes scrubbing and sloshing, Ruby threw her sponge in the bucket and said, 'We're fed up with this lark,' and sauntered off.

So I threw my sponge in the bucket too, and sidled after my sister.

'Hey, come back, you lazy beasts,' Rose shouted, and she threw a sponge at us.

It glanced off Ruby, still sopping wet. Ruby took hold of it and aimed. She's a very good aimer. It caught Rose full in the face.

We ran right away then. We walked round and round the village and up and down the stream and then we went down by the river but it was too muddy and we weren't wearing our wellies and I slipped and got mud all over my bottom. It looked AWFUL. And Ruby made it worse because she kept laughing at me. I tried to rub the mud off with grass but it was useless.

I started to cry and Ruby got cross.

'Why do you always have to be such a baby?' she said. 'Look, it's your own fault for slipping like that. And it doesn't matter anyway – they're only your old jeans. And she *can't tell us off because she's not our mother or any part of our family. So stop snivelling.'*

'I can't go back through the village like this. People will look at me and laugh.'

'No they won't. *They won't even notice, honest,' said Ruby.*

She wasn't being honest. They did notice. This crowd of children fishing by the bridge saw us and stared. First of all because we were strangers. Second because we're twins. But then they saw the muck all over my jeans and then they really *stared. And sniggered. And shouted horrible rude suggestions.*

Ruby caught hold of me by the wrist and gave me a little shake to stop me crying again.

She marched us straight up to them instead of skulking away, like I wanted. Her face was as red as her name.

'What's so funny?' she said, when we were right up close to them. She made me say it too. 'What's so funny?' we said in unison.

They were mostly around our age, but some were bigger. Ruby didn't care.

Some of the littler kids stepped backwards. They weren't just worried about Ruby. It was me too. Because we were walking in step and talking exactly together and when we do that lots of people find it really spooky.

The bigger boys weren't easily fazed though. One fat one with silly sideways hair said something ever so rude and horrible and they all laughed again.

'Ooh! Being covered in mud is funny, is it?' said Ruby.

'Funny, is it?' we said together.

Then Ruby looked at me and looked at the muddy grass and I knew what she was going to do. I knew I had to do it too. We bent, we sunk our hands into the mud, we straightened up – and while they were still all gawking at us we went splat, right in their faces.

'Have a big laugh then,' said Ruby – and we ran.

They started running after us, but we can be very speedy so we soon got clean away. Well. I wasn't clean. I was still covered in mud.

'But so are they!' Ruby spluttered breathlessly. 'Their faces. Oh, Garnet, that was so glorious. Twin-grin!'

'Twin-grin,' I echoed obediently, though I didn't really feel like smiling.

We have this little grinning ritual whenever we're really pleased about something. Ruby puts her fingers at the corners of my mouth and turns it into a huge grin, while I reach out at the same time and do the same to her.

I managed to stay grinning like a Halloween pumpkin, but I kept looking behind me all the same, in case those children might be creeping up on us.

'Relax. They'll have gone back to their stupid fishing,' said Ruby, sussing that I was still scared.

'Maybe. But they'll still be out to get us sometime, won't they,' I said stiffly, trying to keep my grin in place.

'Well, we'll get them back,' said Ruby airily. 'Especially that Big Blobby one.'

'But they'll all start hating us then. And we've got to go to school with them, haven't we,' I said. My grin wavered, and then drooped.

'We won't go to this dumb old school. We'll slope off by ourselves,' said Ruby.

'But they'll find out and we'll get into trouble,' I said. 'And we're in pretty big trouble now. We can't go home because Rose will get us, and we can't go down by the river because those children will get us.'

It looked like we were stuck for ever, hiding up a little alleyway at the edge of the village. I leant against the wall, the cold pebbly stuff scratching me through my T-shirt. My jeans were still wet and sticky with mud. My face ached with trying to smile. My eyes stung with trying not to cry again.

'Garnet?' said Ruby gently.

She put her arm round me and cuddled me close. I snuggled up against her and we held on tight to each other. Our shadows became Siamese.

'Perhaps we'd better go back to the bookshop,' I said eventually.

'No, not yet. We've only been gone an hour or so. She'll just get angry. No, we have to stay away ages and ages, and then she'll be really worried. Better to stay away until after Dad gets back, then he'll be dead worried too, and they'll maybe have a go at each other. Then when we do turn up they'll be so relieved we've not been kidnapped or killed that they won't go on at us. Or not so much, anyway.'

'But what are we going to do?' I wailed.

'We'll do one of our plays,' said Ruby.

That made me cheer up. Ruby hasn't felt like playing one of our pretend games for ages. So we had this really great game together.

And then, when we eventually sloped back to the shop, Rose didn't get cross with us.

She'd done all the front of the shop by herself, but she didn't tell on us to Dad. She even washed out my jeans for me without getting fussed. Gran would have gone nuts.

What's the matter with you, Garnet? Have *you* gone completely nuts? Is this Let's Love Rosy-Posy Day?

No. I can't stick her, you know that. But I'm just trying to write a truthful account, that's all. In our accounts book.

Well, I think we should give a good account of ourselves. And make a bad account of everyone else. That's much more fun.

Rose was OK when that woman in the quilty jacket and the lollopy dog came to complain about the red paint.

Dad looked like he was going to burst into tears, but Rose went 'Oh B-B-B-R-R-R-R-R-R-R-R-R-R!'*,blowing this giant raspberry and said it was our shop and we could paint it whatever colour we fancied and that the video shop two doors along with all its placards didn't exactly add to the authentic Victorian charm of the village anyway. So the bossy lady got into a huff and flounced out with her floppy dog and we were all laughing—*

Yes, but Rose wasn't really that clever, because how many real customers has Dad had?

Well, there was the man who wanted the gardening book . . . and the lady who wanted all the Bills and Moons . . . lots of ladies . . .

Yes, but they only spend fifty pence at a time!

That vicar came. And he bought a Bible – the big one with pictures that cost heaps.

And that's about *it*. They don't want to come, the villagers. They don't like us. Or they don't like books. Or both.

Yes, but Dad says he's really after the Tourist Trade. The people who come at weekends. And holidaymakers.

Who'd ever want to come and have a holiday in this old dump? All right, the shop did get quite busy last Saturday and Sunday, but hardly anybody *bought* anything.

There were the hikers

and they left mud all over the place.

There were the bikers

and they dripped ice-cream everywhere.

And there was that family who asked to use the toilet.

None of that lot bought a sausage.

One of the bikers bought an old Beano *annual.*

Oh, big deal. I'm telling you, Garnet. Dad's going to go bust in six months.

Come on, let's play. Make the most of our free time. Because we're starting at our new school on Monday, yuck yuck yuck.

SIX

It's awful. We knew it would be. It's like a little toy school. There's hardly any playground. There aren't any computers. There isn't even a television. The teacher writes stuff up on a blackboard and we sit at these dinky little desks with lids and inkwells. It's like the sort of classroom you get in a cartoon.

Miss Debenham isn't a bit like that, Ruby! This *is Miss Debenham.*

Yes, and she made me feel positively sick and squirmy inside when she stood us in front of the class and introduced us – and as if we *needed* introducing anyway. We're famous in this dreary dump of a village. Everyone knows us.

Especially Jeremy Treadgold and his gang.

Fancy that great Blob being in our class. It's a wonder he can cram himself into the teeny-weeny desk. Imagine having to sit next to him.

I'm glad we can sit together, anyway. Miss Debenham asked us what we'd prefer. Teachers don't usually ask you stuff like that, they just tell you what they want you to do. And I like some of the lessons, like when we had to write about twins.

You can be a real smarmy little creep at times! I had it all sussed out.

THE GOOD THINGS ABOUT BEING A TWIN

Everything

THE BAD THINGS ABOUT BEING A TWIN

Nothing

And then you were supposed to do your mirror-writing trick. It would have been so brilliant:

THE GOOD THINGS ABOUT BEING A TWIN

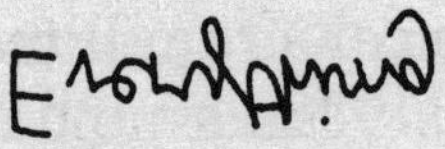

THE BAD THINGS ABOUT BEING A TWIN

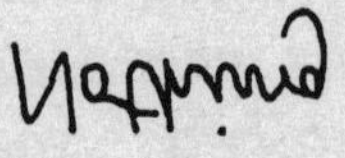

It would have been PERFECT. An answer, and a twin answer. Identical, like us.

But oh no, Miss Suck-up-to-the-teacher-smarty-farty has to write all that rubbish.

THE GOOD THINGS ABOUT BEING A TWIN

There are lots and lots of good things about being a twin. You're never alone, you've always got a best friend to talk to and play with. You can have all sorts of special secrets and make up wonderful games that no-one else can ever understand. You can say things together and do things together so that you can have twice the power.

THE BAD THINGS ABOUT BEING A TWIN

There aren't many bad things about being a twin. Just occasionally it might be peaceful to be alone. Not to have to talk or make up games or listen to secrets. Just to be yourself. Not part of anyone else. You.

Very *bad*, Garnet! Do you *really* want to be left alone? OK, I'll run off the next time that Big Blob tries to get us.

Oh, that was so awful! He crept up on us with this huge great wiggly worm in either hand, and I can't stand *worms.*

Well, I'm not absolutely enchanted with them myself. Especially not squirming down my jumper. But I got mine out. I shoved it straight down the Big Blob's trousers!

Judy said he once put a worm down her neck too. Judy just about went bananas. She said—

I'm not the slightest bit interested in Judy and what she said. I don't know why you wanted to go off with her.

She's quite nice, Ruby, really she is. And I didn't go off with her, you know that. Miss Debenham said she wanted us to do this big Noah's Ark painting to brighten up the classroom wall and she was going round the whole form asking them which animal they wanted to paint, and I kept hoping nobody else would bag a giraffe, because they're our favourite animal, so when she got to us I said, 'Giraffe' quick. And Miss Debenham smiled at you too and said, 'And you'll do a twin giraffe, right, Ruby?'

So I said, 'Wrong, Miss Debenham. I don't want to paint any stupid old giraffe.'

But why *did you say that? And why did you have to choose a* flea *for your animal?*

Simple. One little blob. Flea finished. And if you'd only shut up and waited for *me* to answer old Dumbo Debenham, you could have done a flea too. Then we could have just sat and mucked around for the rest of the lesson. But oh no, you have to go off with that ghastly Judy girl and paint stupid giraffes with her.

I didn't go off – well, not deliberately. I couldn't help it that Judy said she wanted to do a giraffe too. And I tried to back out, you know I did. But Miss Debenham said, 'No, come on, Garnet, you said you'd like to do a giraffe. So you can do the giraffes with Judy. Never mind what Ruby wants to do.'

Yes, never mind *me*.

Oh, Ruby. Don't be like that.

I'll be exactly how I want. If you want to pal around with Judy then fine, you go off with her.

I don't want to pal around with her.

So why did you let her tag around with us at playtime then? Going gab gab gab until I felt like punching her in the gob.

Well, what could I do? I couldn't tell her to go away.

I could.

You did. You were ever so rude to her. And I keep telling you, Ruby, she's good fun, she really is – you'd like her if you could bother to get to know her.

I'm not going to get to know any of them. OK. You go and have good fun with your super new friend. Pal around with her all you like. Just don't expect to pal around with *me*.

Ruby! Don't let's quarrel. I hate it so. Ruby, come back. Please.

SEVEN

Ruby?

I can't STAND it when Ruby won't talk to me. It's as if most of me goes missing. As if my own mouth won't work, my own hands won't hold.

She's right. I was crazy to write that stuff about being a twin. It's awful being on your own.

Ruby wouldn't talk to me all yesterday evening. When I tried saying anything she put her hands over her ears and went Bla-bla-bla so she couldn't hear.

After we'd had tea, Ruby went up to our room and started reading an old Beano *annual. I said I was sorry, but she didn't look up. I tried putting my arm round her but she wriggled away. I took hold of the* Beano *annual to make her look at me but she grabbed it back and hit me on the head with it. It hurt quite a lot, but that wasn't really why I was crying.*

Ruby didn't take any notice at all.

My nose started to run so badly that I had to go and get a tissue. Rose saw me before I could mop myself up.

'Oh, sweetie,' she said, and she pulled one of her chiffony scarves off her neck and wiped my nose with it. 'Hey, I'm just popping down to that video shop because there's nothing good on telly tonight. Come and help me choose a good film, eh?'

I didn't know what to do. I knew Ruby would never forgive me if I palled up with Rose. But it didn't look like she would ever forgive me anyway.

'Come on, we'll get some chocs too,' said Rose. She rubbed her tummy. 'I've put on a good half-stone since we got here. Still, never mind, eh?'

I wanted to go with Rose. Ruby might not even know unless she looked out of our window. No, who was I kidding? It's like Ruby can look through a little window straight into my head.

'I'd better not,' I mumbled to Rose. 'I mean, I don't feel like it.'

'You don't always have to do what Ruby wants,' Rose said.

She can tell us apart now. Unless we deliberately trick her. She thinks she's getting to know us. But she can't ever really understand. I don't always get it myself. But I do have to do what Ruby wants. Because if I don't, this happens. And it's so horrid.

Rose usually chooses love films with big hunky men, but this time she brought back The Railway Children. *It's one of my all-time favourite films, but generally when we watch it Ruby mucks around and mocks all the accents and at the end when Bobbie runs to her father at the station and it's so lovely, Ruby makes sick noises and switches it off before it's finished.*

Dad raised his eyebrows a bit when he saw which film it was, but he didn't say anything. He usually sits on the sofa with Rose, but this evening he sat in the armchair and he caught hold of me and sat me on his lap while Rose put her feet up on the sofa, a box of Cadbury's Dairy Milk balanced on her tummy. She kept throwing Dad and me chocolates. I said I wasn't very hungry thanks, but Dad popped my favourite chocolate fudge into my mouth as I spoke and I couldn't really spit it out.

They were being so nice to me, but it didn't work. The chocolate didn't have any taste. The Railway Children *got started but I couldn't watch it properly. I kept glancing up at the ceiling, at Ruby crouched up above us all on her own.*

'Why don't we ask if she feels like coming down now?' Rose said.

Dad and I looked at each other. Rose certainly doesn't understand Ruby yet.

Rose went up all the same. She left a couple of chocolates beside Ruby. They weren't touched when I came to bed.

Ruby and I always share the bathroom and do synchronized tooth-cleaning, but Ruby barged straight past me and banged the door in my face. When we got into our nighties in the bedroom she seemed to be staring straight through me, as if I didn't exist. That was exactly the way I felt.

When we were in bed with the light off I kept whispering to her, but she wouldn't answer. I lay awake for ages and ages and ages. In the middle of the night I slipped out of my bed and climbed in beside Ruby. She was snoring softly, deep in a dream, but she still wouldn't cuddle up

and after a while I crept back to my own bed.

I think I slept a bit but now I'm wide awake again, even though it's not properly morning.

I think Ruby's awake too.

Ruby?

She's still not speaking.

But I know what to do now.

I did it. And we're friends again now, aren't we, Ruby?

Yeah. OK, OK. Get *off* of me, Garnet!

Make friends, make friends, never never break friends?

I said, didn't I?

Write it too. Write it down here, in the accounts book. Write that you'll never break friends with me again.

I will never break friends with my twin sister and best friend Garnet Barker.

Oh, you've really written it! And put: I swear.

I swear my twin sister and best friend Garnet Barker is driving me completely batty with all this sloppy junk, and if she doesn't shut up soon I might well go back on my promise.

You can't do that. No backsies.

I was only teasing, stupid. Here, what's all this drivel you've been writing? Whimpering on about me for page after page?

Don't look at it now. You're right. It was just rubbish.

So you had chocolate fudge downstairs, did you?

I didn't mean to – I just had my mouth open and—

Oh,well. I might as well eat up my choccies too. One ... Yum yum yum.

And two ... Gobble, gobble, gobble. Don't look at me like that. You had yours last night.

Only one.

Well look, here ...

It's all chewed and slobbery!

Well, we're twins, aren't we? Your slobber is the same as my slobber. My drool is the same as your drool. My spit is the same as your spit.

Your spit is a lot splashier *than mine.*

Hey, wasn't it great today when we got Jeremy Blob splat-splat! Oh boy oh boy! That was the most terrific supersonic idea of mine, eh? Going up to him in the playground and saying stuff ever so ever so softly so he shakes his head and screws up his face. 'What?' he says. 'I can't hear you?'

So we go, 'Then wash your ears out' and you spit . . . SPLAT. And *I* spit . . . SPLAT. In his ears.

I wish Miss Debenham hadn't been walking across the playground though. She wasn't very pleased either when I said I didn't want to

finish my giraffe and I did a twin flea to match yours. And Judy was a bit fed up too, because now she's lumbered doing one and three-quarters giraffes by herself.

Still, we don't care, do we?

It doesn't matter, so long as we've got each other.

So now school's a doddle, because Garnet and I don't do anything. We just sit looking blank when Dumbo Debenham gets on to us. Or I write the barest minimum and Garnet does mirror-writing. Or we copy everything twice – two lots of sums, two maps, two fact-sheets, because we say everything's got to be doubled because we're a double ourselves.

'Double trouble,' said Dumbo Debenham, and she sighed and tried separating us, Garnet right at the back of the class and me at the front.

It didn't work. Garnet just had to keep her eye on me. I'd tilt my head one way, and that was the signal to sneeze simultaneously. Or I'd tilt my head the other way and we'd both tip our books off the desk. Or I'd nod very slightly and we'd both stand up and say in unison, 'Please may I go to the toilet, Miss

Debenham?' and then we'd walk out keeping step, me first, Garnet second, left right, left right, our arms swinging right left, right left, and then when I gave the slightest little cough we'd toss our heads so that our plaits would go left right, left right, over our shoulders.

And all the kids would stare with their mouths open.

We even spook Jeremy Blob!

But it looks like we're in double trouble with Dad. Dumbo Debenham phoned him up and told tales on us!

'So why are you acting so stupidly at school?' Dad demanded.

'I think they act stupidly at home too!' said Rose.

'We only act–'

'Stupid—'

'To stupid—'

'People,' we said.

But then Dad shook us. Hard. I thought he might even bang our heads together.

'Stop it! I won't have you talking to Rose like that. What's the matter with you? I just don't get it. You've always been such good girls. Well, you've had your moments, Ruby, but you've never ever behaved as badly as this before. And you've both always done so well at school. I've been so proud of you. But now it sounds as if you're going out of your way to be as naughty and disruptive as possible. And you're not even trying to make friends with the other children. Miss Debenham says you've got into silly fights with some of the boys – and you really upset one of the girls yesterday. Judy someone?'

That was great. She was carrying on with this boring boring Noah's Ark nonsense and she'd just got started doing the giraffe's long neck with brown paint, so I got Garnet and we did our wanting-to-wee double act and then as we went out we both bumped into Judy accidentally on purpose and her giraffe ended up with this amazing corkscrew neck. Shame.

I couldn't help sniggering just thinking about it, and Dad got madder than ever.

Garnet spoilt it a bit because she started snivelling, as always. Then Dad sighed and said, 'Why do you always have to copy Ruby, Garnet? You obviously tried hard at school at first. But now you're starting to be just as naughty as Ruby.' And then he shook me a bit and said, 'Why can't you ever copy Garnet, Ruby?'

But Garnet was OK.

'I don't copy Ruby,' she said.

'I don't copy Garnet,' I said.

And then I sniffed because I knew Garnet was just about to, and I rubbed my dry eyes and she rubbed her wet ones, and then Garnet knew I'd stare at Dad defiantly with my chin up so she did too.

It unnerved Dad, even though he's used to us. But Rose clapped her hands.

'They ought to go on stage,' she said.

'Well ha ha ha, we're going to,' I said.

Garnet was a bit slow with her response this time. She only managed a '. . . going to,' and she sounded a bit half-hearted. But I'm her other half. The oldest biggest bossiest half. We have to do what I say.

EIGHT

This is it! Our Big Chance!

We were sitting in the kitchen on Saturday, mucking about. Dad was down in the shop. Rose had caught the early bus to the town. We had the place to ourselves. Garnet mixed up some flour and water and started making dinky little dough twins.

She even plaited their hair and gave them little laces in their trainers.

I said I wanted mine to have Doc Martens – all the better for kicking, ha ha – and I tried to change their shoes, but they wouldn't go right. So I squashed my twin up and started all over again, but it just went all blobby. I turned it into Jeremy Blob instead, while Garnet made another me. Then I got some toothpicks and tortured Jeremy Blob until he stopped looking like a doughboy and turned into a porcupine.

I got fed up with dough then and folded up

a newspaper and cut it out carefully the way Gran showed us once and then, when I unfolded it, there was this whole row of paper dolls. The newspaper just happened to be Rose's *Guardian* and she hadn't even opened it yet. Tough.

I got a felt tip and started scribbling in eyes and mouths and buttons down the front of each little paper girl. I'm not dead artistic like Garnet. I can't be bothered to be so finicky.

'I'm turning them all into twins,' I said.

I did a smily mouth for me and a little-o anxious mouth for Garnet, and then a smiley mouth for me and a . . .

And then I stopped, because I saw the word Twin on the paper doll. I read her skirt and then I ferreted around for the left-over paper to try to read the rest. I got the Sellotape and started trying to stick the whole bang-shoot back together again.

'Yes, Rose is going to want to read that when she gets back,' Garnet mumbled, putting the finishing touches to the little dough me.

'Blow Rose reading it. *We've* got to read it!' I said, and I was so shaking with excitement that I stuck myself together with the Sellotape. 'Garnet, come and take a look at this! Oh boy! No, oh *girl*. Oh *twin* girl!'

'Whatever are you burbling about?' said Garnet. 'Hey, don't jog. Look, you've made me muck up your plait now.'

'Leave it. *Look!*'

I shoved the crumpled, Sellotaped sheet of paper in front of her nose.

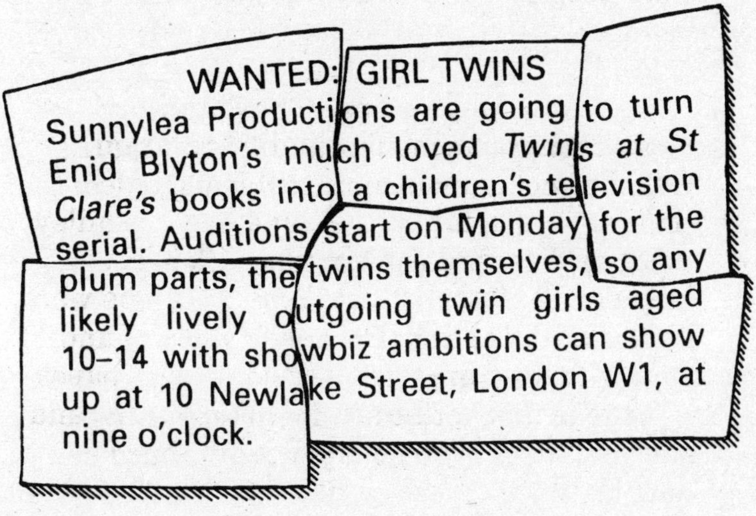

WANTED: GIRL TWINS

Sunnylea Productions are going to turn Enid Blyton's much loved *Twins at St Clare's* books into a children's television serial. Auditions start on Monday for the plum parts, the twins themselves, so any likely lively outgoing twin girls aged 10–14 with showbiz ambitions can show up at 10 Newlake Street, London W1, at nine o'clock.

'This is it, Garnet!' I shouted.

Garnet is usually a quick reader but she seemed to be taking her time getting through one small paragraph.

She was still holding the little dough me.

'Hey, watch out! You're spoiling me,' I said.

Garnet squashed me into a little ball and then dropped me on the kitchen floor.

'No,' she said.

'What?'

'No. I can't.'

'What do you *mean*? We can we can we can. Yes, all right, it's going to be difficult getting to London by nine o'clock. We'll have to get up ever so early. Rose will have to look after the shop herself while Dad drives us. Still, that'll be fun.'

'*No.*'

'Yes. Now, we're going to have to work mega-fast preparing our audition number. Get the book, quick, and we'll learn one of the scenes.'

'Ruby, I can't. I can't act for toffee, you know I can't.'

'Look, it'll be fine. I promise you won't wet yourself this time.'

'Stop it. It's not funny. I don't *want* to be in showbiz. Look, you go if you want, but I'm not.'

'Oh ha ha, very helpful. How can I audition as a twin by myself, eh? Take one of the little dough twins along with me? Don't be such a dope. Now, where's the book, we've got to get cracking. Which twin is which? I'll be the one that says the most. We'll work it so you don't have to say hardly anything, OK?'

'No, Ruby, please, *please*.' Garnet started scrabbling at me, getting dough all over my jumper.

'We can't miss out on this, Garnet. It's our big chance. We've got to go for it.'

'But it says lively. I'm not a bit lively. I don't jump about like you, I just sort of flop in a corner. And I'm not outgoing. I'm as inwardbeing as you could possibly get.'

'You'll be OK. Just copy me.'

Why do I always have to copy Ruby?

I can't act.

I don't want *to act.*

I can't go to an audition in London! I can't say a lot of stuff with everyone watching. It'll be even worse than being a sheep. Why won't Ruby understand? She won't listen to me. She's riffling through The Twins at St Clare's *right this minute, trying to choose which bit we'll act out.*

Only I'm not going to act.

I can't can't can't act.

Remember what Gran says? There's no such word as can't! Now stop scribbling and start spouting. We've got to be word-perfect by Monday!

It's OK! I don't have to act after all. Dad won't let us.

I can't believe he could be so Mega-Mean. He doesn't seem to see this is our one big chance, tailor-made for us. He won't even take it seriously.

'Don't be daft, Ruby. As if I'm going to drive you all the way to London at the crack of dawn on Monday! And I don't want you and Garnet involved in any acting caper while you're still children. I can't stick those simpering stage-school kiddiewinks. You're already enough of a show-off as it is.'

What a CHEEK! He can't be bothered to help us achieve our all-time ambition

Your *ambition*

and yet look what we've had to do for him. We've had to leave Gran and all our friends and our old school and come and live in this horrible dusty old dump in the middle of the boring bleak rainy old country which is all mud and sheep and nothing else and he says we've got to have old Rosy Ratbag as our *mother*.

Stepmother. And Rose said she didn't fancy herself as a stepmother anyway, and she didn't want us to feel she was forever trying to slip us poisoned apples. She said she just wanted to be our friend.

Well, we don't ever ever ever want to be friends with her. Do we? *Do we, Garnet*?

I suppose not. No. But she's not really as bad as all that. And she *said she didn't see why we couldn't go to the audition. She said she thought we'd walk away with the parts.*

She told Dad not to be so stuffy. She said she'd even get up early on Monday and drive us in the van.

Yes, but she didn't really mean it. She knew Dad would put his foot down and say no.

Still, she did stick up for us.

Look, what is this, the Rosy Ratbag Appreciation Society? You'll be writing a fanzine about her next.

Save your appreciation for *us*.

The talented gems of stage and screen, identical twins Ruby and Garnet Barker, who first sprang to stardom in the acclaimed television serial, 'The Twins at St Clare's.'

Only we're not going to be in The Twins at St Clare's.

Oh yes we are.

Dad won't let us. He won't ever change his mind. He's like you. He won't take us.

I know he won't take us. So we'll take ourself.

What???

I'll fix it. We *can't* miss this chance. Come on, Garnet. Twin-grin. *Smile*.

Ruby won't be able to fix it – will she???

I DID FIX IT!!!

I prodded my brainbox into action and charged out on Saturday afternoon to arrange things. I phoned the station to check on train times.

I went into the video shop and ordered the taxi for quarter past five on Monday morning. Mr Baines the video man is also the taxi man. *And* he's also a nosy old git who wanted to know why we were going to the station to catch the early train. I spun him this tale about it being Gran's birthday. He seemed to take it for granted that Dad was going to be visiting her too.

Then I went to the nearest antique shop and tried to sell my silver locket and my wristwatch and a dopey old china baby doll that Gran gave me. I never liked it even when I was little. Garnet played with mine as well as hers. But the doll *was* mine. And the locket and the watch. But the antique shop lady wouldn't buy them. She said I had to have Mummy or Daddy with me.

Well, I haven't *got* a mummy. Or much of a dad.

I tried the next antique shop. No go. And the last one. Useless.

But did I give up? Nope. I went to the car-boot sale in the field by the river on Sunday morning. No-one was very interested in my chain and my watch but I saw them get excited about the doll, even though they tried to act like they couldn't be bothered. They offered me a fiver like they were doing me a favour. I'm not daft. I asked for fifty. Of course they didn't *give* me fifty. But they gave me twenty.

Which wasn't going to be enough for the taxi and the train fare, even with all our savings in our piggybank, so when my alarm went off at four in the morning I sneaked downstairs while Garnet was still asleep and pinched a note or two out the till. It isn't really stealing if it's your own family, is it? If you're going to pay them back anyway? Well, all right, it is – but I *had* to.

Then I went and woke Garnet and we bumbled about in the dark getting ready, in our best clothes

and then we crept downstairs and snaffled some biscuits for breakfast and then stood outside the front door waiting for Mr Baines so that he wouldn't ring the bell and wake Dad or Rosy Ratbag. They were still fast asleep. I checked.

Mr Baines was ten minutes late so I was in a bit of a tizzy in case we were going to miss the train, and then he held things up by asking where Dad was, and he's got this incredibly loud voice and I was sure he was going to wake everyone up. But I rose to the occasion. I spun him this story about Dad having a tummy bug and being unable to travel, but Gran was so disappointed when he rang her that he promised to send us on our own.

'Two little girls like you?' said Mr Baines doubtfully, but I showed him my bulging purse and told him Gran was meeting us off the train, so he shrugged and said OK.

Garnet didn't say a word. She still seemed half-asleep. Then she went green in the taxi. *I'm* the one who gets travel-sick, but I was perfectly OK. I even remembered to give Mr Baines a tip, thought I didn't think he really deserved it, being late and asking hundreds of questions all the way.

I bought the tickets for the train. Garnet wasn't with me. She was being sick behind a hedge. I was worried she might muck up her best jacket. You can't audition attractively with vomit all down your front. But she was quite neat about it, though she looked greener than ever when she came back. Still, our jackets are green, so at least she matched.

She was all shivery, even on the train. I made her rehearse a bit and she got even more trembly and tearful.

'Don't you dare cry,' I said. 'You don't want to be all red-eyed and bleary at the audition.'

She did cry a bit even so, but I mopped her up in the ladies loo.

'You're not going to let me down, are you, Garnet?' I said very fiercely.

Sometimes you've got to be fierce to get what you want. But even I felt a bit timid when we got off the train because it was all so big and busy and we didn't know where to go and we asked someone where Newlake Street was and they'd never even heard of it, and I said we'd get a tube but we didn't know which tube, or where, and we went down the escalator and then back up the escalator and then I saw a taxi sign and we still had some money in our purse so we took a taxi.

It turned out we didn't have quite enough money after all. The taxi driver got a bit narked.

But I wasn't bothered about that. I was bothered about something else. I got out of the taxi and Garnet staggered out after me. And we stared. And hundreds of eyes stared back at us. Twin eyes. Twin after twin after twin after twin.

NINE

It was so weird *seeing so many twins. Ruby and I have seen identical twins before, obviously, but never* hundreds *of pairs. It was as if the whole world had split into two. I felt as if I was splitting too. We've always felt so different. Unique. Special. It's what made us* us. *But standing there in that street we were just part of the crowd. Totally ordinary. With nothing at all to make us stand out.*

'Let's go back home,' I said to Ruby. 'Look at them all. We don't stand a chance.'

'Don't be so ridiculous,' said Ruby furiously. 'I keep telling and telling and telling you, this is our big chance. We're not giving up now. We'll show them all. We'll act better than any of them.'

'But I can't act at all, *Ruby.'*

She just gave me this terrible look, took hold of my arm, and marched me to the end of the very long queue.

We passed big twins

little twins

pretty twins

plain twins

showy twins

shabby twins

girly-girly twins

tomboy twins

even real boy twins.

'They obviously haven't even read the book!' said Ruby dismissively. 'Unless they're going to put on frocks and wigs and play the parts in drag.'

'But look at some of the others. The ones with the big smiles and loud voices. I bet they've been to acting school,' I said.

'Well, so what. I've done my best to school you in acting. Now come on, let's go over our parts.'

'Not out here, in front of everyone,' I said, agonized.

'Look, you're the one who needs heaps of practice, not me,' said Ruby. Then she pulled me close and muttered in my ear, 'We'll just do it in whispers, OK? And I've been thinking – we'll have to inject a little ooomph into our act to make us stand out in front of all these others. So we'll still do the scene with the twins having a battle with Mam'zelle, but we'll act Mam'zelle too. Don't look so scared, I'll do her. I am good at doing zee French accent, ma cherie, oh la la, très bon.'

But it turned out we didn't get a chance to do any of our act. We had to wait hours and hours in the queue and I was desperate to go to the loo so when we did eventually get inside the building I had to walk around with my legs crossed and we had to give our names and addresses and date of birth and school to this lady at a desk and then we went upstairs and I was scared I might really wet myself and it would be the sheep situation all over again only worse but there were toilets along the corridor

and a big cloakroom where you were supposed to change only we didn't have anything to change into, 'cos we were wearing it. But Ruby pinched my cheeks to give me a bit more colour and I tidied our hair although my hands were trembling so I could barely tie a knot and then we got into another *queue, waiting to get into the actual audition room.*

It got scarier and scarier and I had to dash back to the loo once or twice and even Ruby got a bit fidgety and she kept staring round at all the other twins. They were rehearsing their routines and they all seemed so brilliant

that Ruby started to frown and bite her nails.

'I didn't figure we might have to dance,' she mumbled. 'They don't do any dancing in the story do they? Although maybe they're turning it into a musical version? So if we're asked, we'll sing . . . er . . . not a pop song, they'll all do that. We could do "My Bonnie Lies Over the Ocean" with hand gestures.'

'I'm not singing, especially not with gestures!' I said. 'You know we can't sing in tune, either of us.'

'Well, we could just sort of say *the words, with lots of expression,' said Ruby relentlessly. 'And if we have to dance well . . . we'll just have to jump and jiggle a bit. Improvise. You copy me, OK?'*

This was so obviously not OK that I didn't even bother to protest.

'We could work on a routine now, you know,' said Ruby, hopping and skipping and kicking out one leg.

She kicked a little too enthusiastically, and there was an argument with the twins in front of us.

They were dressed up in wonderfully old-fashioned school uniform – gymslips and baggy blouses and lisle stockings and strappy

shoes. One of the lisle stockings had a little ladder now where it had connected with Ruby's kick, and the mother of the laddered-lisle was very cross indeed.

*'Look, it was an accident – anyway, it just adds to her general schoolgirl . . .*authenticity,*' said Ruby, pronouncing this big word with pride.*

The mother didn't seem convinced, and the schoolgirl twins were still getting all shirty too, but then they were called into the audition room so they rushed off in a fluster.

'Us next,' said Ruby. She took hold of me by the shoulders. 'We're going to do great, Garnet. Better than any of this dopey stupid showy-offy lot. You and me. Ruby and Garnet. We'll act it all out and it won't be scary at all, it'll just be like us playing in private at home. Trust me.'

I tried. And then it was our turn. And it wasn't at all like playing in private. We were shown on to this stage and there were lots of people watching us and a camera filming us and I was so frightened I nearly fell over. Ruby grabbed me by the hand and hissed 'Twin-grin' and marched us into the middle of the stage.

'Hi, twins,' said this woman with short hair and a smock.

'Hi there,' said Ruby, imitating her voice, trying to sound all cool and casual, though I could see little beads of sweat on her forehead.

She nudged me, and I squeaked 'Hi' too.

'We've got our audition piece all prepared,' Ruby said brightly, trying to show them we were dead professional. 'I'm Pat and she's Isabel and I'm also Mam'zelle and at the end I'm Janet as well.'

They all laughed, for some reason. I blushed, because I was scared they thought Ruby was silly, but Ruby didn't seem to mind. She laughed too.

'We'd love to see your little number some time, twins, but right now we just want to test out your voices,' said the woman with the short hair. 'Sooo – twin number one. Tell me what you had to eat yesterday.'

Ruby blinked at her. But then she threw back her hair, put her hand on one hip, and got started.

'OK, you want to know what I had to eat yesterday. Well, breakfast was boring old muesli again. Garnet and I used to have Coco Pops and jam sandwiches and they were yummy, but now we have this awful woman living with us, our dad's girlfriend, and she's into health foods so it's bye-bye Coco Pops, hello muesli – all this oat and bran that makes your face ache munching and then there are these little raisins like rabbit droppings, yuck.'

They were all laughing again, but this time even I could see that this was good. They loved Ruby.

'Right, now, twin two, tell us what you had for lunch,' said the woman with short hair.

They stopped looking at Ruby. They looked at me. And Ruby looked at me too. Desperately. Terrified I was going to let us down.

I tried to pretend to myself that I wasn't shy

stupid scaredy-cat Garnet. I made out I was Ruby. I threw back my hair. I put my hand on my hip. I opened my mouth to start.

I had it all worked out what I was going to do. I was going to tell about Rose's garlic crumble and how it not only tasted absolutely disgusting, but people ducked and dodged for days afterwards whenever we breathed in their direction and we'd worn out six toothbrushes already trying to take the taste away. I could be funny too if I really tried. I could be just as good as Ruby. I could.

But then someone came bursting through the door and stood there, staring. Dad!

And I couldn't. I simply couldn't.

He didn't say anything to stop me.

But he didn't need to. I couldn't get started, not in front of him. I opened my mouth – but nothing came out. I tried to speak, but I couldn't even squeak.

'Come on, *Garnet,' said Ruby.*

I gulped, I opened my mouth, I tried. But all I managed was a goldfish impersonation.

'Look, I'll say what we had for lunch,' said Ruby.

'No, sweetie, we've already heard you. We want your twin to talk now. Let's skip lunch. And tea and supper. What time did you go to bed, twin two?'

I saw Ruby flash her eyes at me. I knew she was willing me to tell a funny story about our bed-delaying tactics, our constant unnecessary trips to the bathroom, our midnight raids on the fridge, our frequent nocturnal ramblings – all deliberately done to unnerve Dad and Rose, so that they could never totally relax into unwedded bliss.

I could tell it, but not in front of Dad.

So, after several centuries had gone by and I actually saw the short-haired woman glance at her watch, I started a stupid mumble about 'Well, we're supposed to start getting ready for bed at nine, ten at weekends, but we often try to stay up.'

My voice was this sad expressionless little squeak. I saw Ruby close her eyes in agony. I saw Dad hang his head. I saw the short-haired woman and all her colleagues shaking their heads. I saw it all and I shrank down to mouse-size to match my squeak.

'Thank you, sweetie. Off you go, twins. Next!' said the short-haired woman. She was already staring past us, smiling at the new set of twins.

'No, hang on a minute!' said Ruby. 'Look my sister isn't very well, she's been sick, she's not normally like this, she can speak up and be ever so funny, I swear she can. How about if we just do a couple of minutes of our prepared piece? Give us a chance. We've used up all our savings getting here, and we're going to get in terrible trouble with our dad when we get back . . .'

'Yes, it's a shame, sweetie, but we don't really have the time,' said the short-haired woman, and she put her arm round both of us. It wasn't just sympathy. She propelled us gently but firmly to the edge of the stage.

Even in the midst of her despair Ruby remembered the camera, twisting round and grimacing in agony, and then she sighed and waved her hand.

I could hear a few chuckles.

'That kid's a caution,' said someone.

'Yeah. Pity about her twin.'

It was only a murmur. But it was like a giant roaring in my ears. It wouldn't soften or stop.

I couldn't seem to hear properly even when Dad caught up with us.

'You bet you're in terrible trouble,' he said furiously. 'How dare *you run off here like this, when I expressly forbade it. I couldn't believe it when we woke up and found you both gone. I was so worried I was going to call the police, but Rose insisted you'd both be all right and that you'd obviously gone for this idiotic audition.'*

'Well, it was a complete waste of time anyway,' said Ruby. 'You really blew it for us, Dad. We were doing just great and then you had to come barging in and put us off our stroke.'

'Put me *off. Not you,' I said. 'And it wasn't Dad's fault. He waited. He gave us a chance. But I mucked it up. That's what they said. You were great, Ruby, yeah. But I was useless. They said so.'*

'No they didn't,' said Ruby. 'And anyway, they didn't give you a proper chance. It wasn't fair.'

'You don't want to be an actress anyway, Garnet,' said Dad. 'And even if you'd both been offered the parts, I wouldn't have let you take them. Ruby can act when she grows up, but I don't want my girls turning into

ghastly little child stars, thank you very much.'

'There's no chance of me being any sort of star,' I said, and I started crying. I couldn't bear it. They were both so sorry for me. Dad was still mega-mad because we'd sneaked off up to London by ourselves, but he was holding back his anger for a bit to try to comfort me.

And Ruby wasn't cross with me. She should hate me for ever because I did muck it up. I should have said all that stuff and never mind about Dad being there. I could *have done. Only I didn't. I let her down. I'll always let her down.*

She's the biggest and the brightest and the best.

She's the caution.

She's the star.

It's a pity she's stuck with me.

Pity about her twin.

Pity about her twin.

Pity about her twin.

TEN

What's all this pity piffle??? Perlease, Garnet! And anyway, I did get cross with you. I had a real go at you in the car, because you *were* a bit of a wally at the audition. What did it matter if Dad was there or not? You could have made something up if you didn't want to do a rant at Rose. I mean, I wouldn't go on at you if I truly thought you couldn't do it, but you *can*. Well, you could have. Only it's too late now. We've blown it. Lost our chance. We don't get to be famous child stars. We're drab child nobodies stuck in this dreary dump for ever and ever. *And* we've lost all our savings for nothing. Not to mention my baby doll that Gran gave me.

Garnet? Oh, don't start crying *again*.

Look, *I'm* the one who should be crying. *I'm* the one who wants to act. *I'm* the one that Dad is maddest at. The way he went on and on at me! And then when I argued back and told him he was an old worryguts and that we're big enough to look after ourselves and what possible harm could happen on a simple trip to London, I thought he was actually going to clock me one.

He hasn't ever smacked us, has he? I wish he would, then we could show the bruises at school and get taken into care.

I mean it. I'm sick of living here with him and her.

Hey, let's write to Gran and see if she could possibly squeeze us into her flat. We could sleep curled up on her settee, couldn't we? And she keeps saying how much she misses us on her postcards.

Then we could go back to our old school. We're not going to this stupid new school again, especially now that Dumbo Debenham's told tales on us. We're not going even if Dad picks us up and tries to drag us there. We're not speaking to him, right? And we're certainly not speaking to *Rose*. Who cares if she came out with all that guff about us being ultra-determined and clever getting ourselves to London. We didn't ask her to stick up for us, did we?

Garnet? Look, what does it matter what she's shouting? We don't want to go and watch television with her! Who cares if it's—

It was us! Well, only a glimpse, but they showed me, doing my goodbye bit. The camera came right up close. They didn't show much of Garnet, just a bit of her hair and an elbow but they showed all of me, and there was a voice-over saying, 'And this twin certainly took rejection like a trouper.'

Pity they didn't say our names. Still. We were on the telly. Well, I was.

It was on the News. We missed the first part but Rose videoed it. They did a whole little item about the audition for the *Twins at St Clare's* series as a clever early puff for the programme, seeing as it's going to be made by the same telly company. They showed some of those other twins doing their party pieces. There weren't any as good as us. Well, me. Of course, that's only my opinion.

The twins that they've chosen are absolutely *awful*.

That's the way they talk,too. Oooh absolutely jolly good show, fwightfully, ya, jolly super-duper green-welly wallies.

Perhaps it's just as well we weren't chosen. If they'd got us to talk all twiddly-snooty-pop like that then we'd have been sent up rotten for ever and a day. Kids won't want to watch a pathetic programme like that. Or if they do, they'll just laugh at it.

Still, it looks like they're pulling out all the stops on the production. It's being filmed on location in this real big boarding school during the summer holidays. They showed all the grounds. It was just like a stately home. And there was a swimming pool. And a sort of miniature zoo, where they keep their pets. And inside this huge great house it wasn't a bit like a *school* school. There were ordinary boring old classrooms but they had playrooms with television and videos and music centres and computers and upstairs there weren't dormitories like I thought – they had lots of bedrooms with flowery duvets and teddies on the beds and posters up on the walls, and best of all, this school has its own *theatre*. It's quite small, OK, but it's got a real stage with red velvet curtains and lighting and props and everything, and they put on plays.

I wish we could go to a school like that.

Hey.

Wow.

Yes!

No!

Oh,Garnet, come on! It would be absolutely fantastic! Oh, let's go there. We wouldn't be acting, we'd be the *real* twins of St Clare's. Well, Marnock Heights. It would be such fun. We could play all those posh games – hockey and lacrosse and cricket in the summer. I bet I'd be absolutely ace at cricket. And we could have a pet each in the little zoo place. Twin pets.

Rabbits? Those little ones with shy faces. Dwarf rabbits.

OK, twin baby bunnies. Though I'd sooner have gerbils. Or rats.

I don't like rats. Or gerbils. I don't even like mice.

Right, we're agreed. It's rabbits. We'll go and play with our rabbits every day and we'll have a game of cricket and we'll swim in the pool and in the evenings we'll watch videos in the sitting-room and then, after we've gone to bed, we'll have mega-midnight feasts.

This is a game, isn't it?

No! It can be real. We're going to go to boarding school.

Yes, it's a school, so there'll be lessons all day. We can't just muck about stroking our rabbits and playing games. There'll be English and History and Technology. And hard stuff too like Geometry and Latin.

That's OK. You'll be able to do that. And did

you see that library in the telly clip? All those wonderful books, Garnet.

We've got books here.

Old boring books. We hate this bookshop. We hate this school and this whole horrible dump of a village. So we're going to get out. We're going to go to boarding school. Marnock Heights. We'll write a letter applying. You'd better do it, Garnet, your writing's much neater than mine. I'll tell you what to put.

But I don't want to—

I'm sick of you going on about what you want and don't want. Look, *I* wanted to be one of the twins of St Clare's on the television. *I* planned and plotted so that we got all the way to London by ourselves. *I* sold all my stuff. *I* did my audition thingy so well that they all laughed and they really liked me, and it looked like we'd actually got the part, didn't it? But then *you* mucked it up.

Yes.

There's no need to look like that. I'm not being deliberately horrid. I'm just trying to get you to understand that it would be ultra ultra ultra mean of you to muck up my chances of getting what I want second best in the world. Right?

The Red Bookshop
High Street
Cussop

19 May

Dear Madam - We are sorry, we don't know your name.

We are ten-year-old identical twins, nearly eleven and we hate our school in this village. We don't fit in. The lessons are boring and there aren't any proper books and the only games we play are rounders.

We went to the television audition for The Twins at St Clare's. We very nearly got the part actually. We were featured in the television coverage. Well, one of us was. And you were featured too and your wonderful school and we thought Oooh this is our idea of heaven, the stage and the swimming pool and the games and the animals and all that.

So please can we come to your school in September? We promise to be good pupils and you don't have to worry about us being homesick because we hate our home.

Yours faithfully
Ruby Barker
Garnet Barker.

P.S. Please say yes. You won't regret it. Honestly.

Look at this!

We went rushing to tell Dad. We thought he'd be in a good mood because some nutty old girl had bought all his *Girls' Own* annuals for a lot of money, and as she staggered backwards and forwards to her car with book after book she kept burbling, 'Those were the days, eh? When girls really *were* girls. A hard game of hockey and then toasted teacakes in front of the fire.' She sighed happily, and then saw Garnet and me hanging around.

'Only nowadays it's all disco dancing and McDonald's beefburgers,' she said. 'That's what you want, isn't it, girls?'

'Oh no,' I said quickly. 'Garnet and me, we'd like to play hockey and toast teacakes. That's just what we want too.'

'Well, good for you,' said the old girl, lurching out of the shop with the last of her annuals.

'What's all this about?' said Dad, blinking at us. But he looked pleased. We've had a policy of being rude to the customers recently and that's made him extremely narked. I looked at Garnet. She looked at me. I took a deep breath.

'We're not kidding, Dad. We read all the *St Clare's* books, see, when we were wanting to act in the telly series. And we think it all sounds really great. So Garnet and I want to go to boarding school.'

Dad laughed, not taking us seriously.

'It's not really like it is in books,' said Dad. 'I don't think either of you would go a bundle on real boarding school. You have to work hard and do as you're told all the time. According to poor Miss Debenham, you don't do any work at all and never ever do as you're told.'

'Yes, but that's because she's a silly teacher and it's a silly school. But if we went to a super top-notch boarding school then we'd be mega-good, really truly. A boarding school like Marnock Heights.'

'Like *where*?'

'It's the place they're using for the *St Clare's* film. It's a real school. And so Garnet and I wrote to the headmistress asking to go there and she's sent us this booklet all about it, look.'

I ran to fetch it and shoved it under Dad's nose.

'Oh, for goodness sake! Will you girls *stop*

doing things behind my back,' Dad groaned.

'Say we can go, though, Dad, *please*. You look at all the pictures. It's lovely, isn't it?'

'Oh, very lovely,' said Dad, flicking through. Then he stopped at the back page, where there were two pieces of paper tucked into a little pocket. 'And very lovely school fees too! Eight thousand a year. Each! Oh yes, nice one, Ruby.'

I stared at him and then snatched the paper. There were all these figures on it. The fees. I didn't realize you had to *pay* to go to some schools. You had to pay an enormous enormous enormous fee to go to Marnock Heights.

'Oh no,' I wailed.

'Oh no,' Garnet wailed too. But she didn't sound too fussed, in actual fact. Right, Garnet????

Well . . .

We've got to think POSITIVE. Because all is not lost. Maybe Dad won't have to fork out any fees. Not that he could anyway. We're far too poor. But But But . . . There was a letter tucked into the pocket of the prospectus, along with the note about the frightful fees.

Marnock Heights
Gorselea
Sussex

22 May

Dear Ruby and Garnet

What lovely names! You wrote me a lovely letter too. I'm pleased that you'd like to attend Marnock Heights. Here is the current prospectus. Show it to your parents or guardians.

I'd like to point out that we do award several special scholarships each year. These have already been awarded for the new intake in the Autumn, but one girl is now unable to take up her scholarship because she's going abroad. Perhaps you would like to come to the school and sit the entrance examination to see if either of you might pass highly enough for scholarship consideration?

Please telephone my secretary for an appointment.

With best wishes

Yours sincerely

Miss Jeffreys

Headteacher
(There, you know my name now!)

ELEVEN

Dad still wouldn't hear of it. At first. But we kept on at him.

You *kept on at him.*

On and on and on. And then he started to weaken.

It was Rose too. She said we should go for it. She said she wished she'd had a proper education.

'It's a great chance. It's ever such a famous school. If one of them got a scholarship there then they'd be able to go on, do anything, achieve anything.'

She's just desperate to get rid of us. Because we're driving her crackers.

You sometimes drive me *crackers, Ruby. You won't ever change your mind about anyone.*

Or anything. So we're going to Marnock Heights!

We're sitting the exam, that's all. And I don't see the point, as there's two of us and only one scholarship.

We'll wangle two, somehow. Once Miss Jeffreys gets to know us. She likes us already. She's ever so complimentary in her letter. We're lovely. I'm Miss Lovely Ruby and you're Miss Lovely Garnet, OK? Oh, come *on*, Garnet, cheer up! We've won! We've got our own way!

You've *got your own way. And I'm worried about the exam. She doesn't say what sort. If it's an interview then I'm scared I'll go all stupid and shy and not know what to say. Like at the audition.*

It's OK, I'll do all the talking. You just leave it to me.

So I left the talking to Ruby. We were shown into Miss Jeffreys' study and she shook our hands and smiled and gave us tea and biscuits and as we sipped and nibbled, Miss Jeffreys asked us questions.

They were really hard questions too, like:

'Why do you think education for girls is important?'

and 'What are your ambitions for the future?'

and 'What do you like doing in your spare time?'

and even 'How do you feel about being a twin?'

I feel bad about being a twin because I let Ruby down. I couldn't think of a thing to say. I just tagged on to the end of her sentences. She was brilliant.

Hmm! *Mega*-brilliant.

It was easy-peasy. I didn't say what I *really* think, naturally. I just said all this stuff to impress Miss Jeffreys and make her see that we are ideal pupils for Marnock Heights. I don't care a bit about education but I spouted stuff that old Rosy-Ratbag said the other day. And I said truthfully enough that our ambition is to be famous actresses, but I said we needed to study Shakespeare and if we stay in Cussop you don't even get *started* on Shakespeare until you go to sixth-form college. And I said that in our spare time we acted, and we also read lots, and I named all the books that Garnet likes, and some of Dad's Dickens and Hardy, and Miss Jeffreys looked dead impressed. She asked about the stories but I made some stuff up and I'm sure she swallowed it. And then when she asked about the twin bit I said it was just like being one person, only we were twice as good as anyone else.

She laughed and said that was a really good answer.

So *I* said that it was ever so important that we mustn't ever be separated and that as we always shared everything maybe we could share a scholarship too.

Dad got all fidgety then but she laughed even more. Then she took us all round the

school and the grounds, and it is truly fantastic.

The other girls seem OK too. One looked a bit snobby so I stuck my tongue out at her, but she stuck her tongue out back at me and then we both grinned. She had red hair and little wicked eyes. I think we'll be friends with her when we come to Marnock Heights.

If.

Look, I keep *telling* you, Garnet, we'll get there. OK, we had to sit in the library and do that boring old written exam – and I must admit that got me a bit worked up because that other teacher insisted that we sit at opposite ends so we couldn't work together the way we always do. That was ever so unfair. And then, when I caught your eye and we were sort of conferring, it was mean of that teacher to make me turn round and face the other way. They don't understand. We weren't cheating or anything. It's just the way we work, isn't it? Especially when it comes to all that boring stuff like arithmetic and general knowledge. And that composition was ultra-blobby-boring. 'Snow in Winter'! What did you write, eh?

You'll get mad at me.

Oh no. What did you put???

I just imagined a mountain all over with snow and what it must look like. And how odd it must be for the sheep, all green grass one minute and then white sharp stuff that hurts their teeth. And people always say there's a blanket of snow on the ground and yet if you were under that blanket, buried, you'd be dead. And how once when we were making snow angels in the park I stopped moving my arms and legs to see what it would feel like to be frozen. And snow looks so clean and pure but nothing's dirtier when everyone's trudged through it and it's all grey with yellow patches and how it's always like that, it can't ever stay the same, and yet each time you hope there'll be a way of keeping it looking beautiful.

Oh yucky yucky yuck! What did you have to write that rubbish for? I just bunged a few bits down about robins and icicles and footsteps crunching, like the verses inside Christmas cards. That's what they wanted, you idiot, not all your weirdo ramble.

I'm sorry, Ruby.

Yes, well, so you should be.

Ruby . . . What if you get accepted for the scholarship and I don't?

We're *both* going to get a scholarship.

But what if we don't? Would you go to Marnock Heights without me?

I keep telling and telling you, we're going together.

Yes, and I keep asking and asking . . . if it's

just you that gets accepted, will you go?

No. Yes. I don't *know*.

I think you should. Though it will be horrible without you. But I can't stand it if I'm always going to be the one that holds you back.

Marnock Heights
Gorselea
Sussex
29 May

Dear Mr Barker

I thoroughly enjoyed meeting you and your delightful daughters last week.

Ruby is a charming child, so full of vim and vigour. No wonder she wants to be an actress. I am sure she will succeed in her ambitions one day. I'm afraid we can't offer her a scholarship at Marnock Heights. She is obviously witty and intelligent and her conversation sparkles – though she tends to get rather carried away and bluffs when she's uncertain! Her written work is lively if a little slapdash, but I'm afraid she failed several of our tests. If she could only apply herself more vigorously then I'm sure she could reach a far

We're not going to be held back, either of us. We're going rushing forwards. To Marnock Heights.

higher standard. I feel she's relied on her sister to do all her work for so long that she's failed to reach her full academic potential.

Garnet too might benefit from a term of separation from her sister. She lets Ruby do all her talking for her, and therefore does not interview at all well. However, she came into her own in the written tests. She has a few gaps in her knowledge but on the whole she did very well. Her essay was outstanding – extremely sensitive and mature. We would like to offer her a full scholarship at Marnock Heights, commencing in the Autumn term.

With best wishes

Yours sincerely

Miss Jeffreys

Headteacher

TWELVE

We couldn't believe it. We thought Miss Jeffreys had got us mixed up.

'She means me,' said Ruby. 'She must mean me.'

'Yes, it can't be me,' I said. 'Ruby will have got the scholarship.'

'No,' said Dad. 'It's definitely Garnet.'

'Let me see the letter!' Ruby demanded.

Dad didn't want either of us to see it.

'It's addressed to me,' he said. 'And it's plain what it says. There's no mix up.'

'She's just got our names round the wrong way,' Ruby insisted. 'It's always happening.'

'Not this time,' said Rose.

'Look, it's absolutely not fair if she's read the letter too, when it's got nothing to do with her. She's not our mother,' said Ruby.

'No, but I'm your father, and I want you to calm down, Ruby, and we'll talk all this over carefully.'

'Not till you show me the letter!'

'I'd show both the girls the letter,' said Rose. 'They're not little kids. I think they should see what it says.'

So Dad showed us.

It was like a smack in the face.

Not for me. For Ruby.

I read quicker than she does. I watched her face while she was finishing the letter. I couldn't bear it.

'She's written a whole load of rubbish,' I said quickly. 'She only met us for one afternoon and yet she thinks she knows us. Well she doesn't, does she, Ruby?'

Ruby was getting very red in the face. She screwed her eyes up. She looked as if she was trying hard not to cry. But Ruby never cries.

'Ruby,' I said, and I put my arm round her.

She wriggled away as if my arm had turned into a snake.

'Oh, Ruby,' I said, and I was the one who started crying. 'Look, I'm not going to go to Marnock Heights. I didn't even want to go in the first place. It was you that wanted to, not me.'

I was making it worse.

'I think you should go, Garnet,' said Rose. 'You've done very well. We should all be busy congratulating you. I know it's tough on Ruby, but—'

'You don't know anything,' I shouted.

I couldn't stand it. I didn't want them ganging up on my side. I was on Ruby's *side.*

'Hey, we'll have less of that cheeky tone,' said Dad. 'Rose, love, could you make us all a cup of coffee? Let's talk it over, eh? It's been a bit of a shock for all of us. Ruby? Ruby, where are you going?'

'There's nothing to talk about,' said Ruby. Her voice sounded awful. She was trying to make it sound couldn't-care-less, but it kept catching in her throat. 'Garnet's got the scholarship. I haven't . And that's it.'

'But I'm not going, Ruby! Please believe me. I promise I'm not going to go. I couldn't stand going there. Especially without you.'

'So why did you try ever so hard in all those silly tests and write all that yucky stuff for your essay?' said Ruby.

'I don't know. I just didn't think. Oh, Ruby, I'm sorry.'

I tried to grab hold of her again but she wouldn't let me.

'You get away from me,' she said, ducking.

'Now this is getting ridiculous,' said Dad. 'Pull yourself together, Ruby. I'm ashamed of you. I know you've had a bit of a disappointment, but there's no need to be nasty to poor old Garnet. Why can't you be big enough to congratulate her? She didn't act like this over that television audition, now did she? She was full of praise for you.'

Dad was making it worse. I saw Ruby's eyes, as she ducked. They were brimming over.

'Oh, congratulations, clever goody-goody Garnet,' Ruby gabbled, and then she rushed out the room.

I tried to follow her, but Dad stopped me.

'No, Garnet. Let her go. She won't want you around for a bit, especially as she's crying,' he said. Perhaps he did understand a little bit after all. 'But there's no need for you to cry, sweetheart. Rose is right. You've done brilliantly and I'm very proud of you.'

'I'm not going though,' I wept.

'Well. I can't make *you go. And this boarding school lark certainly wasn't my idea.*

But I do think now that it's a wonderful opportunity.'

'I'll say,' said Rose, handing round the coffee. 'You've got to go for it, Garnet.'

'I can't leave Ruby,' I wailed.

'But Ruby would leave you,' said Rose.

'That's different,' I said.

'But it shouldn't be different,' said Dad, and he pulled me on to his lap. 'This letter has made me see that maybe it's bad for you and Ruby to be together all the time. You're holding each other back, spoiling each other's chances. You're growing up now, and you need to develop as two separate sisters.'

'But we're not separate. We're twins. We can't do without each other.'

'You're going to have to learn to some day,' said Dad. 'You'll both grow up and have different jobs and have different lifestyles and have different families.'

'No, we're going to stay together,' I said.

We'd got it all sorted out.

We'd stick together when we were young

and when we were old

and when we were even older

and if we ever wanted to get married then we'd marry twins

and have twin babies

and then when they grew up they *could stick together for ever and maybe they'd have twins too and then* they *could . . .*

My head was buzzing with all these twins. I wanted my own twin. I could hear her upstairs. She was sobbing.

I don't know what to do.

It's worse than when Ruby wasn't talking to me.

She's talking now, but not properly. *And she only talks when we're with other people. When we're together she hardly says anything. She won't play any of our games. She won't plan any twin-tricks so that we do things simultaneously.*

She doesn't seem to want to be a twin any more.

She won't even dress like me now. She waits until she sees what I'm putting on and then she puts on something entirely different. And she does her hair in a new way too.

I tried to copy her, so she changed it again.

And so I changed too. And then she did something terrible. She got the scissors and I thought she was bluffing. And then I wasn't sure.

'Don't!' I said.

But she did. She cut off all her hair.

'Oh Ruby, what have you done?*' I said, looking at her poor head with the chopped hair sticking up like a scrubbing brush.*

'I'm making me different,' she said, running

her hand through the stubble. She swallowed and sniffed. 'And you needn't look like that. I like it. I wanted it this way for ages. It's . . . sort of punk. Great.'

I didn't know what to do. We've always had long hair, right from when we were little. When Gran made us have plaits I would always do Ruby's as well as my own. Sometimes when I was feeling sleepy I'd forget which was my head and which was hers.

Now when I stared at Ruby I felt as if my own hair had been hacked off even though I could still feel the warm weight of it on my shoulders. It gave me the weirdest out-of-synch feeling, like when you watch a film and the people say things a fraction before their lips open.

Ruby couldn't grow her hair. So there was only one thing to do.

'No you don't!' Ruby hissed, as I reached for the scissors. She snatched them away from me. 'I'm warning you, Garnet. You cut off your hair and I'll cut off your head*!'*

She looked so fierce I felt I believed her.

She looked like she hated me.

She took the scissors and some newspaper and cut out a line of paper dolls. She cut them into twins. And then she chopped through their hands, so they were separate.

She chopped so violently that they tore all the way up their arms.

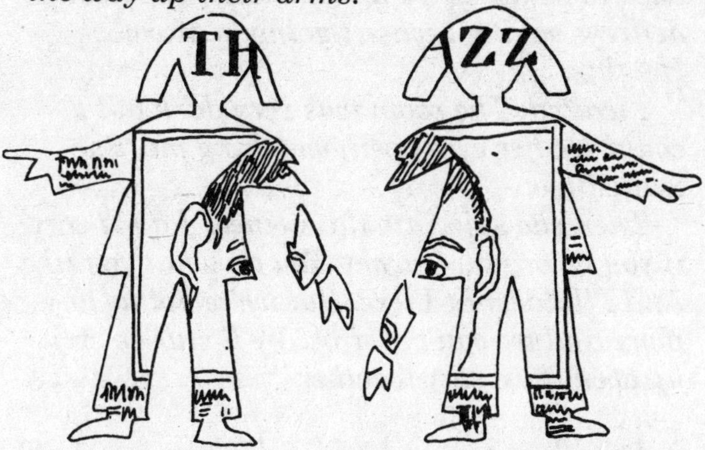

It's me again. Ruby won't write in the book any more. I don't want to write much either. How can I give an account of us when we aren't us *any more.*

If only I could tear out all the pages about the school and the scholarship – scrub them out so that they never happened.

Ruby's acting like she wants to scrub me out altogether. It's the holidays now, but she won't go around with me. She just goes off by herself and when I try to follow her she runs away. She could always run faster than me. And she's better at hiding. I don't know where she goes or whether she joins up with anyone else. But she won't join up with me.

I asked her in bed at night if we could go back to being us if I wrote a letter to Miss Jeffreys saying I wasn't going to Marnock Heights.

I waited. The room was very dark but I could see her eyes open, watching me. She waited too.

Then she said into the silence, 'I don't care if you go or not, Garnet. You do what you like. And I'll do what I *like. But we're not us any more and we can't ever be. We'll still be split up even if we stay together.'*

But it's not what I like. I don't know what I *like.*

I don't want to go to Marnock Heights. Although I've been reading all these books. Not the twins ones. I feel sick whenever I see them. No, there's a whole shelf of old school stories at the back of the shop – girls who go to schools in Abbeys and Chalets and Towers – and I've been reading one in the morning and one in the afternoon and sometimes one in the evening too and sometimes – just sometimes – it sounds as if it might be fun.

Judy thinks so. She's dead envious. She comes round to the shop sometimes. I've been to tea at her house. She's got all these tapes and videos. You just have to sit and watch and listen. Or we go up to her bedroom and play games. Not our sort of games. Board games. And I do get a bit bored playing them. Judy's OK but she's a bit boring too.

She says she's seen Ruby going around with Jeremy Treadgold and his gang! Ruby with the Giant Blob??? I asked Ruby but she just rubbed the end of her nose, indicating that I should mind my own business.

Ruby doesn't want to be my business any more.

She's made herself different.

She even looks different.

People maybe wouldn't even think we were twins now.

Gran nearly did her nut when she came to stay for the weekend. This old man, Albert, drove her in his car. He's her neighbour in her sheltered flats. He came and stayed too, which made it a bit of a squash. Gran said we should call him Uncle Albert, though he's not our uncle.

I looked at Ruby and she looked at me and just for a second it was almost like the old days.

But these are new days and everything's changing and Ruby's changed most of all.

'WhatEVER have you done to yourself, Ruby???' Gran demanded. 'What DO you look like? You're such a scruff. Like a gutter child. And your HAIR! Oh my lord, have you got nits?'

'Leave off, Gran,' said Ruby, fidgeting and scowling.

'For goodness sake, how could you let her run round like a ragamuffin?' Gran said to Rose.

Rose had tried to smarten Ruby up a bit for Gran's visit. She'd washed all her best clothes and ironed them and she'd begged Ruby to let her try to neaten up her new hairstyle. Ruby refused. She wore her oldest dirtiest clothes and deliberately fished her old holey trainers out of the dustbin, even though Rose had bought her brand-new ones specially.

But Rose didn't say any of this.

'Ruby likes to be comfy. And we think her hairstyle really suits her, don't we, Ricky?'

'Sure,' said Dad, putting his arm round Rose.

'Well, at least Garnet looks fairly presentable,' Gran sniffed. 'But what's all this I hear about you being packed off to boarding school, Garnet? I don't hold with that idea at all. What's the matter, do they want to get rid of you?'

'Of course we don't want to get rid of her!' said Dad. 'We just think she should give it a try for a term, seeing as she's got this scholarship. But if she hates it then of course she can come home whenever she wants.'

But like I said, I still don't know what I want. I'm starting to get nightmares about going to the school.

And yet it's horrid at home now that Ruby is a stranger instead of a sister. I'd secretly hoped that I could talk to Gran in secret and ask her if I could maybe go and live with her for a bit – but I'd forgotten how naggy and niggly she can be sometimes. And then there's Albert who isn't our uncle. He's not part of our family but it looks as if he and Gran are a new family all of their own.

Then there's Dad and Rose. They have rows sometimes but they always make it up and when Rose tried ever so hard to cook a proper Sunday lunch for everyone, but somehow the beef got burnt and the Yorkshire pudding sulked and the potatoes wouldn't roast and the beans went stringy and the gravy had lumps, Dad still ate up every scrap on his

plate and said it was super and even asked for seconds.

They're a family too.

I'm part of their family and Gran's family and I used to have Mum as special family but even more than Mum there was always Ruby.

Ruby-and-Garnet.

Only now there's just Ruby. And Garnet.

Ruby?

Ruby.

Oh, Ruby.

MEMORANDUM

THIRTEEN

This is my written work. And I don't give a toss if it's slapdash. Who cares what that stupid jumped-up jelly-belly Jeffreys says?

I wouldn't want to go there anyway. Not now. I'm having heaps better fun here. I am.

Anyway, I bet Garnet doesn't have the bottle to go without me.

Or if she does, I bet she gets terribly homesick and cries heaps and will be sent back a sodden wreck.

She can't manage without me. Even she knows that.

But I'm doing just fine without her.

This is my new notebook and I shall take heaps of notes. It says MEMORANDUM on the cover. I like the first two letters. ME ME ME ME ME ME ME ME ME ME ME ME ME ME ME ME ME ME.

This notebook is going to be all about Me.

I like being just me.

I like it just me. Oh, I've put that bit before. Never mind. It makes it twice as true. I feel GREAT.

I know what Memorandum means, too. I am quite intelligent actually, even if some people seem to think I'm a total thicko. Memorandum means notes of things to be remembered. And I want it officially down on paper that

1. Ruby Barker doesn't give two hoots about not getting that stupid scholarship.
2. Ruby Barker doesn't give two hoots that her sneaky sister is going instead of her.
3. Ruby Barker doesn't give two hoots about said sneaky sister.

She is *absolutely devastated* (there, *I'm* the one who uses ever such posh long grown-up words, so it just goes to show that Miss Jeffreys is talking RUBBISH).

Yuck! Now. Where was I?

Oh yes. Garnet is truly despairing because I have broken up our twinship. She needs me.

She might think she's the clever one now, but not a bit of it! She's utterly lost without me. But *I'm* fine. I don't need her. Not one *bit* of her.

Well, maybe her hand would come in useful some of the time. So she could do the writing when I get bored.

I do get a little bored sometimes. I go out because I don't want to stay in that smelly old shop, but there aren't many places to go to in this horrible dump. So I just sort of mooch about.

I don't need Garnet to make up games for me. I can make up my own. I mostly pretend I'm this intrepid explorer trekking through the jungle, and there are killer snakes and huge hairy poisonous spiders

and ferocious tigers

and I wade through the rapids

and hang by my fingertips from dangerous mountains

and whenever I get the merest glimpse of the enemy I have to hide because in spite of my superhuman powers and mega-brilliance I am hopelessly outnumbered.

I am planning an ambush when the Blob goes unprotected.

The Intrepid Explorer often starves for days and days. She has to make quick raids into enemy territory

but often has to make do with natural resources.

The Intrepid Explorer did ponder about doing a bit of hunting

but she decided she was a vegetarian. Even though she doesn't actually go a bundle on vegetables. Sprouts . . . yuck. Cabbage . . . yuck. Cauliflower . . . double yuck.

If this is a *Memorandum* book, then it's just about *me* . . . and I can jot things down at *randum*. I know what that means too, Miss Jeffreys, so ya boo sucks to you. It means there's no plan, and you just shove things in any old how. So these are my random jottings.

I am Ruby Barker and I am a brilliant actress and if my ex-twin hadn't made such a muck of things then I could be starring in a telly serial this summer.

I tried phoning the television people, telling them I was willing to audition for any other part. They thanked me and said they'd get in touch. But they didn't. So I phoned again and they got a bit shirtier this time and said there weren't any parts going spare, sorry and all that but would I quit pestering them please, and if I really wanted to be an actress I needed to get myself an agent and why didn't I go to a good stage school.

Well, how can I go to a good stage school when my rotten old father won't send me to one, though he's sending my sister to the poshest boarding school in the country.

OK, he doesn't have to pay fees, but her uniform is costing a *fortune*.

You should see it too. Talk about awful and old-fashioned! I wouldn't be seen *dead* in those clothes. Garnet looks *appalling*.

Well, I suppose Dad isn't having to pay out of his own pocket. Rose helped Garnet sell her doll at an auction. The crummy china baby doll, twin to mine. I sold mine at the car-boot sale and they gave me £20.

It is exceedingly painful to have to write this next bit. Garnet's doll went for £600. Yes. Mine would have been worth that too. It's some rare French make and daft doll-collectors are willing to fork out a fortune. I mean, you could probably buy a real baby for that sort of money.

Rose was very very angry when she found out the car-boot people only gave me £20. Not angry with me, with them. She went and found them and kicked up a great fuss, but they argued that it had been a perfectly fair deal and she was in the business and she should know they weren't running a kiddie's charity. But they did very reluctantly hand over £100. As a gesture. Rose was still cross because she said they must have made heaps more, but I was happy because that £100 is mine, and although boring old Dad said I should put it in a building society, Rose said she didn't see why I shouldn't have some spending money as I was having a bit of a tough time just lately.

Only I'm not having a tough time at all. Like I said, I'm fine. Doing great. Couldn't be better. *And* I've ended up with £50 to spend all on ME (plus £50 in Dad's boring old building society).

I don't have to waste it on a horrid, hideous

school uniform either. And special suitcases and hockey sticks and dressing gowns and frightful Clarks clodhopper shoes.

I can spend it on

or

or

or

or

or

or

It's weird. I've never had my very own money to spend before. I've always had to share. So it's great to get twice as much.

It's just I can't quite get used to being just me.

I don't even look like me. It's a shock whenever I see myself in the mirror. My hair's growing a bit but it seems to have lost all idea of gravity. It's growing *up*.

This has attracted comments from certain uncouth local loonies, enquiring whether I'm a boy or a girl.

I soon dealt with them.

But then the Huge and Horrible Blob opened his horrendous gob.

He had *such* an inventive and witty new nickname for me.

So I invented several new names for him and his stupid mates.

So then they got all these grass cuttings and asked me if I'd like a green wig and then they threw them all over me

so I hid behind a hedge until I heard them coming and then I jumped up and yelled that they all talked a lot of rubbish so look out—

and they got this black plastic bag full of rubbish all over them.

I'd just grabbed a bag out of someone's dustbin. I hadn't looked inside. It turned out it was wondrously smelly soggy rubbish, all sour milk and tea-leaves and half-eaten Chinese takeaways . . .

So then they got really mad and yelled, 'Let's get her!'

I couldn't run away quite fast enough.

So they got me.

And they smeared rubbish on me and I hit out at them and they kicked me and I bit them but there was only one of me and there were a lot of them.

And then while Blob and I were bashing away at each other, this horrible boy with ferret teeth got his arm round my neck and started choking me and I tried to reach round and hit him where it really hurts but he was hurting that wobbly bit where you swallow so much that I couldn't move and Ferret-Face yelled, 'Go on then, Jerry, bash her face in!' and I thought, This is it. I've already lost my hair. Now I'm going to lose my looks. I'm going to have to go round with a broken nose and no teeth for the rest of my days, and it's not going to help my acting career one bit, and I had my face all squeezed up ready for the blow but Blob hesitated.

'Leave go of her, Brian, she's choking,' he said.

'Well, hit her then!'

'Not with you hanging on to her. And all you others. It's not fair. We'll just fight it out, her and me.'

Ferret-Face muttered and moaned, but he did leave go. I reeled a bit, rubbing my sore neck.

'Are you OK?' said Blob.

'Course I am,' I croaked.

'Right. Let's fight,' said Blob.

So he gave me a punch on the shoulder. Quite a soft punch. And I gave him a shove in his stomach. But not too hard. And then he wrestled me to the ground. But carefully. And I kicked at him. Though I actually barely touched him. We seemed to have lost interest in a really ferocious fight. We were just sort of going through the motions.

Ferret-Face and the other mates got a bit bored with the whole situation too. And they were fed up being covered in all the stinky guck from the rubbish bag, so they sloped off home.

Blob and I were left.

'Shall we just say that I've won the fight and call it quits?' said Blob.

'You haven't won the rotten fight!' I said indignantly. I gave him another punch, though it was a very feeble one.

'All right all right. Well, how about if we call it a draw?' said Blob.

I thought a bit. And then I nodded.

'OK. Though I could have won, you know,' I insisted.

'You're quite a good fighter. For a girl,' said Blob.

'You're quite a good fighter. For a big fat blob,' I said.

He looked hurt. 'Hey, there's no need to call me names. I stuck up for you! I stopped Brian mangling your neck.'

'Yes, but you call me names. Baldie.'

'Yes, well, you do look a bit bald since you had that wacky haircut.'

'Yes, well, you do look a bit blobby.'

'We *both* look a right sight. Especially now. Covered in all this gunge,' said Blob, wiping bamboo shoots out of his eye.

'You can say that again,' I agreed, picking tea-leaves off my face.

We looked at each other. Then we laughed.

And it's weird. We're not bitter enemies

any more. We're sort of friends.

I sometimes go round in the gang, though I can't stick Brian. Actually, Blob isn't too keen on him either.

So we've started going round together. Just him and me.

He still calls me Baldie.

I still call him Blob.

But it doesn't matter because we're mates.

It's great to have someone to pal round with. Someone different, not someone the same as me.

And both Blob and I are going on to the big school together. I'm glad I'll be shot of that Dumbo Debenham. I'll be a new girl at a new school with new teachers. I could make a whole new start if I wanted. Work a bit.

Well, that's what Dad says.

I'll have to see about that.

But there is one good thing about the new school. They've got a stage. Not quite as posh and elaborate as the one at Marnock Heights, but they've got velvet curtains, and they can put up special lights and rustle up some scenery and they have a proper play in the summer and a pantomime at Christmas. Blob told me, because his sister's been in them.

So I'm going to get to be in them too.

Definitely.

It's all going to be great.

I'm ever so happy.

Garnet isn't happy. She's started crying at nights. She's scared about going to boarding school by herself. But it's not just that. She says she can't bear not being friends with me any more.

I listen. And sometimes my eyes sting a bit, but it's OK in the dark. She can't see.

I open my mouth to say a whole lot of things. But somehow I can't ever get them said into the silence. I can't even manage one word. Sorry.

Well, I don't see why I should say sorry. It's Garnet's fault she's going. She shouldn't have done so well in that stupid entrance exam.

No, she should have tried harder at the audition. Then we'd have got to be the Twins at St Clare's. We'd be acting now. Together.

We've been separate all summer.

It's been a bit strange sometimes.

It's going to be even stranger when she's gone.

It's her last night at home. Rose cooked chicken and chips, Garnet's favourite, and made a cake.

She's never made *me* a special cake.

Garnet could only manage one small slice.

Then we all had to sit around playing daft games like Snap and Happy Families. Pretending we were all one Happy Family. And Garnet looked like she was going to snap.

But she didn't cry. Not even when we went to bed. At least, I don't think she did. I got right under the covers so that I couldn't hear.

I felt as if I was snapping. In half.

I kept pretending it wasn't really happening but then we woke up in the morning and Garnet got dressed in her strange new uniform and we've never looked less like twins in our lives.

Rose came into our bedroom to help Garnet get all her new stuff packed and ready.

I looked at all the new clothes and the pyjamas and the hockey boots and all the other stuff, all exactly my size. But not for me.

And for the first time I was really glad I wasn't going. I knew I'd be scared.

Garnet was so scared she had a funny tummy and had to keep dashing to the loo. One of the times she was missing in the bathroom I picked up her old nightie lying on her pillow and sort of snuggled into it for a second, like a baby with a cuddle blanket.

Rose was bent over Garnet's suitcase but she turned and saw me.

She didn't say anything – but she straightened up and put her arm round me and gave me a quick hug.

I started to wriggle away, but she held on to me. So I found I was kind of hugging her back.

And then I started crying.

'You're the one that never cries. You'll start me off,' Rose whispered.

'Don't be nice to me. I've been so hateful. To Garnet,' I sobbed.

'You haven't been exactly sweetness and light to me, either,' said Rose, laughing shakily. 'Or your dad. But you're right. It's Garnet that really matters.'

It's Garnet that really matters.

My twin. My best friend. My other half.

She came back from the bathroom and I rushed at her, flinging my arms round her neck.

'Oh Garnet, I'm so sorry, I've been such a pig, I didn't mean it really, I was just so jealous, and I felt so stupid, and I felt so left out, but you will still be my twin, won't you, even though you're off to Marnock Heights?'

'I'll be your twin for ever and ever and ever,' said Garnet, and we hugged so hard we seemed like Siamese twins, joined for ever.

Only we were about to be ripped apart.

'It's all my stupid stupid stupid fault,' I wailed. 'Oh Garnet, I'll miss you so terribly.'

'I'll miss you too, Ruby – ever so ever so much. But Dad says I don't have to stay if I really hate it.'

'And you'll come home some weekends – and all the holidays. Oh, how can I have been crazy enough to waste all this summer being so foul? I hate me. Why do I always have to be the bad twin?'

'Why do I always have to be the good twin?' said Garnet. 'Hey, maybe we're changing round. We're starting already. You're crying – and I'm not!'

'You will still be my best friend, won't you? You won't go all posh and snooty and look down on me?' I said.

'Don't talk wet,' said Garnet.

'And you will write to me?'

'Every single day. And you write to me too.'

'I promise.'

'You don't always keep your promises.'

'But this is a promise I'll keep, I swear. And I also promise that I'll never ever be mean to you again, Garnet.'

'You'd better not swear on *that* promise,' said Garnet, laughing.

But she cried a little bit when she and Dad went off in the car. We *all* cried.

Garnet's taken the accounts book with her. She's going to write in it every day and then show it to me when she comes home. I've nearly finished this memorandum book already.

I'll have to get another. Bigger, so I can write more. I'll look and see if there's a Paperchase in Hineford on Saturday. Rose is going to drive me there. She's found out about this Saturday drama club. So I'm joining it.

I was dead chuffed when she told me about it.

'Thanks, Rose,' I said.

Well. It was more of a mumble. But she heard.

'It's OK, Ruby. I'm dying to go to Hineford to see some decent shops. I'll have a lovely time in the shopping centre while you do your drama session and then we'll meet up and have lunch. Yes?'

'You bet,' I said.

She's not quite so bad as I thought, Rose.

It's time I started some serious drama training. For my big moment when the telly people get in touch and ask me to audition. Because they still *might*. If this *Twitty Twins at St Clare's* serial is a success they might want to do another Enid Blyton book. One of the Famous Five stories, maybe. The leading part is this fierce tomboy girl, Georgina. I could play her easy-peasy. I've even got the right haircut now.

When Dad gives me a big cuddle, he ruffles all the bristles and calls me his little

Scrubbing Brush. Dad's needed quite a lot of cuddles. Because he's missing Garnet so much.

We're all missing her.

I'm missing her most.

But she's all right. She sort of likes it.

I'll stick her first postcard on this page.

Dearest Ruby,

I'm here! At Marnock Heights!
I feel just like one of the girls in those old school books. I cried a bit after Dad left but this lovely big girl put her arm round me. She's called Jamilla and she's my Sheepdog. That doesn't mean she barks at me, she just shows me where everything is, the classrooms and my bedroom and the dining-room. We had chicken and chips for supper. And Jamilla gave me half a Kit Kat. I'm in the bedroom now and there are three other girls and we're all setting our alarms for midnight so we can have our first feast! The girl in the bed next to me is called Lucy, and she wears little glasses and she's got a toy rabbit to take to bed and a real rabbit in the zoo and she says I can share it if I want. She wants to be my best friend and I said yes but you're my <u>bestest</u> best friend, Ruby. xxxx

With lots and lots of love from Garnet xxxx

P.S. I do miss you so.

Oh, Garnet. I miss you too. Ever so ever so much.

But we're still Ruby and Garnet, even though you're there and I'm here.

We're going to be Ruby and Garnet for ever.

THE END

Miss Beckworth kept me in at dinner time. She didn't give me any stupid lines to write out, though. She said I could work on my Victorian project.

Boring, boring, boring, I thought – but better than lines. And at least I had the book box to myself. I asked for something about Victorian homes.

'Not a posh house for the rich. What about an ordinary little home for a poor family? Aren't there any books about that?'

She found me one or two pages, but there wasn't much. So I made a lot of it up...

The *Lottie Project* is Jacqueline Wilson's ninth title for the Corgi Yearling list. Her previous titles include *The Suitcase Kid*, winner of the 1993 Children's Book Award, and *Double Act*, winner of both the 1995 Smarties Prize *and* the 1996 Children's Book Award.

Also available by Jacqueline Wilson:

Available from Corgi Pups, for younger readers:

THE DINOSAUR'S PACKED LUNCH
THE MONSTER STORY-TELLER

Available from Young Corgi Books:

LIZZIE ZIPMOUTH

Available from Doubleday/Corgi Yearling Books:

BAD GIRLS
THE BED AND BREAKFAST STAR
BURIED ALIVE!
CLIFFHANGER
THE CAT MUMMY
THE DARE GAME
DOUBLE ACT
GLUBBSLYME
THE ILLUSTRATED MUM
THE LOTTIE PROJECT
THE MUM-MINDER
SLEEPOVERS
THE STORY OF TRACY BEAKER
THE SUITCASE KID
VICKY ANGEL
WORRY WEBSITE
SECRETS

Collections

THE JACQUELINE WILSON COLLECTION
(includes *The Story of Tracy Beaker* and
The Bed and Breakfast Star)
JACQUELINE WILSON'S DOUBLE-DECKER
(includes *Bad Girls* and *Double Act*)
JACQUELINE WILSON'S SUPERSTARS
(includes *The Suitcase Kit* and *The Lottie Project*)

THE JACQUELINE WILSON DIARY

Available now from Doubleday / Corgi books, for older readers:

GIRLS IN LOVE
GIRLS UNDER PRESSURE
GIRLS OUT LATE
GIRLS IN TEARS
DUSTBIN BABY
LOLA ROSE

The Lottie Project

Jacqueline Wilson

Illustrated by Nick Sharratt

CORGI YEARLING BOOKS

For Rupa Patel
(author of The Jacqueline Wilson Quiz Book)
and special thanks to everyone at
Burscough County Primary School

THE LOTTIE PROJECT
A CORGI YEARLING BOOK : 0 440 866227

First published in Great Britain by Doubleday,
a division of Random House Children's Books

PRINTING HISTORY
Doubleday edition published 1997
Corgi Yearling edition published 1998

Corgi Yearling Books are published by Random House Children's Books,
61–63 Uxbridge Road, Ealing, London W5 5SA,
a division of The Random House Group Ltd,
in Australia by Random House Australia (Pty) Ltd,
20 Alfred Street, Milsons Point, Sydney, NSW 2061, Australia,
in New Zealand by Random House New Zealand Ltd,
18 Poland Road, Glenfield, Auckland 10, New Zealand
and in South Africa by Random House (Pty) Ltd,
Endulini, 5a Jubilee Road, Parktown 2193, South Africa.

Made and printed in Great Britain by Cox & Wyman, Reading, Berkshire

SCHOOL

I knew exactly who I was going to sit next to in class. Easy-peasy, simple-pimple. It was going to be Angela, with Lisa sitting at the nearest table to us. I'm never quite sure if I like Lisa or Angela best, so it's only fair to take turns.

Jo said what if Angela and Lisa want to sit together with *you* behind or in front or at the side. I just smiled at her. I don't want to sound disgustingly boastful but I'm the one Angela and Lisa are desperate to sit next to. Lots of the girls want to be best friends with me, actually. I'm just best friends with Lisa and Angela, but anyone can be in our special Girls' Gang. Any girl. No boys allowed. That goes without saying. Even though I just did.

But guess what happened that first day of term. We got this new teacher. We knew we wouldn't be getting Mrs Thomas because when we broke up in the summer her tummy could barely fit behind her desk. Her tummy could barely fit behind her *smock*. You could see her tummy button through the material, like a giant press fastener.

When I was a very little kid I used to think that's how babies were born. They grew inside the mother and then when they were ready the mum pressed her tummy button and out they popped. I told Jo how I'd got it all sussed out. Don't laugh. I was *very* little. *Jo* laughed. 'Dream on, Charlie,' she said. 'If only it were that easy.'

That's my name, Charlie. OK, my full name is Charlotte Alice Katherine Enright, but nobody ever calls me that. Jo and Lisa and Angela and all the kids at school call me Charlie. Some of the boys call me Cake or Carrot Cake or Cakehole, but they're just morons, though they think they're dead original. (Note the initials of my name. Got it?) But right since I was born, all the way through nursery and primary, no-one's ever called me Charlotte. Until this new teacher.

Miss Beckworth. She was new so I thought she'd be young. When you get a new young teacher they're often ever so strict the first few weeks just to show you who's boss, and then they relax and get all friendly. Then you can muck about and do whatever you want.

I *love* mucking about, doing daft things and being a bit cheeky and making everyone laugh. Even the teachers. But the moment I set eyes on Miss Beckworth I knew none of us were going to be laughing. She might be new but she certainly wasn't young. She had grey hair and grey eyes and a grey and white blouse and a grey skirt and laced-up shoes, with a laced-up expression on her face to match. When she spoke her teeth were quite big and stuck out a bit, but I put all thought of Bugs Bunny imitations right out of my head.

There are some teachers – just a few – who have YOU'D BETTER NOT MESS WITH ME! tattooed right across their foreheads. She frowned at me with this incredibly fierce forehead and said, 'Good morning. This isn't a very good start to the new school year.'

I stared at her. What was she on about? Why was she looking at her watch? I wasn't late. OK, the school bell had gone as I was crossing the playground, but you always get five minutes to get to your classroom.

'It's three minutes past nine,' Miss Beckworth announced. 'You're late.'

'No, I'm not,' I said. 'We're not counted late until it's five past.'

I didn't say it cheekily. I was perfectly polite. I was trying to be helpful, actually.

'You're *certainly* not off to a good start,' she goes. 'First you're late. And then you argue. My name's Miss Beckworth. What's your name?'

'Charlie, Miss Beckworth.' (See, *ever* so polite – because I could see I had to proceed d-e-l-i-c-a-t-e-l-y.)

'Your proper name?'

'Charlie Enright.'

'We don't seem to be connecting correctly, Miss Enright. Charlie isn't a proper name. It's a diminutive.'

She was trying to make *me* look pretty diminutive, obviously. I tried to act cool but I could feel my cheeks flushing. I have this very white skin that can be a real problem when I get mad or embarrassed. When you have a lot of long red hair and you get a red face too you start to look as if someone's put a match to you.

'Are you *Charles* Enright?'

I can't *stand* it when teachers go all sarcastic on you. A few of the kids tittered nervously. That posh prat Jamie laughed out loud. Typical. Angela and Lisa were looking all anguished, dying for me.

'I'm Charlotte Enright, Miss Beckworth. But I've never been called Charlotte at this school, only Charlie.'

'Well, I'm going to call you Charlotte, Charlotte. Because in my class we do things differently,' said Miss Beckworth.

You're telling me we do things differently. (Well, *I'm* telling *you*, but you know what I mean!) I wasn't allowed to go and sit with Angela. She'd promised to get to school ever so early to grab the best desk (and the one next to it for Lisa) and she'd done well. The desk right next to the window, with the hot pipe to toast my toes on when it got chilly. But all in vain.

'No, don't go and sit down, Charlotte,' said Miss Beckworth. 'I was just about to explain to the whole class that while we get to know each other I'd like you all to sit in alphabetical order.'

We stared at her, gob-smacked.

Miss Beckworth spoke into the stunned silence, holding her register aloft.

'So, Anthony Andrews, you come and sit at this desk in the front, with Judith Ashwell beside you, and then—'

'But Judith's a girl, Miss!' Anthony protested in horror.

'Cleverly observed, Mr Andrews,' said Miss Beckworth. 'And kindly note, I call you Mr Andrews, not plain Mister. I would prefer you to call me Miss Beckworth. Not Miss.'

'But boys and girls never sit next to each other, Miss,' said Anthony. He's as thick as two short planks – *twenty*-two – but when Miss Beckworth's forehead wrinkled he rewound her little speech inside his empty head and took heed. 'Er, Miss Beckworth, Miss. I don't want to sit next to Judith!'

'Well, you needn't think I want to sit next to *you*,' said Judith. 'Oh Miss Beckworth, that's not fair!'

Miss Beckworth didn't care. 'I said things would be different in my class. I didn't say they would be fair,' she said. 'Now, get yourselves sorted out and stop fussing like a lot of silly babies. Who's next on the register? Laura Bernard, right, sit at the desk behind Anthony and Judith, and then . . .'

I hovered, signalling wild regret with my eyebrows to Angela, who'd got up half an hour early for nothing. Angela's surname is Robinson, so obviously we wouldn't sit together. But Lisa is Lisa Field, right after me on the register, so it looked as if we were OK after all. It wasn't really fair on poor Angela if I sat next to Lisa two years running, but it couldn't be helped.

But it didn't work out like that.

'James Edwards, you sit at the desk at the back on the left,' said Miss Beckworth. 'With . . . ah, Charlotte Enright beside you.'

Jamie Edwards! The most revolting stuck-up boring boy in the whole class. The whole year, the whole school, the whole town, county, country, world, *universe*. I'd sooner squat in the stationery cupboard than sit next to him.

I thought quickly, my brain going whizz, flash, bang. Aha! Sudden inspiration!

'I'm afraid I can't see very well, Miss Beckworth,' I said, squinting up my eyes as if I badly needed glasses. 'If I sit at the back I won't be able to see the board. Sometimes I still have problems even at the front – so if Lisa Field can come and sit next to me again, then I'm used to her telling me stuff in case I can't read it for myself. Isn't that right, Lisa?'

This was all news to Lisa, but she nodded convincingly.

'Yes, Miss Beckworth, I always have to help Charlie,' said Lisa.

But Miss Beckworth wasn't fooled. 'I'm not convinced that you're short-sighted, Charlotte. Quick-witted, certainly. But until you bring me a note from your mother and another from your optician I'd like you to sit at the back beside James.'

That was it. I was doomed. There was no way out. I had to sit next to Jamie Edwards.

He moved his chair right up against the wall and shuddered elaborately as I flopped down furiously beside him.

'Charlie Cakehole! Yuck!' he said. But under his breath, because he knew Miss Beckworth was watching.

Jamie Edwards is the smarmiest little swot, and always wants the teachers to have him as their pet. Which he is anyway. Because he's such an infuriating Clever Clogs, always coming top top top.

Well, who on earth wants to be top of the class?

'Why can't you try harder at school, Charlie,' Jo always says. 'You're bright. If you'd only stop messing about and work hard you could do really well. You could come top if you really tried.'

I asked Jo why she always nagged so about my boring old education.

'Maybe you're not so bright as I thought you were,' Jo said. 'Can't you work it out for yourself?'

That made me feel bad. But it's hopeless. Maybe I could do better. I'm not bottom of the class, mind you. Just a nice comfy middle. But I suppose if I worked like stink then I could do better. I can generally beat Lisa and Angela if I want. Maybe I could come top of all the girls. But I couldn't ever beat Jamie Edwards. And I'd far sooner be bottom than second to Smarty Pants.

So I slid down in my seat and sulked for most of

the morning. It was hot but Jamie kept me well-fanned, waving his hand frantically all the time because he kept wanting Miss Beckworth to pick him. Pathetic. I wouldn't put my hand up even when I knew the answers. Even in English, which is my best subject. I've always got ticks and stars and *Very Goods* all over the place for my stories.

Miss Beckworth started a poetry lesson and it was actually quite interesting and then she read this poem by some dippy American lady and you had to guess what it was about. Like a riddle. And no-one knew. Jamie guessed it might be about a river and Miss Beckworth said it was a very good guess – but it was wrong. Ha. *I* knew what it was. Easy-peasy, simple-pimple. It was a train. And I sat there with this pleased feeling throbbing through me, though I acted all cool and bored, slumped in my seat, arms folded . . . waiting. Waiting until she was just about to give up and then I was going to put my hand up after all and maybe yawn a bit or fiddle with my hair and then I was going to go 'It's a train' like it must be obvious to everyone. One up to me. And ya boo sucks to Jamie.

'Think really hard,' said Miss Beckworth. 'Can't anyone guess?'

And she looked straight at me, almost as if she could see inside my head and look at the train going puff puff puff round my brain.

I still waited. I waited just a fraction too long.

Because she stopped looking at me, and just as I was unfolding my arms ready to put my hand up she said, 'It's a train!'

And everyone else said, 'Oh, a train', 'Of course', '*I* get it', and Anthony and those of his ilk scratched their heads and said, 'You what?' and 'Why is it a train?' and 'I hate this soppy poem stuff.' I drummed my fingers on the desk in irritation and muttered, 'I knew it was a train.'

Jamie looked at me with those snooty eyebrows of his disappearing right up under his floppy fringe. 'Oh, sure,' he said sarcastically.

Well, I wouldn't have believed me either. But I *did* know. So I felt even less like joining in now and I drew trains all over the back of my new school jotter – large looming trains about to mash and mangle small snobby boys tied to the railway tracks.

Then we had to write our own poem about trains. I can usually write poems quite quickly so I did a silly one first on a piece of paper torn out of my jotter.

And Miss B is a Bore
Her train theme's a chore
Want to sit with my friend
I'm going round the bend
I feel so Blue
Choo choo choo!

I folded it up and put TO ANGELA AND LISA – PASS IT ON – and then quickly passed it on myself while Miss Beckworth's head was turned. It got about halfway across the class. Miss Beckworth looked up at the wrong moment. Uh-oh.

'Ah!' said Miss Beckworth, pouncing. 'Someone has written a poem already, and they're so proud of it they want to pass it round the whole class.'

She glanced at it. 'Who is the author of this little rhyme, hmm?'

I put my hand up. I had to. Half the kids were craning round to look at me already.

I thought I might be in dead trouble. Miss Beckworth was such a funny old-fashioned teacher. I didn't know what she might do to punish you. Maybe she had a cane tucked up her skirt and she'd whip it out and whack me one.

But all she did was crumple up my poem and say, 'I don't think this is quite Emily Dickinson standard, Charlotte. Now write me a proper poem please.'

I decided she maybe wasn't such a bad old stick after all – so I tried hard with my poem. I decided to be a bit different. I chose to write about a tube, because they're underground trains, aren't they, and it was all about the dark in the tunnels and how that weird voice that says 'Mind the gap' could be the voice of the Tunnel Monster.

Jamie peered rudely over my shoulder. 'You're writing rubbish,' he sneered.

'Yours is the real rubbish,' I snapped back, reading his pathetic twee twoddle about the Train going through the Rain, in the Midst of the Storm, the Train will keep you Warm . . . Yuck!

But when Miss Beckworth walked round the class to see what we'd written so far she said he'd made a Good Attempt. And do you know what she said about *my* poem?

'Try to stick to the subject, Charlotte.'

That was *it*!

'Told you you were writing rubbish,' said Jamie.

So I put down my pen and didn't write another word. I had Angela and Lisa and all the other girls in hysterics in the cloakrooms after lunch doing my Miss Beckworth imitation. Even back in class I just had to put my front teeth over my bottom lip to have all the girls in giggles.

'Settle down, please,' said Miss Beckworth sharply. 'Now, History. I thought this term we'd do the Victorians.'

I ask you! Who wants to study the stuffy old Victorians? Well, guess. Jamie Teacher's Pet Edwards.

Miss Beckworth began telling us about the Victorians, starting off with Queen Victoria herself – that fat little waddly Queen with the pudding face

Queen Victoria

who said, 'We are not amused.' Well, I wasn't amused either, especially when Miss Beckworth started on about the Queen Vic pub down the road and Albert Park and how she lived in these old Victorian mansion flats, and did any of us live in a Victorian home by any chance?

I slumped to one side with the boredom of all this just as Jamie stuck his hand up so violently I *very* nearly got two fingers impaled up my nostrils.

'I live in a Victorian house, Miss Beckworth,' he said, showing off like mad. 'In Oxford Terrace.'

I sat up straight. I knew he was a right little posh nob – but I had no idea he lived in one of those huge grand houses in Oxford Terrace, all steps and little lion statues and incy-wincy balconies as if the people who live there might come and do a Royal Family and wave down at you.

Oxford Terrace is on our way home from the town. Sometimes when Jo and I are trailing back with our Sainsbury's bags cutting grooves in our hands we make up stuff and we sometimes play we live in Oxford Terrace and we're Lady Jo and Lady Charlie and we have champagne for breakfast and we go for a workout in a posh club every day and then we have a light lunch someplace snobby and then we shop until we drop, going flash flash flash with our credit cards, and then we eat out

Oxford Terrace. Wow!

and go dancing in nightclubs and chat up film stars and rock stars and football players but we just tease them and then jump into our personal stretch limousine and whizz home to our five-storey half-million mini-palace in Oxford Terrace.

'You live in Oxford Terrace???' I said.

Even Miss Beckworth seemed surprised. 'Do you live in a flat there, James?'

'No, we've got the whole house,' said Jamie airily.

'Well, perhaps you can help us understand what life was like in a big Victorian house, James.' Miss Beckworth rummaged amongst a whole box of books about the Victorians. She pounced on something about Victorian houses and held up a picture of a Victorian parlour. 'I don't suppose your house looks much like this inside, though, James?'

'Actually my mum and dad have this real thing about the Victorians and they've tried to make the house as authentic as possible, so we've got stuff like William Morris wallpaper and Arts and Crafts tiles – though we've got ordinary modern things like televisions and computers and stuff.'

I felt I was sitting next to Little Lord Fauntleroy. He carried on in this sickening fashion for ages until eventually even Miss Beckworth got tired of it.

'Thank you very much, James. If anyone wants to know more about Victorian houses then you're obviously a mine of information. Now, we'll be studying the Victorians all this term in class, but I want you all to work on your own special project at home too.'

I groaned. I hate home projects. 'You don't sound

ultra-enthusiastic, Charlotte,' said Miss Beckworth.

'Well. I don't know what to do. I don't know anything about the Victorians. Not like some people,' I said, glaring at Jamie.

'I'll copy a whole lot of suggestions for topics on the board. See if you can get your famously defective eyes to focus on them,' said Miss Beckworth briskly. 'It might be worth your while. I intend to award a prize for the best project at the end of term.'

So I copied out all her suggestions:

boring boring boring boring boring boring boring boring boring boring

HOME. FOOD. TOYS AND BOOKS. SCHOOL.
WORK. THE FAMILY. COURTSHIP. SUNDAY.
LAW AND ORDER. SEASIDE. CHRISTMAS.

boring boring boring boring boring boring boring boring boring boring

I didn't fancy any of them.

'Can we do more than one topic, Miss Beckworth,' said You-know-who. 'Can we do them *all* if we want?'

'Yes, if you like,' said Miss Beckworth.

He was quite sickening in his enthusiasm, grabbing all sorts of stuff from the book box, though he's probably got his own private library in his Victorian mansion.

'Here, it's not fair, you're bagging all the best books,' I said, trying to snatch at a book on Victorian hospitals that looked as if it might be promisingly gory.

'OK, OK. Here's one specially for you,' said Jamie – and he bungs me this book on Victorian domestic servants! 'Know your place,' he goes.

I was about to bash him on his big head with the servant book but Miss Beckworth got narky and told us to settle down and start the research for our projects with the books we had in our hands. So I was stuck with the servant book.

I flipped through it furiously – and then stopped. There was a photo of this girl about my age. She even looked a bit like me, skinny and pale. It was a black-and-white photo so it was hard to make out if her hair was red too. It was long, like mine, but scraped back tight behind her ears, with a little white cap crammed on top. She was surrounded by little kids, but they weren't her brothers and sisters. She was a nursery maid. She had to look after them. She was their servant.

I was a bit stunned. I didn't know they used to have children as servants. I read a bit about these nursery maids and kitchen maids and housemaids. They had to work all day and into the evening as well for hardly any money. Girls as young as eleven and twelve. No school. No play. No fun. Just work work work.

I decided I'd do a project on 'Servants'. I was all set to write quite a bit about it actually. I decided I'd show that Jamie.

But Jo was already at home when I got back from

school and she had such terrible scary news I forgot all about my servant project.

I didn't remember until the next day when everyone was showing off their project books. Jamie had done ten whole pages about 'School' and he'd stuck in this old photo of kids in rows in a Victorian classroom and got his mum to do some lines of special copperplate handwriting.

'I've finished my school topic already,' he boasted.

So I whipped out an old exercise book and scribbled out a page at playtime.

'I've finished my school topic too,' I said, sticking my tongue out at Jamie.

SCHOOL

My name is Lottie. I am eleven years old. I left school today.

My teacher, Miss Worthbeck, nearly cried when I told her I could not come back. She thinks the world of me. I am her most talented pupil. I am not being boastful, this is exactly what she said:

'Dear Lottie, you are the best at English and writing and arithmetic, you know your geography and history perfectly, you play the piano well, you paint beautifully and you sing like a lark.'

There! I am also useful to Miss Worthbeck, because she is the only teacher at our school, and she has to control a class of forty mixed infants and twelve of us older pupils. I am not the eldest by any means. There is one great lad of fourteen, Edward James, but he is very slow. He is a head taller than Miss Worthbeck, and she finds it hard to control this boy. In fact many of the boys are great lummoxes, stupid and surly. Miss Worthbeck has to use her cane on them to keep them in order.

I do not need to resort to the cane when I am left in charge of the boys though I take delight in swishing it in front of them! But I usually instruct the little ones, and they all try hard for me and give me apples and bites of their gingerbread and scratch 'I love Lottie' on their slates.

Miss Worthbeck has always said I am a born teacher. She has always wanted me to stay on at the school until fourteen, and then she will give me a position as a pupil-teacher, with a proper wage. But I cannot wait two years. I need to earn a proper wage immediately.

HOME

Jo and I haven't always had a home. We lived with Grandma and Grandpa at first. That was pretty bad. Grandma is the sort of lady who keeps a damp flannel neatly folded in a plastic bag and she's forever whipping it out and smearing round imaginary sticky bits. On me. Even at my age. That's nothing. She does it to Jo too.

She doesn't do it to Grandpa because he's one of those pale men in stripy suits who don't ever get sticky. I can't imagine hanging on to his sharply creased trousers or bouncing on his bony knees when I was a baby.

Grandma and Grandpa didn't want Jo and me around, but we didn't have any place else to go. Then we got told about the Newborough Estate and asked if we wanted a flat there. Grandma and Grandpa just about died. You've probably not heard of the Newborough Estate unless you live around here. You'll *definitely* have heard of it if you do. The police get called out every night. And the fire service, because the kids keep setting fire to the rubbish in the chutes. The ambulances are always there too, because there are so many fights and people getting battered. Sometimes they come to scrape up the bodies because people throw themselves off the balconies because they're so fed up living in a dump like the Newborough Estate.

But we went to live there, Jo and me. There was this HUGE row and Grandma and Grandpa said they were really washing their hands of us this time. But Jo stood up to them. Funny that. Jo can't say boo to a goose. She lets everyone walk all over her. Especially me.

She worries terribly about Grandma and Grandpa and she tries so hard to please them. When they come over nowadays and pick faults – Grandma's thc worst, pick pick pick, and Jo winces like she's scraping at her actual skin – she still stands up to them over me. It's as if it's easy-peasy, simple-pimple where I'm concerned.

I asked her how come once.

'Because you mean more to me than anyone else,' said Jo.

She does to me too. She's my mum. You guessed that, didn't you? You wouldn't guess it though if you saw us out together. Big sister and little sister, that's what you'd think. With me the big sister. No, that's just a joke. Though it won't be long before I'm taller than her. She's only little and I'm getting big.

There's only that much in it now.

There's not much between us age-wise either. She was still at school when she had me. Shock Horror Disaster!

That's what Grandma and Grandpa thought. Of course, I wasn't observing much in those days but I can imagine it all too well. Jo's told me lots of stuff anyway. They didn't want her to have me. And then after I got born they wanted Jo to put me in a Home. The sort with a capital H. So that Jo could start a new life all over again.

'This is my new life,' said Jo. 'As if I'd ever give my baby away! I'll make a proper home for both of us.'

She did too. It wasn't so bad on the Newborough Estate. Well, it was some of the time. Like when we got our door kicked in and boys wrote stuff all over the walls. Or the day this loony cornered us in the lift. Or the time our telly got nicked the day after it got delivered.

But we made some great friends there too.

It was our home, even though we didn't have any cash to do it up and make it look pretty. We were on benefit at first, and then Jo got a job once she'd got me into nursery, but we didn't spend much even then. We were saving.

Grandma and Grandpa stopped being so huffy and offered us lots of money to get us out of the Newborough Estate. I thought Jo was mad to say no. But she said we had to do it all by ourselves. To show them. Because they didn't think we stood a chance.

But we made it! Jo worked hard at her job selling televisions and washing machines and we saved like crazy and then Jo got a promotion and another and then guess what. She was made the manageress of the big branch down in the shopping centre, in charge of a staff of twelve. And so we started hanging out around estate agent windows, looking for anything going really cheap because people keep getting made redundant in our area and so they can't keep up the payments on their homes and they get taken away from them.

There were a few ex-council flats we could have managed, posher than the Newborough Estate, but Jo wasn't having that.

'We want something Private,' she said. 'Small but select.'

And that's what we've got. A one-bedroomed flat in a quiet private block with laid-out gardens. No-one tore out the roses or smashed the windows or peed in the lift. The people living there were mostly elderly ladies or young married couples or schoolteachers who don't usually tear and smash and pee publicly. They looked a bit nervously at Jo and me when we moved in – especially me – but Jo insisted we had to be on our Best Behaviour at all times.

'Well, at least till we get accepted,' she said. 'So we'll keep the CD player turned down *low*, right, and we'll smile at everyone and say stuff like Good Morning and Good Afternoon ever so polite and we won't go barging straight past someone to get in the lift first and if we're having one of our famous ding-dong rows we'll have to do it in a whisper, get it?'

I got it. I stuck to all these rules. Most of the time. And we've *got* accepted. Oh, one or two of the truly stuffy old bags have asked me pointed questions about Daddy and then they mumble with raised eyebrows, but even those ones say hello and offer me toffees and tell me how tall I'm getting. We're friends with just about everyone in the flats.

But we don't really need all the other people, of course. When we shut our blue front door (I wanted red, but Jo said we had to blend in with the others along the balcony) then we're home and it's all ours and we can be our family. Small, but select, like the flats.

We still haven't got much money to do it all up because most of Jo's earnings go on the mortgage. We've got a good telly and video and CD player and washing machine though (because Jo gets them at a serious discount) and we've painted all the flat so that it looks great. Jo wanted white for the living room (boring) but she let me choose this amazing dark red for our bedroom, and we've got these truly wonderful crimson curtains we found at a boot fair and a deep purply-red lamp and when it's a treat day like a birthday we draw the curtains and switch on the lamp and have a special red picnic in our beautiful bright bedroom. Cherries, plums, jam tarts, strawberry split ice creams, Ribena for me and red wine for Jo, yum yum.

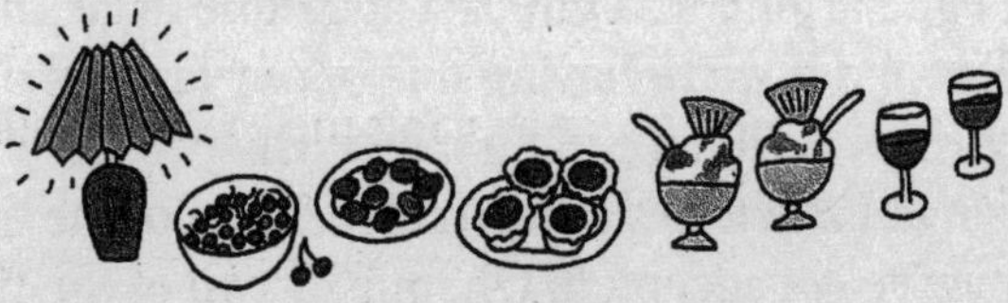

I was kind of hoping Jo and me might be having a bedroom picnic that evening because she had an appointment with the manager for the whole of our area and she was hoping it might be about further promotion.

It was scary opening the door of our flat and seeing Jo because she doesn't usually get back from work till six at the earliest. But there she was, sitting in the middle of the living-room floor. Not doing anything, just sitting with her hands clasped round her knees.

'Jo? What's up?' She looked so small sitting there like that. I towered over her as I stood beside her. 'Jo, why are you home from work? Don't you feel well? Have you been sick?' I thought maybe that was it. She looked so white. No, *grey*, and her eyes were all watery.

'Oh, Charlie,' she whispered.

'*What?*'

'The most terrible thing's happened,' she said in such a tiny voice that I had to bend right down close to hear.

All these different possibilities came bubbling up inside my head until I felt as if it was boiling. 'Tell me,' I said.

Jo opened her mouth again but her voice was just a wisp now.

'*Tell* me, go on. You're scaring me,' I said, giving her shoulder a little shake.

I could feel she was shivering even though it was hot in the flat and she hadn't bothered to open any of the windows when she came in.

'Jo?' I sat down properly beside her and put my arm right round her.

She gave a little stifled sound and then tears started dribbling down her face.

'It can't be that bad, whatever it is,' I said desperately. 'We've still got each other and our flat and—'

'We haven't!' Jo sobbed. 'Well, we've got each other. But we won't be able to keep the flat. Because I've lost my job.'

'What? But that's ridiculous! You're great at your job. They think the world of you. How could they get rid of you? Was this the area manager? Is he crazy?'

'He's lost his job too. We all have. The firm's closing down. We all knew things had been a bit tight recently, and some of the smaller shops closed, but no-one thought . . . They've just gone bust, Charlie. They can't find a buyer so that's it. They've ordered us to lock up all the shops. I'm out of a job.'

'Well . . . you'll get another one. Easy-peasy, simple-pimple,' I said.

'I wish you wouldn't keep saying that,' said Jo, sniffing. 'It sounds so stupid. And you're being stupid. How am I going to get another job? All the electrical goods chains are struggling. There's no jobs going there. I've been to the Job Centre. There's nothing going in retail at all. There's some office work, but they want all sorts of GCSEs and certificates. Which I haven't got, have I? I'm the one that's stupid.'

'No you're not,' I said. Even though she'd just said I was stupid.

'I should have tried to keep up with my school-work. Gone to evening classes,' Jo wept.

'You had me.'

'I could have been catching up these last few years. But I didn't think I needed to. I was doing so well at work . . .'

'You'll get another job, Jo, honest you will. There *must* be shop jobs going somewhere. You'll get a job easy . . . You'll get a job, I promise.'

I promised until I was blue in the face but of course we both knew I could turn positively navy but it wouldn't make any difference.

Jo didn't come to bed till very late that night and then she didn't sleep for ages. She tried not to toss and turn but whenever I woke up I knew immediately she was awake. Lying stiff and still, staring up at our crimson ceiling. Only it doesn't look red at night. It's black in the dark.

I woke up very early, long before the alarm. At least the ceiling was dimly red now. Jo was properly asleep at last, her hair all sticking up, her mouth slightly open. She had one hand up near her face, clenched in a fist. I propped myself up on one elbow, watching her for a bit, and then I slid out of bed.

Jo won't let me stick any posters or magazine pictures up in the living room. We've got a proper print of a plump lady cuddling her daughter with a white frame to match the walls. I didn't want to mess up the round red glow of the bedroom but I've stuck up heaps and heaps of stuff in the loo. Want to see?

Of course, it's a bit weird with all these eyes watching you when you go to the toilet. Lisa and Angela always have a giggle about it when they come to my place.

They both like my home a lot. They've got much bigger houses but they think mine's best. They're thrilled if I ever have one or other of them to stay over. (They have to come separately – and even then Jo has to sleep on the sofa in the living room.)

Angela's house seems quite small too but that's just because she's got a big family, not just brothers and sisters but a granny and an auntie or two. It's fun at Angela's house and she's got a super mum who

laughs a lot and she cooks amazing food. Angela and I stayed up half Saturday night and got the giggles so bad when we went to bed that we still couldn't get to sleep for ages. I nearly fell asleep in church. That's the disadvantage of staying over at Angela's. We went to church *twice* on Sunday. I might even have had to go *again* in the evening if Jo hadn't picked me up in time.

Lisa's got an even bigger home with a huge garden and a swing. We put up this tent in her garden and camped out in it, though I'd have sooner slept in her bedroom which is pink and white and ever so pretty, with special twin beds with pink and white flowery duvets. Lisa's mum is all pink and white too and she smells very flowery but she isn't always as soft and gentle as she looks. She nags Lisa about all sorts of stuff. But Lisa's dad adores her. He calls her his little Lisalot and when he comes home from work he gives her such a big hug he lifts her right off her feet.

Lisa said it must be awful for me not having a dad. I said I didn't care a bit. And I don't. I've got Jo.

Sometimes Jo and I play this silly game that we're both male, because we've both got funny names. I'm little-boy Charlie and she's this big gruff funny bloke Jo who's my dad. We often have games together where we muck around and play at being different people. When I was little my favourite game of all was me being Jo and Jo being me, so that I was the mother and got to tell her what to do.

I wandered out of the loo and into the living room and stared at the space on the carpet where Jo had sat yesterday. I felt as if I was the mother now and she was the little kid – but it wasn't a game.

The minute Jo woke up she said, 'What are we going to do?' As if *I* knew.

I felt worried about leaving her at home when I went to school. I kept wondering if she was sitting on the living-room floor again, all hunched up. I was thinking about Jo and her job and our home so much I didn't listen in lessons and Miss Beckworth got really narked with me. So I acted cheeky and then I was in serious trouble, but I didn't really mind. That just made things more normal.

Miss Beckworth kept me in at dinner time. She didn't give me any stupid lines to write out, though. She said I could work on my Victorian project.

Boring boring boring, I thought – but better than lines. And at least I had the book box to myself. I asked for something about Victorian homes.

'Not a posh house for the rich. What about an ordinary little home for a poor family? Aren't there any books about that?'

She found me one or two pages, but there wasn't much. So I made a lot of it up.

HOME

There is nothing for it. I have to leave home.

I love my home very much, although it is only a tumbledown cottage, stifling hot in the summer and bitter cold in winter. The winters have always been the worst. Two little brothers and one infant sister died during the winter months, and Father passed away last February when the snow was thick on the ground.

I did not cry when Father died. Perhaps it is wicked to admit this, but I felt relieved. He treated Mother very bad, and though he earned a fair wage he drank a great deal of it. So we were always poor even then, but Mother kept our simple home shining bright. She made bright rag rugs to cover the cold stone flags of the floor and each bed upstairs had a pretty patchwork quilt. I cut out pictures from the illustrated papers and pinned them to the walls. I even pinned pictures out in the privy!

There was always a rabbit stew bubbling on the black–

leaded range when we came home from school. We'd dig potatoes or carrots or cabbage from the garden, and in the summer Rose and Jessie and I would pick a big bunch of flowers to go in the pink jug Frank won at the fair.

Mother always liked us to wash our hands and say Grace at the table before eating. Father never washed his hands or said Grace, but Mother could do nothing about that. Sometimes Father did not come home until very late. One night last winter he fell coming home in the dark and lay where he was till morning. They carried him home to us and Mother nursed him night and day but the cold got to his chest.

Mother used up her sockful of savings on Father's funeral. She bought us all a set of black mourning clothes, even little Ada-May. I thought this a waste of money, but Mother is determined that we stay respectable.

Our grandmother and grandfather did not want Mother to marry Father. They thought he was a wastrel, far too fond of the Demon Drink. I privately agreed, but I did not like them saying this to Mother. They came to Father's funeral and said it all over again. They asked Mother how she was going to manage now.

Mother said she would take in washing and do fine sewing for ladies.

Grandmother and Grandfather sniffed. They took a shine to my sister Rose, who is pretty, and offered her a home with them. It will be one mouth less for you to feed, they said. Mother asked Rose if she wanted to live with Grandmother and Grandfather and she cried and said no. So Mother said we would all stick together.

'You will be sticking together in the Workhouse then,' said Grandmother.

Mother stuck her chin in the air and said we would manage fine. But I heard her crying at night. I went to comfort her. 'We *will* manage fine, Mother, you'll see,' I said.

But it has become very hard. Mother washes all day and sews half the night. She has become very pale and thin and coughs a good deal. I am very frightened that she will get really ill in the winter if she keeps working so hard. Frank and Rose and I tried to help out this spring and summer, running errands and selling nosegays and sweet lemonade at the market. But we can only earn pennies. We need pounds to keep us out of the workhouse.

So it is up to me. I am the oldest. I must go and earn money and send it to Mother. There is only one job a girl my age can go for. I must be a servant.

WORK

The phone rang. I answered it automatically. Lisa and Angela are always ringing me up – and some of the other girls in our class. I don't want to sound disgustingly boastful but I am quite popular.

But it wasn't a girl. It was Grandma.

'Hello, Charlotte dear,' said Grandma.

I told a teeny white lie to Miss Beckworth. Grandma always calls me Charlotte, pursing her lips and clicking her teeth. If you're standing right in front of her you get sprayed with spit. I found I was holding the telephone at arm's length just in case.

'Can I speak to Mummy, please?' said Grandma.

That's another weird thing she does. I've never called Jo Mummy in my life. But Grandma always does. As if Jo is *her* Mummy. Though Grandma treats Jo as if she's a silly little toddler, not a grown-up woman with a practically grown-up daughter of her own.

Grandma's voice is so loud it boomed right across the room to Jo. She shook her head in a panic. 'Say I'm not here!' she mouthed at me.

She'd been crying and she'd got to that sodden stage where everything is still dribbling. She fumbled for a tissue and blew her nose dolefully.

'I'm afraid Jo's just nipped out to the shops, Grandma,' I lied.

'Don't be silly, Charlotte. It's half past seven in the evening,' Grandma said briskly.

'There's heaps of shops still open round here, Grandma. There's the video shop, and the off-licence, and the Spar down the road—'

Grandma gave a disdainful snort. 'Please don't argue with me, Charlotte. I know Mummy's there, I can hear her blowing her nose. I want to talk to her.'

'Well, she doesn't want to talk to you,' I said – but in a little squeaky-mouse mumble as I passed the phone over.

'Josephine?'

'Hello, Mum,' said Jo wearily, sniffing.

'Are you crying?' Grandma demanded.

'No, I – of course I'm not crying,' said Jo, a tear dribbling down her cheek.

'Say you've got a cold!' I whispered, miming a major bout of sneezing.

'I've got a cold,' Jo said, nodding at me gratefully. 'Why on earth should I be crying?'

'Well, you tell me,' said Grandma. 'Your father's just read a most disturbing item on the financial page of his newspaper. It says Elete Electrical have folded.'

Jo shut her eyes and said nothing.

'Josephine? Are you still there? Is it true? Is it a

nationwide collapse? You are being kept on until they find a new buyer, aren't you? And if the worst comes to the worst, they will give you a substantial redundancy payment, won't they?'

Jo sniffed again but still couldn't speak.

'Do say something, dear,' said Grandma. 'We're very worried about you. We've always said you're in a very precarious position. How on earth are you going to keep up the payments on your flat if you lose your job? You and Charlotte can barely manage as it is. We do worry about you so.'

Jo opened her eyes. She stood up straight. She gave one last giant sniff and then spoke.

'Honestly, Mum, you do get into a silly state. There's no need to worry. We're fine. I feel I was ready for a change from Elete anyway. Of course I've known for a long time that things have been precarious with the firm – which is why I applied for my new job. I have this brilliant managerial position, and a much larger salary too – so Charlie and I are very comfortably off at the moment. I really must go now, Mum, I badly need to get a hankie, my goodness, this is a terrible cold, I think I'd better have an early night with honey and hot lemon, well, goodbye, thanks for phoning.'

She said this without pausing, absolutely gabbling the last bit and then slamming the phone down quick. Then she took the receiver off again, so that Grandma couldn't call back.

'What?' Jo said to me, wiping her cheeks with the cuff of her shirt.

'You know what! You told her one socking great lie,' I said admiringly.

'Well, I couldn't stand her going on and on like that.'

'But she'll find out that it's not true,' I said.

'I'm going to *make* it come true,' said Jo. 'You'll see.'

All the tight feeling in my tummy untwisted. It was OK. Of course Jo would get another job, easy-peasy, simple-pimple.

She was up early the next morning, hair washed, all made up, blouse fresh on, skirt carefully pressed. When I woke up she was walking up and down the bedroom, practising.

'Good morning. My name's Jo Enright. I've been the manageress of a large shop for the last year but now I feel it's time for a change. Are there any new job opportunities in your company?' she asked our bedroom wardrobe, shaking the sleeve of her dressing gown.

'Good morning. I am Mr Wardrobe. Yes, Ms Enright, you can come and manage my clothes for me and I'll pay you a million pounds a week,' I said from under the covers.

'Charlie! You didn't half give me a fright!' said Jo, finding my tummy through the duvet and tickling it.

'Don't make me laugh! I need to go to the loo. I'll wet the bed, I'm warning you,' I giggled, rolling around.

'Well, get up and go, you lazy thing,' said Jo, trying to tip me out. 'Come on, you'll be late for school. And I thought this new teacher of yours is dead strict?'

'You're telling me! Lisa and Angela and me didn't feel like playing boring old rounders yesterday so we hid in the girls' toilets. We've done that heaps of times and no-one ever thought a thing about it before, but Miss Beckworth came looking for us, right into the toilets, and when we all hid in a cubicle she peered underneath the door and said, "Will the girl with six feet please come out of this toilet immediately." We thought we were really in for it, but she said she'd hated games at school too and as she'd already picked the two rounders teams we didn't have to play just this one time and we thought *great* – but do you know what we had to do instead? Run round and round the playground without stopping for the entire lesson. We were absolutely *knackered*. And every time we ran past her and begged for mercy she

said brightly, "Aren't you lucky to be taking part in *my* rounders game, girls?" She's so . . . slippery. You can't suss out what she's going to do next. Every time you get ready to hate her she's funny and then when you start to think she's an old softie she plays a trick on you.' I was in the bathroom by this time, sitting on the loo.

'She sounds a good teacher,' Jo called. She

followed me into the bathroom. 'Do you think I look a bit older and more professional with my hair up? Yeah, I think so. Help me pin it up at the back, eh?'

She's usually great at fixing her own hair but her hands were all fumbly this morning, and she couldn't eat any breakfast because she said she was too nervous.

'You've got to eat something. You don't want to faint dramatically in the middle of a job interview,' I said.

'Maybe I won't *get* any interviews,' Jo said. Then she stopped and took a deep breath. 'No. I've got to think positive. Right, Charlie?'

'You bet. Good luck, Jo,' I said, hugging her.

I hoped and hoped Jo would get a job that day. She went into town and she walked round in her high heels with this big bright smile on her face, going into all these different shops and introducing herself and asking and then nodding and walking out again, over and over, all day long. She came home and she kicked her shoes off and she howled. But then I made her a cup of tea and rubbed her feet and she stopped crying and the next day she tried again. And the next.

A shop selling weird way-out clothes was advertising for staff but they said Jo wasn't wacky enough. A big store wanted a sales assistant for their ladies' dress department but they said Jo wasn't mature enough. A snobby shop selling designer clothes made it plain Jo wasn't posh enough.

'This is hopeless,' said Jo, sighing.

She tried record shops, but she didn't know enough about modern music. She'd been too busy bringing me up to dash down the disco. She tried bookshops, because she likes reading,

but the only shop with a vacancy was full of all these studenty boys in jeans making jokey remarks, and the one with the scruffiest hair and the grubbiest T-shirt turned out to be the manager and although Jo said he was friendly it was obvious she didn't fit.

She charged out at seven in the morning on Friday to buy the local paper and she skimmed through all the small print looking for jobs.

'Nothing!' she said despairingly. 'Well, no proper jobs. There's bar work. But I'm not leaving you alone in the evenings.'

'Don't be daft. I'll be fine. Go for it, Jo! You could learn how to make all those great cocktails with the little cherries and toy umbrellas. It would be fun,' I said.

Jo went to the pub to see what it was like.

'It would not be fun,' she said. 'I wouldn't be making any cocktails there. Just serving pints of bitter to a lot of boring old men trying to look down my front. I could put up with that, but I wouldn't be free till half past eleven every night and then I'd have to walk miles home unless I forked out for a taxi – and they were only paying fifty pounds for five full evening shifts. We can't pay the mortgage with that.'

Jo went back to the local paper. 'The only other jobs are cleaning,' she said.

'What do you mean, cleaning? Like at Sketchley's?' I said.

'No, not a dry cleaning shop. Cleaning ladies. You know.'

I looked at Jo.

'I can clean, can't I?' she said.

'But you hate cleaning. Look at all the fights we have over whose turn it is to vacuum.'

'OK, OK. But this is in a supermarket. You get socking great industrial cleaning machines. I quite fancy charging about with one of those.'

She didn't mean it, of course. She was just being brave.

'It's two hours every morning, that's all. Sixty-two pounds,' said Jo, tearing out the advert.

'That's not enough to pay the mortgage.'

'I know. But look, there are heaps of other adverts for cleaners. I could go after them too. Listen. "Private house, cleaning, some ironing, nine to twelve, Mondays and Thursdays, thirty pounds". And then there's this one here, they want two hours' cleaning daily plus someone to look after a little boy after school.'

'You don't want to be lumbered with someone else's little *boy*,' I said.

'I don't want to be lumbered with my own great

big girl if she's going to be so picky,' said Jo. 'Look, Charlie. I haven't got any choice. I'll keep on trying to get a proper job but until that happens I might as well earn what I can. It's lousy money but it all adds up. So shut up about it, OK?'

I shut up. Jo phoned the supermarket and they told her to come along for an interview. She rushed off. I sat by myself, feeling fidgety. Then I got out my notepad and a big fat felt tip pen. I wrote out my own advert.

STRONG RELIABLE SCHOOLGIRL
WANTS WORK. WILL DO SHOPPING,
RUN ERRANDS, WHATEVER YOU WANT.
APPLY MISS C. A. K. ENRIGHT,
NO. 38 MEADOWBANK.

WORK

I've got work. I earn eleven pounds a year. One pound for every year of my age.

I did not tell anyone my real age. I swore I was thirteen, going on fourteen. I do not know whether anyone believed me. I put my hair up and lowered the hem of my skirt as far as it would go. At least I looked respectable in my mourning clothes.

I went to a domestic service agency in town. They said they had just the job for me. But when I went to the house and saw the cross sulky face of the Mistress I wasn't so sure. I did not find out what the Master did for a living, but it was easy to tell he was not a gentleman. They wanted a maid-of-all-work and I could see at once I'd be toiling all day long and well into the night, and scolded all the time no matter what pains I took. I am willing to be a servant but I will not be a slave.

I went back to the agency and said the first position wasn't suitable. They seemed astonished at my effrontery, but sent me after another position. I thought at first this was more likely. It was in a grand house with six servants. I was to be the nursery maid, helping the upper–nurse care for a little boy.

I do not care for little boys. My brother Frank has always been a great trial to me. I believe he takes after Father. I certainly did not care for *this* little boy, who stuck out his tongue in a very rude manner and then kicked me hard upon the shin. I did not care for the upper–nurse either, who had a face like a boot and long nipping fingers like button hooks. But I would have taken the position even so, if it weren't for the Master of the house. He was a widower, and I was all prepared to feel sorry for him if he were still mourning his late wife. Ha!

This gentleman patted me at the interview and said I was a fine–looking girl fresh from the country. His eyes slid sideways and I detested the way he was looking at me. He might be a gentleman but he didn't act like one. I knew he would be quick to take liberties and if I complained I would be sent packing with no reference. I am young but I am no fool.

I went back to the agency yet again and said the second position wasn't suitable either, and I said why, too. This time they were appalled at my impertinence. How dare I criticize my Betters? But they gave me one last chance. I knew I had to take it this time.

I do hope it is third time lucky. I am employed by a mistress who wants a young nurse for her three children, Victor who is six, Louisa who is four, and baby Freddie who is still in petti-coats. I did not meet the Master, but I shall have to hope for the best. There are two other servants in the household, a cook and a housemaid. I hope they will be friendly.

I am not sure about this mistress. She does not look cross but she seems very firm. She told me my duties in great detail. I must light the fires when I get up and dust the day nursery, I must dress Louisa and help Victor with his boots and buttons, I must attend to the baby, and then we have breakfast. Victor and Louisa are then to be sent down to their mother while I wash and dress baby Freddie and give him his bottle and put him back in his cot. I must then clean and tidy the night nursery and then dress the children in outdoor clothes and take them for a walk. They will have a rest on our return while I brush their clothes and clean their boots, and then I must get them ready for their dinner. We are to take another walk in the afternoon when possible, and then after a light tea I must put baby Freddie to bed while Victor and Louisa go downstairs. Then I must put them to bed and tidy the nurseries and eat my supper and then go to bed myself.

'Do you feel you can manage all this?' she said. 'You look very little.'

'But I am strong, Madam. I will manage,' I said determinedly.

'Very good. You can start on Monday. I will give you the print for your uniform and a bolt of cotton for your apron and caps. I hope you are satisfactory at sewing, Charlotte?'

I blinked at her. 'Charlotte, Madam?' I said foolishly.

'That is your name, is it not?' she said.

'No, Madam. I am called Lottie, Madam. It was the name of Mother's doll when she was small. No-one's ever called me Charlotte.'

'Well, I do not think Lottie is a suitable name for a servant. You will be called Charlotte whilst you are working for me.'

FOOD

Jo phoned me from the town.

'Guess what! I've got the job.'

'Great!'

'Well. It's not really. It wasn't even a proper interview. It obviously doesn't matter what you're like when you're a cleaner.'

'Still. I bet you're going to be the best-ever squeakiest-cleanest cleaner they've ever had,' I said.

'The start of a whole new career,' said Jo. 'Do you think I'll make it to the Champion Floor Cleaning Polish trials, hmm?'

'You bet. So you'd better get into training quick. When do you start?'

'Tomorrow.' I heard Jo gulp. 'At six. In the morning. Oh, Charlie, I must be mad. I could claim income support and lie in bed till noon.'

'Still, you don't have to fib to Grandma any more. You really have got a job.'

'I can just imagine what she'll say when she finds out I'm a cleaner.'

'No, you're not a *cleaner*. You're . . . you're a state-of-the-floor supervisor, right?'

'You're a sweet kid, Charlie.'

'I was a snotty kid earlier. You coming home then? I'm starving.'

'Yes, I've just got to buy something for tea. I hoped I might get staff discount at this supermarket but that's only for the women working the tills.'

'Get some red treats for a bedroom picnic to celebrate your job.'

'Hey, we're economizing.'

'Very cheap red treats?'

'Do you think baked beans could be called red?'

'Just. Get some red plums for pudding.'

'Or red apples. And a block of raspberry ripple ice cream?'

'Yes! And what about a strawberry gâteau?'

'I think that's coming it a bit, old girl. Beans, plums and ice cream, that'll do. I'll be home soon then. You get the trays ready.'

I padded about the kitchen thinking we really should have a cake to celebrate properly. I remembered this ancient packet of cake mix I'd won on a tombola at the school fête donkey's years ago. I had a poke around the kitchen cupboard and found it crumpled behind some tins of soup. Jo didn't go in for making cakes and the only sort I'd ever made were pretend pink dough ones when I was a little kid, but this packet sort looked a doddle. You just had to add an egg. I found one egg in a box at the back of the fridge. I thought back to when we'd last had scrambled eggs and it was only about a fortnight ago so it should be all right.

I tipped the contents of the cake mix packet into

a bowl, swished the egg around until it was all sticky, scooped the lot into the tin and shoved it in the oven. Easy-peasy, simple-pimple.

'What's that lovely smell?' said Jo when she came in the door.

'A surprise. Hey, congratulations.'

'I've got *two* jobs! I phoned the number where they want someone to look after the little boy as well as do a bit of cleaning. That's in the afternoon, so it'll be easy to fit that in too.'

'Where are you going to look after this little boy then? Not round here, I hope,' I said. 'I don't want him messing up all my stuff.'

'He sounds a nice sensible little boy, though he's very shy. I spoke to him on the phone. And his dad sounds nice too, though ever so sad. His wife left and he's trying to cope on his own.'

'We cope fine on *our* own,' I said. 'Look, you're a cleaner now. Why don't you just stick to cleaning jobs. You don't want to be a nanny too.'

'It's seventy-five pounds a week. That's not bad. If I could find just one more job like that to fit in mid-morning then we'd be laughing,' said Jo. 'Hey, is your surprise all right? It's not burning, is it?'

It had burnt just a little bit, but only around the edges. I decided to cut them off – and then I went on cutting and trimming, turning the round sponge into two letters, a big 'J' and a small round circle for the 'o'. We didn't have any icing so I smeared some

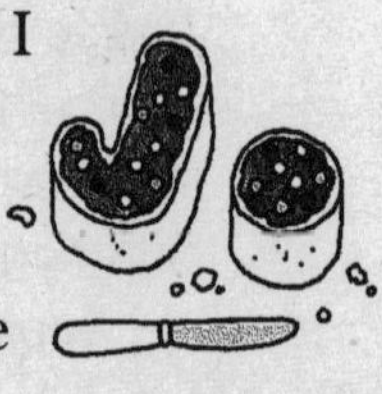

strawberry jam on the top and then studded both letters with Smarties.

'That looks wonderful,' said Jo. 'Hey, you're really good at this.'

I don't want to sound disgustingly boastful, but it really wasn't bad for a first attempt.

I added a line to my work advert:

MAKES EXCELLENT CAKES.

I didn't show Jo my advert. I wanted to surprise her. But when I took my advert into the newsagent's and asked Mr Raj to put it in the window he shook his head.

'You can't work. You're just a little girl,' he said.

'Girls work just as well as boys. *Better*,' I said indignantly.

'It's not because you're a girl. You're too young. You couldn't do any proper work.'

'Yes I could! Look, a hundred years ago I could work full time as someone's servant. I could be scrubbing all day. I'm doing this project about it for school, see.'

'That's what you should be doing at your age. Concentrating on your school work.'

'You don't get paid for doing school work.'

'You kids. Just wanting money money money. What do you want? A bike? Roller blades? A computer? My kids want all these things, nag nag nag. If the boy don't turn up to deliver the newspapers and I ask my boy to help me out then it's "How much money will you pay me?"'

'*I'll* do a newspaper round,' I said.

'You can't. You're too little. It's against the law, see. Times have moved on since your history project. Kids aren't allowed to work.'

I could see I was wasting my time. I tried the newsagent's down in the town but he said the same. So I decided to use my initiative. I'm quite good at that. I spent most of my spare cash photocopying my advert and then I went round sticking them through people's letterboxes in our flats and the flats over the road and half the houses down the street.

I'd put my phone number, so I sat by the phone and waited. And waited. And waited.

'What's up with you?' said Jo.

'Nothing.'

'Come on. Are you waiting for a phone call?'

'I might be.'

'Don't play games with me, Charlie, I'm feeling too dopey to work it out,' said Jo, yawning.

She'd started her job at the supermarket and was finding it an awful struggle to get out of bed at five.

'Look, why don't you go to bed now, get a really early night. You look exhausted,' I said.

'Why do you want me out the way? Who is it who's going to phone, eh?' Jo's sleepy eyes suddenly sparkled. 'Hey, it's a boy!'

'What?'

'You're waiting for some boy to phone you!'

'I am not.'

'Yes, you are. You've got a boyfriend,' said Jo, giggling.

'Don't be so stupid. I hate boys.'

'So you *say*. I know. It's . . . what's-his-name? The one you keep going on about at school. The one you sit next to.'

'Jamie Edwards! You have to be joking. I can't *stick* him. Sitting next to him is driving me absolutely crazy.'

I couldn't believe Jo could be so crackers. I truly detested that Jamie. He was just the most annoying person in the whole world to have to sit next to. He waved his hand in the air so often to answer Miss Beckworth's questions that I was in a permanent breeze. And every time he got the answer right – which was nearly flipping always – he gave this smug satisfied little nod, as if to say, see, what a super intelligent smartie-boots I am.

I hated the way when Miss Beckworth set us some work he'd start straight away, his posh fountain pen bobbing up and down as he wrote, while the rest of us were still scratching our heads and ruling margins and looking at our watches to see how long it was till playtime.

I hated the way his work came back from Miss Beckworth, tick tick tick at every paragraph, and *Well done, Jamie!* written at the bottom. I got lots of crosses and *You could try much harder, Charlotte,* and *Tut tut, this is very shoddy work,* and *You can't fool me by making your writing enormous and widely spaced. You can only have spent five minutes*

on this work at the most. This is not good enough!

I didn't want to be bothered with anything else but learning about the Victorians. I was starting to kind of enjoy writing my project. It was weird. I read stuff in books and then started writing and it was as if this other girl entirely was scribbling it all down. The servant girl. Lottie the nursery maid. She'd started to feel real, like I'd known her all my life. I knew her better than I even knew Lisa or Angela. I just picked up a pencil and all *her* thoughts came rushing out on the paper.

I couldn't stand the thought of Miss Beckworth speckling it with her red biro. It was private. At least we didn't have to hand our projects in till they were finished, and we had weeks yet.

Of course You-know-who had practically finished his project already. He didn't want to keep *his* project private. He kept flashing it around at every opportunity. He even took it into the canteen with him at dinner time. Well, he did that once. I just happened to choke on a fishfinger and so needed an immediate drink of Coke and in my haste I happened to tip the can over and the merest little spitty bit of froth spattered Jamie's precious folder. Only the outside. But he declared the posh marbled paper was all spoilt. The next day he carted his project to school, completely re-covered with repro-Victorian wrapping paper, all fat frilly girls in bonnets and soppy boys in sailor suits, yuck yuck. And inside there was page after page of Jamie's neat blue handwriting with his own elaborate illustrations, carefully inked pictures of railway engines and mineshafts and factory looms, but he didn't have any train drivers or miners or factory hands because he can't draw people properly.

'I'll draw them in for you, Jamie,' I offered.

He turned down my generous offer. He didn't trust me. I wonder why!

He had lots of proper pictures too, cut out of real old illustrated Victorian papers, and samples of William Morris wallpaper, and photos of Victorian families standing up straight in their best clothes, and real Victorian coins carefully stuck in with Sellotape. Jamie's file was bulging already. My notebook was small and slim and there were still only a few pages of writing.

'You haven't done much yet, Charlie,' said Jamie, snatching it up and rifling through it.

'Give it *back*,' I said, trying to grab it.

'Why have you done it in this funny pencil writing? What's all this stuff? It's like a diary. "Well, I do not think Charlotte is a suitable name for a servant." What are you on about?' said Jamie, holding it just out of my reach.

'Don't you *dare* read it!' I said, and I gave him such a smack on the head he dropped my book instantly.

'Oooow! What did you do that for?' he gasped, clutching his head.

'I warned you,' I said, clutching my book to my chest.

'You're mad! If you weren't a girl I'd sock you straight back,' said Jamie.

One side of his face was bright red and the shape of my hand. There were tears in his eyes. I felt a bit worried. I hadn't meant to hit him quite as hard as all that.

'You can try hitting me back but I wouldn't advise it,' I said. 'Just stop messing about with my private stuff, right?'

'It's just your Victorian project, for goodness' sake. And you're doing it all wrong, not a bit the way Miss Beckworth said.'

'I'm doing it *my* way,' I said.

'You'll get into trouble.'

'See if I care,' I said.

Miss Beckworth came into the classroom just then. She gave us all one quick glance – and then fixed her gaze on Jamie.

'What's the matter with you, James?' she said.

I held my breath. It looked as if I was in trouble right that minute. I expected Jamie to blab. He looked as if he were going to. But then he shrugged and shook his head. 'Nothing's the matter, Miss Beckworth,' he said.

I was amazed. And even more astonished when Miss Beckworth didn't pursue it. She just raised her eyebrows as if to say 'You can't kid me,' but then she sat down at her desk and started the lesson.

Jamie started working right away, one cheek still scarlet. I watched him for a while. I struggled with myself. Then I leant towards him. He flinched, as if he was scared I might slap him again.

'Why didn't you say I slapped you?' I whispered.

Jamie blinked at me nervously. 'I'm not a sneaky tell-tale,' he said.

'Well. Thanks,' I mumbled.

He didn't say anything back but his other cheek went red too.

So perhaps Jamie isn't one hundred per cent revolting and disgusting and infuriating. Just ninety-nine per cent. But as if I'd ever sit chewing my nails waiting for his phone call!

Nobody rang. Not a single soul required the services of the strong reliable schoolgirl.

'Why don't you ring him?' said Jo, still dopily deluded.

But the next day Miss Pease from downstairs waylaid her as she was stumbling back from her morning shift at the supermarket.

'Yes, Miss Pease wanted a little word about you, Charlie,' said Jo, hands on her hips.

'If she's nagging on about my music again she's nuts. I keep it turned down so soft I can barely hear it myself. She must have ears like Dumbo's,' I said, munching toast.

Jo snatched half of it from my plate. 'Here, spare a crumb for your poor hardworking mother,' she said. 'I'm starving.'

'So am I. You make your own. I've got to go to school.'

'Yes, well, you can wait a minute. Miss Pease says you've been soliciting.'

'I've been *what*?' I said.

'Well, that's the word she used,' said Jo. She was trying to sound stern, but she looked as if she might giggle any minute. 'Yes, that's what she said. "I really must bring this to your attention, Josephine. Charlotte has been soliciting."' Jo's voice wobbled.

I chuckled tentatively. It was a mistake.

'No, it's not funny, Charlie. What have you been playing at, posting all these little letters in people's flats offering to do work?'

'I was wanting to help out.'

'Oh, Charlie. You are a nutter. Miss Pease is right for once in her long and boring life. You can't advertise yourself like that, especially when there are such loonies around. Some weird guy might have read about this little schoolgirl wanting work and got some terrible ideas.'

'I'm not little, I'm big. And strong. But I take your point. Still, you don't have to fuss. No-one's phoned. Not a single sausage, and after all that money I spent on photocopying. It's daft. The whole idea was to *make* a bit of money.'

'Don't worry. That's my job. And anyway, it has worked in a way. Miss Pease says she's got a job for you.'

'Really?' I tried to feel pleased, but Miss Pease is such a pain. She's the sort of old lady who pats you on the head like a puppydog and relentlessly asks you how old you are, as if you might have aged five years since the last time you told her a week ago. Still, work is work.

Only this work was worse than most. You'll never guess what she wanted me to do. *Read* to her.

I don't really like reading aloud at the best of times. I don't like hearing my voice go all silly and showing-off. And that's when I can pick and choose my own book. Miss Pease wanted me to read her library book, one of those large big-print books that make your arms ache when you hold them up. My arms ached, my back ached, my head ached, my throat ached, my entire body was in ache overdrive after I read to Miss Pease for a whole hour.

It was this terrible stupid story about some dippy woman who kept being pursued in the desert by this total nutcase in a striped nightie. Well, that's what he was wearing on the book jacket. Instead of telling him to get lost sharpish the heroine simpered and swooned into the sand. I kid you not. And Miss Pease obviously adored this utter rubbish. She sat back literally licking her chops. Mind you, that might have been because of all the Cadbury's Milk Tray she was eating. She got through a good half of the box.

'Of course I'd offer you one, Charlie dear, but you can't really read with your mouth full, can you?' she said.

'I can try,' I said hopefully.

She thought I was joking. And *I* thought she was joking when she handed over my wages for the reading session.

'Here you are, dear,' she said, fumbling in her purse. She handed me a ten-pence piece.

I stared at it. Had she mistaken it for a pound coin? Even so, what a totally mingy rate of pay!

'Pop it in your money box, dear,' said Miss Pease. 'And come back and read to me tomorrow.'

Not flipping likely! I was dead depressed, and annoyed when Jo just laughed and found it funny. But she was in a good mood because she'd got herself *another* job, cleaning this big posh house three days a week from ten to twelve.

'*Three* jobs!' she said, and she sent out for pizza with three extra toppings to celebrate.

'You'll exhaust yourself,' I said. 'What with getting up at five and doing the supermarket and then looking after the silly little sprog in the afternoons.'

'I'll be OK. And this new job's a doddle. The house is big, but they keep it very tidy. She's ever so worried about the idea of employing another woman to do her dirty work. I bet she runs round with the vacuum before I get there.'

'Where is it?' I asked, my mouth drooling cheese fronds.

'Oxford Terrace,' said Jo.

I stared at her, so shocked that my half of the pizza slipped out of my fingers onto the floor. I didn't care. I wasn't hungry any more.

FOOD

Oh, how I long for Mother's cooking. One of her meaty stews, bubbling with barley beans and carrots. Or rabbit pie. Mother has such a light touch when it comes to making pastry. Her fruit lattice pies are famous all over the village. And her suet puddings. If I could only have a plateful of Mother's jam suet pudding and custard! Or even a big doorstep slice of bread and dripping . . .

I have to slice up the bread so thin here I slice my fingers too, and Louisa won't eat her crusts even then. The baby likes *his* bread pounded into mush with warm milk. Mother would never dream of pampering us so. We always ate what we were given and chewed it cheerily. Well, mostly. But Louisa always plays around with her food and cries and complains something chronic, and Victor is extremely pernickety for a boy, fuss fuss fussing if he swallows a little lump in his custard. Sometimes it's all I can do not to grab their plates and eat it up for them because I'm so hungry. I have to manage on nursery food too, no meat at all during the week, and just one slice off the roast on Sundays. I am allowed one egg a week too, but it's a pale watery thing compared with the deep gold yolks laid by our hens at home.

I have to make do with this niminy-piminy fare with the merest scrape of butter. The only food that is plentiful is milk pudding. I shall start mooing before long.

'We don't want you to fall ill with too rich a diet,' says the Mistress, as if servants have different stomachs from posh folk.

Mrs Angel the cook and Eliza the maid are supposed to survive on this frugal diet too, but they eat their meals down in the kitchen and Mrs Angel is adept at keeping back the choicest portions for their own plates before Eliza serves the Master and Mistress in the dining room. I have my meals in the nursery so I miss out on these perks. Mrs Angel and Eliza treat me like one of the children anyway. They whisper and have secrets and laugh unkindly at the things I say. They are excessively tiresome. *They* are the childish pair. I do my best to ignore them, but then Mrs Angel calls me hoity toity and Eliza pulls my hair so that it tumbles down out of my cap. It is hard to bear sometimes. At home I was always a favourite. At school I

was definitely Miss Worthbeck's pet. All the children loved me. Even the boys. Yes, even that great lummox Edward James. But now I am openly despised and it makes my heart sore. At night I cry into my pillowcase, the sheets pulled right over my head so the children will not hear me.

Victor sees my red eyes in the morning and says that I have been blubbing.

'Nonsense,' I say firmly. 'I have a slight cold, that is all.'

Perhaps that was tempting fate. Now the whole household has gone down with colds, even little baby Freddie. Mrs Angel has taken to her bed and Eliza is trying to take charge of the kitchen, but with very bad grace. The Mistress says her ailing children must have calves' foot jelly served to them at every meal. I ask Eliza to prepare it but she utterly refuses, saying she has her work cut out as it is and she cannot abide messing around with lumps of messy meat.

So I have to make the jelly. The whole kitchen reeks and the walls glisten as the calves' feet boil and boil and boil, and I skim and skim and skim, and then when I go to strain the liquid through the jelly bag my hands slip and . . . disaster! By the time I have run out to the butcher's for six more calves' feet and started the whole business in motion all over again I am in such savage spirits that I would cheer if a whole herd of calves stampeded through the house and trampled everyone within it with their poor feet.

TOYS AND BOOKS

I was so scared! Jo could be cleaning Jamie Edwards's house. I could just imagine Jamie lounging on a velvet chaise-longue in his posh William Morris-papered parlour, snapping his fingers imperiously at Jo.

'Hey, you! Cleaning lady! Get me another cushion,' he'd command. 'I've spilt crumbs all over the carpet so get cracking with the hoover. And don't sigh like that or I'll dock your wages.'

I could see it as clear as anything. Poor Jo would have to wash Jamie's clothes and tidy Jamie's bed and dust all Jamie's possessions. Maybe Jamie had a brace of younger brothers just as bratty as him, and she'd have to wash their clothes and tidy their beds and dust their toys. If he had a baby brother she'd maybe even have to wash and tidy and dust *him* down.

'It's not your Jamie Edwards's house,' said Jo. 'This is the Rosen family, Mr and Mrs, with two teenage daughters.'

I practically passed out with relief.

'Are you disappointed?' said Jo. 'Did you hope I'd get to go in your Jamie's bedroom, eh, to tell you all about the posters on his wall and whether he still has a teddy on his bed and maybe even have a sneaky peek in his diary to see if he ever writes anything about you?'

'He's not *my* Jamie!' I shrieked. 'You are so nuts, Jo. I keep telling you, I can't stick him.'

Jo wasn't the only one who teased me about terrible Jamie Edwards. Lisa and Angela had started up this stupid game too. I was starting to get seriously annoyed with them. I didn't know what had got into them this year at school. Last year we were the three leaders of nearly all the girls and we had this special club badge with GAB on it, short for 'Girls Are Best', and we all called each other Gabby and we had this cheerleader chant I made up: 'Girls are best, Never mind the rest, Boys are a pest, So *Girls are best!*'

Some of the other girls got a bit fed up and drifted away but Lisa and Angela and I kept up our special girls' gang all the time, and the three of us always went yuck and pulled a face whenever any of the boys spoke to us. I wanted to extend the rules to cover men too, but Lisa said that was daft because her dad was a man and she loved him better than anyone else in the whole world, and Angela was equally awkward and got this immense crush on this pop star and squealed whenever she saw him on the telly and she stuck hundreds of pictures of him all over her bedroom walls and kissed every one of them goodnight when she went to bed and she did inky designs of his name entwined with hers all over her school books and her ruler and her bag and even on the sleeve of her jacket, though her mum got very narked about that.

Lisa and I thought Angela had gone incredibly crackers because this guy she likes is *pathetic*. Angela agrees with us now, and she's torn down all his pictures and crossed out his name and she's got a new jacket – but she's in love with another pop group now, *all* of them, and she's forever striking up these boring boring boring conversations about what she'd do if she could only get to meet them.

I knew that if only I'd been able to sit next to Angela at school as I'd planned then I'd have been able to be a good influence on her and keep her under control. She was starting to get on my nerves so much I was wondering about whittling my best friends down to one. But then Lisa fell in love too.

And that was worse. Because she started to go crazy over David Wood – and he's certainly not a famous star in a band, he's just this ultra-boring boy in our class at school.

'He's not ultra-boring!' Lisa squeaked. 'He's dead cool. I love the way he does his hair. And his eyes. And he looks really old for his age, doesn't he, because he's so tall.'

'He might look old but he acts like a

toddler,' I said, disgusted. 'Didn't you see him in the canteen throwing his lunch around?'

'That was just his bit of fun,' said Lisa. 'One of his chips landed right in my lap!'

'Oh wow! How could you contain your excitement,' I said, dead sarcastic.

'She ate it too!' said Angela. 'After he'd drooled all over it.'

'I wouldn't mind if he drooled all over *me*,' said Lisa.

'Oh shut *up*,' I said. 'Honestly. I think you had a lobotomy in the summer holiday.'

'A lobby-what?' said Lisa.

'It's an operation they perform on your brain,' I said. 'Don't you know anything?'

'I know one thing, Charlie Enright. You're getting a right pain, always showing off and looking down your nose at other people. You're getting just like Jamie Edwards.'

'Yeah, maybe it's rubbing off on her because they sit together,' said Angela, giggling in this particularly irritating way. 'Hey, Lisa – Charlie and Jamie, what a pair, eh?'

'They're always yacking away together, certainly. Miss Beckworth had to tell them off the other day, they were getting so carried away,' said Lisa, giving Angela a nudge.

'You're the one who's in danger of getting carried away – in a body bag,' I said, giving them both a simultaneous example of *my* sort of nudge. I have very very sharp elbows. 'I hardly *ever* speak to Jamie

Edwards – and when I do it's just to have a ferocious argument with him.'

However, I needed to speak to Jamie in a dead-casual, almost-friendly way to find out exactly where he lived in Oxford Terrace. He knew what Jo looked like. We'd both been going to this school since we were practically babies. For years and years our mums had delivered us or collected us. I had noticed that Jamie's mum was plump and beady-eyed like him, with lots of hair and jazzy jumpers and coloured tights and bright boots, none of them matching. He had probably noticed that Jo was much younger than the other mums, and dyed her hair to match mine and wore high heels to make her just a tiny bit taller.

It's awfully hard to strike up a dead-casual, almost-friendly conversation with someone you can't stick. We're barely allowed to breathe in Miss Beckworth's classes anyway, let alone converse. But at playtime I took ages putting away my books and let Lisa and Angela go off by themselves. Jamie always took his time too, not at all keen to go out into the playground. He's not the outdoor type. He's hopeless at football and he can't even run properly, his arms and legs go every which way. He isn't bullied by the other boys because he can be quite quick and cutting with what he says, but he's not exactly number one popular person with his peers. (Not like *some* people I could mention if I wanted to be disgustingly boastful.)

He generally slopes off into a corner by himself and reads a book. I watched him take one out of his satchel. It was covered in the Victorian wrapping paper so you couldn't see the title.

'What's that you're reading then, Jamie?' I asked.

He looked at me suspiciously. 'Why?'

'I just want to know, for goodness' sake,' I said.

'With you it's usually for badness' sake,' said Jamie.

'Let's have a look, then,' I said, reaching for it.

He hesitated, holding it away from me. 'Are you going to hit me again if I don't let you?' he said.

'That was different. That was *my* book. So what's yours? Why have you got it all wrapped up like that? Hey, it's a dirty book, that's it, isn't it! Shock, scandal, swotty old Jamie's reading a rude book. And you didn't want anyone to see you're reading it. What is it, eh? Show me!'

'Get off!' said Jamie, trying to push me away, but he was still wary of me. I snatched his book easily and opened it.

'"Esther Waters",' I read, flicking through the pages. 'Oooh! What a swizzle. It's just some boring boring boring old Victorian book. Typical you, Jamie Edwards. You're just doing some extra swotting up for your project, aren't you?'

'The Victorians thought it was a rude book,' said Jamie. 'They were ever so shocked when it came out.'

'Well, they were shocked by anything. They were

so stupid they even covered up their piano legs! If a woman raised her skirt a few inches above her ankles the chaps practically fainted dead away,' I said scornfully. 'So what does this Esther Waters get up to, Jamie? Is she so dead brazen she flashes her kneecaps?'

'Oh, ha ha,' said Jamie, sighing.

I saw he had his bookmark more than halfway through.

'Gosh, have you read all that? It looks *terribly* dull and difficult. You're mad,' I said.

'It's a good story actually,' said Jamie. 'It's about this girl Esther—'

'No!'

'—and she's a servant and—'

'She's a servant?' I said, stopping messing about.

'Yes, and she goes to this big place in the country and this footman chats her up and she doesn't really want to go out with him but he forces her and she ends up having a baby and she doesn't know what to do because she's young and she's not married and she's lost her job . . . Why are you staring at me like that?' said Jamie. 'What is it?'

'Nothing. It just doesn't sound quite as boring as I thought. Maybe I'll borrow it after you, OK?'

I mostly stuck to reading horror stories, the spookier and scarier the better, but I wanted to find out more about this Esther.

'What happens to her? Does she keep her baby?

Does she get a job? She doesn't get married at the end, does she?'

'I haven't got that far yet. OK, you can borrow it after me. Or some of my other books if you want. I've got a whole lot of Victorian ones sorted out because of my project.'

'Oh, Jamie, you would!' I said. Then I suddenly realized this was my golden opportunity. 'So, I might come round to your famous Victorian house sometime and see your books. What number Oxford Terrace, eh?'

'Number sixty-two,' said Jamie.

I felt my stomach squeeze. Number 62. Jo's Rosen family lived at Number 58, next door but one to Jamie. What if he saw her going into their house? What if Jamie's mum nipped along the road to have a cup of coffee with Mrs Rosen when Jo was dashing around with a duster? What if Jamie's mum thought Jo looked dead handy with a hoover and offered her a job? I was proud that she was working so hard but I couldn't *stand* the idea of her cleaning all Jamie's junk.

'Has your mum got her own cleaning lady?' I blurted out before I could stop myself.

Jamie blinked at me, baffled. 'What? Why? Are you scared you'll get all dusty if you come round to my house?' he said.

'Does your mum do her own dusting?' I persisted.

'No. Mum's hopeless at any sort of housework. We did have a cleaning lady once but then she got ill and—'

'You're not looking for another one, are you?' I asked, horrified.

'My dad does the housework now. The hoovering and that. Mum might do the bathroom, and I'm supposed to do some stuff, me and my brother, only we skive off mostly. *Why?*'

I shrugged elaborately. 'I – I've got interested in the whole idea of housework and stuff because of my servant project,' I said.

Angela and Lisa put their heads round the class-room door.

'Come *on*, Charlie. Playtime's nearly over. What are you doing?' said Angela.

'Of course, we don't want to interrupt anything if you and Jamie are *busy*,' said Lisa, giggling.

'I'm *coming*,' I said, charging over to them.

But then that idiotic Jamie put his great big foot in it. 'So, you're coming round to my house after school tonight, right?' he said, in front of Lisa and Angela. Their mouths dropped open. Mine did too.

'Wrong!' I said, and rushed off.

Lisa and Angela rushed too.

'We were just kidding you before. But you really have got a thing going with Jamie, haven't you?' said Angela.

'You're going round to his *house*!' said Lisa. 'Oh, I do wish Dave would ask me round to *his* house.'

'I'm not *going* round to Jamie Edwards's house,' I insisted. 'He was just going on about these boring

boring boring Victorian books and he seemed to think I was mad enough to want to look at them, that's all.' My heart was thumping a bit as I said it. I knew I was kind of twisting the truth. But I had to stop Lisa and Angela getting the wrong idea once and for all.

So all that day I sent them notes under the quivering Beckworth nose as often as I dared, with silly caricatures of Jamie and rude little rhymes about him. Jamie saw his name and must have thought I was writing a note to him. He peered over my arm and read it. I'd just written a *very* rude bit about him. (Sorry: far too rude to be repeated where adults like Miss Beckworth might whip this book out of your hands at any minute!) Jamie read the very rude bit. He blinked. He didn't look baffled this time. He looked upset.

Still, it was his own fault, wasn't it? He shouldn't have been nosy enough to read my private note. I passed it to Angela and she cracked up with silent laughter and then she passed it on to Lisa and she read it and snorted out loud and had to protest to Miss Beckworth that she had a horrible cold and couldn't help it. Lisa and Angela and I all fell about helplessly when we came out of school.

I certainly didn't go round to Jamie's house after school. Lisa and I went round to Angela's house first because her big brother had just got some dead flash roller blades for his birthday and we were hoping we'd get to her home from our school a good half-hour before he got back from *his* school, so we could all maybe have a sneaky go on his blades. But he'd got wise to Angela's wily ways and installed a brand-new padlock on his bedroom cupboard. We found his old skateboard stacked in a corner but we weren't really into skateboarding any more, and anyway, one of the wheels was all wobbly.

Angela's mum was doing a day shift at the hospital so she couldn't fix us anything exciting to eat so we all went round to Lisa's instead. That was far more promising, because Lisa's mum was being a hostess for a jewellery party that evening and so she was making all these fiddly little vol-au-vents and tarts. She let us sample them while she got busy icing a cake. Lisa wanted us to go straight up to her bedroom, but I hung around her mum for a bit, watching how she did the icing with this natty little squeezy bag.

'I always wondered how people wrote those little messages,' I said. 'Is it difficult?'

'No, pet, it's easy as anything,' said Lisa's mum, and when she had finished she let me practise icing these cookies she'd baked. I iced my name and then Lisa's and then Angela's. That was dead crafty, because we got to eat them!

I asked Lisa's mum how she made the cake and she thought I was angling for a slice of that too.

'Sorry, pet. I'm saving it for the ladies at my party. Hey, maybe your mother would like to come?'

She hesitated. 'I mean, just for the chit-chat at the party. I know she's not really in a position to buy any jewellery right this moment.'

'She goes to bed really early now. Because she has to get up at five for this new job,' I said.

Lisa's mum's smooth face went into a crease of pain.

'Oh my goodness. She's being so *brave*,' she said, as if Jo went and wrestled with a pit of poisonous snakes instead of one unwieldy industrial cleaner.

'But I really would like to know how to make a sponge cake like that. We don't make cakes at home,' I said.

'Well, it's so simple. And really not very expensive. Tell your mother you just need to put the butter and the sugar and the flour in the blender and—'

'No, we haven't got a blender.'

Lisa's mum stared as if I'd said we hadn't got a *kitchen*.

'Oh. Well. I suppose you could mix it all by hand. I know!' She went to her shelf of cookery books beside the spice rack and pulled out an old fat book; the pages had gone a little yellow. She flicked through it.

'Aha! This was *my* mother's cookery book. She certainly didn't have a blender. Yes, there's a whole section on cake-making. Do you think your mother would like to borrow it?'

'It's not for Jo, it's for me. I'd *love* to borrow it,' I said eagerly. 'I want to

suss out how to make cakes. Proper ones, not the packet sort.'

'Well, good for you. I wish my Lisa would get interested in cookery. You're a strange girl, Charlie. You've always seemed such a tomboy. I never thought you'd get keen on cake-making. Still, you're all getting older. It's only natural you're changing.'

'I'm not changing,' I said quickly.

'What's that saying? "Too old for toys but too young for boys." Though my Lisa has certainly started on boys already. It's Dave this and Dave that until we're sick of the sound of him! Which boy do you like, Charlie?'

'None of them,' I said firmly.

'Give it another six months,' said Lisa's mum, smiling at me.

I had to stay polite because she'd just lent me the cookery book but when I got home to Jo I moaned like anything.

'She's treating me like I'm retarded or something,' I said. 'Like I still play with my Barbie dolls.'

'What's wrong with Barbie dolls?' said Jo.

She used to buy me lots of Barbies with all their different outfits and we'd dress them up and drive them round in their Cadillac and take them to the disco and make them bop up and down on their tiny high heels. I think Jo liked playing Barbie games just as much as I did. If not more. I wanted to chuck all mine out ages ago but she wouldn't let me.

'Store them in a drawer and keep them for *your* daughter,' she said.

So they're stored. I took off all their glitzy little outfits and laid them on their backs in my underwear drawer and covered them with bits of old pillow case, playing one last ritual game with them. Mortuaries.

Jo got totally unnerved when she opened the drawer looking for spare socks.

'Have you come to view the corpses?' I said.

'You are a seriously weird child.'

'It's coming from a single-parent family,' I said. 'I'm seriously deprived. It's no wonder I'm weird.'

I was only joking of course. I *like* being a select family of two. Jo and me. And that's the way it's always going to be.

TOYS AND BOOKS

I cannot believe the toys the children have here! Victor has a dappled rocking horse as big as the old pony in the field behind our cottage at home. It's such a splendid creature, with a curly mane and a long tail of real horse's hair, a red saddle and reins and great green rockers. Louisa begs and begs Victor to let her take a turn but he will rarely agree. Once when the children were downstairs with the Mistress I stood staring at the rocking horse. Before I knew what I was doing I had hitched my skirts above my knees and clambered into the saddle. I fingered the curly mane and stroked the smooth shining wood, and then I dared lean forward and rock once, twice, three times. The rockers creaked and I did not dare persist in case they could hear me down below.

Louisa's china doll seemed to watch with her blue glass eyes. Her painted red lips were open as if she might tell. But I must not be fanciful. She is only a doll. But a beautiful doll all the same, with golden ringlets and three sets of fine clothes. She even has little lace mittens for her tiny china fingers, imagine! I have had to help Louisa on and off with those clothes, stripping the doll right down to her white silk drawers. She has three petticoats, two silk and one flannel, and white cotton stockings and little soft kid shoes, three pairs, in black and grey and pink for parties. Three pairs of shoes for a doll that cannot walk. Rose and Jessie and I have never had soft shoes. We'd run around barefoot in the summer and plod in our old boots throughout the winter. How Rose and Jessie would love Louisa's dolls, and the dolls' house with all the furniture – little chairs and tables, a four-poster bed no less, and even a miniature mop and mangle in the scullery!

We had our own halfpenny dolls at home, one each in our Christmas stockings, and we'd sew them little dresses and make them a home in an old wooden crate, the same crate that was once our Frank's boat and carriage. Sometimes I gave baby Ada-May a ride in that old crate and she crowed with delight . . .

Oh, how I miss her. How I miss Rose

and Jessie. I even miss Frank. I miss dear Mother most of all. I write to her once a week, unburdening my heart. I hope Rose reads my letters properly to Mother. She can read well enough when she wants, but she hurries so over the words. Mother was kept at home as a child to mind her own young brothers and sisters so she never learnt to read. She used to marvel after I went to the village school and learnt to spell out words.

Miss Worthbeck let me read aloud to the children on Friday afternoons from wonderful story books, *Alice* and *The Water Babies* and some of Mr Dickens's books. I do not wish to boast but she once said I had Shining Intelligence.

My Shining Intelligence is tarnishing rapidly now I am a nursery maid.

FAMILY

It was Grandma and Grandpa's Pearl Wedding anniversary in a couple of weeks.

'We're not having a party,' said Grandma. 'That's not our way.' She spoke as if parties were incredibly vulgar, on a par with naked mud wrestling in pig sties. 'We thought we'd like to celebrate the occasion with a special Sunday lunch.' She paused. 'Just for the family.'

She meant Jo and me. Once she was off the phone we moaned and groaned, trying to think up wild excuses to get out of it. We don't like going to Grandma and Grandpa's at the best of times.

'And this will be the worst,' said Jo. 'They'll talk about their wedding and their anniversaries, all thirty of them. Grandma will fiddle with her wedding and engagement and eternity rings. She might *even* get out their wedding album. Oh help, she might even delve in the trunk upstairs and come out with this truly horrible yellowy-white lace veil and then her voice will go all shaky when she says she kept it specially for me to wear at my wedding. And then she'll stop and sigh because I didn't ever have a wedding. Watch out, Charlie. She'll be saving it for you now.'

'*I'm* not going to get married!' I insisted. 'I'm going to stay here with you. I look old for my age and you look young so by the time I'm grown up we'll just be like two sisters. I'll be earning too so it'll be easy-peasy, simple-pimple paying that old mortgage.'

'I wish!' said Jo.

We didn't have any spare cash for Pearl Wedding presents so we had to be inventive. Jo bought a half-price droopy pot plant and fed and watered it until it stood up straight and grew new glossy leaves. She bought some pearl-white ribbon and then tied thirty tiny bows all over it.

'There? Do you think it'll do?' she said, tying the very last bow.

'It looks lovely.'

'It's nowhere near as impressive as your cake.'

Yes, I'd made Grandma and Grandpa a proper cake! I used Lisa's mum's recipe book. I couldn't do a fruit cake because the ingredients were too expensive. I just did a sponge. Well, I did three sponges if you must know. I didn't quite get the hang of it the first time and failed to realize you had to mix it all like crazy until your arm practically falls off. There was just this surly sulky crust at the bottom of the tin when I took it out of the oven. The second go was better, but I was too eager, opening the oven door a couple of times to see how it was getting on.

It didn't rise properly and so I left it in longer and then it got a bit burnt. I cut off the burnt bits and made it into a trifle, but even so, I was starting to think I was squandering money instead of saving it. Jo said I should have one more go and *this* time it was third time lucky. My sponge was *perfect*.

Now I could get started on the best bit. I covered it with apricot glaze to stop any crumbs getting mixed up with the icing. Then I piped *Happy Anniversary* across the top of the icing and made little rosettes all the way round and studded it with tiny pearly balls. It took ages but I was so proud when I'd finished. Jo looked worried when I showed it off to her.

'What?'

'It's beautiful,' she said. 'They'll love it.'

Ha! They didn't love it. Or Jo's plant. Grandpa nodded and said, 'How delightful. Thank you so much. How thoughtful of you. But you really shouldn't have.'

That sounds OK down on paper. But my grandpa speaks in this slow serious voice with hardly any expression. He doesn't go *Wow!* or hug or kiss. If he ever touches me accidentally he wipes his hands on his hankie afterwards, as if I'm sticky.

Grandma uses enough expression for two. 'Oh, darlings, we weren't expecting *presents*. Especially in your current circumstances. Josephine, I've been very worried about your new job, you've hardly told me anything about it.'

'Look at the cake Charlie's made you. She did it all herself. It took her ages,' said Jo.

'Yes, it's *lovely*, dear. Yum yum. We'll all have a slice for tea.' But Grandma sighed. 'What a pity!'

'What?' I said.

'I can't wait to sample this cake,' said Jo quickly. She was sending signals with her eyebrows to Grandma. Grandma ignored them.

'It's such a shame you left out the "n", dear.'

I'd left out one of the 'n's in *Anniversary*. Even though I *knew* how to spell it. I couldn't stand it. I'd thought it really was perfect.

'As if that matters,' Jo said, furious with Grandma for pointing it out.

'Well, as a matter of fact, I *do* think spelling matters although I know they don't pay much attention to it in school nowadays,' said Grandma, putting my cake on her kitchen table. She took the pot plant to the sink.

'It doesn't need watering yet. I did it yesterday,' said Jo.

'I just want to perk it up a little,' said Grandma.

She should have watered Jo and me. We were visibly drooping. I can never work out if Grandma knows what she's doing. She's certainly an expert at chewing you up and spitting you out in tiny pieces. No wonder it took Jo months and months before she dared tell them she was going to have me.

Grandma and Grandpa still treat her like a schoolgirl in disgrace. Grandma kept on and on about her old job while she put the vegetables on to cook, prodding Jo as sharply as the potatoes. Jo lied a lot but she's not as good at it as me. Grandma didn't even shut up when we started eating.

'What do you *mean*, Josephine? What does this new supermarket job entail?' Grandma attacked her grapefruit, jabbing at it with a serrated spoon. 'You're being deliberately evasive. Are you sure you're not working as a cashier on the tills?'

Jo suddenly flung down her own spoon, going as red as the glacé cherries Grandma used for decoration. 'I am not a cashier,' she said. 'I am a cleaner at the supermarket. So now you know.'

Grandma sputtered like the hot fat cooking her roast beef. She gave Jo a roasting all the while we chewed on our meat. She told Jo it wasn't a suitable job when she'd been a manager for nearly a year, as if Jo had deliberately turned down umpteen other manager's jobs just to be contrary. She told Jo she was being an irresponsible mother going out early in the morning and leaving me, and that made me so mad I had to put in my two-pennyworth.

'I think *you're* being the irresponsible mother to Jo, telling her off and being so horrible when Jo's tried so hard to sort things out. I think she's wonderful to get up so early and trudge off like that. *I'm* OK, I'm still in my bed. Jo has to get up early every single morning except Sunday, and she should be having a lovely long lie-in today, but she couldn't, because we had to get the train and the

bus right over to your place to wish you a Happy Anniversary – *two* 'n's – only you're just mucking it all up.'

They were all staring at me.

'That's quite enough, young lady!' said Grandma.

'You're not my mother so you can't tell me off,' I said. 'Jo? Do you want me to shut up?'

'Yes!' said Jo. 'Come on, Charlie, we'd better go home.'

'Now don't be ridiculous. We haven't even started on pudding yet,' said Grandma.

'Why don't you all do a lot more chewing and a lot less yapping,' said Grandpa, calmly working his way through his second helping of roast beef.

So we sat still and no-one said anything. Jo and I left a lot on our plates. So did Grandma. But Grandpa didn't even leave a glisten of gravy.

I didn't think I'd be able to eat pudding. It was pineapple upside-down cake and my own stomach felt upside-down too. But I tried a tiny bit and it was actually good, so I ate a bit more, and then a bit more still, until I'd finished it all up.

Grandpa nodded in approval. He finished his last mouthful too.

'Now that you've all calmed down, perhaps we ought to discuss your financial situation, Josephine,' he said.

I wanted to tell him it was none of his business. But even I didn't quite dare cheek Grandpa.

Jo stammered a little as she told him that we were managing, and she'd sorted things out with the building society to give us a little leeway, and she didn't just have the one job, she had three, and she was still looking for another supervisory position all the time. She said it all as if he was giving her a formal interview. Grandpa nodded, occasionally easing the collar of his shirt where it rubbed his neck. He never wears casual clothes, not even at weekends. I couldn't remotely imagine him in something like a T-shirt. I can't even picture him in his underwear. I don't think Grandpa has an ordinary body at all, he's just hard smooth plastic underneath like a Ken doll.

Grandma wanted to know all about the other cleaning jobs. She raised her eyebrows and looked pained when Jo told her about the Oxford Terrace job, but she actually leant forward and looked interested when she heard about Robin, the little boy Jo picks up from school.

'So what's his father like?' said Grandma, suddenly all ears. I could actually see them getting pink underneath her neat grey curls.

I sighed and flopped back in my chair. This was so *typical* Grandma. She can't even get it into her head that Jo *likes* being a single mum and isn't remotely interested in meeting any men. Grandma used to keep trying to introduce Jo to all these creeps, and she nagged her to join a Singles club and she even once advertised Jo in a Lonely Hearts column. She did, I kid you not. She thinks if she can only get Jo married off then she won't have to be ashamed of us any more.

I waggled my eyebrows at Jo, expecting her to wink back. But she wasn't looking at me. She wasn't looking at anyone. She was staring at the shiny yellow pudding on her plate as if Robin's father was reflected there.

'He's very nice,' she said. Her tone was brisk – but she blushed.

I stared at her. Grandma was staring too.

'Very nice?' said Grandma impatiently. 'What *sort* of very nice? What job does he do? What does he look like? What's happened to the boy's mother?'

'He's very nice – what more can I say?' said Jo. 'He's something in the Civil Service.'

'Which grade?' said Grandma.

'As if I know!'

'Is he good looking?'

'I suppose so. In a kind of lean, lost sort of way,' said Jo.

'Mmm!' said Grandma. 'And is he a widower?'

'No. His wife left him. She had custody of Robin at first, but he didn't get on with the boyfriend, so now he's back with his dad.'

'And Dad doesn't have a girlfriend?'

'No. Well. He could have. But he hasn't mentioned one,' said Jo.

'She's just his cleaner,' I said crossly. 'She doesn't have anything to do with him, do you, Jo?'

'No. That's right. Yes,' said Jo, sounding muddled.

I frowned at her. What was she on about? And why did she have that stupid little smile on her face? I suddenly got terribly anxious. What was going on?

Jo hadn't ever said anything about this man to me. Well. She'd said he was nice. Very nice. But that's such a limp nothing sort of comment that I didn't even notice it at the time.

I didn't have a clue what he was really like. I'd never met him. I had met Robin. It was easier for Jo to bring him round to our place after she'd met him from school.

'It's so I can be here for you too, Charlie. We can all have a snack together,' said Jo. 'Then I can take him home and do a spot of cleaning before his dad gets back.'

I wasn't at all keen on this idea, but I couldn't really object much to Robin. He wasn't like an ordinary boy of five at all. He was very little, with a long thick fringe and huge dark eyes in a white face. He gnawed nervously at his bottom lip all the time, and he trembled for the first few visits. He was like one of those small furry nocturnal creatures you see in the zoo, hunched at the bottom of their cage.

He certainly didn't run amok, messing up all my things. He sat where he was put, picking anxiously at the scabs on his bony bare knees, going nibble nibble nibble at his lips. Jo brought him books and he looked at them obediently. Jo found him paper and crayons and he drew neat square houses with a mummy on one side and a daddy on the other and a very tiny Robin in the middle, under the house. He wasn't any good at perspective so it looked as if the house was falling on him, about to crush him completely. Or maybe that was really how he wanted it to look, I don't know. I asked him but he wouldn't talk properly. He'd just nod if I said, 'Is this your mum?'

I'd only got him going once. I noticed he had a little pocket in his school sweatshirt that he patted every now and then. I thought he was checking up on his handkerchief. Robin was the sort of little boy who always breathes heavily and has a runny nose. He kept sniffling one afternoon so I told him rather sharply to use his handkerchief.

He looked stricken. He didn't move.

'Your hankie! Your nose is running. Yuck!' I said.

He shrivelled away from me, practically going inside the neck of his sweatshirt.

'Stop nagging him, Charlie. Here, we've got some tissues somewhere,' said Jo.

'But look, he's got his hankie with him,' I said, putting my hand in his pocket and pulling something out.

It wasn't a hankie. It was a little fluffy toy.

'That's mine! Give him back!' said Robin, and he darted forward, grabbing.

'Hey, OK! Don't get in such a flap. Here's your

little toy. What is it?' I said, peering.

Robin held it tight against his chest.

'Is he shy, your little animal?' I said. 'Oh yes, he is, isn't he? Sorry. Didn't mean to frighten him. He's looking at me with one big beady eye. I think he really wants to make friends. Are you going to get him to say hello to me, Robin?'

Robin didn't seem sure. He fidgeted, not meeting my eyes – but he seemed almost to be joining in the game.

'Hello, little shy animal,' I said into Robin's clasped hands.

'He's not an animal,' said Robin. 'He's a bird. He's Birdie.'

Birdie edged his beak into the air so that I could see.

'Oh, so he is! Hello, Birdie. Can you fly?' I said.

Robin nodded, and made Birdie nod too.

'I don't believe you,' I said.

'He can!' said Robin, and Birdie's beak went up and down.

'No. I'm sure he can't possibly fly,' I said.

'Yes, he can, I'll show you,' said Robin, and he unclenched his fist so that Birdie's woollen wings flapped free. Robin stood up and skipped round the kitchen, making his arm swoop up and down. Birdie flew along with him. He had two black bead eyes, a yellow beak, and big brown wings, carefully scalloped at the edge. He wore a bright-red knitted waistcoat.

Birdie

'I get it! Birdie's a Robin, like you,' I said.

Robin nodded happily, and Birdie flew faster.

'Did your mum make him for you?' I said without thinking.

Robin stopped. Birdie lost height rapidly and landed. Jo frowned at me from across the kitchen. Robin went and sat on a chair without saying another word. I didn't know whether his mum had made Birdie or not.

'I'm sorry, Robin,' I muttered.

I wondered what it would feel like if your mum didn't really want you. I knew what it felt like not to have a dad, but then that was OK. I didn't want one. Certainly not one like mine. When I was really little, younger than Robin, Jo used to tell me all these fairy tales about a lovely daddy who was so sad he couldn't see me, but I soon twigged she wasn't telling the truth. I asked her straight and so she told me straight. My dad was Jo's first boyfriend. She loved him like crazy but he was never so keen on her. Then when she found out she was going to have me she told him and he didn't want to know. 'That's your problem,' he said. I've been Jo's 'problem' ever since but we manage just fine.

Robin doesn't look like he's managing very well, even if he's still got this very nice dad. If he *is* very nice.

I don't like the sound of him.

FAMILY

It is our Jessie's birthday today. She is five years old, quite the little lady. I have been fretting over what to send her for a birthday present. Louisa has so many discarded toys in her trunk. There's a little china tea-set our Jessie would adore. Louisa packed it away so carelessly all the little teacups fell out of their cardboard setting and the lid of the sugar pot seems to be lost for ever.

'I don't care about that old tea-set, not now I have my new willow-pattern set,' said Louisa.

I very nearly asked her if I could have it for my little sister. Louisa might have said yes, but I didn't think the Mistress would like it. There are many many many things the Mistress doesn't like!

I did not risk taking so much as one tiny teacup for Jessie's present. I cut up one of my old black stockings that had worn away to holes and sat up sewing half the night, turning it into a little toy monkey like the one that sits on the organ-grinder's shoulder. I wanted to give him a little jacket and cap too, so I cut a square out of my red flannel petticoat. It will not show, after

all. The monkey looked splendid in his fine red clothes. My eyes were red too the next day from sewing by candlelight and I was desperately tired, but I did not care for once. I wrapped the monkey in a piece of last week's newspaper and tied it with string and inked the address really large and clear upon the front and posted it off in plenty of time.

I felt happy for the first time since I have been working here. But now I feel sad, because I cannot see Jessie opening her present. I cannot give her a birthday kiss. I am so scared Jessie might forget all about me as I can only go home one day a year, on Mothering Sunday. Baby Ada-May will think me a total stranger. It makes my heart break.

The Mistress came into the nursery unexpectedly and found me weeping with my head in the wardrobe.

'Whatever is the matter, Charlotte?' she said. 'You are not ill, are you?'

'No, Madam.'

'Then why are you crying? Make haste with Miss Louisa's dress, or the child will get a chill.'

'Yes, Madam. Sorry, Madam. I'm just sad because I miss my family so.'

'You are part of *this* family now,' said the Mistress.

She said it as if she were granting me an immense

privilege. But I do not care for this family. How can I be part of it when I can never answer back or say what I really think? How can I feel really close to these children when I have to call them Miss and Master? I have to look after them all the time but there is no-one to look after me.

COURTSHIP

'I look such a mess,' Jo wailed.

'You look fine,' I said. Though she didn't. She had two spots and her hair needed washing and her sweater had shrunk and her leggings were all baggy at the knee.

'I'm going to have to change,' said Jo, diving into the bedroom. 'Keep an eye on Robin for me.'

I frowned after her. I went and fetched a drawing pad and felt tip pens. I put them in front of Robin on the kitchen table.

'Right. You can do a drawing with my own personal set of super felt tip pens – so long as you promise not to press too hard on the points, OK?'

'OK,' said Robin eagerly, because I didn't often let him borrow them. He was used to making do with his own little-boy wax crayons.

He picked up the red, ready to draw his usual neat square house.

'Don't draw any of that boring old house and mummy and daddy stuff. Why don't you pretend

Birdie's grown ginormous and you get on his back and you both fly away to a Magic Land where anything can happen. Draw that.'

Robin blinked at me doubtfully.

'Go on,' I said, giving him a little nudge. 'I'm just going to go and have a talk with my mother, OK? Do not disturb us unless it's a dire emergency like you've been seized with an uncontrollable desire to stick two felt tips simultaneously into your eyes and you need immediate medical attention.'

Robin nibbled his lip, glancing nervously at the tin of felt tips as if they might spontaneously attack him.

I sighed and marched into the bedroom. Jo had pulled off her old cleaning clothes and was standing in her underwear, making faces at her clothes in the wardrobe.

'Yuck,' she said. 'They're all old and grotty and rubbish.' She scratched her head. 'Double yuck. So am I. I've *got* to wash my hair. I was going to do it yesterday but I was so blooming tired and then there wasn't time to do more than splash my face this morning. Oh God, I think I'll climb into the washing machine at the Rosens' tomorrow morning and give myself a good soaping . . .' She went burbling on like this, to herself rather than me, as she made for the bathroom in her knickers, remembered Robin, went back for her tatty old dressing gown, and then stripped off and stepped into the bath. 'Do you think we'll ever have enough spare cash to have a shower installed?' she shouted over the roaring taps. 'Pass us that Snoopy mug, Charlie

– and the shampoo. What is it, eh? 'Cause I'm in a tearing hurry.'

'Why are you fussing about what you look like?' I said, sitting on the loo.

'What?' Jo said, tipping water over her head.

'Why are you washing your hair *now*?'

'Oh, for goodness' sake. My hair's all lank and disgusting, that's why,' said Jo, exasperated. She lathered shampoo in and then wiped the bathroom mirror clear of steam and looked at herself. '*Look* at me. Spots all over the place. And huge great bags under my eyes. It's not fair. I thought all this hard work would make me super fit at the very least and yet I look a wreck.'

'Why does it matter so much?' I said sternly.

'Of course it matters,' Jo snapped, rinsing. 'I haven't quite given up on myself yet. I don't want to go round looking so dirty and disgusting that people in the streets run away from me screaming.'

'You don't mind what you look like when you go out to the supermarket,' I said.

'Well at that time most people have their eyes tightly closed – even the ones that are up,' said Jo, sluicing more water over herself and then getting up. 'Pass us that towel and stop being so stupid.'

'You're the one that's being stupid in my opinion,' I said. 'You don't care what you look like when you go to the Rosens' either, you just wear any old gungy thing. You don't care what you look like when you go and collect Robin from school and bring him back here. But suddenly, when it's time to take him home to his dad, it's flap and fuss and you getting worked up into a right flap-doodle.'

'I don't know what you're on about,' said Jo, towelling herself dry.

'Yes you do. What's the matter with you, Jo? Why are you trying to impress that wimpy little kid's father, eh?'

'I'm not. I just want him to see he's got a competent and reasonably clean person looking after his son. Stop looking so *fierce*, Charlie.'

'But you like him, don't you?' I asked.

'I don't even know him properly. He's just my employer.'

'You're not going to do anything really gross and go out with him, are you?' I said.

'Oooh, now, that's a great idea,' said Jo. 'And you and your Jamie could come too on a double date, how about that?'

'You shut up teasing me. I'm serious!' I said. 'I'm having grave doubts about you, Loopy Mum. We don't like men, remember? *Especially* the lean lost ones. Honestly! What a description. You are a *fool*.'

'Don't you tell me I'm a fool. I'm your mother!' said Jo, trying to act all dignified. 'Now go and keep an eye on poor little Robin and stop bugging me. Do as you're told!'

'Who's going to make me? You and whose army?' I said, standing my ground.

'Go!' said Jo, giving me a push.

'No!' I said, giving her a push back.

'You do as I say,' said Jo, pushing with both hands.

'I don't want to,' I said, pushing back.

We went on pushing and shoving and Jo's towel fell off and she tried to grab it and I snatched it first and slipped on the bath mat and Jo fell on top of me and we rolled around, starting to giggle as we wrestled.

'Oh!' said a little voice.

We looked up and there was Robin at the bathroom door, his mouth open in astonishment.

'Sorry, Robin!' said Jo, grabbing the towel back and wrapping it round herself.

'Are you fighting?' Robin enquired timidly.

'Yes,' I said.

'No, of course we're not,' said Jo. 'Take no notice of Charlie, Robin. She's a wild child, totally out of my control.'

'Grrrrrr!' I said, baring my teeth dramatically.

'Will she fight me?' Robin asked.

'No, of course she won't, she's only teasing,' said Jo.

'Yes, I will,' I said, and I swooped on him and picked him up under his armpits and swung him round wildly so that his spindly legs kicked in the air.

He squealed noisily but he seemed to be enjoying it.

'Stop being so rough with him,' Jo called, pulling on her clothes in the bedroom.

'Is he lean and lost like his daddy then?' I said, setting Robin back on his feet. His face was flushed robin red, his eyes dark with excitement. He took a step and staggered. I caught hold of him.

'It's OK, you're just giddy,' I said as he clung to me. His hands were like little monkey paws. I wondered if he'd ever clung to his mum the way he was clinging to me.

'Giddy,' Robin repeated. This was obviously a new experience for him. He moved tentatively.

'There, it's getting better, isn't it? Hey, did you put all the tops back on my felt tip pens, yeah?'

'Oh yes. Honest,' said Robin.

'Did you do a drawing?'

'I started.'

'Let's see then.' I walked him over to the kitchen table. He'd drawn a very big Birdie as I'd suggested, with a tiny Robin clinging to his back. They were just landing in the Magic Land, Birdie's wings outstretched.

I touched the strip of green below Birdie's claws. 'Is this the Magic Land then?' I asked.

Robin nodded. 'Yes! Shall I draw it for you, Charlie?'

'OK. Go on then. What's in your Magic Land, eh? Pink candy-floss trees and rivers with tame dolphins and unicorns you can ride and it's never ever bedtime?' I suggested, trying to conjure up a dinky little Magic Land that might take his fancy.

Jo and I elaborated endlessly on our own Magic Lands. It was one of our favourite games. Jo's current Magic Land was a huge turquoise swimming pool and she'd float endlessly on a white lilo sipping champagne and eating white cream chocolates all day long.

My special Magic Land was an immense jungle and I'd hack my way through, not the slightest bit scared even when huge pythons wound themselves round my waist or tigers roared at me or elephants suddenly charged. I'd whistle a magic tune so that the python swayed in a hypnotic trance, I'd roar right back at the tiger, and I'd catch hold of the elephant's trunk and get him to lift me up on his head between his mighty ears and we'd thunder across the land together.

I started drawing my own Magic Land, concentrating on the immensely tall trees, home of great gorillas and hairy orang-utans and tribes of funny furry monkeys, and I was Queen of all the Apes and swung through the trees faster than any of them.

'Look, this is my Magic Land. See the monkeys?' I said, showing Robin.

He was kneeling up on his chair, drawing intently, his tongue sticking out he was concentrating so hard. I peered at his picture.

'That's not a Magic Land!' I said. 'You're just drawing your mum and your dad again.'

'Yes, they're in my Magic Land, and we all live there and it's magic,' said Robin. He bent his head very near his drawing, as if he was trying to step inside it.

'It's nearly time we were off, Robin. We'll show Daddy your lovely picture, yes?' said Jo.

That wasn't all they were going to show off to Daddy. Jo was wearing her shortest skirt and her little angora wool jumper. I usually call her Fluffy Bunny when she wears it. I didn't at all feel like flattering her with babyish nick-names now. What was she *doing*, getting all dolled up to deliver little Robin back home? She was supposed to do some housework when she was there too, so why dress up like she was going dating, not dusting?

'What?' said Jo, all wide-eyed, as I glared at her.

'You know what,' I said.

She was hours getting back home too. Well, an hour late. Just over half an hour. But she was still *late*.

'What are you playing at, eh?' I said furiously.

Jo burst out laughing.

'It's not funny!' I exploded.

'Yes it is. Talk about role reversal. Watch it, Charlie. You're starting to sound just like Grandma. "Why are you so late back, Josephine? This simply isn't good enough. And wipe that smirk off your face, it's not funny."'

'Well, maybe if you'd listened to Grandma instead of thinking you knew best then you wouldn't have ended up as a single parent having to go out cleaning for other people to keep a roof over our heads,' I said.

There was a sudden silence. We were both shocked. Jo's never minded if I shout back at her but I've never tried to hurt her like that before. I put my hand over my lips to try to get them under control.

Jo was struggling too, no longer laughing. 'OK. Maybe that's a good point – if a cheap one. Though I'm glad I made that major mistake because I got you out of it. And you're the best thing that's ever happened to me, even if you're acting like a right old ratbag at this present moment in time,' said Jo. 'I'm sorry if you were worried I was late. I didn't realize. Mark and I just got talking and—'

'So it's Mark, is it?'

'Oh come off it, Charlie. He's not the sort of man you call Mr Reed.'

'No, he's the little-boy-lost type, yeah?'

'I don't know why you're being so *stupid*,' said Jo. 'You're acting like I'm going out with him or something.'

'Well – don't you want to?'

'Of course not. He's my employer. He's a nice quiet friendly man who adores his son and he's still hurting after the break up of his marriage and he's lonely and he just likes to talk a bit, that's all. And – and – I like to talk to him too.'

'Why? You're not lonely. You've got me.'

Jo looked as if she might giggle again. 'You're sounding like my husband now!'

'Well, why do you have to get all prettied up in your best clothes just to talk to this Mark?'

'*Definitely* like a husband. Oh, Charlie!' Jo put her arms round me, her angora tickling my cheeks.

'Get off. You're getting fluff all over me,' I said, sneezing.

'Well, stop being such a prize berk, eh? Look, if it keeps you happy I'll tell Mark tomorrow that I'm not allowed to say another word to him because it annoys my fierce bossy man-hating daughter.'

'Right, you do that,' I said.

I knew I was being ridiculous. But I couldn't help it.

I was fed up at school too. Angela and Lisa were being stupid stupid stupid. Angela had joined this dippy fan club and had a special magazine and a signed photo of her new favourites and a T-shirt with all their heads on which she wore every day under her school shirt. She endlessly read aloud the most amazingly trivial facts about her new darlings, like one had a thing about red-and-white striped toothpaste and another had a wacky Scottish auntie and another fell about laughing every time he saw Bugs Bunny. Well, so what??? But Angela kept giving great excited whoops and yelling, 'Listen to this, listen to this!'

Lisa was getting pretty cheesed off with this too, but she was just as bad over Dave Wood. Worse even. She went bright red whenever he came remotely near her, and when one day in singing the music teacher had her standing right next to Dave, Lisa was so overcome she couldn't sing a note, she just opened and shut her mouth like a goldfish.

'I was so *embarrassed*,' she kept saying afterwards. 'I mean, we were practically touching.'

'Yuck! I wouldn't touch Dave Wood with a bargepole,' I said.

'Oh *you*,' said Lisa. 'Look, do you think Dave likes me?'

'*I* don't know,' I said impatiently. 'Why don't you ask him?'

'I can't *ask* him! No, I've got to find some subtle way of finding out.'

'I'll ask him, if you like,' said Angela, reaching down her school blouse and blowing kisses to the faces on her T-shirt.

'No, that's not subtle enough,' said Lisa.

'Angela, stop doing that, it looks seriously weird,' I said. 'And you're trying to be so subtle it's just a waste of space. Never mind whether that twerp likes you. He most likely doesn't have a clue that *you* like *him*.'

'Well, I can't tell him that!' said Lisa.

'Why not? Though *how* you can like him I just can't fathom. I can't stand the way his hair flops forward into his eyes so that he has to keep flipping it out the way!'

'I think that's seriously cute,' said Lisa.

'Yuck!'

'Yes, double yuck,' said Angela, giving me hope, but then she started on about the hairstyles of all her pop darlings until I was ready to tear out *my* hair. In fact I got so seriously bored that I stalked off by myself.

I was feeling so fed up that when some stupid boys kicked their football and hit me right on the head I found I had tears in my eyes. I blinked rapidly, horrified. I never ever cried at school, no matter what. Even when I was a little kid right back in Year One and some big boys gave me a Chinese burn I didn't cry.

'Watch it, you stupid idiots,' I said, and I took their football and threw it as far away as I could, right over behind the bike sheds.

'Oh, you rotten pig, why did you go and do that?' they groaned. 'What's up with you, Cakehole? Just because you've had a tiff with your little girly gang there's no need to take it out on us.'

I responded with a very rude gesture. Miss Beckworth was on playground duty. I hoped she hadn't seen. I made off sharpish in the opposite direction, dodging behind the Portakabins.

Jamie Edwards was sitting on the steps, head deep in a book. He looked startled when he saw me – but he smiled nervously.

'You still reading about that Esther?' I said.

'I finished that book ages ago. I read ever so quickly,' said Jamie, unable to resist a little boast.

'So what you reading now then, eh?' I peered at the densely printed pages. 'It looks even worse. Ever so hard.'

'Ever so Hardy,' said Jamie, chuckling, showing me the spine.

'*Tess of the D'Urbervilles* by Thomas Hardy – oh, I get you, ha ha, very droll. It sounds awful! Is it French with that funny name?'

'No. It's English, about this girl Tess and she goes to work on a farm and this man has his wicked way with her,' said Jamie, eyes gleaming.

'Oh, another one of *those*. You are awful, Jamie.'

'And it's ever so sad, because Tess has a baby and then she falls in love again but it all goes wrong and I know it's not going to have a happy ending.'

'Oh, hang about! I've seen it on the telly, I think. There's a bit about Stonehenge at the end – I watched it with Jo and we both wept buckets.'

'Is Jo your sister?'

'No, my mum.'

'And you're allowed to call her by her first name?'

'I can call her whatever I like,' I said.

I felt like inventing some new and incredibly nasty names for her because I was still so annoyed with her. I kept thinking about her with this creep Mark. I didn't know what he looked like, so I imagined him like Robin but big. A *total* wimp. So why why why did Jo want to bound round to his house in her bunny jumper and twitch her nose at him?

'Are you planning to go round to Lisa's or Angela's on Friday night?' Jo said that evening.

'Maybe. I don't know. I've got a bit fed up with them recently,' I said gloomily, chucking my school copy of *Victorian Life* on the floor. None of Miss Beckworth's books went into the sort of detail I wanted. 'I might just go round to Jamie's house because he keeps telling me he's got all these Victorian books he'll lend me.'

'Oh, round to Jamie's house, eh?' said Jo.

'So?' I said fiercely. 'It's just to borrow a book.'

'OK, OK. But if you stay for tea or anything, can his mum or dad run you home? I can't come and fetch you because . . . I'm babysitting for Robin.'

I stared at her. So Mark was going out?

'Who's this Mark going out with?' I asked.

Jo shrugged uneasily. 'I don't know. Look, he just asked if I could – could come round and babysit, so I said OK, but I won't be back late, and I can always say no if it's not all right with you, Charlie.'

'It's fine with me,' I said. It obviously wasn't fine with Jo. I felt a bit sorry for her. But I was also thrilled for me. The wimp had got himself some girlfriend so he couldn't be interested in Jo. He just wanted her to look after little Robin.

Or so I thought.

I was so stupid! I didn't twig at all. Not that first Friday, or even the Friday after. I was so pleased and relieved I was extra nice to Jo.

We had a wonderful Sunday, having a really long lie in and then a dozy hour or two snuggled up in bed playing Magic Lands and then, when we eventually got up, I made us special little fairy cakes.

We ate them hot out of the oven for breakfast and then later when they'd cooled down I iced them pink and then changed to white in my little icing bag and piped funny messages over them – HELLO and I LIKE YOU and FUNNY FACE – like those little love heart sweets.

I took them to school the next morning. There was a lot of silly teasing about Cakehole making cakes – but everyone seemed dead impressed when they saw them. Everyone wanted one, but they were only for a select few. I gave Lisa an I LIKE YOU and told her what to do with it. She giggled and blushed and protested and wouldn't give it to Dave Wood outright – but he saw her leave it on his desk, so the message got through.

I gave Angela another I LIKE YOU and she pretend-fed it to the grinning faces on her T-shirt and then gobbled it up herself.

I gave more cakes to the girls I'd liked best in our old gang, and then Lisa and Angela and I had another two each. There was just one left by the time we went back into school.

'Did you make those little cakes yourself, Charlie?' Jamie asked.

'Yup.'

'They looked ever so nice. Really tasty,' said Jamie wistfully.

I looked at him. And then I sighed and reached in the tin and gave him the last one. It didn't say HELLO. It didn't say FUNNY FACE. It said I LIKE YOU.

COURTSHIP

It was bitterly cold in the park today. Louisa cried because she could not feel her feet inside her boots and baby Freddie's nose kept running in a most unattractive way. Victor ran ahead with his hoop to get warm, so I stuck Louisa into the pram beside Freddie and ran too. We raced all the way home, careering round the corner and practically running over the butcher's boy. He did not seem to mind.

'Whoops-a-blooming-buttercup!' he said. 'Mind what you're doing with that perambulator, Miss. It's a dangerous weapon!'

No-one has ever called *me* Miss before. I must admit I liked it, though I stuck my nose in the air and called the butcher's boy a saucepot.

Trust Victor to hang back at that precise moment. 'What were you saying to that errand boy, Charlotte?' he enquired.

'It's none of your business, Master Victor,' I said haughtily.

'Is he going to be your gentleman caller?' Victor asked.

'Certainly not!' I said, and I took Victor's hoop and bowled it so hard he had to run like the wind to stop it going into the road and under a carriage.

That settled *his* hash. He well knows that his mamma does not allow the servants to have gentleman callers. I had to protect Eliza when she was canoodling in the kitchen with her current sweetheart, the draper's assistant, who had come to deliver the Mistress's new shawl and gloves. In finest cashmere. If only I had a warm woolly shawl and mittens! I have chilblains that throb and itch like the devil.

Anyway, I was down in the kitchen fetching the children's hot milk and biscuits when I heard the Mistress clip-clopping down the stairs in her neat kid boots.

'Quick, Eliza, the Mistress is coming!' I hissed, and then I bounded *up* the stairs and waylaid the Mistress by telling her a very long story about Miss Louisa-not-drinking-her-milk-even-though-it's-so-good-for-her, and by the time I'd done and the Mistress had made her way down to the kitchen Eliza had had time to bundle any number of gentlemen callers out of the back door.

She didn't say anything to me, but Eliza and Mrs Angel stopped calling me Baby and laughing behind my back – and yesterday when the children were asleep Eliza slipped into the nursery with a bowl of Mrs Angel's special sherry trifle for my supper.

Mrs Angel is Mother's age but she has gentlemen callers too! The fat policeman for the street calls on a regular basis for his piece of pie and Mrs Angel's patter. I was astonished to see a woman so old go rosy-cheeked and chuckle when he praised her pastry.

I received a letter from Rose today and now I am starting to worry that Mother herself might be courting!!! Rose says that Mr Higgins from the Dog and Duck brings Mother a jug of ale from time to time, and in return she cooks him a meal. I do not like the sound of this!

Rose's letter makes me feel *so* homesick. It is a poor ill-spelt half-page but I have read it as avidly as if it were a masterpiece by Mr Dickens. Rose has never tried hard enough at school. She writes that Miss Worthbeck sends her kindest regards and can scarce manage without me. And a certain Edward James sends a most impertinent message to Dear Little Lottie. Hmm!

SUNDAY

I found it seriously weird going round to Jamie's house. I mean, this was Jamie Edwards, the worst boy in the whole class, old chubby-chops super-swot wimpy-wuss Jamie. I made pretty sure all the boys in our class treated me with respect but I wanted a capital 'R' from Jamie.

Yet in his huge great famously Victorian villa he was so different. As if he'd grown to fit his fourteen-roomed house. (I counted.) And I felt different too. As if I'd shrunk considerably. It felt strange just going into his house through that dark-blue front door with the big brass lion knocker. I felt as if I should slink round the back or down the basement steps like my Lottie.

If Jamie and his family had lorded it over me I'd somehow have felt easier. I could just dismiss them as horrible snobs and sneer at them. But they were ever so friendly. Even Jamie's elder brother Jules.

Elder brothers are usually a race apart. Angela's elder brother charges straight past you without even bothering to say hello. He doesn't even mean to be rude, it's just that you don't register with him. But Jules said Hi and chatted like I was his age and he made me and Jamie a toasted sandwich. We ate it in the kitchen – but *what* a kitchen! I stared round, scarcely able to swallow.

There was a shelf of cookery books and I had a quick peer but I couldn't see anything special on cakes. When Jamie's mum got home much later I saw she wasn't really a cake-maker. She came in clutching all these files and folders, her cardie falling off her shoulders, her scarf trailing on the ground. She said hello as if she was really pleased to see me, and then she unpacked some shopping and made us an amazing treat of cream cheese and smoked salmon in a strange round roll. (No wonder Jamie is chubby round his chops with all these delicious snacks on offer.) Jules had one of these bagel things too, and then went up to his room to get on with his homework.

All Jamie's family are seriously brainy. Jules is going to take *twelve* GCSEs, and then there are two older brothers, both at university. Jamie's mum and dad *lecture* at the university. He teaches French, she teaches Politics and Economics.

'The Economics is a bit of a laugh,' said Jamie.

'Mum can hardly add up. She's meant to pay me when I do stuff like vacuuming and that, two quid an hour, plus appropriate percentage for ten minutes extra, say, and *can* she work it out? Nope! Clueless, aren't you, Mum?'

I didn't think his mum clueless at all, paying Jamie a measly two quid per hour when the rock-bottom going rate was £3.50 and the Rosens right next door paid Jo a fiver an hour – dead Economical! Things got a bit awkward when Jamie's mum started chatting about how she remembered me from way back when I had my hair in a pony tail (yuck!) and then she said: 'And you always looked so cute because your big sister had a pony tail too, so you both walked along to the school, hair bobbing away.'

I smiled in a strained sort of way and decided to keep my mouth shut. But Jamie didn't.

'Oh, Mum, honestly! That wasn't Charlie's sister. She's her mum.'

Jamie's mum looked startled. 'Good Heavens! Oh Charlie, what a lovely young mum you've got! Not an old bag like me, eh? What does your mum do?'

I swallowed. 'Well . . . she used to be sort of a lecturer like you.' It was true in a way. She was always having to give her staff a right lecture in her shop.

'So now . . . ?'

'Now she's – well, she's been made redundant, I mean, it's not her fault, she didn't get the sack or anything, it's just—'

'Oh, tell me about it! We're in a sticky situation at

the moment too. We're all very worried. So has your mother found another post at all?'

'Well. Not – not lecturing. She's having to do temporary work.'

'I see. Well, I do hope things sort themselves out soon for her. Is it . . . ?' She paused delicately, trying very hard not to put her foot in it again. 'Is it just your mother and you at home?'

'Yes.'

Just Jo and me in a home we're hanging on to by the skin of our teeth. If Jamie's mum loses her posh job then they'll maybe have to swop from smoked salmon to tinned, but they'll still be able to live in their huge great house. OK, they have actually got a couple of lodgers right upstairs, two students from the university. They've got a bedroom each, a shared living room and kitchenette, and their own bathroom and loo. The students' rooms are bigger than our flat.

It still leaves the Edwards with so many different rooms. This includes a *library.* They've got books in absolutely every room, even the downstairs loo, and there are shelves in the hall and the living room downstairs, but there's this huge great room on the first floor absolutely crammed full of books, and there are shelves and shelves of Victorian stuff.

'See,' said Jamie proudly, pulling various volumes down and displaying them in front of me.

I saw. No wonder Jamie's Victorian project was

so brilliant. Still, he was letting me look at the books if I wanted.

'You've still got time to do a proper project instead of that old diary thing,' he said. Unwisely.

'Cheek! I don't want to do a boring old project. Who wants to be like everyone else? I'm doing my diary – and yes it is "old", it's *supposed* to be old, it's meant to be written by a Victorian, for goodness' sake.'

'OK, OK. You don't have to get all heavy with me,' said Jamie. 'You're so fierce, Charlie.'

'Fierce?' I said. I said it again, savouring the word. I felt as if he'd paid me a real compliment.

'So don't you want to borrow any of the Victorian books, then? Because we can go and play a game on my computer if you want. Or I'll show you my dinosaur stuff. Or we can play War.'

'War? You mean fight?' I said, grinning. 'I know who's going to win.'

'No, it's a game, with all these little soldiers – *they* fight, and there are little guns and land mines and all that stuff. It's great to play but Jules won't play it with me, neither will Mum or Dad or anyone because they're all pacifists.'

'I'm not. I'll play you. But just let me look at this book a tick.'

I'd found a whole set of Victorian girls' books. I wanted to see if there might be any Lottie could have read. There was one huge fat annual with lots of pictures, like a magazine. There was one coloured picture of a huge table groaning with wobbly jellies

and puddings like castles and all sorts of dinky sweets and teeny sandwiches . . . and fancy cakes.

'Hey, look! I just want to take a couple of notes, OK?'

'OK. Though why don't you borrow it?'

'You mean I can take it home with me?'

'Sure.'

'Oh. Well. Great.' I tucked the huge book under my arm. 'So let's play War.'

We played War for hours. It was a great game. And guess who won!

Jamie's mum ran me home in her car. I was worried she might object about the book because it was probably valuable as it's so old but she didn't turn a hair. Her hair is already grey. I wonder what it's like to have a mum old enough to be your granny. I think it's much more fun to have a mum young enough to be your sister.

'We've heard so much about you, Charlie,' said Jamie's mum.

I blinked.

'You've made a big impression on Jamie,' she said.

I thought about it. I'd made a *literal* impression on Jamie several times.

'We're going to the V and A on Sunday afternoon,' she said.

'The what?'

'Sorry. The Victoria and Albert Museum. I know Jamie would love it if you'd come with us – and it would be very useful for this famous Victorian project.'

'Well. Thank you very much. But Sunday is sort of special. Jo and I do things together.'

'She's very welcome to come too.'

'Thanks, but . . . I don't think we can.'

'Well, another time maybe. And do come round to our house any time you want. It'd be lovely to see you,' said Jamie's mum.

I was a little bit dubious. Did Jamie have an actual thing about me? He hadn't acted all lovey-dovey when we were in his room. The mere thought of Jamie Edwards acting lovey-dovey was enough to crease me up. Just let him try! And anyway, I didn't want to go to some stuffy old museum on a Sunday. Like I said, Sundays were just for Jo and me.

So I was utterly shocked and stupefied when Jo dropped this ginormous bombshell.

'We're going out on Sunday,' she said.

'Oh yeah?'

'How would you like to go to Red River Theme Park?' she said.

I stared at her. I'd been wanting to go to Red River ever since it opened. Lisa had promised she'd get her dad to take Angela and me for her birthday treat, but that wasn't until next year. And it wasn't a certainty anyway, because it cost a fortune to get into Red River.

'We can't afford it,' I said to Jo.

'We're being taken out,' she said. 'Isn't it great?'

'*Who's* taking us out?' I said, starting to smell a rat. A great big rat with twitchy whiskers on its lean lost face. And I was spot on.

'Mark was talking about taking Robin this Sunday and he thought it would be so much more fun if we all went together. He's paying, and I'm getting a picnic together. It's going to be a fantastic day out.'

'We don't have days out on Sundays. We have days in. Just you and me. As a matter of fact, *I* was asked out on Sunday, the Edwards family asked me, they wanted to take me out for this bumper day in London, a drive all round the sights and lunch in Planet Hollywood and then this museum for Victorian stuff and then tea at one of those really posh hotels, scones and cream cakes and all that, and then – then we were going for dinner at the Hard Rock Café and – and *then*—'

'Then you were going to be violently sick, I should think,' said Jo. She reached out and ran her finger up and down my lips, the way you do a baby to make it go wibble-wibble-wibble. 'This is a bad mouth,' said Jo. 'It is telling fibs.'

'They did ask me out on Sunday, honest,' I insisted.

'Well, you can't, because I've already said we're going to Red River with Mark and Robin,' said Jo. 'Come *on*, Charlie! You've been desperate to go to Red River for ages. I thought you'd be over the moon. I think it's absolutely great of Mark to invite us.'

'Why us, though? Why isn't he going with this girlfriend of his?' I said.

'What girlfriend?' said Jo. She frowned.

'The one he's started seeing on Friday nights when you babysit,' I said.

'Oh. I see. Ah,' said Jo.

'What?' I said. '*What?*' Although I suddenly *knew* what.

'I think you maybe got hold of the wrong end of the stick,' said Jo. 'I never said Mark had a girlfriend.'

'So where did he go when you went round to babysit?'

'Well . . . the first Friday he was going out, just to see this film he fancied, but we got chatting, and then we watched this film together on the telly instead, so—'

'So you're the one who's been telling dirty great lies,' I said.

'No I'm not!'

'And *you're* his girlfriend now, aren't you?' I said.

'Of course I'm not. Don't be so silly. I'm not Mark's girlfriend. I work for him. I've only known him a few weeks. Oh, Charlie, don't be so difficult.'

I felt like being difficult. I was Mega Mad. No-one seemed to understand why. Lisa and Angela and I went round the shops on Saturday afternoon and they thought I was completely nuts.

'Can't you get this guy to take us too?' said Lisa hopefully. 'Say we're your all-time best friends and you can't go without us. After all, I promised I'd get my dad to take you two on my birthday.'

'This guy isn't my dad though. He isn't anything. He's just this creep who's started chatting up my mother.'

'Still, who cares if he's a creep? You still get to go to Red River,' said Lisa.

'Yeah, I'll go in your place if you don't want to,' said Angela. 'I just go to church on Sundays. You count yourself lucky, Charlie.'

'No, you've got to be a good girl and go to church,' said Lisa. '*I'll* go instead of Charlie. I just have to go to all these boring antique fairs with my mum while my dad plays golf, it's not fair.'

'Neither of you are going,' I said. 'And *I'm* not going too.'

I told Jo that on Saturday evening, while she was busy getting all this picnic stuff together.

'OK,' said Jo, mashing up hard-boiled eggs.

'I really mean it. I'm not going. And you can't make me,' I said.

'Right,' said Jo, mashing harder.

'So that's settled,' I said.

'Yep,' said Jo, pounding so hard that the bowl rattled.

'I'm not going to Granny's or anything. I'll just stay here. By myself. I'll be fine,' I said.

'Aha,' said Jo, and her hand slipped and she banged it hard on the edge of the kitchen top. She bent over, clutching her wrist.

'You're not supposed to mash like that. You're hopeless when it comes to cooking,' I said. 'Jo?'

She didn't answer this time. Her head was so bent I couldn't see her face for hair. I went over to her. I saw a tear trickling down her cheek.

'I've really upset you, haven't I?' I said.

'No. I've just hurt my wrist, that's all,' said Jo.

She can be as stubborn as me sometimes. Her wrist wasn't really hurt. And she stopped crying when I put my arms round her and told her that I would go to Red River on Sunday if she really really really wanted me to go.

I even made some more little fairy cakes for the picnic. With messages.

Mark was exactly how I imagined him. No, worse. The sort of bumbling Bambi-eyed boy-man that makes some women go bananas. He had a tuft of hair sticking up on top and little round glasses and a big check shirt and faded jeans and one of his socks was black and the other was navy. *Pathetic*. Mark almost made little Robin look macho. He was ever so scared of me. 'Hi, Charlie,' he said, trying to sound dead casual, but he stuttered – and when he attempted this silly little wave, spreading his fingers, I saw his palm was all sweaty. Yuck.

But there was something far far worse. Jo. She was better at acting cool, of course. If you didn't know her you'd think she was dead relaxed, making a fuss of Robin and flappy little Birdie, chatting nineteen to the dozen to Mark, telling some silly story about her supermarket job, the day her machine ran away with her and attacked a pile of loo rolls. I don't think it even happened, she was just making it up as she went along, but it made Mark laugh and even little Robin tittered behind Birdie's wing. But she was just pretending all the time, her voice too high, her eyes blinking, her hands gesticulating wildly. She was like a clockwork toy that had been wound up too tightly.

I yawned and started humming to myself while she was in mid-flow to show her I wasn't impressed. I hardly said a word the entire car journey to Red River Theme Park. Jo was going jabber jabber jabber so there was no point anyway.

Mark seemed so impressed that he could barely keep his eyes on the road ahead. 'Yeah? Mmm? *Really?*' he'd go, and every so often he'd crack up laughing.

I slumped back in my seat, weary with this deeply disgusting performance. Mark caught sight of me in his driving mirror. 'Are you all right, Charlie?' he said.

I didn't bother to reply.

'She's not feeling sick, is she?' Mark asked Jo.

Jo turned round. 'Stop being a pig,' she mouthed at me.

I gave one small snort for her

benefit. Robin blinked at me in surprise.

'She's OK,' said Jo.

'And you're OK too, Robin?' Mark asked. 'You don't feel sick or anything?'

'I don't think so,' Robin mumbled. 'But maybe Birdie does a bit.'

Oh great. I didn't care for the idea of Robin chucking up all over me.

'Talk to Robin, Charlie,' said Jo. 'Take his mind off it.'

I didn't want to talk to Robin. Or his dad. Or my stupid mother, all got up in her fluffy pink top and her tiny skirt. To match her new shrunk tiny brain and her fluffy pink persona. Bimbo Mum. Out with Bambi Man and Birdie Boy.

'What's *up* with you, Charlie?' Jo said, her voice sharp.

There was nothing up with me. I was the only person in the car acting anywhere near normal.

'She's shy,' said Mark.

Me, shy! I snorted again.

'She's not shy,' said Jo. 'Are you, Charlie? I'm the one who always gets into states about things and can hardly say boo to a goose. Charlie's always had far more guts than me. She was born a fighter, eh, Charlie?'

She was sucking up to me now. It was sickening. Robin seemed to find it sickening too. Literally.

'Birdie's starting to feel *very* sick,' he gasped, his face pale green.

I snapped into action mega fast, opening his

window and sticking his little head out just in time. He was sick all over the car, but at least it was outside, not inside. We had to pull up in a lay-by and get him mopped up and the car wiped down. I backed away from both these proceedings. As Mark had to deal with the car Jo had to sluice the sicky dribble off Robin. She's always had a weak stomach. Still, she was the one who wanted to play Happy Families. Let her be Mother.

Robin started wimpering that he smelt, and eventually Jo had to waste a bottle of the picnic water washing him. Then Robin snivelled that Birdie smelt too, because one tiny tip of his wing had got stained. Birdie had to have a regular little bird-bath too.

I was practically at screaming point by the time we drove off in the car. The day didn't improve. The world and his wife had decided to visit the Red River Theme Park. We were not the world and we certainly weren't ever going to be anyone's wife, but we were stuck in their traffic jam. It took hours before we got there, and then there was a huge queue to park and by the time we staggered through the entrance we felt as exhausted as if we'd already had a day out.

Still, I decided I might as well make the most of this opportunity and I clamoured straight away to go on the really scary famous Red River Run.

'Let's go a bit gently first,' said Jo. 'Robin still looks a bit pale. What would you like to go on, Robin?'

He twittered and skittered and eventually decided

he wanted to try the Treetops ride because Birdie might see a lot of big birds up there. I was getting heartily sick of all this twee Birdie nonsense by now. I wished Birdie would flap his wings and fly away, sharpish.

We went on this Treetops ride and it was a bit babyish because you rode round this aerial scenic railway ever so slowly, absolutely no swooping up and down or looping-the-looping. Big birds were very few on the ground too. Well, few in the air, shall we say. I'd have stuck stuffed parrots to every branch and dangled a few eagles in the air just to make the view a bit livelier. You couldn't rely on the real birds to put on an entertaining aerial display. A few sparrows flapped far away and that was our lot.

It was all very tame. For me. Not for Robin. He went a familiar pale green.

'Put your head over the side of the truck,' I said quickly.

But when he did as he was told he looked down *through* the treetops and got so scared he couldn't even be sick (which was just as well for all the unsuspecting folk wandering around underneath!) Robin just opened his mouth and screamed.

'Hey, Robin! It's OK, son. Don't yell like that. It's meant to be fun,' said Mark, turning round and trying to put his arms round him.

'Don't look down, Robin.

Look up at the trees. Look, there's a pigeon,' said Jo.

'Can't anyone shut him up?' I said. 'Robin, you're giving Birdie a headache. Look, he's had to put his head under his wing. Shut up, OK?'

It wasn't OK. He didn't shut up until we'd finished the ride and hauled him off. Mark picked him up and he buried his head in his shirt and gradually adjusted the scream to an intermittent sob.

'Well, he's having a whale of a time,' I said.

Jo gave me a shove. 'Will you stop being so hateful?' she hissed. 'Poor little Robin.'

'Yes, poor little wimpy-pimpy,' I said. 'Come on, Jo. He's not a baby. He's five, for goodness' sake. In Victorian times he'd be old enough to shove up a chimney.'

'I wish I could shove you up a chimney,' said Jo. 'Look, he acts like a baby because his mum's cleared off and he feels like his whole world has fallen apart. Can't you understand?'

I was starting to feel that way myself. Like my own mum had cleared off. Jo turned her back on me and started fuss fuss fussing over Robin, and all the time Mark was looking at her with this sickening soft expression so that now I was the one who felt like throwing up.

Robin wouldn't go on any other rides, apart from a twiddly little roundabout for tiny tots. He sat bolt upright in a little car and held on to that steering wheel so tightly his knuckles were practically bursting out of his skin. Jo and Mark waved like crazy every time he came round but he never once looked at them. He stared straight ahead, as if he were watching the road.

He wanted another go. And another.

'Look, this is loopy,' I pointed out. 'It costs a fortune to get in and you're supposed to go on all these incredible rides and all we're doing is watching Robin go round and round a roundabout that would only cost fifty pence at a summer fête.'

'At least he's liking it,' said Jo.

'But this is his last go. I agree with you, Charlie. Hey, we'll go on the Red River Ride, eh, you and me?' said Mark.

I couldn't stand the way he was trying so hard to get on with me.

'I'll go on my own, thanks,' I said.

But for some infuriating reason they didn't let kids under twelve ride on their own.

'You come, Jo. Go on. Please,' I said, practically begging.

But it was no use. I ended up surfing the Red River with Mark. It spoilt it all utterly. People seeing us together might have thought he was my *dad*. I sat as far away from him as I possibly could. He kept yelling, 'Isn't this fun! Isn't this great!' though he'd gone almost as green as his son. When we lurched up to the very top and then swooped down like crazy he screamed so that I could see the fillings in his back teeth. When we got to the last and largest hill of steel before the watersplash he actually tried to put his arm round me.

'Do you mind?' I said, and I wriggled as far away as I could just as we went over the top. My head jerked forward as I hurtled down and I banged my nose hard on the safety bar. Pain exploded in my head as water splashed right over us and soaked us to the skin.

'Wow!' said Mark. 'Hey, Charlie, what's up? Did you bump your head? Your poor nose is all red.'

'No. I'm fine,' I said thickly, trying to blink my tears back. I didn't want his soggy sympathy. Even though it was all his fault. Him and his silly snivelly son.

Jo was still so busy fussing over Robin that she didn't even *notice* that my nose had suddenly turned into a tomato. So I decided I wouldn't bother to tell her. Even though it was more than likely broken, and my looks would be marred for all time.

We went to the picnic area but I wasn't really hungry. My nose throbbed so much and chewing aggravated it. The picnic wasn't up to much anyway. The sandwiches had gone limp inside and hard out because Jo had made them the night before. She'd packed the crisps under the cans of Coke so that they were all broken into little bits. The grapes had got so squashed that one more trample would have turned them into wine.

The only good part of the picnic were my fairy cakes which I'd packed myself in a nest of paper tissues inside a big tin. They were delicious. And carefully iced with witty messages. I handed them round so that everyone got the right one.

Mine said HEY, BEAUTIFUL.

Jo's said TRAITOR.

Mark's said DEADLY POISON.

Robin's said GET LOST.

'What does it mean, g-e-t l-o-s-t?' said Robin, licking his message tentatively.

'Oh, it's just Charlie being silly,' said Jo, glaring at me. She didn't even touch her cake. Mark gave a great false roar of laughter and ate his in two gulps.

'Yum yum, delicious,' he said, and then he gasped and pretended to choke.

'Daddy?' said Robin.

'It's OK, Daddy's just dying,' I said.

'It's a silly joke, Robin,' said Jo, cramming the lid back on the rest of the cakes. She looked like she wanted to cram me inside too. Without any airholes. 'How would you like another go on that little roundabout, Robin?'

He had many more goes. And I went on some other rides too, but somehow they all seemed a waste of time. My whole head was hurting now, not just my nose. Sometimes I went on the rides with

Mark while Jo looked after Robin. Sometimes I went on the rides with Jo. That wasn't any better, because we weren't speaking.

Then we got to the Stardust Sparkle ride. It was all pink glitter and hearts and flowers outside.

'That's pretty,' said Robin.

'Pretty yucky,' I said.

'Would you like to go on the Stardust Sparkle ride, Robin?' said Jo. 'We could all go on it, eh?'

Robin watched the ride warily. A couple got into a pink pretend Cadillac and it drove through a door in the shape of a big heart. You couldn't see inside the door. It was all dark.

'No,' said Robin. 'Too dark. I don't like the dark.'

'Surprise surprise,' I said. 'Well, *I* certainly don't want to go on the Stardust Sparkle ride either, if anybody's interested. Not that anyone is.'

'I'd like to,' said Mark. 'Come on, Jo.'

I stared at her. But she didn't even look at me.

'Look after Robin, Charlie,' she said, and she rushed off with Mark.

The two of them together. In a pink Cadillac. Disappearing through a big heart into the dark.

'They've gone,' said Robin.

'Too true,' I said.

'They'll be back soon?' Robin asked.

'How should I know?' I said.

The ride was mostly enclosed, but the first couple's Cadillac suddenly shot through a door overhead and rode through the air in full view of everyone for several seconds. The couple didn't seem to realize. They were kissing.

'Look!' said Robin, giggling.

The first couple disappeared through another dinky door. We waited for the second couple. We waited a long time, and then suddenly they burst through the overhead door. They rode through the air in full view of everyone. They didn't realize either. They were kissing.

'Look!' said Robin, giggling again. And then *he* realized. 'It's Daddy and Jo!'

I didn't say anything. My nose was still hot but the rest of me had turned icy cold.

'But they were kissing. Why were they kissing? They don't kiss,' said Robin, sounding perplexed. He rubbed Birdie's wing against his cheek like a cuddle blanket.

'Looks like they certainly do kiss,' I said. 'So there you go, Robin. Your dad. And my mum. Well, he's not going to be my dad. And she's not going to be *your* mum.'

'I've got a mum,' said Robin.

'Yes, but she doesn't want you any more, does she?' I said.

'Yes, she does,' said Robin uncertainly. 'Daddy said. It's just her new man who doesn't want me.'

'Well, my mum's obviously got herself *her* new man. So she doesn't want me. And your dad's got himself his new lady. So he won't want you either now. Tough, isn't it?'

It made the pain ease just a little if I made Robin

smart too. His face crumpled as he clutched Birdie. I started to get scared.

'Hey, don't cry again. I was only joking,' I said.

But we both knew I'd been serious.

SUNDAY

Sunday is meant to be a day of rest. Well, ha ha. There's no rest as far as I'm concerned. Baby Freddie wakes up screaming just the same as always and I have to crawl out of my warm bed and change his napkins and give him his bottle, and by the time he's settled Louisa comes trailing in clutching her doll and Victor leaps up and starts bouncing on his bed in his nightgown and I have to do my best to quieten them, because it's Sunday.

They have to wear their Sunday best, even the baby, and by the time I've got all three laced and buttoned and booted, my chilblains throb so bad I can barely do up my own clothes. It's my Sunday best too, though my hideous servant uniform is nothing to show off about. We all have to go to church after breakfast. Louisa and Victor are supposed to sit still in the pew, but of course they swing their legs and nudge each other and

giggle and I get the blame. If Freddie cries the Master and Mistress glare at me and expect me to stop him – but if he really gets going then I'm allowed to take him out of the church to carry him around outside. When the Vicar is droning on and on I sometimes feel like giving baby Freddie a sly pinch just to escape!

We were never really church folk at home. When Father was alive us children were sent off to Sunday School every week – but I think that was just so Mother and Father had a bit of peace and quiet without us. I liked Sunday School well enough, because you were given a book every year if you attended regularly. I liked singing the hymns too, though the words sometimes made me ponder. 'All things bright and beautiful' is pretty enough, but I do not care for the part where it says God made us high or lowly and each to our estate. In other words, us servants must know our place. Fiddlesticks!

I talked about this with Mrs Angel and Eliza when we were having a cup of cocoa together at the end of the long day. Eliza giggled but Mrs Angel was shocked. She said I was being bad and blasphemous and shooed me out of her kitchen. But Mrs Angel was in a bad

mood anyway because she was so tired. Sunday is such a long boring day that everyone wants to eat all the time and she is forever serving meals, her huge roast beef and Yorkshire, with three puddings to follow, and scarcely have they eaten the last morsel than they're ringing the bell for afternoon tea.

The children are bored silly too, because they are not allowed to play with their usual toys. I am supposed to lock away Louisa's favourite doll and bring out her grand Sunday doll with her golden curls and cream silk clothes from France. Louisa admires this doll but does not dare carry her around for fear of mussing her. Victor is not allowed to play any rumbustious boys' games. He is supposed to occupy himself with a suitable Sunday story book, all instruction and no adventures. Victor finds this very dull fare.

It is usually easy to get the children to go to bed on Sundays because they are so eager for it to change to Monday!

I have been tormented these last few Sundays thinking of Mother. Mr Higgins closes the Dog and Duck on a Sunday. I have a terrible feeling that they might be stepping out together. I shall not be able to bear it if Mr Higgins becomes my new father. I did not care for my old father, but I shall care for this one even less.

LAW AND ORDER

We were all very quiet in the car going home. Jo and Mark kept giving little quick glances at each other. I couldn't stand it. They both seemed to have forgotten that there were passengers in the back.

I started singing stupid songs as loudly as I could.

'Charlie!' said Jo. 'For heaven's sake, you can't even sing in tune.'

'It's fun to sing in the car,' said Mark. 'Let's all have a sing-song, eh? What about "Ten Green Bottles"? We know that one, don't we, Robin?'

Robin didn't reply. He was scrunched up with Birdie's wing right over his face.

'Are you feeling sick again, Robin?' Jo asked, peering round at him.

No response.

'Is he asleep?' she whispered to me.

'I don't know,' I said, taking a deep breath for my next song.

'Shut up,' said Jo. 'Don't you dare wake him up.'

He wasn't actually asleep. Whenever we were on a brightly lit road I could see the gleam of his eye.

And when I went quiet I could just hear his snuffling above the car engine.

I should have reached out and given him a cuddle. I should have told him that he mustn't worry, of course his dad would still want him. I should have told Mark and Jo that he was crying.

I didn't. Oh, how I wish I had. But I didn't. I stayed hard and hating.

Mark dropped me and Jo off outside our flats.

'Thank you for a fantastic day out,' said Jo, putting her head so close to his that I thought she was going to kiss him again right in front of me. But she straightened out and he started to wind up his window.

'Say thank you, Charlie,' said Jo.

'Thank you,' I said, with absolutely no expression, total Dalek daughter.

'What the hell is the matter with you?' Jo exploded, the moment we were inside our own front door. 'You've been foul the entire day.'

'I'm surprised you noticed. You've only had eyes for one person all day long. Oooh Mark, how lovely, what a treat, gee-whizz how fantastic,' I said, imitating her gushing tone.

She blushed, but she tried to stare me out.

'Grow up a bit,' said Jo. 'You're acting like a toddler whose mum has started to talk to someone else. Surely you don't seriously mind that I've made one nice friend all by myself? You've got hundreds of friends, you always have done, and I've been thrilled you've got such a good independent social life. I've always been useless at making friends. And now for the first time ever I've found someone I get on with, why do you have to make all this fuss?'

'But he's not just a friend, is he?' I said.

'Yes, he is!'

'Don't give me that rubbish. I don't go round snogging my friends.'

'What?'

'You heard. I saw you. On that stupid Stardust ride.'

She went redder than ever, and now she couldn't meet my eyes.

I couldn't stand to look at her either. She looked so stupid and flushed and girlie, like Angela swooning over her beloved rock group or Lisa dithering over Dave Wood. But she was Jo. She was my mother. She was mine.

I didn't say another word to her all evening. We both went to bed early but we didn't sleep. We tossed and turned separately, a great gap in the middle of the bed.

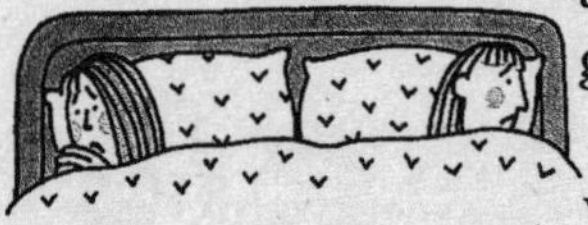

It still seemed like night-time when the phone rang. Jo sat up, looking dazed. 'Have I slept in for work?' she said.

I peered at the alarm clock. 'It's only three o'clock. So who on earth's phoning . . . ?' I said, as I jumped out of bed and ran into the living room. 'Hello?' I said, as I snatched up the phone. 'Hello, who is it?'

'It's Mark here, Charlie.'

I couldn't believe it!

'Can I speak to Jo, please? It's urgent.'

I dropped the receiver as if it were burning me. Jo came rushing into the room.

'Who is it? What's going on?'

'It's only your *friend*,' I said. 'And he says it's *urgent*. Well, would you mind asking him to save his urgent little lovey-dovey messages till it's actually daylight. I'd like to get some sleep before I go to school, if it's all the same to you two lovebirds.'

'Do shut up, Charlie,' said Jo, picking up the receiver. 'Mark? What is it?' She was silent for a few seconds.

I started to do a mime of exaggerated kissing and then pretended to puke. But then I saw the shock on her face and I stopped the pantomime.

'What's happened?' I said.

'It's Robin,' said Jo. 'It's little Robin, he's gone missing.'

The words sizzled in my brain like an electric shock.

'Missing?' I whispered.

Jo was asking Mark heaps of questions, and I could hear the frantic tone of his answers.

'You're *sure* he's not just hiding somewhere? Under his bed? In one of the cupboards? Let me come over and search,' said Jo.

More talk.

'No, I want to come anyway. I'll be with you in ten minutes,' said Jo, and hung up.

She ran to the bathroom. I followed her.

She was on the loo, cleaning her teeth at the same time, shaking her head to wake herself up. She shook it again at me.

'Look, Charlie, I can't take any sneering from you just now. This is nothing to do with Mark and me. It's serious.'

'I know,' I said, biting my knuckle. 'Has Robin really run away?'

'I don't know! Mark woke up and he just popped his head into Robin's room to check up on him – he'd been a bit funny when he put him to bed after the day out – and – and he wasn't there. Mark says he's searched everywhere. I don't see how Robin could have got out the door and run off somewhere, I mean, he's such a timid little thing – oh God, I keep thinking of awful possibilities . . .' Jo was nearly in tears as she rushed round the bathroom and then ran back into the bedroom, pulling on jeans and a jacket over her nightie.

I started yanking on my own clothes too.

'Charlie? Look, you'd better not come. Go back to bed. Maybe you could phone the supermarket later if I'm not back. And you get yourself off to school and—'

'No! I'm coming too! Oh, Jo, something awful will have happened to him, won't it?' I clung to her as if I were a tiny kid myself.

'Hey, hey. We'll find him. He'll be OK,' said Jo, although neither of us believed it. 'Someone will have found him wandering about and—'

'But that's what I'm scared of. What if some really

creepy pervert gets hold of him and—'

'Don't. No. Look, he'll have just wandered down the road – maybe sleepwalking, something like that – and he'll be curled up in a doorway somewhere, perfectly safe, sound asleep.'

'But it's cold out – really cold for a kid like Robin. And if he was just wearing his pyjamas . . .'

'Mark said his school jumper's missing too – and his slippers.'

The thought of Robin setting off in his new too-big school jumper, his pyjamas and his scuffed slippers made me bite my knuckle almost to the bone.

The lights were all on in Mark's flat – and there was a police car outside.

'There! They've found him,' said Jo, taking my hand and hauling us both up the stairs.

But they hadn't found him. Mark had called the police and was telling them over and over again how he'd looked in on Robin's room, and he wasn't in his bed, and he'd gone to the bathroom, he'd gone to the kitchen, gone round and round every room in the house, calling and calling . . . His voice was hoarse now, and his face looked dreadful, pale grey and shiny. He caught hold of Jo but this was different; he was just so desperate to get Robin back safe and she might be able to help.

I might be able to help.

I had to tell them.

I opened my mouth but I couldn't get the words out.

'Don't worry,' said this young policewoman, patting my shoulder. 'We're doing our very best to find him. We've sent out his description and everyone's searching. Children go missing every week – and they nearly always turn up safe and sound.'

'Not kids as little as Robin. It's all my fault,' I said. 'I made him run away. I even gave him that little cake with GET LOST on it.'

'Oh, come on, Charlie – that was silly, yes, but that's got nothing to do with it,' said Jo.

'But I said . . . I said all this hateful stuff . . . when we saw you kissing . . .' I waited.

Mark put his hands on my shoulders. His hands dug right into me. 'What did you say, Charlie?'

'I – I – it was so awful . . .'

'I don't care how awful. You've got to tell us. It might give us some clue where he's gone. I've been running round the streets this past hour, everywhere he goes, down to the shop on the corner, up the road to the park, he's not anywhere – I've looked, I've called – and yet how could he have got further, just wearing his slippers, and he hates going for walks, and he'd never go off willingly without me . . .' Mark's voice cracked.

'I told him you wouldn't want him any more,' I whispered. 'I didn't really mean it, I said I was joking, but – but it was a horrible thing to say to him, I'm so sorry, it made him cry in the car going home and I didn't tell and it's so awful and if anything's happened to him—'

'Nothing will have happened to him,' Jo said, putting her arm round me. We're nearly the same height and yet I seemed to have shrunk and she'd become a great big enveloping mother. 'We'll find him, I promise you, we'll find him.' She was promising Mark too, saying it over and over, trying to convince us.

'What did Robin say when you said all this?' Mark persisted.

'He mentioned his mum. Could he have run away to see her?' I asked.

'She lives in Manchester. How could he possibly . . . ? But I know he's been missing her ever since his last visit. Though he always said he wanted to stay with me when I talked to him about it. Oh, Charlie, *how* could you tell him I didn't want him?' said Mark, tears running down his face.

He wasn't angry with me. Yet. This was far worse. I started to cry too.

'It was a terrible thing to say but you were angry and upset,' said Jo. 'Everyone says terrible things when they feel really bad. Stop it Mark, she's only a kid herself. Can't you see how desperately sorry she is? Don't blame her, blame me. I forced her into that day out. She wasn't ready for it. We've been too close . . .'

I listened to Jo sticking up for me, making all these excuses. It made me feel worse, the worst person in the whole world.

Messages kept crackling over the police radio clipped to the policewoman's shoulder. We froze each time – but it was never to say they'd found him.

'I've got to go and search for him again myself,' said Mark.

'It'll be light soon. I should wait till then,' said the policewoman.

'But Robin's frightened of the dark—'

'He's probably tucked up in a corner somewhere, fast asleep. We've alerted everyone available. They're all searching. We've got the helicopter up too. It's got this special thermal imaging sweep that works even in the dark. The scanner picks up heat from the body—'

'The body?' said Mark, his voice cracking.

'From the person, from your little boy, and it gives off a green image. It's an amazing invention; we've had great success with it.'

But Mark couldn't wait, couldn't stay still, so he went off in one of the patrol cars cruising the area. Jo and I waited in his flat with the policewoman. She made us a cup of tea but when I drank it down it made me feel so sick I only just got to the toilet in time. I splashed cold water on my face afterwards and stared at myself in Mark's bathroom mirror. I felt I was looking at a murderer.

I've never really felt bad about myself before. I could be cheeky, I could be bossy, I could be fierce – but I'd always thought I was one of the good guys. If any little kid at school was getting bullied I'd always charge in and send the bully flying. If anything needed sorting out then all the other kids would turn to me. Everybody liked me. Even the boys.

But now I'd done the meanest thing in the whole world. It didn't matter that I was sorry. Robin had run away and maybe he was going to be lost for ever.

I felt myself folding up so that I was crouching on the bathroom floor, my head banging against the cold edge of the bath. I shut my eyes tight, banging and banging, trying to knock myself backwards, trying to make time tick backwards, so that I could undo and unsay everything. But no matter how I tried I couldn't stop the hands on my watch moving forward, and every minute Robin was still missing.

I heard the whirr of the police helicopter overhead. I wondered if they'd be able to spot Robin staggering along a grass verge, crouching down beside a hedge, curled beneath a tree. He might look up and show Birdie this immense mechanical relation . . . No, if he heard the whirling noise he'd probably be frightened and hide in a doorway, a cardboard box, behind a dustbin, and then he'd never be spotted.

I could see him so vividly in my head, crying, shivering with the cold, clutching Birdie desperately. And then I saw a sinister shadow beside him, someone reaching out and grabbing him, a hand over

his mouth so that he couldn't scream . . .

'Charlie? Charlie, let me in.' It was Jo, knocking on the door.

But I needed to stay in there by myself. I scrunched up tight into a ball and I closed my eyes and I mumbled, Please let Robin be all right, Please let Robin be all right, Please let Robin be all right, over and over, until the words concertinaed. I didn't dare stop even for a second – not until I heard the front door bang.

I rushed out of the bathroom. More police. And Mark – holding something small and shabby in his hands.

'Robin?' I whispered.

Mark shook his head. 'I went to the park,' he said, his voice breaking. 'It's still too dark to see properly, but I thought I'd check the pond – I always take him there to feed the ducks. And he's not there – no sign of him – but over by the gate the police officer stood on something. He thought it was a dead bird . . .'

Mark held out the cloth wings and the stained scarlet chest. Birdie.

LAW AND ORDER

Oh my Lord! Baby Freddie is missing and I fear it is all my fault.

I was worn out and near to despairing with all three children. Freddie kept me up half the night wailing and whimpering, then Louisa would *not* wear her proper day dress and insisted on putting on her party silk – and then spilt her porridge all down the front. Victor gave me cheek all morning and when I remonstrated he kicked me hard upon the shin.

I was so cross with my disagreeable and disobedient charges that when we were in the public gardens together I parked the perambulator and stormed off for a few moments by myself, calling all three children as many bad names as I could think of under my breath. When I had calmed down a little I went back again. There was no sound from the perambulator so I assumed baby Freddie had gone to sleep at last. Louisa was over by the pond, feeding the ducks with crusts of stale bread begged from Mrs Angel, while Victor bowled his hoop round and round the pond, singing a vulgar song at the top of his voice.

I told him to hush and begged Louisa to take care because she was standing right on the edge. Louisa took no notice and hurled a crust wildly, lost her balance and toppled over into the water! The pond is not deep but Louisa went headlong. I had to hitch up my skirts to wade in and grab her. Louisa clutched at me wildly, convinced she was drowning – and over I toppled too.

Victor shrieked with laughter at the pair of us. I had duck–weed streaming from my hair when I struggled out at last, Louisa under one arm. We were both sopping wet.

'Quick! Home at once before we catch our death of cold,' I said, shivering, conscious that we made a right spectacle. I took hold of the perambulator handle – and peered at the pillow. No baby Freddie! I pulled back the blankets frantically, tossing the pillow to one side. He was gone! I ran desperately around the perambulator, wondering if he could possibly have clambered out by himself. I wondered if Victor was playing another prank on me but one look at his white face made me see that this time he wasn't joking.

Someone had snatched baby Freddie and stolen

him away! I stopped passers–by and asked them if they had seen the little mite. Someone said they'd seen an infant in the arms of some scoundrelly looking creature and I started shrieking. I ran home with Victor and Louisa, pushing the empty perambulator. I had to tell the Mistress. I could scarce get the words out. She had a fit of the vapours at the terrible news and Eliza had to fetch the smelling bottle. Mrs Angel ran down the road to find her policeman friend and he took all the particulars. He swears he will search every thieves' den in the town, for he thinks Freddie has been stolen to be held to ransom. He is going to write to the police station in the neighbouring district, and a piece will be put in the *Police Gazette*.

He said that once he catches the varmint responsible he will have him publicly flogged and if he has harmed the baby then he will hang by the neck until he is dead.

Oh my Lord, I am so scared. If only I hadn't stormed off like that. If only I had kept a watch on the perambulator all the time! If only, if only, if only!

SICKNESS

'They'll find him,' Jo kept saying. 'He'll be in the park. Or nearby. They'll find him when it's light. He'll have just fallen asleep now, Mark, that's all.'

'The helicopter hasn't tracked him down. And we've looked everywhere. All over the park,' said Mark, hugging Birdie to his chest. 'We called and called. They're still there now, calling. If he was asleep he'd wake up and hear. He could be in the pond – they're going to dredge it. He could be lying in a ditch somewhere—'

'Don't think like that, Sir. There's no reason to think the worst,' said the policewoman. 'I've been with parents so many times, and they've been going through agonies like this but it's always turned out well in the end—'

'That's right, Mark. We've got to be positive,' said Jo, putting her arm round him. She held her other arm out to me. 'Come here, Charlie.'

But I couldn't go. I felt too ashamed.

Police came, police went. The phone rang but it was Mark's ex-wife, ringing from an all-night motorway café. She was on her way here with her new man, desperate to know if there was any further news. The policewoman made more tea, endless cups, although no-one took more than a few sips of each fresh brew. Someone switched on the radio at six and tuned it into the local station.

'*A five-year-old boy is missing from his home in Newcombe Way,*' said a voice. '*Little Robin West is small and slight, dark hair, dark eyes, believed to be wearing nightclothes and a grey sweater . . .*'

It made it all so horribly real hearing Robin's name on the radio. Everyone's head jerked at the sound.

More news bulletins kept tuning into my head. Imaginary ones with terrible news. I put my hands over my ears, but I couldn't block out the sound of my own thoughts.

Then the police radio crackled again, and the policewoman answered it.

'You're sure? He's OK?'

We all stared, hardly daring to hope.

'Robin?' said Mark, springing up.

'Yes, I think it is!' said the policewoman. 'Small boy, dark hair, found at the railway station. He'd crawled behind a whole pile of parcels awaiting delivery, so no-one spotted him at first.'

'He's all right?' said Mark, tears pouring down his face.

'I think so, Sir – but freezing cold, so they're taking him straight to the hospital. We'll take you there right away.'

'We have to go too,' said Jo, pulling me up.

I didn't dare believe it until we got to the hospital. I kept thinking it would be some other little boy – it couldn't be Robin because I was so sure he was lost for ever now, and that it was all my fault, and that I would hate myself for the rest of my life.

Jo knew, and held my hand very tight all the way there, and when Mark ran forward at the hospital Jo elbowed our way through too.

'She has to see him, just for a few seconds,' she said when nurses tried to catch hold of us.

There was something so commanding in her voice that they let us through. There were more nurses at a bed, a doctor with a stethoscope, a policeman, all circling a narrow bed containing a small tinfoil parcel like a chicken ready to be roasted for Sunday dinner. A flushed face peered out of one end, a smaller bird than a chicken. A Robin.

'Oh, Robin!' I whispered. 'It really is you!'

He didn't hear me. He was too busy blinking up at Mark.

'Daddy!' he said. 'What are you doing here?'

'What are *you* doing here, you silly sausage?' said Mark, and he bent and kissed the tiny bit of Robin that was exposed. 'Oh, Robin, you've led us a merry dance! What did you run away for? We've been so scared.'

'I was scared too. I wanted Mummy—'

'Mummy's coming. She'll be here soon. And you can see her for as long as you like. But Robin, you do know we *both* love you and want you. You're the most important little guy in my life. I was so frightened when I found your bed empty.'

'I had a nasty dream and I wanted Mummy so I got Birdie and we thought we'd go and see her.'

'In Manchester? But Robin, how could you possibly think you could walk to Manchester?' said Mark.

'You get the train. You took me once. We went through the park to the station so that's what we did, Birdie and me, but when we went past the pond the ducks woke up and quacked at us and scared us and then . . . and then . . .' Robin burst into tears.

'You dropped Birdie – but look, Robin, look!' said Mark, producing Birdie, who flew down onto Robin's chest, one wing touching his cheek. 'Birdie's got more sense than you, Robin. He flew home to Daddy.'

I wanted to talk to Robin myself, to tell him how sorry I was.

'Not now,' said Jo, pulling me away. 'He just needs Mark. And we don't want to be here when his mother comes. We'll go home.'

It seemed extraordinary to be back at our flat, having breakfast at the usual time. Whole weeks seemed to have gone by since yesterday.

'You ought really to go back to bed,' said Jo. 'You look exhausted.'

I was far too wound up to sleep. 'I still can't believe he's safe!' I said.

'I said he would be!' said Jo, hugging me.

'Don't, Jo. You've been so nice to me. When I was so wicked.'

'But you didn't mean it.'

'I should still be terribly punished.'

'Well, what do you want me to do? Whip you? Shut you up in a cupboard for a week? Shave all your lovely long hair off and paint you purple?'

'I mean it, Jo. I feel . . . bad. Robin *will* be all right now, won't he?'

'Yes, of course. Once they've got him all warmed up and checked over then I'm sure he'll be able to go home.'

'And can we go round and see him straight away?'

'Well, not if his mother's there too. I don't want to look as if I'm butting in. And maybe this might bring them back together again as a family . . .'

I didn't dare ask her if she'd mind terribly.

Jo went off to the supermarket to explain why she was so late – and I went to school.

Lisa and Angela came charging up to me the minute I set foot in the classroom.

'Hey, Charlie! Did you hear on the radio? That little boy who went missing, Robin. Isn't he the one your mum looks after?'

So I had to say yes, and then when I told them we'd been with Robin's dad half the night and that I'd actually seen Robin in the hospital they asked me dozens of questions, and practically all the class

gathered round wanting to hear. So I had to turn it into a proper story and spin it out a bit while they all gasped and exclaimed. They didn't even quieten down when Miss Beckworth swept into the room and told everyone to go to their seats.

'Miss Beckworth, Charlie's practically headline news, she helped find that little boy. Tell Miss Beckworth, Charlie!'

So I told the story all over again, though I was starting to tire of the whole tale. It didn't seem right that even Miss Beckworth seemed mildly impressed. But then she asked the one question I was dreading. Trust her.

'Why did the little boy run away, I wonder?'

I just shrugged and backed away to my desk, sharpish.

Jamie stared at me, looking a little puzzled. 'I love the way you tell things, Charlie. Making it ever so exciting and funny,' he said.

I made little slurpy noises with my lips, to show I thought he was sucking up to me.

'But did it all really happen?' Jamie persisted.

'Yes! What do you think I am, some kind of nutter with a compulsion to tell blatant lies to everyone?'

'But how come your mum looks after this little boy? I thought you said she was a lecturer, like mine?'

I took a deep breath, thinking hard. A blatant lie indeed. Well, call it an elaborate evasion. It was time for another.

'She lost that job, right? So for the moment she . . . she teaches little Robin.'

I had to tell my story all over again at playtime to kids in different classes, and they went off and told other kids, so that by dinner time it was all over the school. There were many different versions by this time. Some assumed that my mum and Robin's dad were already a definite item, which infuriated me.

Others gave me an even more prominent role in the story, so that I'd gone out in the early morning and tracked Robin through the park to the station all by myself. It was starting to turn into a story about how I'd saved little Robin's life.

It was a relief when school was over at last. I went rushing straight home, wondering if Jo would be round at Mark's place with Robin.

But she was at home, looking tired out herself, pulling fluff out of her bunny jumper, pick pick pick.

'Is Mark's ex-wife round at his place then?' I asked delicately.

'I think she's at the hospital. With Mark,' said Jo.

'What? Is Robin still there then?' I paused. 'He is OK, isn't he?'

Jo's fingers fidgeted down the sleeve of her fluffy jumper. 'Well, I'm sure he's going to be OK, yes, but . . .'

'But what? Tell me!'

'I don't really know much. Mark only had ten pence for the phone. He just said that the doctor was a bit worried about Robin's chest—'

'His chest?'

'Apparently he's always been slightly asthmatic, and he did get very chilled, so now he's got a touch of pneumonia.'

'Pneumonia! People die of pneumonia!'

'Now calm down, Charlie. There's no need to get yourself all worked up. I promise Robin's not going to die—'

'You promised he'd be as right as rain, out of hospital as soon as they'd got him warmed up.'

'Well, he *will* be as right as rain. They'll just need to give him some antibiotics.'

'And people always get completely better after pneumonia if they take antibiotics?'

'Well, nearly always. How do I know anyway?'

'Let's go and see him now.'

'I shouldn't imagine he can have too many visitors. He'll need to be kept quiet. He's got his dad – and his mum.' Jo's jumper was going to be picked bald quite soon.

'Couldn't we go to the hospital just to ask if we could see him for two minutes?' I said.

'No, we can't just keep pushing in,' said Jo.

I kept going on at her. I can always wear her down. I had to see Robin again. I hadn't been able to talk to him when he was trussed up in tinfoil like a tiny turkey. I had to tell him something.

But I still didn't get a chance. We found our way to the children's ward and it was still visiting time so we walked the long length of the polished floor, looking for Robin. There was no sign of him.

We walked back again, pausing at every bed. There was one empty one and I suddenly took Jo's hand.

'Can I help you?' said a nurse, hurrying past.

'We're looking for Robin West,' said Jo anxiously. 'He's the little boy who was lost.'

'Yes, I know. He's in the side ward up at the end – but I'm not sure he should have any more visitors,' said the nurse.

'There, Charlie,' said Jo. 'I told you.'

'Couldn't we just put our heads round the door to say hello?' I pleaded.

'I suppose you can take a quick peep, if you promise to be quiet,' said the nurse.

'As a mouse,' I said.

When we got near the side ward we walked on tiptoe, though the polish made our shoes squeak like real mice. We were still hand in hand. Our clasp was clammy.

I put my head round the door first. There was Mark, sitting right by the bed, his head in his hands. A pretty blonde woman with a pinched face was wiping her red eyes. And there was Robin lying very still in bed, his face milky white, his eyes closed. Birdie was on his chest, wings spread.

'He's dead!' I burst out, forgetting all about my promise to be quiet.

Robin stirred and whimpered.

'Who on earth . . . ?' said the blonde woman, glaring at me.

'What do you want, Charlie?' said Mark, standing up. His grey face was going patchy red with anger. 'Haven't you done enough?'

'I just wanted to say . . . I'm sorry,' I said.

'Oh, that makes all the difference in the world, does it?' said Mark.

Jo was tugging at me to get me to go. 'We shouldn't have come. We were both just so worried about Robin,' she muttered. 'Come *on*, Charlie.'

'He is going to get better, isn't he?' I said desperately.

Mark ignored me but touched Jo on the shoulder to reassure her. The blonde woman tightened her eyebrows.

'He's still got a high temperature but they're pumping him full of antibiotics and they keep saying he'll be fine,' he said. Then his eyes swivelled to me. 'No thanks to you.'

I let Jo tug me out of the doorway and out of the ward. We had to wait a long while for a bus outside the hospital and then it was a twenty-minute walk home. Jo kept talking to me but I hardly said anything.

She thought it was because I was scared of crying

in public. When we got home at last she put her arms round me and said, 'Right, you can let it all out now. Have a really good cry and then you'll feel better.'

I did cry a bit. Jo did too. I don't know whether she felt better. I didn't.

I felt really bad at school the next day. Angela and Lisa still kept on about Robin, asking if I'd seen him and how he was, wanting me to tell them all about it.

'Look, I don't really want to talk about Robin,' I said.

'What are you on about? You did nothing *but* talk about Robin yesterday,' said Lisa.

'OK, OK. That was yesterday. This is today, right? Let's talk about something *else*,' I said.

Angela immediately started burbling about the birthsigns of her beloveds and I groaned and pretended to gag.

'There's no need to take that attitude,' said Angela, hurt. 'You told me to talk about something else, so I did. There's no pleasing you sometimes, Charlie.'

'Hey, my dad says he's still taking us to the Red River Theme Park for my birthday,' said Lisa. 'Which rides are the best, Charlie? Come on, you didn't get a chance to tell us yesterday.'

'No!' I said fiercely.

'You can be a right pain sometimes, Charlie,' said Lisa huffily. 'There's me inviting you out on my birthday treat and yet you just shout at me.'

'Yeah, I can't stick it when you throw a moody like this,' said Angela. 'You think you can treat us like dirt, Charlie Enright, but we might just start to get fed up with it. Isn't that right, Lisa?'

'You bet,' said Lisa. 'Come on, Angela.'

They walked off across the playground arm in arm. I was left all by myself.

I decided I didn't care a bit. There were lots of other girls desperate to be my friend. Or even boys. Like Jamie.

I went and found him in his usual place, head deep in a book. Still *Tess of the d'Urbervilles*, but he'd nearly finished it, even though it's hundreds and hundreds of pages long.

'You'll go cross-eyed reading so much,' I said, flopping down beside him. 'Are you really enjoying that?'

'It's great,' said Jamie. 'Here, Tess murders this guy at the end, the one who had his wicked way with her – Alec.'

'The one she had the baby with?' I said. I tried to remember the film, but I just had this hazy picture of pretty girls in white frocks doing a dance, and afterwards Jo and I had done our own dance in our white nighties. 'Did Tess have a daughter or a son?'

'A little boy.'

'So what happens to him? I don't think there was a little boy in the film.'

'No, he dies when he's a baby.'

'What of?'

'I don't know. I don't think it says.'

'Babies don't just *die*.'

'They did then. Especially little puny ones. They just need to get a little cold and then it develops into pneumonia or something—'

'Shut up!' I shouted.

Jamie jumped. 'What's up?' he said. 'Hey, Charlie – where are you going?'

I didn't know where I was going. I wanted to get away from him, away from Lisa and Angela, away from the whole school . . .

I made for the gate, deciding to make a dash for it and bunk off school for the afternoon. But Miss Beckworth was on playground duty and her eagle eyes were beady-bright.

'Charlotte Enright! Where on earth do you think you're going, young lady?' she called.

I was so desperate I kept on running but I collided with a bunch of little kids coming back into school after going home for dinner. I tripped as I dodged them and fell flat.

I heard them squealing excitedly. Ominous footsteps paused by my side. I didn't try to get up. I just lay where I was – and cried.

'Out of the way, children. There's no need to gawp. Off you go. Shoo!' said Miss Beckworth. She seemed to be bending down beside me. 'Charlotte?'

I howled harder.

'I need to know if you've really hurt yourself badly and need medical attention,' said Miss Beckworth. 'Can you try and sit up so we can examine the damage?'

So I had to sit up, snivelling and snorting. I'd cut my knee and grazed the other, but it was nothing much. Certainly nothing to cry about. Though I was spouting like a fountain.

Some other kids were coming nearer, eyes popping at the sight of Charlie Enright bawling her eyes out.

'Will you go *away*, please?' Miss Beckworth said briskly. 'Charlotte, you'd better come with me.'

She put her hand under my armpits and got me to my feet. She walked me across the playground, shielding me from the stares. She took me right into school and sat me down in the empty classroom.

'There.' She looked at me, and felt up her sleeve for a tissue. 'Use this.'

I blew and mopped.

'That's better. Now. What's the matter?'

'I'm not crying because I fell over,' I said.

'I realize that.'

'And I'm not crying because I shouted at Jamie. Though I feel bad about that.'

'I expect Jamie's used to your shouting at him,' said Miss Beckworth drily.

'And I shouted at Lisa and Angela too and I think they've broken friends with me, but I'm not crying about that either,' I said.

'So . . . what are you crying about?'

I said nothing.

'The little boy who was lost?'

I nodded. 'He's ill. He's got pneumonia. Everyone says he's going to be all right, but I'm so scared that maybe . . .' I cried harder.

'Now, calm down, Charlotte. I haven't got any more tissues! You mustn't worry. Look, I've had pneumonia myself and I recovered perfectly. I know you're obviously very fond of this little boy—'

'No, I'm not! I've been horrid to him. *That's* why I'm crying. You think I'm being all kind and concerned but it's because I've been so bad.'

'Oh dear,' said Miss Beckworth. 'Go on. I think I'm pretty shockproof after twenty-five years of teaching. So tell me.'

So I did. All of it. And stuff about Jo and me from way back. Stuff I'd never dream of telling anyone – let alone *Miss Beckworth*.

She listened to it all – and then she put her arm round me and let me cry on her shoulder even though I was all slurpy and snotty.

'I know you think you're all-powerful, but the little boy didn't run away *just* because of you,' said Miss Beckworth. 'You're only a little part of all this. You were a bit silly and spiteful but you're truly sorry now – and you certainly didn't mean any of this to happen. I'm sure the little boy will get better.'

'You're really sure?' I said, sniffing. 'Because you're never wrong about anything, are you?'

'That's right!' said Miss Beckworth. 'Now, you'd better run along and wash that poor old face. Try to cheer up, Charlie.'

It wasn't until I was right along in the girls' cloakrooms that I realized. Miss Beckworth had called me *Charlie*!

SICKNESS

He's been found! I can scarcely believe it. Little Freddie is back with us – though we are all still so worried about the poor lamb because he is sick.

He wasn't taken by thieves and robbers. It was a woman half-demented because all her own babies had died. She watched us in the public gardens, she admired Freddie's chubby cheeks and golden curls – and when Louisa fell in the pond and I rushed in after her this woman snatched our Freddie and made off with him.

She was all set to make him her child, but her brain was so addled she scarcely fed our poor little boy and left his napkin unchanged. She covered him with just one thin sheet at night and of course the poor child caught a chill. She took fright as he grew dangerously sick and eventually she wrapped him in her cloak and left him on the doorstep of the foundling hospital. (She was observed and followed, and is now in police custody.)

The Master and Mistress were sent for when Freddie was found and great was their rejoicing – but their joy turned to terror when they saw the state of their poor darling. They took him home and we put him straight to bed and called the doctor. He listened to Freddie's rasping breathing and felt his fevered brow.

'There is nothing I can do,' he said sorrowfully. 'Keep him warm, feed him sugared water, and let us hope the Good Lord sees fit to spare him.'

The Mistress and I have been taking turns to nurse him. For once we are not like Mistress and servant at all. We are more like sisters, united in our desire for Freddie to recover. I feel as much for Freddie now as little Ada-May at home.

Victor and Louisa are being as good as gold. Eliza is looking after them, while I nurse Freddie. Mrs Angel is forever bringing him bowls of nourishing broth but the poor mite is too poorly to even suck the spoon.

Oh, please let him be saved!

SEASIDE

We were back to Charlotte the next day. We had English first lesson, one of those boring writing exercises – a formal letter of apology. It seemed a perfect opportunity to make things up with Lisa and Angela. (I didn't need to go to letter-writing lengths with Jamie as I was sitting right beside him. I could just give him a nudge and mumble, 'Sorry I yelled at you to shut up. You can tell me to shut up some time if you want.' Jamie blinked at me. 'I'd have to make sure you were in a good mood first!' he said – displaying his famous intelligence.)

Anyway, I got cracking with my apology letter. I think I did it beautifully, in my very best handwriting, no blotches, no smears. I put my address at the right-hand corner, I remembered the date, I flaunted an amazingly varied vocabulary, I didn't make a single spelling mistake, I signed off appropriately, and I even personally decorated my piece of paper. You look:

My Desk
Miss Beckworth's Class
Avondale Junior School

Truly Terrible Tuesday

Dear Lisa and Angela,

Do not rip this letter up in disgust when you see it's from the appalling, beastly, crosspatch, dolthead, egotistic, foul, gross, horrible, irritating, jealous, knavish, loathsome, mangy, nerve-wracking, odious, presumptuous, quarrelsome, ratty, spoilt, terrible, unkind, verminous, wicked, X-rated, yucky, zero called Charlotte Alice Katherine Enright (commonly known as Charlie), who used to be your friend. No wonder you both broke friends with me! I have been Utterly Foul (though with just cause seeing as I've had Terrible Things on my Mind) but that is no excuse to be hateful to you two, who are the dearest sweetest kindest friends any girl could ever wish for. And if I had a wish it would be this: Please will you make friends with me again?

Yours utterly sincerely – and with lots of luv and XXXXXXXX

Charlie

Jamie read my letter over my shoulder (I let him because I was trying so hard to be a new sweet person) and he cracked up laughing.

'That's a merry sound, James – but a little inappropriate in a classroom,' said Miss Beckworth. 'Please tell me why you're laughing.'

Jamie had long since stopped laughing. He had gone red and stammery. 'I – I was just clearing my throat, Miss Beckworth,' he said.

'I not only have all-seeing eyes, James. I also have all-hearing ears. You were not clearing your throat. You were laughing. Why?'

Jamie shifted desperately on his chair. He's so weird, he gets so worried the rare times he gets told off. I expected him to blurt out that he'd laughed because of my letter but he kept his lip buttoned to try to keep me out of trouble. Which was sweet of him, but a total waste of time.

Miss Beckworth was looking at me, eyebrows raised, one arm extended. 'Bring me that piece of paper, Charlotte. How dare you mess around instead of getting on with your set written work.'

'It *is* my written work, Miss Beckworth,' I said, taking it out to her.

She read my letter. For one second her lips twitched – and I thought I was going to be OK.

No such luck.

'This is *not* a formal letter of apology, Charlotte,' said Miss Beckworth.

'It *is* – sort of,' I insisted unwisely. 'You know what I'm like, Miss Beckworth. I always have to do things my way.'

'I appreciate that, Charlotte. There is just one small point you seem to have missed. This is my class, not yours. In my class we do things *my* way. And you will do me a proper sensible sticking-to-the-rules formal letter of apology now, and you will write out another *five* formal letters of apology, all different, at home tonight. That might make you reflect a little and learn that it makes more sense to do things my way right from the start.'

That was the most amazingly atrocious punishment of all time – especially as I wanted to do something extremely important and very time-consuming that evening. But even I realized it would be unwise to argue further. It seemed utterly unbelievable that such a cruel unbending beastly teacher could have let me cry all over her jumper just yesterday, but there you go.

The one weeny good thing was that she gave me my original letter back, so I could give it to Angela and Lisa at playtime. They laughed too. Lots. And we're best friends all over again, so at least that's something.

I got started on my five foul letters the minute I got home. It took me ages but I knew it would be foolish to fudge them. I actually wrote a sixth letter, just a little one.

Dear Miss Beckworth,

This is partly yet another formal letter of apology. I am sorry I mess around at everything. I will truly try to do things your way. Though it will be very very difficult.

This is also an informal letter of thanks. Thank

you for letting me say all that stupid stuff on Monday. Sorry I used up your tissues! And you were right, because Robin is lots better!

Yours sincerely,

Charlotte

Mark might have made it plain that he wanted nothing to do with me, but he phoned Jo to tell her that Robin's temperature had gone down, his chest was clear, and the antibiotics were obviously doing their job well.

'So is Robin properly awake now, sitting up and able to look at things?' I asked.

'Yes, but I'm not taking you to the hospital again, no matter what you say,' said Jo.

'It's OK. I can see we can't go. Mark really hates me now, doesn't he?' I said.

'No, of course he doesn't. He's just still terribly wound up and anxious over Robin,' said Jo.

'And he blames me.'

'He wasn't thinking straight.'

'Look, *I* blame me. But it's just sort of weird. Being hated by someone.'

'He doesn't hate you, I keep saying that. And anyway, it doesn't even matter if he does because you don't have to see him ever again. He probably won't want me to work for him any more, let alone . . .' Jo's voice tailed away. She looked so miserable I couldn't bear it.

'Jo? I'm sorry I've mucked things up for you and him,' I mumbled.

Jo gave me a push. 'What rubbish! You're not the slightest bit sorry about that, Charlie! You did your level best to spoil things right from the start. And I don't know why you're carrying on about Mark not liking you, because you made it amazingly plain that you hated him.'

'Yes, I know. I couldn't stand it when he smarmed all over me, and kept trying to take my side. But now . . . I still don't like him but I want him to like me.'

'That's just typical of you, you spoilt brat,' said Jo. 'Have you finished all your letters? Shall we go to bed and watch telly for a bit?'

'*You're* the one that spoilt me! Not that I blame you, of course. Seeing as I'm so chock full of charm.'

'Ha! Come on, I can't be too late. I daren't mess them about at the supermarket after missing my Monday shift.'

'I want to do a bit of drawing first. You go. I promise I won't wake you if you go to sleep first, I'll creep in ever so quietly.'

I sat up for hours doing my drawing. I drew a bed in the middle of the page, with a pale little boy and a tiny toy bird propped up on the pillows. Then in all the rest of the space I did an immense flock of birds come to wish Robin and Birdie better. I did great eagles and albatrosses swooping round the ceiling, parrots and cockatoos and canaries singing silly songs, soft doves fanning him with their feathers, lovebirds billing and cooing above his head, tiny wrens whizzing every which way while swallows

flitted in strict formation, ostriches and emus picking their way cautiously across the polished floor, little fluffy chicks cheeping in clumps, proud peacocks spreading their tails as screens around the bed.

I coloured it all in as carefully as I could, until my

eyes watered and my hand ached. But it was done at long last – and I just hoped Robin would like it.

Jo came rushing in to tell me *she* liked it at half past five in the morning.

'Hey! I didn't wake you up last night,' I grumbled under the covers. 'Can you stick it in an envelope and post it to Robin at the hospital?'

Jo said she would – but when I got home from school that day she told me she'd taken it to the hospital herself.

'It would have spoilt it, folding it all up to fit into an envelope. So I took it to the hospital after I'd been to the Rosens'. I was just going to give it to one of the nurses but then I bumped into Mark quite by chance . . .'

'Oh yeah!'

'What are you looking at me like that for? Anyway, he seemed quite happy about me having a peep at Robin, and he's doing wonderfully. They think he can come out of hospital by the end of the week. And I showed him your picture and he just loves it, Charlie; he spent ages and ages looking at all the different birds and now he's got it pinned up on the wall beside his bed. Mark was so pleased. He looks a bit better himself now that Robin's recovering. He's taken the next week off his work too, and he's talking about taking Robin to the seaside.'

'With Robin's mum?'

'Ah. No. She's had to go back to Manchester – when she knew Robin was going to be all right.'

'Has that upset him?'

'Well. He obviously misses his mother a great deal, but Mark was always the one who looked after him most even when they were together.'

'She looked a right cow to me,' I said.

'Charlie!' said Jo. But she looked pleased.

'What about Mark? Does he miss her too?'

'Well . . . He doesn't seem to, no. He said things were never very good between them, and they had all these rows—'

'Yeah, listen and proceed cautiously, Josephine! *That's* what marriage is all about. Rows,' I said, wagging my finger at her. 'Don't you dare think of ever getting married, right?'

I did another picture for Robin that night. This time I drew him in a warm red woolly jumper with a pair of massive feathery wings sticking out the back, brown to match his trousers, real robin colours, and he and Birdie were flying over the sea with a flock of sea-gulls, and they all had sticks of rock or candy-floss

or portions of fish and chips in their beaks and way down below there was a beach and everyone was waving and pointing and smiling up at them.

Jo took it in to Robin at the hospital. This time I got my own picture back. It was a portrait of me. Well, it had my name on it in very wobbly letters. My hair was an orange scribble right down past my knees. My eyes were crossed. My arms stuck straight out of my neck. My legs were mostly hidden beneath a triangle of green frock, but my feet were vast and stuck out sideways.

'Hmmm,' I said. 'Is this supposed to be flattering?'

'He tried ever so hard,' said Jo. 'This was his third attempt.'

'What's this pointy thing sticking in me? A dagger? Did Mark add that?'

'It's an arrow, pointing to you, to show you're Charlie. And Mark doesn't want to stick any daggers in you, you daft girl. In fact he wants you to come to the hospital tomorrow to see Robin.'

'Oh, wow, His Lordship has given his orders, eh?' I said.

'Charlie?' said Jo. 'Oh, don't be like that.'

'Don't look so worried. I'll go. To see Robin.'

'Are you going to do him another picture?'

'How about one he can eat?'

I wanted to make him a proper robin cake in the shape of a bird, but I couldn't work out how to do it, and the wing tips and little claws would be far too fiddly and break off. So in the end I made two ordinary round sponges and sandwiched them together with lots of butter cream and jam and then I made up this super brown butter icing with a bit of cocoa powder and smeared it over most of the cake, doing an extra feathery layer each side for wings, and then I stuck on two brown smarties for eyes and a yellow one for the beak, and I filled in the gap with new bright-red butter icing.

It all took much longer than I'd thought, and the robin cake still didn't look quite right.

'It's wonderful!' said Jo.

'No, it looks like the robin's been severely squashed,' I said, sighing.

I really wanted to stay up all night and try again, but I'd used up all the eggs and icing sugar and practically half our housekeeping money, so I couldn't.

I kept worrying about the stupid cake the next day at school. Or maybe I was worrying about going to the hospital. Or something.

I took my time going home from school.

'Come on, what kept you?' said Jo. 'We won't get there in time for Robin's tea at this rate.'

'I don't feel like trailing all the way over there,' I said. 'You go.'

'After you've made Robin the fantastic cake?'

'It's a stupid cake. But you can take it if you think he'd really like it.'

'You're the one that's being stupid. Dump your schoolbag, find your jacket, and let's get cracking,' said Jo. Firmly.

So I went to the hospital clutching my cake in a tin. Mark didn't smile at me, but he nodded. Robin put his head on one side shyly, but he had this great big grin on his face.

'It's *Charlie*!' he whispered – as if I were someone important.

I don't like little kids much. Especially little boys. But somehow I dumped my cake tin and put my arms round Robin and gave him a great big hug. He'd always been a skinny little thing but now he felt like one of those little glass animals that snap off an arm or a leg when you just look at them. I tried not to hug him too hard in case I hurt him. Then I had to hug Birdie too. His general appearance hadn't been improved by Robin's recent adventures. I didn't really enjoy having this filthy piece of cloth rubbed round my face, but I didn't complain.

My cake had got a bit bashed about inside the tin, but it was still just about recognizable as a robin. The real Robin didn't want to cut it at first, but I made Birdie pretend to be starving hungry and nibble a corner of the cake, so Robin gave in.

It wasn't a work of art *ornithologically* (ha!) but it certainly tasted good. Robin had a great big slice. So did Mark and Jo and two nurses and a couple of kids in the main ward that Robin had made friends with. I had a great big slice as well. Two, actually, just to check it tasted good all the way round.

'It's a lovely cake,' said Mark, giving me another

nod. Then he smiled at Jo. 'I expect you helped Charlie with it?'

I spluttered. 'Jo can't even make *toast*!'

I felt like clouting him with the cake tin. But I didn't. I sensed our relationship was still dead precarious. I still couldn't stick him. I didn't ever want to make friends with him. But I did want to be friends with Robin.

Mark took him to the seaside the next week. Bournemouth. I'd never been there.

'I have,' said Jo. 'Your grandma and grandpa used to take me there on holiday when I was little. In a big white hotel and they played tennis all day and whist in the evening and I just mooched about, too shy and stupid to make friends with any of the other kids.'

'Aaaaah!' I said, teasing her. 'Don't worry, *I'll* play with you next time we go to the seaside.'

'We could go to Bournemouth on Saturday,' said Jo, trying to sound casual. 'Meet up with Robin and Mark. Mark phoned and suggested it.'

Jo still had to do her supermarket shift early Saturday morning, but I met her at eight o'clock and we went straight to the station and set off for Bournemouth. Robin and Mark met us off the train. Robin looked a bit bigger and bouncier out of bed, though he was so well wrapped up against the sea breeze that he could barely move. Birdie's appearance had deteriorated even more because he'd dived into the sea by mistake when Robin was paddling in wellie boots – but at least he'd had a good wash.

It was a bit nippy for the beach but we walked right along the sands and I laboured long and hard making a sandcastle for Robin. He twittered beside me and Jo and Mark billed and cooed in the background. I was beginning to think I'd maybe done enough hard labour and that it was time I was let off for good behaviour – but I perked up a little when Mark bought us all ice creams.

It was far too cold to go swimming in the sea, of course, but we went to the Leisure Pool instead. Birdie took a nap in a locker while Robin splashed around happily with me. Robin still looked a bit too thin stripped to his bathing costume but he was very perky. Mark looked a right berk in his trunks. I practically fell about laughing.

We spent ages drying every tiny bit of Robin afterwards and wrapping him back in his one hundred and one layers and then we had hot chocolate to make sure he was well and truly warmed up before going out into the wind.

We went on the pier and Mark spent a small fortune on the cuddly-toy cranes. He's useless at them . . . but *eventually* he won a lop-sided parrot for

Robin and a simpering blue bunny for Jo. And then he got this hideous bug-eyed troll with long orange hair – and gave it to me.

I wasn't particularly charmed with that little seaside souvenir. But I tell you what I *did* get. There's an amazing museum place in Bournemouth called the Russell-Coates Gallery. It's this big Victorian house and it's stuffed full of everything Victorian and I went round and round peering at everything, pretending I'd really stepped back into the past. No nurseries, though – my Lottie wouldn't have had a job.

Robin needed to have a wee so I took him into this lavatory – and it was a genuine Victorian one, with a special picture down the pan and a great big wooden seat. I tried it out too.

I hoped I'd be able to buy a postcard of it, but no such luck. I bought lots of other postcards, though. Not for Lottie's diary. It had become obvious to me that Miss Beckworth was not going to approve of my project. It was very much *my* way, not hers. And yet there was no way I was going to change it now. So I decided if I couldn't win a prize for best Victorian project then I might as well make sure that Jamie did. I bought all the postcards for him.

SEASIDE

Dear little Freddie pulled through! One night his fever rose alarmingly and he didn't know any of us and we all really felt this was the end – but towards dawn he quietened and grew calm and suddenly opened his eyes and said 'Mamma' as clear as anything. He took a long drink and then settled down into a peaceful sleep. He woke at lunchtime almost his old self, though his sweet curls were all in a tangle and his face pale and drawn. He lapped up all his broth and made it plain that he wanted more.

The Mistress cried, Mrs Angel cried, Eliza cried – and oh how I cried too!

We were all so tired and strung out watching over little Freddie that the Master decided to take a week away from his business and hire rooms for us all at the seaside as soon as Freddie was fit to travel.

We went on the steam train, an amazing adventure! Victor was beside himself with glee, asking questions nineteen to the dozen – and Louisa insisted on sticking her head out of the window and got herself covered in sooty smuts.

It was dark when we arrived at long last and there was such a to-do getting the children to bed and all our belongings unpacked that I simply crawled into my own bed and fell fast asleep while Eliza and Mrs Angel were still joshing and giggling (we three share a room in the seaside lodgings and it is very companionable). But I awoke early. I looked in on Freddie but he was still fast asleep, and there wasn't a peep from Louisa or Victor either. So I wrapped myself in my cloak and ran down to see the sea.

I could not believe it. I knew it would be a very large stretch of water, but I'd pictured it like the river at home. I had no idea it would shimmer as far as the eye could see. And it moved so, wave after wave rolling over and over.

It was very cold in the early morning air but I tore my boots and stockings off and paddled in the shallows just to say I had done it! A fat old woman told me I could use one of her bathing machines if I cared to, but I was happy enough just to let the water whirl about my ankles. My feet were blue with cold all morning but I didn't care.

Then, when I took the three children to the beach later that morning there was an ice-cream man selling hokey-pokey for a penny a lump, even though it was the winter season. I had three pennies so I bought one for Louisa, one for Victor, and one for Freddie and me to share.

My first ice cream! This time my lips turned blue but I licked them warm again.

I still cannot say I enjoy being a servant – but it has its compensations!

CHRISTMAS

Jamie's Victorian project *did* win. Well, it was obvious it was going to. It was easy-peasy, simple-pimple to work it out. Though my postcards from Bournemouth certainly helped. They made Jamie's project much thicker and the pages clicked enticingly as you turned each page. These postcard pages were so bright and glossy that Miss Beckworth couldn't *help* being dazzled. All right, she puts lots of ticks and stars and *Well Dones!* on his sections on railway engines and factories and coal mines, and she liked his town and country pages and all his maps in the British Empire bit, and she went a bit overboard on his Crimean War with an *EXCELLENT!* underlined. My postcards just got a tick or two, but that was obviously because she didn't want to deface the beauty of the page.

Miss Beckworth held Jamie's project up and showed it to the class and all the goodie-goodies went Oooh and Aaah and all the baddie-baddies went Yuck and Boring and Swot and Teacher's Pet. I would normally count myself the baddest baddie-baddie – and yet I found myself thumping old Jamie on the back and saying, 'Well done, Clever Clogs.'

He went very red when I said that. Maybe I thumped a bit too hard. Then he had to go up to Miss Beckworth and shake her hand and *she* said 'Well done' too. She said she'd like to give him a little prize. She gave him a £5 book token and a little painted Victorian soldier. Jamie was dead chuffed.

I couldn't help feeling a bit wistful then. I waited for Miss Beckworth to hand out the rest of the projects. I was sure mine would have red lines all through it and *SEE ME, CHARLOTTE!* in cross capitals. But you'll never ever guess what! Miss Beckworth paused theatrically.

'Jamie's brilliant project tells us almost all there is to know about Victorian times. But there's one other project here that tells us what it *feels* like to be a Victorian.' And she held out MY project!!! 'I'm so impressed with your diary of Lottie the Nursery Maid that I'd like to award you a prize too, Charlotte.'

'Great! Good for you, Charlie,' said Jamie.

Yep! Good for me! Miss Beckworth beckoned me out to the front of the class and I had to go through the hand-shaking ceremony too, which was OK – but I kept thinking, am *I* getting a prize like Jamie? And I did! A £5 book token, and a tiny reproduction china doll the size of my little finger.

'Oh, she's sweet! Thank you very much, Miss Beckworth,' I said.

'Do you know what they used to call that sort of doll? They were called Frozen Charlottes,' said Miss Beckworth, and she actually grinned at me.

I appreciated her little joke. I actually sort of appreciated *her* for once. She asked me to read out some of my diary entries for Lottie. So I did. Everyone got a bit shuffly and sighing to start with – but by the time I'd got to the bottom of the first page *they were riveted*! I read on and on and not a single person said Yuck, so there!

Lisa and Angela got a teensy little bit snotty afterwards. Lisa especially, because her dad had done all her Victorian project on his posh computer with special loopy writing and graphics and it hadn't even had a special mention.

'You're really getting to be a teacher's pet now, Charlie,' said Lisa. 'I don't know who's the swottiest now, you or your precious Jamie.'

'He's not mine. And he's not precious either, come to that,' I said, snorting.

'*We* saw you putting your arm round him when his project won,' said Angela, giggling away.

'Purlease!' I said. 'Don't be so pathetic, Ange.'

'You're the one that's pathetic, Charlie, getting all matey with Jamie Edwards. He's the nerdiest boy in the whole class.'

'So?' I said fiercely.

'So what do you *see* in him?' said Lisa.

'He can be quite good fun sometimes. OK, he

does look a bit weird—'

'You're telling me!' said Lisa.

'And he wears the grottiest clothes,' said Angela.

'Yes, right, he's a total Arnie-Anorak, but I don't care.'

'She's gone off her rocker,' said Lisa to Angela.

'Completely nuts,' said Angela to Lisa.

'Yeah, you're mad, Charlie. You could probably get any boy in our class keen on you – well, apart from Dave Wood – yet you choose *Jamie* for a boyfriend.'

'He's NOT my boyfriend. You two aren't half slow at catching on. He's a friend who happens to be a boy – OK a nerdy, grotty, swotty boy – but so what?' I shouted. A little too loudly. Jamie himself came out the boys' cloakroom and stared. Lisa and Angela doubled up laughing. I felt myself going red. Totally screamingly scarlet.

'Better leave the two lovebirds together,' said Lisa, and she tugged Angela away.

They went giggle giggle giggle down the corridor.

'Idiots,' I muttered. I blew hard up my nostrils, fluttering my fringe. 'Phew, isn't it hot in here?' I paused. 'What are you staring at?'

'Did you just say I was nerdy and grotty and swotty?' Jamie asked.

'Oh,' I groaned. 'No.'

'I heard you,' said Jamie, looking wounded.

'Well, all right, yes. But it wasn't my description,' I said.

'So everyone thinks I'm nerdy and grotty and swotty,' said Jamie.

'No. Yes. Well, a few of the girls maybe. And the boys. Don't look all upset, Jamie, I'm trying to make things better.'

'I'd hate it if you were trying to make things worse then,' said Jamie.

'Look, you're not daft, you must have twigged that's what they think,' I said.

'You *are* making it worse,' said Jamie.

'But you don't really care, do you, Jamie?'

'Don't I?' said Jamie.

'Well, *I* don't care what anyone thinks of me,' I said.

'Yes, but that's because everyone likes you,' said Jamie.

'No they don't. Not even Lisa and Angela much, and they're supposed to be my best friends.'

'And . . . did you say *I* was your friend too?' said Jamie, looking a bit perkier.

I shrugged. 'Mmm,' I said.

'You mean it? We're really friends? Even though I'm a boy? And a nerdy grotty swotty one at that?' Jamie didn't seem at all upset now. I wondered if he'd been pretending before. I wouldn't put it past him.

'I generally can't stick boys,' I said. 'But you're OK.'

'So are you,' said Jamie.

We stood there looking at each other. For two ultra-chatty people we suddenly seemed lost for words. And then there were these s-t-u-p-i-d slurpy kissy-kissy sounds. Angela and Lisa had crept back towards us.

'Look at them!'

'Gazing into each other's eyes, dumb-struck!'

'Go on then, Jamie, kiss her.'

'They'll be snogging at the school disco next week!'

They collapsed with laughter.

'Take no notice,' said Jamie calmly. 'Let the lower mortals prattle.'

'You what?' said Lisa.

'He's talking in some foreign lingo now,' said Angela.

'See if you two can understand plain English then,' I said – and I used some very short sharp shocking words to indicate that I wanted them to go away.

'Who is using that disgusting language?' said a familiar voice.

A teacher came stalking down the corridor. The one with the all-hearing ears. You've guessed right.

She gave me a detention too, even though it wasn't really my fault at all that I'd been reduced to blunt language. But I still felt *quite* fond of her, even though she was always so snappily strict. So when our top year had our special disco party and Miss Beckworth organized it and asked us to bring some refreshments from home I went overboard.

I went round to Jamie's house and hunted through the Victorian books – and found a great big fat one with lots of recipes called *Mrs Beeton's Book of Household Management*. I flipped through it until I found the *perfect* cake.

It needed quite a lot of ingredients but that was no problem. (For reasons I will divulge later!)

It took ages to make the special cake. I had to make this special lemon jelly and then pour a little bit into a big tin and then stud it with glacé cherries like jewels, and then I did another layer of jelly and stood sponge fingers all the way round the tin and *then* I made a special eggy custard and poured that on and let it all set and THEN the next day I dunked the tin very quickly in hot water and then, holding my breath and praying, I gently tipped it out onto a pretty plate like a little kid turning out a sandcastle. You know what often happens with sandcastles? They crumble and break, right? But my special Victorian cake came out whole and perfect, easy-peasy, simple-pimple.

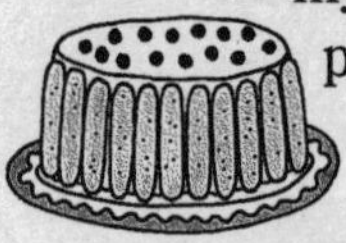

It was a bit of a mega-problem getting it to school, though. I had to carry it on a tray and hope it wouldn't rain. My arms were aching terribly by the time I got to school. I was a bit late too, because I'd had to walk so carefully to keep my cake intact.

'Charlotte Enright, you're late for school,' said Miss Beckworth.

'Only half a second, Miss Beckworth. And it's in a very very good cause,' I said, propping my heavy tray on a desk and peeling back the protective tinfoil I'd arched over it.

'And what's this very good cause, might I ask?' said Miss Beckworth.

'You!' I said, pulling the last of the foil off with a flourish. 'I've made you a cake, Miss Beckworth. Well, it's for all of us at the disco, but it's in your honour and you've got to have the first slice. It's a Victorian cake. And you'll never ever guess what it's called!'

Miss Beckworth looked at my wondrous masterpiece. She blinked her all-seeing eyes. They twinkled as she met my gaze.

'I *can* guess,' said Miss Beckworth. 'In your own ultra-irritating phrase, it's easy-peasy, simple-pimple! It's an absolutely magnificent Charlotte Russe.'

She really *is* all-knowing! We shared the cake-cutting ceremony when it was nosh-time. I got a bit worried my Charlotte cake would collapse, but it stood its ground splendidly. And it tasted great too, mega-yummy. It was all gone in a matter of minutes – just a lick of lemon jelly and a few sponge crumbs left on the plate.

I made sure all my special friends got a slice. Then the disco started up. It wasn't a *real* evening disco with a proper DJ and strobe lighting. It was just an afternoon Christmas party in the school hall for

Year Six, with the headmaster playing these mostly ropy old discs. Hardly the most sophisticated exciting event of the century – though you'd maybe think it was, judging by the fuss Lisa and Angela and some of the other girls made.

We were allowed to change into our own home clothes, you see. The boys didn't think it much of a big deal. They looked *worse* out of school uniform.

I didn't try too hard either. I was too busy creating my cake to fuss about my outfit. And I can't actually win when it comes to cool clothes way in the front line of fashion. My kit comes from the label-free zones of Oxfam, Jumble and Car Boot Sales, especially nowadays. Though this might change soon. (Second hint of changes in the Enright family fortunes!)

Lisa and Angela and lots of the other girls tried very hard indeed. Lisa looked particularly lovely.

But Angela was the big surprise. She usually wore ordinary old jeans and jumpers when we were hanging round after school. But now her mum had bought her this new party-time outfit down the market. Angela's got too tall for kids' clothes so this was really grown-up gear. And Angela looked ultra-adult in it too.

'Look at *Angela*!'

You couldn't help looking at her. Everyone did. It was as if she'd become an entirely new girl to match her new outfit. When she danced the boys all circled round. Even Dave Wood.

Jamie's jaw dropped when he saw Angela too, but he didn't try to dance with her. He didn't dance with anyone at first. I danced with lots of people. Then I went and stood near Jamie. I waited. It started to get on my nerves.

'Come on, Jamie. Let's dance,' I said commandingly.

'I don't think I'm very good at dancing,' said Jamie.

He was right about that. He just stood and twitched a little at first.

'Let yourself *go* a bit,' I said, jumping about.

Jamie let himself go a bit too much. His arms and legs shot out all over the place. I had to stay well back to stop myself getting clouted. But I suppose he was trying.

Lisa was standing near us. I prepared myself for some ultra-sarcastic comments. But Lisa's eyes were a little too bright, her smile showing too much teeth. She wasn't watching Jamie and me. She was watching Angela and Dave.

'Hey, Jamie. I want to dance with Lisa for a bit,' I said.

'Good! I need a rest,' Jamie puffed.

So I danced with Lisa for a bit. And then I danced with some of the other girls. And some other boys. So did Lisa. And at long last Dave Wood came slithering up to her, because he'd been elbowed away from Angela by the rest of the boys. I expected Lisa to send Dave Wood off with a flea in his ear. I'd have added a swarm of stinging wasps and a buzz of killer bees. But would you believe it, Lisa just gave him this stupid smirk and danced with him devotedly. Lisa has got a very pretty head but it contains *no brain whatsoever*.

'Do you want to dance again, Charlie?' Jamie asked eagerly. 'I think I'm getting the hang of it now.'

He was a little optimistic. But we had fun all the same. The party ended at three and we were allowed to go home then.

Lisa and Dave Wood went off together, so she was happy.

Angela went off with half the boys in our class, so she was happy.

I decided to go back to Jamie's house because I was still a bit peckish in spite of my Charlotte Russe (the other refreshments weren't up to much) and I fancied one of his brother's toasted cheese sandwiches. We walked along Oxford Terrace together. I peered up at all the attic rooms right under the roofs and imagined Lottie looking out.

Jamie kept walking closer and closer to me, so that his schoolbag banged my shins several times. I turned to tell him off – and he kissed me on the cheek!

'What are you playing at?' I said furiously.

'I – I – well, you kept sticking your chin

up and looking up in the air so I thought you wanted me to kiss you,' Jamie stammered.

'Well, you got it seriously wrong, matie,' I said, giving him a shove. I scrubbed at the little wet patch on my cheek with the back of my hand. 'You do that again and I'll clock you one,' I said.

'Don't worry, I won't,' said Jamie. He sighed. 'I wish I could figure girls out. I especially wish I could figure *you* out, Charlie.'

'It's part of my deeply mysterious feminine charm,' I said, chuckling.

Jamie's brother came up trumps with another toasted sandwich and his mum asked if Jo and I could go round to their house on Boxing Day. They have a party every year. Jo got a bit worried when I told her and said she didn't think it sounded her cup of tea – well, glass of punch – but she's agreed to come with me because I've been astonishingly agreeable about *her* Christmas plans.

I shall give Jamie his Christmas present then. I've bought him a big fat paperback Victorian novel. *Jane Eyre* – by Charlotte Brontë, and inside the cover I've written: *This is a present by a Charlotte, from a Charlotte!*

I'm going to make Jamie's mum a special cake to eat at her party. I've got it all worked out. It's going to be a square cake, iced all over with a cake lid on top and marzipan ribbon, so it looks like a special gift box – for Boxing Day, get it?

I'm going to be so busy busy busy

making cakes in the Christmas holidays. I've got to make one for Grandma and Grandpa when Jo and I go over there on Christmas Eve – yuck! I had all sorts of good ideas but Jo talked it over with me and she thinks they'd like an ordinary conventional Christmas cake, white icing and HAPPY CHRISTMAS, boring boring boring – but I've said I'll do it.

I'm making one more cake – and this one's a special one.

Jo fixed a beautiful red breakfast in bed for us on Sunday (ruby grapefruit and raspberry Danish pastries and cranberry juice). When we'd eaten it all up we cuddled down in bed again and I started up one of our games and Jo tried to join in but I could tell she wasn't concentrating.

'Jo? What is it, eh?' I could feel her tense.

'Well . . . I want to talk to you about something,' she said.

I felt as if all the delicious red food inside me was being whisked in a blender. This was it. I knew what she was going to say. I wriggled away from her and lay stiffly in bed, waiting.

'It's about . . . Robin,' she said.

'And Mark,' I said, through clenched teeth.

'Well. Yes, I suppose so. Oh, Charlie. I don't know how to say this.'

'I'll say it for you,' I said. 'It's easy-peasy, simple-pimple. You

and Mark are going to get married and Robin's going to be my little brother and you'll be giving up all your jobs to look after him full-time and we'll have to sell our flat and go and live with them and I expect you want me to make you a flipping wedding cake as well, but if I have to come to your wedding I warn you, I won't throw confetti, I'll start throwing rocks at you,' and I turned over on my tummy and started to cry.

'What?' said Jo. '*What?*' And she started to laugh.

'It's not funny!' I sobbed. 'I want to stay here. With you. Just the two of us.'

'So do I,' said Jo. She shoved my tangled hair out of the way and said it straight into my ear. '*So do I!* That's what we're going to do. Now listen, Charlie! You've got it all wrong. Mark and I aren't getting married. He's still too fussed about his first marriage – and I don't think I ever *want* to get married. OK?'

'So you don't love him?'

'I don't know what I feel. I just want to let things develop. Slowly. In their own time. I hope I'll still see a lot of Mark and Robin – but I might not carry on working there. You know this Christmas job?'

You don't know about the Christmas job. Jo's stopped working at the Rosens'. The last big electrical goods shop in the town advertised for part-time staff to help them out over their busy Christmas trading time. Jo jumped in there and they took her on right away, working from nine to three. So we've got enough to keep up the mortgage payments – *and* a bit over. *That's* what I was hinting at earlier.

'You mean it's too tiring, working there and then going to look after Robin?' I said, leaning up on my elbows.

'The thing is, the shop manageress is going to have a baby. She wants to start her maternity leave in January – and even though I'm only temporary they're asking if I'm interested. It won't be for ever, of course, though she might decide she wants to stay at home with the baby – but it would still be great to get back to the work I like. But of course it would be full time, through till half past five.'

'I see. Well. You'll have to take it, Jo. I mean, it's great. But . . . what about Robin? He likes you a lot.'

'He likes you even more, Charlie. Mark hopes he'll be able to juggle his working hours and pick Robin up from school himself. Or maybe he'll have to find another child-minder. But in an absolute emergency I said you could always pick Robin up from school and look after him until Mark could come.'

'Mark wouldn't ever trust me with Robin!' I said.

'Yes he would. He knows that you're really very sensible and responsible,' said Jo.

'Me?' I said. 'OK. Tell Mark he can count on me. As long as he pays me!'

'Charlie!'

'So we can really stay here in our own flat, Jo?'

'You bet.'

'And we'll have our first Christmas here, just us two?'

'Ah. Well. That's the other thing I wanted to discuss.'

This time I did guess right.

'You want Robin and Mark to come round here for Christmas?'

'If that's all right with you, Charlie?'

I didn't want Mark to come at all. Still, it might be fun to have Robin bobbing about at Christmas.

So . . . I decided I'd better come up with something pretty special for our Christmas cake. I baked a square fruit cake and then carved out part of the front and made up a brown butter icing and did this posh basket weave all over to make it look like . . . a stable! With a big gold marzipan star and a fat pink marzipan angel perched on the roof.

(I'm going to get to eat the angel on Christmas Day – because I'm currently so angelic!) Then I made a marzipan Mary (Jo can eat her) and a marzipan Joseph (I suppose I *might* offer him to Mark) and a dear little marzipan baby Jesus clutching a white marzipan lamb (specially for Robin).

I piped a long message in front of all my Nativity figures.

PEACE ON EARTH.
GOOD WILL TO ALL MEN.

I never ever thought I'd be wishing Good Will to *any* man! I decided to add a bit.

AND GOOD WILL TO ALL WOMEN
AND BOYS AND ESPECIALLY GIRLS!

THE END